MW00761815

An Artful Affair

An Artful Affair

A Novel

∽

CORINNA P.S. CLENDENEN

Copyright © 2004 by Corinna P.S. Clendenen.

Library of Congress Number: 2003099132
ISBN: Hardcover   1-4134-4156-4
                Softcover   1-4134-4155-6

All rights reserved. No part of this book may be reproduced or transmitted in any form or by any means, electronic or mechanical, including photocopying, recording, or by any information storage and retrieval system, without permission in writing from the copyright owner.

This is a work of fiction. Names, characters, places and incidents either are the product of the author's imagination or are used fictitiously, and any resemblance to any actual persons, living or dead, events, or locales is entirely coincidental.

This book was printed in the United States of America.

To order additional copies of this book, contact:
Xlibris Corporation
1-888-795-4274
www.Xlibris.com
Orders@Xlibris.com
23036

For all the artists out there,
Poets and painters alike.

Acknowledgements

Many thanks go to all the teachers, friends and family whose helpful advice and encouragement sustained me through the writing of this novel. They include Adria Arch, Jonis Agee, Maura Boyd, Vicky Chave Clement, Susan Cohn, Wendy Godfrey Sanderson, Betty Chmielniak Grace, Gail Harper, Laura Jarett, David Lesser, Tom Perrotta, Annie and Bill Schley. Thanks also to my father, Gordon Ross Smith Sr., whose love of art and the written word got me started; for the cheerful confidence of my children Allison, Derek and Luke; and with special gratitude for the unwavering support of my husband, Bill.

Cover art: *Ta Matete* by Paul Gauguin, 1892, oil on linen, 73 x 92 cm., Kunstmuseum, Basel. Paul Simon lyrics from the refrain of *50 Ways To Leave Your Lover.*

Prologue

I t wasn't so much the graffiti in the cell that troubled Bo, but that it brought to mind the work of a painter he particularly disliked. When his weary eyes glazed over, the scrawl of jumbled names and expletives blurred, forming a random but intricate pattern on the solid wall of institutional green. It looked just like the abstract chicken scratchings of Cy Twombly. And for this reason he decided halfway through his first night behind bars that it must be his last.

How had it ever come to this? From a simple, one-shot-deal intended only to solve his temporary cash flow problems . . . he hadn't hurt anybody, or chiseled anyone who would have missed the money, or misrepresented anything they would have noticed anyway.

Talk about snowballing, events had turned into a veritable avalanche. Why hadn't he stopped when he'd finally become solvent? But every time the dealer offered him another wad of bills, he thought he was almost home free, just a little bit more.

He shifted his glance out of the cell and grabbed the bars, wincing as he hit the spot where the handcuffs had pinched his wrist, where the cop had twisted his fingers that were already sore from too many hours of holding a paintbrush. He'd always planned to keep on painting no matter what shape his hands were in, but this wasn't exactly what he'd had in mind.

His eyes closed and a chill ran through him. Then an image appeared: a green field, a spreading oak, sunlit clouds in a summer sky . . . worthy of Constable, of Corot, of Winslow Homer. He lowered his head against the bars. *Please, beam me up Scotty, get me the hell out of here. Just give me back my life and I'll redeem myself, I'll paint my own masterpiece, a hallelujah chorus for the ages.*

He looked down the corridor to where the guard sat.

"Hey, excuse me, I need to use the john," he called.

The guard glanced back and gave a curt nod. Slowly, he pushed his chair back from the desk, stood, and ambled down the corridor, keys dangling from his belt.

Bo's heart began to race and he shut his eyes; he envisioned himself running down the city street, sirens wailing, the bitter winter air burning his lungs as he ran farther and farther into the night.

Chapter 1

By the end of the summer Bo had gotten used to the drip from above. He knew by then it meant the photographer upstairs was washing his prints. The pattern had become familiar: first he heard the water in the pipes, then he saw the moistening on the ceiling. The water gathered on the molded tin between two of the cast iron columns that ran down the center of the loft. The white paint had discolored into a rusty brown at the spot where the bubble formed, shimmering like copper as it grew until the tension broke and released the drop to plummet downwards 15 feet. Then it began all over again.

When it first started Bo had his easel set up directly beneath and the drip fell on to the canvas of the portrait he was painting. It landed right on the back of the red wing chair the woman sat in and dribbled down into her yellow dress, carrying some of the pigment with it . . . the brilliant cadmium red running like a tear into the palest strontium yellow . . . he admitted it did add a certain spontaneity, a *je ne sais quoi.* But he was not that kind of painter, an "I don't know what" had no place in his painting. For him, each stroke, each image, needed to be deliberate, an "I know *exactly* what." So he moved the easel and painted it over.

He told his landlord about the drip the next time he saw him. Gozzi grumbled and groused in his usual way. "What do you think this is, Park Avenue? The Ritz? I'll get to it when you start paying your rent on time." Bo wasn't surprised – Gozzi was always such a warm, caring guy.

Eventually Bo grew fond of the drip. After all, it was a demonstration of gravity, of the stickiness of water. The way he figured it, a raw loft was supposed to be raw; it suited him. He always liked a little character in a place. Jeanette – the girl he had been painting at the time – said the drip reminded her of him.

"It's like a feckless lover. It comes, it goes. When it comes, it's not committed. And when it goes, it's not for good. It has neither the strength to pull the plugs nor to dry up altogether."

He smiled, took the cap off a tube of paint and pressed an inch of cerulean blue pigment onto the palette, a flat slab of white glass set on a table next to the easel. He always knew she was clever. But what the hell, if you're going to be put down it may as well be with a little style. His friend Clyde warned him not to get involved with his models. But hey – there she sat, half-clad, with those gorgeous legs and a sultry smile, what could you expect? Was he supposed to turn into a eunuch or something?

He pressed several other pigments onto the palette until half a dozen lined up, squeezed out like so many soft, colorful turds. From a Chock-Full-of-Nuts can filled with clean brushes, the upturned tips fanned out like a flower arrangement from the wide brim, he selected an ox hair mixed with red sable, its bristles firm and springy against his fingers. He dabbed the end of the brush into cerulean blue – what a great color, the flawless blue of an endless summer sky. Blended with a little zinc white for a cold tone, it captured the glacial iciness of Jeanette's eyes. He touched the brush to the canvas, reveling in the perfection of the shade, and her eyes awoke, cool and placid. This was the great satisfaction in painting, getting exactly the right color and using it to create another person, another place, another reality.

Jeanette didn't stay long after her little soliloquy. When the temperatures dropped in the fall she said she couldn't sit around the loft in that scanty dress anymore. Especially with the minimal heat Gozzi supplied. When she left he was flippant. Okay, he told her, I understand. Sayonara. Auf Wiedersehen. Ciao, bella. But her image haunted him, he kept seeing her in the yellow dress, hearing her laugh at his bad jokes, remembering the smooth satin of her dress against his skin. Cool as she was, at least she had been some female company. But she had wanted more than he could give.

After tossing around several background possibilities for the portrait of Jeanette, none of which seemed quite right, the answer suddenly came to him yesterday while he was stretching a canvas. In his mind's eye he saw her sitting primly in the wing chair set atop the fountain in front of the Plaza Hotel, water lapping at her feet like Botticelli's *Venus* poised on a scallop shell. As soon as the image appeared he knew it was right.

Since he was a kid he'd been struck with these kinds of visions. Suddenly, out of nowhere, a vivid picture would present itself, projected in his mind's eye with the heightened clarity of a dream. This was followed by an irresistible urge to capture the image on canvas.

The setting was perfect for her – Jeanette the Queen, she was regal enough to handle it. And if ever she had the fortune to see it hanging in a gallery, maybe she'd understand, maybe she'd forgive him, maybe she'd be happy that she had staying power in his art if not in his life.

After Jeanette left he realized the loft was too crowded with her there, anyway. Not that it wasn't big enough – 2500 square feet – but since he used it as both living space and studio, one person was plenty. All that was left of Jeanette was the red nails she painted on the lion's paw feet of the bathtub.

A sharp rapping came at the door. Bo lifted the brush from the palette and looked at the door without moving. He couldn't think of anybody he wanted to see. With the possible exception of Clyde, but Clyde always rang the buzzer. The rapping came again, this time louder. The muscle in Bo's neck twitched. There was only one person this could be.

"Come on, Ryder, open up!"

He didn't move.

A moment later a key turned in the lock and the door swung open.

Gozzi's big, burly form barged in and, seeing Bo, stopped. "What the hell's the matter with you? Why don't you open the door?"

Bo shrugged. "I'm in the middle of something. What can I do for you?"

"You know damn well what you can do for me. Pay me two months' back rent."

Bo took a deep breath. "I don't exactly appreciate you barging into my loft like this."

"What's that you say? *Your* loft? I got news for you, sonny, this is *my* loft."

Bo bristled. Gozzi was such an asshole.

"I don't remember anything in the lease allowing you to come in here whenever you want to just because you're the landlord."

"Don't start with your lip, Ryder. I've sent you three rent notices already, and now I'm here to collect."

He tossed a yellow invoice on the giant cable spool that served as a table.

Bo put down the brush and crossed his arms. Gozzi glared confrontationally. Bo didn't want to piss him off too much. He was huge – massive shoulders and a neck like a walrus. He could have played one of those Roman gladiators.

Bo stuck his hands in his pockets and walked around the back of the couch.

"Yeah, I know I'm behind. Couple of things I had going last month didn't come through, so I'm a little in the red."

Couple of things, thought Bo. Right. He hadn't sold a painting in over a year.

"I ain't here to listen to your problems. This ain't no charity building I'm running. I got plenty of bills myself. If you can't pay the rent I'll get somebody in here who can."

"All right, now, don't get all upset. You'll get your money."

"When?" Gozzi demanded.

Bo looked at him resentfully.

"Soon as I can get it."

Suddenly the image of Gozzi's white El Dorado Cadillac parked out at the curb rose up in Bo's mind; his fist came down hard on the couch.

"Christ Almighty, you own half of Soho! You're not hurting! Give me a break!"

Gozzi stepped forward and pointed his finger, his craggy face with its fleshy jowls turning bright red.

"Look, punk, you got a break already. Two months worth. And you're not even supposed to be camping out here the way you are. Now I want my money and I want it by the end of the week. Or you're out!"

Bo clenched his teeth in an attempt to hold his temper. One more remark might start Gozzi swinging.

"I hear you," Bo said, staring back.

Gozzi dropped his finger, gave Bo a warning look and stalked out.

Bo walked over and slammed the door shut.

"Goddamn it!"

Nine hundred bucks! Where the hell was he going to get that kind of money? He had fifty dollars in his wallet and he didn't get paid at the parking lot until the end of the week. He kicked at a sweatshirt lying on the floor. The gray cotton flew up on a cloud of dust bunnies and landed on the couch, covering a large hole in the upholstery.

Shoving the rent notice into his pocket, he reached for a long metal pole with a hook on the end. He needed some air. Glancing up at the transoms above the windows that lined the street, he jiggled one open and realized that last summer he'd spent half a month's rent having all the transom glass replaced. Which he did *not* regret. Large and obliquely angled, the windows were handy for releasing the acrid vapors that gathered from volatile paint, turpentine, and varnish. But several had been broken, letting in more city soot than he liked powdering his pigments. So when he had the broken ones replaced, he decided to go ahead and replace the whole bank since the others were so grimy. Why lose any of the ideal northern light? What was money for?

Any amount used improving his studio space was money well spent. Although the loft would not have suited everyone, for him it was now nearly perfect. The big black squares that marked the floor where the former printing company presses stood were now splattered with his own paints. And that was about as close to Jackson Pollack as he was ever going to get.

Besides, he wanted to stay in Soho. He moved to New York to try to break into the art world, not to live in Queens. He leaned the pole up against the wall and slowly walked around the spool table. It seemed he'd need another job. The hours at the parking lot just didn't pay enough.

He picked up a cup he'd gotten at a Bicentennial celebration last year. Printed with a top border of *1776-1976,* the clear plastic sported cracked liberty bells on either side and a border of red, white and blue stars and stripes along the bottom. He stared into the glass at the dried pulp remaining from yesterday's orange juice and made a face.

The rear of the loft served as a makeshift kitchen, and he carried the soiled glass back and turned on the electric burner under the teakettle. The portable two-burner stove sat on a counter top made of an old oak door laid on top of some orange crates. He had found the door at a demolished building on the lower east side and it proved to be a hell of a chopping block.

He always made tea when stressed. His sister turned him on to Ginseng and it did seem to calm him. He drank it and thought of the ancient Buddhists; he aspired to oneness, to inner peace.

The trouble was, he couldn't really afford to live anywhere else. The only reason the loft was so cheap was that it wasn't zoned residential. Gozzi had rented it to him as studio space, not to live in. He seemed willing to look the other way when Bo set up house. At least, he had until now.

There was always waiting tables.

Along the wall between the studio and the kitchen stood the loft bed. Using 2 x 4's and some discarded boards, he built it five feet off the floor to keep the mattress away from the cockroaches. This gave him a fine view of the roofs of Soho out the back window, a crazy landscape of water towers and fire escapes he had grown to love.

He stopped and looked at the pencil and charcoal drawings tacked up on the outside wall of the bathroom across from the loft bed. Done when he was in art school at the École des Beaux Arts in Paris, these copies after Picasso, Daumier, Gauguin, and Matisse recreated the work of his mentors. He believed drawing was the basis of any image. If an artist couldn't draw he couldn't paint. For him, there was nothing finer than the human figure in the early stages of Modernism – the sublime line of the body, its sensuous modulations. As a student he did study after study of the great Modernists until he mastered their forms, their styles, their thinking.

Back in the States, he used this classical training as the basis for a new style of his own. Starting with representational forms, he combined them in illuminating ways with fresh, even unorthodox subjects that he believed took realism to a new ground.

His vision was not always viewed as he intended. It wasn't easy working in a traditional style in the current environment of comic book art. Some termed his art "reactionary," "retro," or "a throwback." But he had an answer to these objections: fuck 'em. It was easy. If they couldn't look past their prejudices and see what he was *doing* in a traditional style . . .

His friend Clyde, a conceptual artist, amused himself by writing above the drawings hung on the wall, *RYDER MUSEUM – Modern Masterpieces*. Clyde was always fooling around with artsy questions of reality – what is art, what is life. Bo wasn't sure exactly what point Clyde was trying to make, but he didn't object. In his isolated work of applying paint to canvas, he was glad when Clyde dropped by at the end of the day.

Stopping in the bathroom he stared in the mirror: pretty grungy, he had to admit. He wasn't going for the Rastafarian look, but he was pretty close right now, pretty close. His brown hair tended to curl when it got long; at the moment it hung in ringlets. As he shook his head his curls danced in unison. For Christ's sake, he looked like some male Shirley Temple – even down to the rosy cheeks and crinkling eyes.

His unkempt self stood in interesting contrast to the mirror, hung in an ornate Rococo frame, its coils twisting and turning around the edges like the curls around his face. But the mirror frame was gilded and its spirals spilled away from the frame in burnished gold. His mother had picked it up in Paris for practically nothing, but when she got it home it didn't fit in with her Americana decor so she packed it up and sent it along. He accepted it as a piece of camp and parked it in the bathroom where its gleaming form hung above the chipped enamel sink.

The kettle whistled and he walked back and flopped a ginseng tea bag into a mug. He poured in the water and glanced at a postcard picturing a colorful painting propped up against the back of the sink. Ah, yes, the opening was this weekend: Frank Stella's retrospective at the Museum of Modern Art. The invitation pictured one of Stella's recent 3-D paintings, which looked to him like the Color Field School having a head on collision with Abstract Expressionism. This was not his taste in painting and he didn't particularly like openings, but it was hard to turn down one at MoMA. Clyde said the food was always great.

Standing under the portraits that lined the wall above him, he dipped the tea bag up and down. They seem to be forming a series, one he'd entitle *Portraits in the City*. Each pictured a figure set in an incongruous but fitting place somewhere in Manhattan. Each was tantalizing in its own way, seemingly realistic until closer inspection. This morning he saw a flyer calling for submissions for an exhibition of young New York painters called *Under 30*. What the hell – there was a cash prize – he'd enter one of these.

From his pocket he took out Gozzi's yellow rent invoice; it had to be good for something. He smoothed out the crumpled paper on the flat counter and neatly folded it into an airplane. Drawing back his arm, he launched it into the air. Carried on currents from the open window, the yellow paper dipped and glided past the canvases until, with an abrupt turn, it swooped into one of his favorites. He grinned – the fates had chosen.

The selected portrait, the first of the lot he painted before he introduced the red wing chair, pictured a naked woman (Jeanette) reclining on a Central Park bench. Her torso raised on one elbow, her other hand held the top slat of the bench. Her curvaceous body, creamy skin heightened by the surrounding verdant foliage, faced away but her head turned over her shoulder to gaze indifferently at the viewer like Ingres's *Odalisque*. Strewn around under the park bench were various items: a horseshoe, several playing cards with a queen of spades and a joker showing, a fur muff, and a party mask with red feathered eyes and a long yellow beak. The palette was rich, the colors so vivid they seemed to exude a light of their own, reeling the viewer in to look and look again because the more you looked the more you saw.

Picking up his mug, he tossed the tea bag in the sink and leaned against it, blowing on the steaming brew as he looked along the row of paintings, their eyes watching him like a bevy of eccentric guardian angels. He was happy with them; he believed in his work, even if nobody else did. Someday these paintings would hang in a major gallery, in a museum, on a collector's wall. He just hoped he didn't have to die first.

Chapter 2

Megan looked across the table at Ned whose fork was poised with a skewered piece of meat. His face was flushed, from what she was not sure: the wine, his still tightly-knotted tie, his anticipation.

"The travel agent called this morning," he said. "We're booked for the honeymoon package, a suite right next to the golf course looking towards Maui. She said the waiters walk right up the beach to take drink orders. You won't have to lift a finger. It'll be perfect, a paradise."

He smiled across the table.

"Sounds like it," she answered as she struggled with her knife and fork. She was having trouble getting the meat off the bones of the dish she ordered, Auk à la Maison. The waiter arrived and wrapped a linen napkin around the neck of the wine bottle, lifted it deftly out of the cooler, and refilled their glasses.

"Could I have a sharper knife please?" she asked the waiter.

"Of course, Madam," he answered with a small bow.

Ned continued expansively. "Hill and Stone is such a great firm. The Personnel Department told me I can take off three extra days in addition to my accrued vacation as long as I make it up in comp time."

"Great."

She turned her fork to the dilled new potatoes which somehow looked much more appetizing than the meat.

"I heard from Todd today, too. He's agreed to be the best man. He says he'll do anything for a trip to New York." He laughed heartily.

The waiter returned and handed her a serrated knife.

"Is the bird to your satisfaction?" the waiter asked. "These wild Auks are flown in from Greenland. They are caught with nets while they fly in mid-air. They are young and should be tender."

She looked up and said, "No, it's fine. I guess I'm just not very handy with a knife."

"Would you like something else instead?" the waiter offered.

She did want something else, but she couldn't think what, and suddenly she didn't feel hungry at all.

"No, thank you. I can manage now."

Ned looked across the white linen tablecloth. "Get something else if you want to. There's no point eating a dish you don't like."

She shook her head and picked up the knife, intent on trying again. The meat cut easily with the new knife and came cleanly off the bones. Suddenly, from out of the mass of skin and meat, she saw the entire carcass of the little bird, lying lifeless on her plate. Her stomach churned and she felt a wave of nausea. She looked up and the motion made her dizzy.

"I just can't do this," she said.

"Order something else, then, sweetheart," he said.

She looked over at Ned, at his neatly combed hair, at his white collar, spic and span above his vertically striped shirt, at his earnest eyes behind the horn-rimmed glasses.

"No, what I mean is, Ned, I can't marry you."

*   *   *

The Soho Weekly News office had a sound of its own, a sound that revealed its mood, like an old car that starts up with a roar or a sputter. From the moment Megan walked in the door she could feel the hum of the place: phones ringing and typewriters clattering, punctuated by laughter, cries, shouts and retorts.

The morning after her dinner with Ned the newsroom had never sounded so good. She pushed open the front door and entered the noisy office, already in full swing, and felt immediately comforted. For as insane as this place could be, and as rocky as her job had become since the arrival of the new managing editor, it seemed infinitely saner than her last twelve hours.

The office was on the first floor of an old cast-iron-front warehouse on Prince Street in Soho. Desks set haphazardly around the high-ceilinged room left a criss-crossed walking space littered with stacks of newspapers and crumpled balls of paper. She made her way through the familiar maze to her desk, take-out coffee in hand. Awash in papers, the desktop was not in sight, so she set the coffee gingerly next to a stack of unopened mail. Her hand shook slightly as she put down the cup.

She had not slept well.

For the first half of the night she wrestled her pillow, the events of the evening hounding her. She kept replaying the awful scene with Ned, the conversation that kept circling round and round, an infinite loop of accusation and recrimination. It finally broke when Ned had to rush to the airport to catch a flight for a business seminar in Los Angeles the next morning. So she had gone to bed alone, thankfully, but lay wide awake far into the night, vacillating between trying to figure out what made her break up with Ned and questioning how she ever got engaged to him in the first place. But most of all she wished that, behind his staunch assertions about the viability of their relationship, he hadn't looked so crushed.

She woke up with an oppressive feeling and wondered only momentarily before the depressing reality hit her. She lay in bed for a little while pondering whether she should send Ned flowers with a note wishing him well or pack his belongings into a suitcase and put it by the door. Or maybe both.

At the desk next to hers, Ron Horvath typed away, absorbed in his writing and seemingly unaware of her arrival. She sat down and kicked her shoes into the corner. For once she was glad he could be so oblivious. She was feeling too shaky for observation.

Horvath's tiny television blared away like a Lilliputian from his desk. The size of a pack of cigarettes, it fed his news habit. He claimed being the staff news reporter justified his continual playing of news, talk shows, and documentaries. From the tiny set an even tinier head was talking: President Carter making a plea for the Egyptian-Israeli accords. Megan found the constant barrage incredibly monotonous, but she had learned to filter it out with the rest of the newsroom racket. She once asked Horvath to wear headphones but he didn't take her up on it. It seemed only fitting that she should find the news dry because Horvath had more than once made it clear he thought her Arts section was fluff. He could think what he wanted. Better fluff than sawdust. The only problem was that the new managing editor, Jack Fogelman, seemed to agree with him.

She sighed, picked up a framed photograph picturing two couples and inspected it closely: she, Ned, Lizzy and Lizzy's now-defunct boyfriend, taken on a Cape Cod dock last summer. How odd, really, that a snapshot, a captured moment, could give such a false impression. The bright sun in the picture lit Megan's auburn hair in gold around her shoulders, a color it rarely was. And the big smiles on their faces made them look like happy couples. She remembered the week as having been fun, but now that she thought about it, most of the fun had been with Lizzy. She opened the bottom drawer and shoved the photo to the back.

She stared blankly at the Arts section in front of her, the section that, after much hard work, had finally become hers to edit when the previous arts editor left to work on a novel. The possibility of offspring with Ned was dimming quickly: *this* was her baby. As she searched the printed page for some sign of response, suddenly the newspaper's center illustration came into focus. It pictured a large painting from a gallery review she wrote on the painter Carol Winter, but the image was upside down. She sat up and seized the paper. No, no, they couldn't have done this again! The painting's abstract, billowing forms should move from the bottom left, expanding outwards, releasing energy and motion into an airy upper right. But upside down the forms had the opposite effect, the deep purples and indigos were top heavy, weighing down the composition. She stood and walked quickly across the room.

Midway down the long wall sat the newly-appointed Fogelman, positioned so he could see the entire room. The leather chair and desk he brought with him were bigger than anyone else's and surrounded by a wide space like an invisible moat. Since coming, he had presided over the newsroom like a king over a court. Which may have been an improvement over his predecessor's waffling lack of leadership, which, under the guise of fair-mindedness, had practically beached the paper. But he at least had let Megan alone to pursue her coverage of the less-established fringes of the art scene.

From her standing vantage point Megan could see Fogelman's thinning dark hair. But whatever he lacked on top was made up for by a jauntily waxed mustache, one end of which he was twirling between thumb and forefinger.

She held up the newspaper. "The printer got the illustration wrong again."

Fogelman glanced at the reproduction. "What's the matter with it?"

"It's upside down."

He laughed dismissively. "Who could tell?"

She tried not to look reproachful. Maybe Fogelman couldn't tell the difference but other people would and the painter would be devastated.

"It changes the whole look of the painting, it totally skews the movement and balance. And it makes us look like idiots."

With exaggerated patience, as if he were talking to a willful child, Fogelman said, "What makes us look like idiots, Megan, is when we put out a newspaper with no news of any consequence."

He picked up the phone from the cradle and began to dial.

She turned and walked back to her desk. How could he be so unconcerned? To dismiss a glaring error by claiming a priority for consequential news – what kind of nonsequitur was that? Where was his integrity, for the sake of the newspaper if not for the artist? But there was clearly no talking to him. She would call the printer herself and have the illustration reprinted in the next issue, right side up, with a correction.

Gradually she cleared her desk of correspondence, making way for the appearance of the ink blotter, which she hadn't seen for weeks. The sight of it cheered her, its grassy green the color of spring, of new growth. It was covered with a variety of designs she had doodled in her four years at the newspaper: the circular looping patterns made as a copy editor straight out of college, the checkered squares from her early days as a fledgling reporter, the elaborate tiers of interlocking triangles penned on her rise to Arts Editor.

Inserting a piece of paper into the typewriter, she rolled the platen until the sheet of virgin white clicked around and stood, pert and ready. She typed in the title of the coming week's lead article: *California Proposes New Legislation: Royalty Rights for Artists.* As she typed, Fogelman's big form appeared in front of her desk. Although only in his thirties, he already looked like a man who spent too much time sitting down. His paunch was accentuated by a shirt of yellow circles on forest green, one in a collection of polka-dot shirts that were his trademark. He handed her some stapled papers.

"Here's something that might interest you."

At his first staff meeting Fogelman had announced that he would read the Manhattan police report daily, that this newspaper would not miss a thing, not if he could help it.

She took the papers and looked at the paragraph Fogelman had circled in red.

Battery Park: Mogidliani painting en route from London detained in customs due to complaint from Italian embassy that it was stolen from Italian owner.

As she read, he addressed her in a pedantic tone. "This is what I'm looking for in the Arts section. Not a lot of hand wringing over lack of funding or obscure art theory nobody understands, but some real newsreaders can sink their teeth into. Think of the competition. What's the hottest story in the dailies right now? Son of Sam. That's what sells newspapers." He glanced at her briefly before asking if she knew the artist.

"Of course. He's an early 20th century Modernist. They spelled his name wrong – but it has to be Modigliani." She pondered the paper for a moment. "Don't paintings require papers to be sold internationally?"

"That's for you to find out, my little Lois. Get the full story. I want to scoop every other city paper on this one. If we're going to have an Arts section, it's got to be first rate."

She looked up at him. "*If?*"

He smiled down and twisted the end of his mustache. "*If.*"

He walked away and she sat very still in her chair. How had someone so narrow-minded gotten so far? But damned if she would give him the satisfaction of failing his challenge.

Horvath peered over at the police report from behind thick glasses that made his eyes look as big as an owl's.

"Stolen paintings? Sounds like a news story to me."

"Indeed it is," she said, taking a deep breath. "An *art* news story."

Horvath grinned. Since Fogelman made clear his bias towards muckraking news, Horvath had been strutting like a cock.

"I see. Art mixed with just enough action to make it tantalizing, is that what you mean?"

She shot him a disparaging look.

"*Titillating* I believe is the word you want."

"Titillating, tantalizing, what's the difference?"

"There's a big difference. Titillating means to excite agreeably, tantalizing connotes frustration."

"Must you always correct me?" he asked.

"I should think you'd be grateful. Don't you want to say what you mean?"

He turned back to his typewriter.

"What I *mean* is, it's nice you've got the chance to get a real story out of something."

The phone rang and Megan reached for it, glad to be spared the necessity of responding. But when she heard the voice on the other end she wished she had asked the receptionist to take her calls.

"Honey, I'm so glad I caught you." The urgency in Ned's voice came though along with the long-distance crackle. "Listen, I just talked to Griggs, and he says he'll cover for me after the big presentation on Thursday. I'll be coming home early so we can sit down and fix this."

Her stomach twisted into a knot. "Ned, I'm sorry but there's nothing to fix."

"Megan, you're wrong. Every couple has problems, we just need to be mature about handling them. I think we should sit down with a piece of paper and make a list of the pros and cons in our relationship . . ."

She glanced at Horvath who was typing away again and lowered her head, her heart hammering.

"Ned, please don't do this. I'm sorry, but it's over."

His voice rose to a shout. "Damn it, Megan, you can't do this to me! For five years I've put up with your crazy schedule and that damned cat of yours, and now you think you can just blow me off like this?"

"Good-bye Ned."

She dropped the receiver into the cradle. Putting her hands to her head, she stared at the ink blotter as the doodles blurred together. No, Ned, don't keep pressing it, don't make it harder than it already is. Although, knowing his insistent drive, he would try to steamroll her into marrying him. The thought was unbearable. She would have to move out of the apartment before he returned.

She stared at the newspaper and tried to collect herself. How much could she lose in one day? A fiancé, an apartment, and possibly a job? She steeled herself and drew a small sun on the ink blotter. This was going to require a major shot of attitude. *Fiancé-free*, that sounded better. As for the apartment, there were others. But the job, no, that was not an acceptable loss.

Searching for a distraction from these thoughts she picked up yesterday's edition, grimaced again at the inverted illustration, and shakily paged through the rest of the section: articles covered a performance piece staged under the Brooklyn Bridge, a screening of "Pull my Daisy" at Film Forum, and a guest columnist comparing the music of Philip Glass and John Cage. She had a flash of uncertainty: *were* these stories interesting enough? They had seemed so last week. Would readers find them engaging or were they as stale as Fogelman claimed?

She put down the paper, tucked a colorful invitation to a Frank Stella opening into the margin of the ink blotter, and picked up the police report about the detained Modigliani. As she read it, her guilt over Ned and the pressure from Fogelman began to fade. She had always loved Modigliani's fluid lines and ethereal faces. This was a story she would enjoy going after, and if it involved a scandal, clearly all the better as far as Fogelman was concerned.

The report recounted statements by several of the people involved, including Agostino Celluci, the Italian consul who, on the part of the avowed Italian owner, contended that the Modigliani was owned by a family of Italian Jews and hung in their Umbrian villa for years until it was confiscated by the Nazis in 1941. The report stated that the claiming Italian owner saw the painting offered in Sotheby's London Modern Painting catalogue. By the time he got in touch with the authorities the painting had been sold and was in transit to a buyer in New York.

The phone number for the Italian embassy was listed in bold print in the directory and she dialed it eagerly. The exchange was brief: Agostino Celucci was not in; the receptionist assured her he would return the call.

She hung up to see Fogelman standing in front of Horvath's desk, both of them eyeing her skeptically.

"So?" Fogelman asked.

"The consul is supposed to call me when he gets back tomorrow."

Horvath snorted and Fogelman shook his head.

"If you want to be an investigative reporter you're going to have to do more than leave a message," Fogelman said.

Horvath wagged his finger at her and turned back to his typewriter. Megan's blood pressure rose like a geyser as Fogelman walked away. She looked back at the police report and stared at the line *"confiscated by the Nazis"* until the print began to dance. Yes, he was crude and rude with an unfortunate penchant for sensationalist journalism. But if she wanted to stay in print she would need to show him that a writer on conceptual art could just as easily produce a headline grabber.

Chapter 3

A pigeon cooed softly outside the open window. To Alastair, in his fragile state, it sounded more like an air raid whistle. He turned over to escape the bright daylight and his head hammered loudly in protest. Oh Lord, what a head. What a hangover.

Fresh morning air wafted in across his bare shoulders in a vain attempt to revive him. The pigeon cooed again, its magnified warbles sounding very close. It must have been right outside, strutting around on the balustrade of the terrace that overlooked Hyde Park. He opened his eyes to stare at the burled walnut wardrobe his godfather had shipped over from Scotland, the grain of the eddied wood swirling at he tried to orient himself. No, no, not Hyde Park, *Central Park*. This was New York, not London.

A voice said, "Good morning."

He sat bolt upright to see a tallish woman with brown hair in a pageboy cut standing in a navy suit in the bedroom doorway. In her hand she held a saucer and teacup.

"Good Lord," he said, his head pounding as he sat up against the headboard, pulling the covers up over his naked waist. "Good morning."

The woman smiled and walked to an armchair where a draped raincoat followed the curves of the Queen Anne legs. The coat looked a bit like his, but from the plaid lining he could see it was a Burberry, so it must be hers. She set down the cup and picked up the raincoat. She turned towards the bed but he couldn't see her face well because of the light from the window behind.

"Thanks so much for the delightful dinner and the tour of the Frick," she said. "I've had some tea in one of those lovely teacups and now I've got to catch a cab to Kennedy. My plane leaves at eleven."

He reached for his robe lying on a nearby chair but when he tried to grab it the satin slid to the floor.

"No, no, don't get up," she said. "There's no need. I can let myself out. I'll call next time I'm coming through."

She leaned down and pecked his cheek and before he could rally to rise she was gone. Her pumps clicked efficiently along the hall and down the stairs. The front door opened and closed, quickly and quietly.

He slid down the headboard and groaned, his head as thick as pea soup. What on earth was he doing? Slowly, it all came back to him . . .

Evelyn. She was the Contemporary Paintings expert from the Los Angeles office. She had been in town all week and somehow they had ended up together last night at a cocktail party at the Frick Gallery. He hadn't intended on going out to dinner with her but they were both hungry after all those appetizers so getting some dinner seemed like a reasonable thing to do. He really didn't feel like dining alone again.

Of course, he didn't have to ask her back to his house, but as the candle burned lower on the table between them she started looking less like a colleague and more like a woman. So that was that. It had been a while.

He did find her nice, in that Californian, professional way. All smiles and warmth on the surface. But several times last night she called him Duncan and she certainly didn't waste any time getting out the door this morning. This must be love American style, a drive-through, a disposable. Alastair stretched his arms over his head. Ah, well . . . when in Rome . . . he'd have to suffer through it.

Superficial as it may have been, he was feeling rather more cheerful this morning, despite the throbbing head. Although he was surprised he let himself go like that. It had always been his personal policy not to get involved with people at work even if they were stationed on another continent. With the art auction market being international, he saw people from opposite ends of the earth with fair regularity. A major sale in London often brought in experts from Los Angeles, Zurich or Hong Kong.

The phone rang and he sat up and reached for the receiver, knocking his cufflinks off the bedside table in the process.

"Alastair here."

"Alastair, it's Jane. I'm sorry to call you at home but I have an urgent message from Colin. He told me to cancel your morning appointments. He's sending a cab for you at 9:30 to go out to Woodlawn Cemetery in New Jersey."

"Whatever for?"

"The note doesn't say. But at the bottom he's underlined, 'You must come. Will meet you there and explain.'"

Alastair rolled his eyes. Wasn't this just like Colin. If he couldn't dictate to Alastair at the office he'd dictate to him through his secretary at home.

"All right then, I guess I'm going. Is there anything else pressing for this morning?"

"There's a telex from Brompton in London. Would you like to hear it?"

"Fire away."

"Rumor has it the Getty Museum has consigned a Picasso self-portrait to Sotheby's for sale. I trust you're rounding up some equally enticing pictures."

His head pounded harder. That was a half-million dollar picture, a challenge to match.

"All right, thank you, Jane. I'll see you this afternoon."

He picked up the cufflinks and dropped them onto the dresser. So – another great consignment for Sotheby's. That weasel Terrence Young, how did he do it? He pulled his bathrobe loosely around his tall, lanky frame and headed for the bathroom. "We'll just see about that then, won't we?" he remarked to the moon face in the grandfather clock that stood at the top of the stairs, its stately finials almost touching the ceiling. He certainly was not going to be beaten by any rival at that *other firm* – tag-sale hawkers as far as he was concerned. Well, all right, they did get a decent picture once in a while but . . . nonetheless. His straight, sandy-blonde hair bounced buoyantly as he walked down the hall to the bathroom. He'd meet Young's bid and raise him one.

Not too worse for wear, he thought, as he stood in front of the mirror and whisked a boar's bristle brush around in the shaving cup. But he'd need an extra dab of hair cream to take care of that ridiculous cowlick. The night must have involved more acrobatics than he remembered. He lathered his face and then began shaving his throat at the edge of the strawberry birthmark that crept up out of his bathrobe. Fortunately, when he wore a collared shirt the birthmark didn't show. It covered his left shoulder and collarbone, its topmost finger spreading onto his neck and stopping just below his Adam's apple. The stain was pale strawberry in color except when he was angry, when it brightened into red.

Popping two aspirin, he turned on the shower and turned his thoughts to the day ahead. Going to a funeral was not exactly at the top of his list. What he really should be doing was rounding up consignments for his next sale, making calls to clients, curators, estate lawyers, dealers – rooting around for paintings like a pig for truffles. You would think he were back in London, being at Colin's beck and call like this. But at least it would give him the morning to clear his head. He cranked open the casement window to let out the steam and the leaded panes reminded him of England. He'd certainly had successes there, he must think of those.

He closed his eyes and let the shower drum steadily on his back. *"Picasso, Picasso, Picasso,"* the hammering water seemed to say. He could, he should, he would, solicit an equally enticing picture. For there he was, just as he had wanted, heading up the Modern Painting department of Lyndhurst and Lloyd's, New York. After five years in the London office with its musty corridors and stale politics, he had welcomed crossing the Atlantic and starting afresh. What a wonderful opportunity it seemed, to take everything he had learned to America, to apply a tradition of excellence in a new world. It certainly sounded good in theory. But in practice he was finding it a bit more difficult than he'd imagined. And matters were not helped by the arrival of Colin, who should have stayed in London where he belonged.

He turned and stuck his face directly under the pounding water: *"Picasso, Picasso, Picasso,"* it pounded. If he could organize a record-breaking auction in London he could do it here. Or so Brompton had told him when he sent him off with a hearty clap on the back: "With those ruddy cheeks and that ready smile, you'll do very well with the New York dowagers."

What Brompton left out of the equation was that Alastair didn't know any of the New York dowagers and was having difficulty finding them. Which felt very odd, since in England his surname opened all the right doors. But in America the name Cavendish seemed to ring a bell with only a few as the distant cousin who discovered hydrogen.

The steam built until the rows of black and white checkerboard tiles misted over and the closeness of the night momentarily returned. The softness of her smooth hair brushing against his face as she moved on top of him, her breath warm in his ear. He drifted into thinking of Amanda back at Oxford whose hair had the same silky feel, of those magical nights in her rooms. The six-year-old image was as vivid as last night.

Out in the hall the grandfather clock bonged quarter past, rousing him from his reverie. He shut off the shower and shook his head free of water and memories. Towel wrapped around his waist, he padded back down the hall leaving a trail of wet footprints behind him.

He pulled on a white shirt, turned up the collar and wound

around a diamond-patterned yellow tie – most anything went with gray pinstripes. He looked around the top of the dresser for his wristwatch.

Propped up against a clock in the middle of the dresser was an invitation picturing a vibrant painting by Frank Stella. Right, the opening was this weekend. A client had invited Alastair to join his party, and he thought he would go. The clock rang gently, a single chime to signal the half hour. He picked up his watch and smiled at the clock, one of his favorite possessions.

The French mystery clock stood six inches high, the rock-crystal body mounted on a black onyx base. Suspended in the middle of the clear crystal was a jade circle mounted with onyx Roman numerals. Floating in the center of the circle, the slender, black hour and minute hands pointed outwards with no visible means of support.

He peered suspiciously at the clock. It ran fast and had already gained five minutes since he last set it back. That was the trouble with these old clocks, much as he loved them, few of them ever kept the proper time. But give or take five minutes, he really had to get going. He strapped on his watch and headed downstairs to look for his shoes.

He seemed to have disrobed in every room in the house last night. He found his vest draped over the newel post, his jacket hung on the back of a dining room chair, and his shoes sitting on the gaming table in the front room alongside two brandy snifters. Ah, yes, the cognac. He could thank the cognac for his hangover.

Next to the brandy snifters were Evelyn's earrings. He glanced at them while he tied his shoelaces, hoping this didn't mean she wanted to return. But they were rather pretty and she'd probably like them back. He dropped them into his shirt pocket. He'd send them to her in the interoffice mail; no, no – that was too obvious – by post would be better. One mustn't underestimate the boys in the mailroom.

A horn beeped outside, his chariot awaited.

He quickly donned his vest and jacket, first giving each a quick sniff. Sandwiched between shirt and overcoat, these didn't require frequent cleaning. He pocketed his house keys from the mantle and was out the door. Nothing like hitting the ground running. Saturdays back in London tended to be quiet, but not so in New York. It was one of his busier days.

Out on the front stoop rain was falling so he nipped back inside and grabbed an umbrella from the stand. A lovely, soft rain, really – just like home.

* * *

The road inside Woodlawn Cemetery wound around under autumnal maple trees, orange leaves fluttering against black trunks. Rows of granite tombstones and massive mausoleums bore names hearkening back to an earlier New Jersey: Buckby, Hedden, Kendrick, Ross, Hamilton, Crane. The rain had stopped and the sun broke through the clouds, sending down through the treetops luminous wedges of vaporous air.

Presently they came to parked cars lining both sides of the road: white stretch limousines, Jaguars, Mercedes, BMWs. He spotted the Lyndhurst and Lloyd's town car and chauffeur. Good; he'd ride back with Colin.

"Here we are," he said to the driver as he handed the bills over the back seat, including a generous tip.

"Enjoy," the driver said, and pulled off.

He couldn't remember when he had seen so many black-clad people, shuffled together like a clan of penguins. They swelled in an enormous circle between two large maple trees. Approaching slowly, he looked for Colin. It would be nice to know whose funeral he was attending.

The minister was well into the service:

"... *none of us will ever forget Edwin's giving nature, his generous contributions to civic causes, his tireless fund-raising energies ...*"

The crowd looked remarkably well-heeled in its grief: trimly tailored suits, smart dresses. He glanced over the heads, scanning the faces. Well, of all people, there was Terrence Young, his Modern Paintings counterpart at Sotheby's. And that looked like Martin Bauman, a trustee of the Whitney Museum. And Brooke Astor, the grand old dame of the New York art world. This *was* quite a gathering.

Finally he spotted Colin standing down at the opposite end from the minister. He eased his way through the crowd with a smile: "So sorry," "Please excuse me," "Forgive me, could I just get by?"

Colin looked dapper but appropriately solemn. He nodded as Alastair stepped in next to him.

"*. . . so hard for those left behind to understand the motives of a loved one who hurries God in calling home His flock . . .*"

"To whom are we paying respects?" Alastair whispered.

"Edwin DuBois."

"Ah."

He knew the name. DuBois and his wife had one of the biggest collections of Impressionist paintings in New York.

The gravediggers lowered the coffin into the ground.

"Doesn't his wife survive him?"

"She does," Colin whispered and nodded towards the minister. Alastair looked closely. The coffin was strewn with flowers like an Alpine hill in spring. Before it stood a petite woman, her gloved hands clasped, her veiled head bowed.

"Then why are we here?" Alastair asked.

The digger shoveled a mound of dirt into the hole.

"*The Lord is my shepherd, I shall not want. He maketh me to lie in green pastures . . .*"

"Haven't you been reading the papers? Edwin was running a gigantic Ponzi scheme that collapsed. This week he was indicted for fraud and embezzlement and he jumped out of a 27th floor window. They're ruined."

"*. . . Yea, though I walk through the valley of the shadow of Death . . .*"

Colin raised his eyebrows. "It's simply a question of how many paintings she will need to sell."

Chapter 4

Bo moved slowly towards the cupboard, keeping his eye on the cockroach. Not that it was hard to keep track of – it was huge, a giant among roaches.

"You goddamn monster, you're not going to get away this time," he muttered as he opened the cupboard door and fumbled around on the shelf for a glass. All he felt was a flat, empty surface.

"Damn!"

Looking around the loft he could see accumulated glasses and mugs strewn everywhere, as if he had had a party. They sat high on the frame of the loft bed, atop the spool table, along the windowsills. But none were within reach.

This time he was going to get the roach; he'd seen this one before. It had to be over two inches long, not including the antennae. Usually he just stepped on them, but this one was so big he didn't relish the idea of splattering its insides all over the floor.

As a rule he had nothing against indoor wildlife and was actually somewhat fond of the occasional mice that visited him. But cockroaches he couldn't warm up to. When he opened the potato drawer and found a mass of crawling roaches, it wasn't exactly appetizing.

He pushed up the sleeve of his frayed blue work shirt and rooted around in the sink brimming with water and dirty dishes, trying not to slop the water out, until he found the Bicentennial cup – plastic, so less breakable. Since he fished it out of the soaking water it would have the advantage of being covered with a layer of Raid, thanks to his new and improved method of washing up. When the sink was piled with dirty dishes, he filled it to the top with scalding water and detergent to loosen any stuck food. Then he sprayed Raid over the surface of the water to keep out the wretched insects. After a good soak the dishes rinsed right off. Worked like a charm.

Cup in hand, he crept stealthily toward the giant roach. It took off just as he reached it, but with one lunge he clapped the cup down over it.

"Ha! Caught you, you monster!"

He watched with satisfaction as the roach ran around and around inside the cup. It stopped and waved its antennae from between the liberty bells, then turned and ran in the opposite direction.

"Lousy parasite."

He returned to washing up, more quickly now as people should be arriving soon. For today was Open Studio Day, organized by a Soho artists' group. His door would be open and he was hoping for a lot of traffic. He felt he could use some positive feedback; a year of living in the artistic Mecca of Manhattan felt oddly like working in a vacuum. The nurturing fold of art school had not prepared him for the silence of the real world.

He wiped the sponge over a plate and tried to keep his expectations realistic. Clyde warned him that a lot of the people who came were tourist types, adventuring from the upper east side or Teaneck to check out the Soho art scene, hoping to catch a whiff of the avant-garde. Then they ended up over on Broadway buying Leroy Neiman posters in chrome frames.

These people really got to him at the parking lot. Weekends brought their big cars wheeling in with Jersey plates. They would step out in their pant and leisure suits, tossing dollar bills left and right as if Gino who ran the sausage truck and Bo were some gutter urchins they deigned to be charitable to.

Where was the justice here? Why did they have so much money when he had none?

The truth was that with his current cash flow problems he couldn't afford to be too picky about who bought his work as long as they paid. So, in the interests of self-preservation, he would try to make his studio as attractive as possible.

On the adjacent wall and well-lit from the windows hung the bigger canvases in the *Portraits of the City*, marked at $700 a piece which seemed like a fair price. The small watercolors and charcoal drawings were priced at under $150. Wouldn't it be great if selling his vision of the city would support his staying.

A favorite was a view of the downtown skyline he painted up on the rooftop. In the foreground, in dark grays and browns, ran a jagged silhouette of cornices, pot-bellied water towers and fire escapes. In the background, the World Trade Towers shot up in a luminous blue sky, their monumental forms glinting with the fiery light of the setting sun.

A pastel depicted the wide plaza below the towers viewed from the low angle of the sidewalk. A line of people of every age, race and dress led to the entrance of the Trade Tower which rose up behind them like a stairway to heaven. He was especially fond of this one, as it captured the feeling he had so often in New York: at the same time the city seemed to dwarf him, he felt important merely by virtue of being there.

Picking up the last stray mug that sat on the easel holding the portrait of Jeanette, he wondered if he should put the painting away since it wasn't finished. He hadn't gotten her hair right yet, the way he wanted the black strands to blow away from her face as she sat atop the Plaza fountain. But people might enjoy seeing a work in progress; he decided to leave it.

He grabbed his jacket and hammered down four flights of stairs, his bright whistling of *Got my Mojo Working* reverberating in the narrow stairwell. Some of the stairs' rubber matting had come loose and lay at cockeyed angles on the treads; he landed carefully on these, having hit one wrong once, which sent him flying.

The door opened onto a clear, cool day, the late September light already slightly fainter. Broome Street was quiet on Saturdays except for an occasional car and it seemed like a holiday compared to weekday mornings when the trucks banged through hitting each pothole with a wallop that ricocheted up the warehouse facades leaving a wake of rattling windows.

He looked down the street, surveying his block with pleasure. The location couldn't be better, right between Greene and Mercer. There wasn't much in the neighborhood but warehouses and that suited him just fine. Just a few blocks north on Prince Street was Fanelli's, where he'd stop in for a beer on nights when he felt like some company and sit at the bar with other local artists. This was exactly why he came to New York, to get away from the small Midwestern towns and farms and live in a city where he could go down to the corner bar and talk about art instead of the wheat crop.

He propped open the heavy door with a wooden wedge and taped up a sign: OPEN STUDIO, RYDER, 4th FLOOR. Groups of people were already meandering down from Spring Street, *Gallery Guide* maps in hand.

His mailbox, filled with jumbled envelopes, sprang open as he turned the key in the lock. He lifted out the pile, sat down on the loading dock, lit a cigarette and paged through bills, a flyer from a new restaurant, a letter from his mother, and an envelope with the return address of *Honthorst Gallery*. That one looked interesting. Having delivered slides to dozens of galleries, he couldn't remember exactly which one this was. He shoved the rest of the mail under his thigh and opened the envelope.

Dear Mr. Ryder,

We are interested in your work as part of the figurative revival and would like to include it in a show. Please contact us so we can discuss the terms.

Sincerely,
Phil Honthorst
Director

"Holy shit," he exclaimed. The mail spilled onto the sidewalk as he stood up and read the letter again. Could this possibly be the break he'd been waiting for, a show of his own?

He bounded up the stairs two at a time and breathlessly threw open the loft door. Spotting the entrapped cockroach, he ran to the cup and lifted it off the floor.

"Hey you louse, I got a show!"

The roach scuttled off and disappeared under the spool table.

Bo tossed the cup on to the loft bed and zipped around the loft nabbing the last stray socks and T-shirts. Rolling them into a ball, he tossed it across the room towards the cardboard box that served as a hamper. As the clothes flopped over the side he let out a hoot and spun around into the perplexed faces of two young women standing in the doorway.

"Excuse us, we thought the studio was open . . ."

"No, no, not at all. I mean, yes, yes, come on in."

One of them handed him his mail and asked, "You are Mr. Ryder?"

"Yes, m'am, I surely am. Please – come see the paintings."

He gladly showed them around. As the day passed, with dozens of people coming and going, he remained the affable artist, welcoming his public. Finally he was on his way to achieving what he'd wanted ever since he'd won the St. Louis *Future Choices* oil painting competition in 10th grade: to be a recognized, self-supporting painter.

Two small pieces sold, two he was proud of. A watercolor of the Brooklyn Bridge at night, its web of silvery cables strung against a starry sky, went for $125. A charcoal sketch of the pigeon coop on the roof with the grey-blue birds circling in the sky brought $100.

"Well, I'll be damned," he murmured, counting the bills. It wasn't exactly big money, but it was $225 he didn't have before. It would take care of Con Ed for a couple of months, if not the rent. But he was gaining on it, he'd get past this starving artist stage – and sooner rather than later, thank you very much.

The visitors dwindled as the afternoon wore on since the

loft was off the beaten track of West Broadway. But he didn't mind. In fact, he wished they would all clear out so he could call the Honthorst Gallery.

About five o'clock a couple came in whom he took special notice of because they looked particularly upper-upper. She wore some kind of fur coat, her red hair swirled up in a French twist, which on her looked fashionable instead of dowdy. At her side walked a somewhat shorter man, slightly built but impressively dressed in a dark suit, which somehow made him look taller than he actually was. Bo glanced at his shoes: almost anyone could dress nicely if they tried, but it was the shoes that gave away just what kind of investment a person might be capable of. This man's shoes gleamed, the black leather opaque but reflective. These two were definitely not hurting.

They looked around with mild interest. Bo thought they seemed better left alone, so he picked up a palette knife and began to clean the paint-encrusted palette. Presently the woman approached him.

"I'm so sorry to infringe on you, but I wonder if I could use your bathroom?"

"Sure, if you're not too choosy. It's right around the corner there," he said, gesturing towards the back.

"Perfect," she answered.

You'll find out how perfect it is when you get in there, he thought, with its rust-stained sink and broken old bathtub.

Her high heels clicked across the floor, turned the corner and stopped. "Oh my!" she exclaimed. Without looking up Bo guessed she had spotted the rococo mirror. It *was* unusual. He continued scraping the stubborn hunks of dried paint.

"Where ever did you get this, in the gilt frame?"

Ah, yes – the mirror. He kept scraping.

"My mother gave me that."

"Is it genuine?"

"Oh, yes. She picked it up in Paris years ago. She's a regular art hound."

Mom did have a good eye and a knack for finding things at a fair price.

"This is some find. What a wonderful example, with the full style and exuberance."

He smiled and kept scraping; that was an interesting way to describe Rococo: *exuberant.*

"It sure is," he said. "You know those French and their *joie de vivre.*"

After a momentary silence she said, "Would you consider selling it?"

This woke him up. He put down the palette knife and walked back to the bathroom, but when he turned the corner he nearly banged right into the woman, for she wasn't in the bathroom at all but was standing outside the door looking at the drawings on Clyde's *Ryder Museum* wall. They had not been talking about the same thing. And he was flattered, because she had been oohing and ahhing not over the Rococo mirror but over his own watercolor study after Matisse's *Joy of Life.*

"Can we take it down and look at it in the light?" she asked.

He was so pleased he didn't know what to say. He hadn't meant to deceive her, but her praise felt so good he wasn't inclined to correct the misunderstanding. He lifted the gilt frame off the wall and carried it to the window where she looked at it closely.

Languorous forms lazed about a sylvan scene, some embracing, others posing suggestively, a Pan figure playing a flute and in the distance, out from under the trees, a circle of nude dancers cavorted hand in hand. The colors were light and clean, the forms simple but classical, evoking a joyful and timeless serenity.

"It's fabulous! These studies for the *Joy of Life* are very hard to find. I have one of them, a smaller one," she said proudly. Then she confided, "Matisse is *my* master, you see. I collect him."

This was funny. But sure, please continue, his lines *were* as fine as Matisse . . . He couldn't resist playing along with her.

"He's one of my favorites, too."

"Reinhold," she called to her companion, who was now looking closely at the drawings on the *Ryder Museum* wall, "Come take a look."

The man walked towards them, his close-set eyes as opaque as his shoe leather. Raven-colored hair that looked almost too black to be true matched his goatee. As he approached he reached not for the drawing, but for Bo's hand. Small but surprisingly vigorous, it pressed around Bo's, giving a quick, hard shake, released with equal speed.

"Reinhold Gerhardt," he said, his Germanic accent clipped and precise. Then he added approvingly, "Very nice work."

"Thanks," Bo answered, feeling flattered. Somehow this compliment sounded more professional than the others he'd heard over the course of the day.

"And I'm Susan Jacobson," offered the woman. She held the Matisse study out for Gerhardt to see and turned to Bo with a laugh. "Reinhold is my art advisor. He has full veto power, my husband insists."

Gerhardt handed the drawing back to the woman with a smile for Bo. "Lovely."

"To add to my collection?" she asked.

"Why not?"

She nodded thoughtfully and turned to Bo. "I'll give you a thousand dollars for it."

He stepped back and laughed in surprise.

"Okay," she said diplomatically. "Fourteen hundred. I know one went recently at Sotheby's for that. But we don't have to pay the commission. I think that's fair, don't you, Reinhold?"

He nodded agreeably. "Absolutely."

Bo shook his head. Some businesswoman. But as much as he was enjoying this, it really had gone too far.

"Nope, can't do it. Sentimental value."

She sighed. "Yes, I suppose, since it was a gift from your mother."

She held up the drawing and pondered. "It would fit so

nicely in with the others." She hesitated a moment. "Are you quite sure? I can give you cash."

He glanced at Reinhardt, whose steady smiled was accompanied now by twinkling eyes. Bo pursed his lips. This was hard, this was really hard. Here he was with barely two nickels to rub together and she was offering him $1400 in cash.

"I'm sorry. I appreciate the offer but I really can't do it." Then he added brightly, "The paintings in the studio are all for sale." He had a loaded collector here, he couldn't just let her walk away.

The woman shook her head. "They do have a certain appeal, but you know I'm just not brave enough yet to buy contemporary art."

"Well, you've got to start sometime. Sure, Matisse was great, but his art is a little passé, wouldn't you agree?" He gestured at the canvases on the walls and the portrait of Jeanette on the easel. "This is New York, this is what's happening now."

He felt like a car salesman. The woman nodded dubiously.

"I understand. It's just that you can't be sure of the resale value."

He gave a little laugh.

"You could buy it because you like it and not worry about reselling it."

Then it was her turn to laugh. She threw a knowing look towards Gerhardt.

"I love to look, but buying is a commitment I never make without being sure of some equity."

She reached into her bag and pulled out a business card.

"If you ever change your mind," she said, handing over her card. "I will never lose my interest in Matisse."

He nodded and took the card. What a silly thing she was. At this point he was happy to let her go; he had better things to do.

As he headed towards the door, Gerhardt turned, his dark eyes intense and suddenly serious. "Your talents will not go unnoticed, you can be sure of that." He clicked his heels and departed.

Bo stood a little taller as he listened to their steps descending the stairs. Well, not too shabby a comment, especially from a connoisseur like him. But compliments were one thing, a contract was another. He quickly found the Honthorst gallery letter. Throwing himself into the swivel chair, he pulled the old black phone with the cracked cord into his lap and dialed, but the receiver just rang and rang in his ear. He looked at his watch. Of course! It was 6:30 and the gallery had closed and, today being Saturday, wouldn't open again until Tuesday morning.

Damn! He almost had a deal in his pocket, and now it was once more out of reach. He stared at the portrait of Jeanette on the easel, thinking that he should keep working and try not to think about it. His eyes dropped to the base where the slats were reinforced with duct tape, and he felt as restrained as the wood. No, his talent would not go unnoticed, he was surely about to land a gallery, but how the hell could he wait three more days to find out?

Suddenly, out from between the legs of the easel, scurried the cockroach. It scuttled across the floor and stopped, waving its antennae. Bo leapt up and flew towards it with an ear-splitting yell, skidding across the floor as his heel landed on the shell. He smiled triumphantly. At last.

Scooping up the squashed remains with the palette knife, he raised the window sash and tossed the carcass into the darkening fire escape. Then he returned to the easel, squinted at Jeanette's hair, and dipped the brush into mars black.

Chapter 5

Megan's eyes skirted every surface in the living room; where could she have put the invitation to the Frank Stella retrospective? It was nowhere to be found at work so it must be here. Searching the apartment, she experienced a strange déjà vu. Every object seemed infused with meaning, emblematic of the irreconcilable differences between her and Ned. The furniture, selected by Ned from Scandinavian Design, looked stale and unimaginative. The peach place mats on the teak veneer table seemed fussy and unnecessary. The Haitian cotton couch appeared overstuffed, as if it didn't know when to stop eating.

When she and Ned first planned to move to New York from the small New England town where they graduated from college four years ago, they decided to live together, which at the time seemed like a good idea. She thought she was ready for the commitment and her mother didn't object, she was so glad Megan wouldn't be living alone in the big city.

Ned found the apartment – he insisted on having a 'good address' – and the truth was it never really suited her. She always disliked the low ceilings with the insulated panels that looked as if they'd escaped from a dentist's office, which didn't keep the apartment quiet anyway with the street noise from the corner of Lexington and 55th. And the neighborhood offered so little in the way of interesting restaurants. The only place Ned ever wanted to go was the French bistro on the corner because they always had filet mignon on the menu. He didn't like to eat out unless he knew he could get steak.

She stopped momentarily in front of some of the art objects she and Ned had acquired together, but then shook her head. No, they weren't worth the argument. She'd just take what she needed. And better do it quickly, because the opening started in an hour and she had to drop off some belongings with Lizzy, who had kindly offered to put her up until she could find a place of her own. The offer was a lifesaver – finding a decent apartment in Manhattan could take weeks, even months.

Behind the potted jade plant she spotted her purse. The purse was never hard to find because it was so enormous. 'Purse' was really the wrong term; this was a bag, definitely a bag, large and leather and big enough to throw over a saddle. It came in handy when she was running late because it often had what she needed and saved her a trip back to the apartment. Her mother called her 'the vagabond' since she'd been carrying it.

She swung it up onto the table. As it hit the surface the contents clunked and settled lumpily, like a seaman's duffel. For her birthday Lizzy got her a plastic shovel and a flashlight, for her 'purse excavation', as she called it. Lizzy thought it was a good joke, but they actually came in handy.

She rooted around inside looking for the invitation. In the process out came a half-eaten package of smoked almonds, a cassette tape recorder, a dog-eared copy of *The Sound and the Fury*, a slide viewer, a polished horse chestnut, a Paris metro map, and a purple swimsuit. Flattened along the bottom was the invitation from the Museum of Modern Art. She took it out and stuffed everything else back in – you never knew.

The invitation was printed with one of Frank Stella's vibrant new three-dimensional pieces. She loved his work and had been looking forward to this retrospective – even more so now with the prospect of further information to be had on the detained Modigliani. Before leaving the office she'd called customs, which informed her that the bill of lading listed the purchaser of the Modigliani as one Catherine DuBois of upper 5th Avenue. Megan had promptly called Mrs. DuBois. A protective voice answered the phone (a butler, no doubt, considering the address) and informed her that Mrs. DuBois was not taking calls due to the death of her husband and that all art matters were being handled by Reinhold Gerhardt of Gerhardt Fine Arts. She reached Mr. Gerhardt easily at his gallery. However, he had no time for a telephone interview as he was on his way to the Frank Stella opening. How auspicious, she'd said, and he'd agreed to meet her in the MoMA sculpture garden at 7 PM.

She checked the bag again to make sure it had her black notebook. Smooth and worn from years of nestling in the palm of her hand, the leather case had held many a spiral pad, its hollow spine a multitude of pens. She would need this if the interview were as fruitful as she hoped. She smiled, suddenly feeling better. What better diversion from heartache than a newspaper mission.

She grabbed two rayon dresses, some underwear, socks and stockings and shoved them into her bag. She paged through the *The New York Times* lying on the table until she found the Classified Real Estate section. This she folded into quarters and stuffed into her bag.

Oreo appeared out of nowhere, purring loudly, his tail curling around her leg. In one deft jump the animal was up on the table, his motor running like an idling car. He rubbed his whiskers against her hand.

"You never liked him anyway. He always kicked you off the bed at night."

She stuffed Oreo's kibble bowl into her bag and hoped Lizzy's old tomcat wouldn't mind sharing his litter box.

As she glanced around at the room her throat tightened unexpectedly. Life with Ned hadn't been all bad. Nor had their visions of the future: a roomy house on a tree-lined street, a screened eating porch, a big dog romping on the lawn, children filling the air with shouts and laughter. She ran her hand along Oreo's arched back as the tears spilled down her cheeks. Never mind; another time, another man. Because in truth that life never would have worked for her, not the way Ned would live it. He needed someone who wanted to move up to Greenwich, who would welcome him and his briefcase full of work home in the evening. He needed a woman who would be happy to join the PTO and the Garden Club and fuss good-naturedly about how his golf shoes left mud on the floor. But it wasn't her; she would turn into the mad housewife.

She turned to pick up her things and her eye caught a print of Titian's *Assumption*. A glorious vision of the miraculous rise of the Virgin Mary, her outstretched arms beckoned from across the room. Megan walked swiftly to the print and looked at the Virgin's euphoric expression as she ascended to salvation, cherubs lifting her upwards on cottony clouds, her face full of joy and wonder. She took the picture off the wall. She could use a little heavenly assistance here herself this evening. Surely Ned wouldn't mind if she took this souvenir of their trip to Venice, if he even noticed. He had barely looked at the great painting when they stood in front of it at the Frari but left the church to find an espresso. He said looking at paintings made his feet hurt.

Print tucked under one arm, she picked up her bag with the other. Oreo just fit into the top, his paws resting on the open zipper, his curious look accented by white whiskers fanning out from his black face. As Megan opened the door to leave the phone rang and she paused, her stomach tightening.

The answering machine picked it up.

"Hi Megan, it's me. Look, I'm sorry I lost my temper. I know you're right about a lot of this stuff. But I'm sure we can reach a compromise, maybe even keep an apartment in the city if you want to . . ."

The air was refreshingly cool in the hallway as she closed the door against Ned's negotiating tone. She hoisted her bulging bag up on her shoulder with Oreo's head bobbing out the top, picked up the *Assumption* print, and headed for the elevator.

> *Just slip out the back, Jack*
> *Make a new plan, Stan*
> *You don't need to be coy, Roy*
> *Just get yourself free*

* * *

Alastair stepped into the black stretch limousine idling at the curb outside his host's town house on Sutton Place. Their party was eight, so seating everyone was a bit tight. But laughing and joking they all piled into the car and he found himself crammed into the corner with his host's sister wedged in beside him like a newborn kitten. She wore a black dress with a slit up one side and a mink coat which she hadn't bothered to button.

Alastair was feeling pleasantly inebriated and didn't much mind when the limousine careened into the cross-town side street, practically throwing the woman into his lap. She shrieked with laughter and said, "*Poor* Alastair, let me make some room for you."

His host, Hank Campbell, lifted a bottle of champagne from the ice bucket in the car door and twisted out the cork, silently, expertly; the gases wisped airily out the top. "One more for the road," he said, handing fizzing champagne flutes all around.

Alastair accepted the glass with a smile. It had been a very long day.

The woman sipped hers daintily. "I'll never finish this before we get to the museum. How about a turn around the park first?"

Hank winked at Alastair and said, "You wouldn't be trying to sidetrack us, would you?"

"Of course not, darling, it's just that we're all having such a good time, it seems a shame to break up the party."

"But aren't you eager to see Stella's new work? I thought he was a favorite of yours, Stella the Fella?" Hank said.

"Always a brother," she answered, rolling her eyes and crossing her legs in the other direction, spreading the slit in her skirt farther up her leg. "Yes, I *am* looking forward to the show, and especially to my personal tour with Alastair. After all, he's the expert." She lowered her eyes demurely.

"Stella's a bit out of my league, I'm afraid," Alastair said.

"Ah, but you're good on any art, I'm sure of that," Hank said. "You're my Berenson."

Alastair smiled deferentially. His host was a budding collector of German Expressionist paintings and if he wanted to compare Alastair to the 19th century's most influential art advisor, far be it from Alastair to dissuade him.

Hank topped off Alastair's glass with the last of the bottle and said, "Let's regroup afterwards for dinner. Those canapés only go so far. We can always get into the 21 Club without a reservation."

"I love 21," seconded his sister. "It's like going home to your own dining room."

The east side streets were slick and gleaming from the rain. While the party chattered on, Alastair looked out the window, enjoying the reflections in the wet pavement – streetlights, storefronts, red and green traffic lights – illuminating the night in festive colors, sparkling against the dark streets as if the whole city were dressed for a party.

But what he felt most like celebrating was that he knew Hank was going to make a great collector. Because for all of his fooling around, Hank had a passion for German Expressionism that was just being kindled; last week he had stood in awe before a Lyonel Feininger, marveling at its masked faces and distorted buildings. This was the kind of reverence that Alastair could cultivate into acquiring a major collection. And Hank had the money to back it.

The limousine turned onto 5th Avenue; they shot down a block and around the corner into 53rd Street, and pulled up to the burgeoning crowd at the curb.

*   *   *

The Spring Street subway stop was as damp as a cave. The tile walls glistened with moisture and a raw mist permeated the station like an uninvited guest.

Bo walked along the platform waiting for the uptown IRT. Water from the earlier rain dripped down through an overhead street grate and lay in puddles on the concrete. The atmosphere was close and dank. He turned and walked back closer to the tracks for a whiff of the fresher air that blew out from the tunnel. The opening in the rough-hewn rock was dark and showed no sign of a coming train.

He took the Stella invitation out of his pocket. From the looks of it, Stella had evolved from primary block painter to whirling dervish. The image was intriguing. Good thing – Bo hated to go to a reception just for the food.

He pocketed the card and turned as a deep rumble sounded from within the tunnel, and momentarily the lights of the E train came into view. The train braked with a squeal and he nipped inside the brightly lit car. The car lurched forward and swayed out of the station.

From the puddled floor of the subway car he could feel the dampness beginning to come through the soles of one of his boots. He turned up the bottom of his boot – sure enough, there was a hole in the leather. They would have to be re-soled; they were just starting to get comfortable. Now, the $2400 in cash that lady had offered for the Matisse study would have bought one hell of a pair of new boots . . . But then, so would the proceeds from his first show at Honthorst. For once in his life, he'd be patient.

He peered between the spray-painted graffiti on the window and watched the stations pass, each marked by street numbers on the tiled walls. The numbers rose as the car banged and hummed its way uptown: 4th, 14th, 23rd, 34th, 42nd, 50th Street, elevating him into the stratosphere; he couldn't remember the last time he'd been north of 14th Street. He'd have to do this more often before he turned into a complete downtown denizen. The wheels screeched as the tunnel turned east and in one more stop delivered him to 53rd Street.

The 53rd Street station was tall and arched like the nave of a Romanesque cathedral. Bo looked up at the lofty ceiling as he walked down the platform and stepped onto the escalator. The rubber railing vibrated slightly under his hands and he leaned back as the moving stairs carried him up and up, rising through the shiny tiled tunnel, gleaming white ahead. Suddenly in his mind's eye he saw Clyde floating above the arch, Clyde in the red chair with wings on its feet, a hovering Hermes. Now there was a portrait worth painting.

Out in the fresh air of 53rd Street the evening had darkened, but from down the street to the left shone the brightly lit windows of the Museum of Modern Art, illuminating the milling crowd. He straightened his jacket and walked briskly towards the light.

Chapter 6

M egan paid the cabby and got out on the corner of 53rd Street. The night air felt cool and soothing, a tonic to her tumultuous week. Once she dropped Oreo and her belongings at Lizzy's, her stomach magically began to settle down from the bilious state it had been in. And now, as she approached the crowd gathered around the museum entrance, she was surprised to find herself looking forward to the evening, to losing herself in engaging art, and especially to talking with Reinhold Gerhardt.

Frank Stella had a big crowd for his opening. A semi-circle eight people deep surrounded the entrance; as she stepped up and took a place she wondered if she'd ever find Gerhardt or Lizzy. Everyone pressed towards the lobby. The entrance was bottlenecked because only two doors were open, and on the inside a single attendant was collecting invitations. She moved forward, trying to avoid an umbrella waving uncomfortably close to her face. But the crowd pressed in on all sides and the umbrella jabbed her in the back of the neck. Ready with a glare for the offender, she turned to see a tall, fair-haired man standing behind her.

"I'm terribly sorry," he said with an English accent. "Please forgive me, it's just that it's so crowded." He looked chagrined.

"That's all right," she replied and turned back to the entrance. It was hard to be miffed with someone who looked so genuinely sorry.

As an empty wedge of the revolving door came around she nipped into it, but the lobby was so jammed there was no room to get out. The door kept turning steadily and she circled back around. A guy with dark, curly hair was pushing the door in the compartment behind her. She shook her head at him; why didn't he just stop and wait? He shrugged and shouted through the glass, "Try again!"

This time the door stopped on the inside and she stepped into the space that had opened up. He followed behind and said in her ear, "Some door, huh?"

"Some *push*," she answered, turning to him. Brown eyes twinkling, he stood at just her height.

"Hey, this is New York. The art world. A pushy crowd. What can I say?"

His cheeks dimpled. She smiled and turned back to the ticket taker. It had been a long time since she came to one of these affairs alone.

She made her way through the wide lobby, maneuvering amongst the tightly packed people, trying to steal a glimpse of the paintings on her way to meet Gerhardt. Bursts of laughter and the clink of glasses rose above the lively crowd. Mounted all around them Stella's huge canvases hung suspended, scintillating spectrums of color. She couldn't help admiring them, noting how utterly different they were from his early color field painting. One she stopped in front of looked like it had exploded. The canvas erupted into three dimensions, pigments expanded into texture and metallics, shapes squirmed out of the geometric into organic freeform. It was as if Stella's creative energies had gotten so expansive they could not be contained and burst out of the picture plane.

On the far side of the escalator she looked out the enormous plate glass window into the sculpture garden. At the appointed meeting place, in front of the John Chamberlain sculpture whose crumpled parts managed to evoke a multi-colored flower more than a crashed car, stood a short, 50-ish looking man dressed impeccably in a double-breasted Armani suit which looked as if it had been designed for a larger frame. He held two glasses of champagne and looked around expectantly. Megan glanced at her watch; she was a minute late.

"Mr. Gerhardt? I'm Megan Trico," she said, approaching him with outstretched hand.

He smiled and bowed his head, at the same time giving a small click of his heels. With a German-sounding accent and a polite reserve he told her how charmed he was to meet her and offered one of the champagne flutes with a smooth and hairless hand, the fingernails gleaming faintly as if they'd been polished. She accepted the glass and a shiver ran through her; the night air in the garden was chilled.

With an expansive sweep of his small hand that took in the surrounding sculpture, Gerhardt solicited her agreement on the worthiness of MoMA, how marvelous it was to have a thorough sampling of European modernism right here in New York, even if it meant one of Gustav Klmit's masterpieces must live away from his native Vienna. Megan smiled inwardly. So . . . his accent was Viennese. What was it about cultivated Europeans that always made her feel like Annie Oakley?

She steered the conversation around to the Modigliani held up in customs. Not having developed the brashness of a true investigative reporter, she gently broached the claim of the Italian consulate on behalf of the Umbrian that the painting was stolen during the occupation. Gerhardt gave a short, ridiculing laugh. "That is absurd. The painting has been part of a French collection for years – the Garnier family of Paris. I was lucky enough to be in London and see it at Sotheby's in time to advise my long-time clients about it, Edwin and Catherine DuBois." Here he sighed and lightly ran his finger around the rim of the champagne glass, the colorful reflections of Chamberlain's crumpled sheet metal shining in the stem. "Poor Catherine, you know, has just been widowed . . . a terrible thing, really very sad. And with her other legal troubles, the last thing she needs now is an unnecessary fuss over a painting that she bought and paid for and is rightfully hers. Wouldn't you agree?"

He looked directly at Megan, his eyes so dark brown she could barely make out his pupils, his face containing such an expression of injustice, it seemed heartless to be anything but sympathetic.

"That is a shame. But I guess the Italians must feel about the Modigliani just as you do about the Klimt, that they are entitled to a proprietary interest." Gerhardt lifted his eyebrows and gave an acknowledging smile. Megan continued. "I've read the police report and the Umbrian is certain the painting is the one he grew up with. He has identified the sitter as a cousin. They are demanding that the stolen art be returned, and even that Germany pay additional damages for the years of loss."

Gerhardt smiled, unruffled. "This is politics, nothing more. Believe me, I know. I lived in Austria during the Third Reich. Yes, the Nazis confiscated many art collections, but this Modigliani was not among them. It has a perfectly legitimate provenance from Sotheby's. The Garniers are the original owners. They lent the painting for exhibitions, all of which I'm sure is documented. I have been an international dealer for many, many years, my dear, and I do business with only the most reputable firms. I trust that despite your youth you are experienced enough to know that Sotheby's falls into this category."

He smiled so charmingly that his words sounded admiring rather than patronizing.

"Yes, most people do accept a Sotheby's provenance," answered Megan.

Gerhardt raised his hands in a gesture of magnanimity. "I'm sure the Umbrians have made an honest mistake and that it will all be settled shortly. And it must be admitted, as lovely as Modigliani's portraits are, they can look quite similar. Clearly it was a comparable portrait that the Umbrian knew. After all, it's been 30 years since he has seen it . . . we all know how memory distorts."

He smiled confidently and nodded towards the bright rooms inside. "Tell me, how do you like the show?"

Megan was satisfied. Back inside she excused herself from Gerhardt and made a few quick notes. Then, with the crowd thickening around her, she walked through the exhibition rooms, keeping one eye open for Lizzy as she drank in the enormous canvases.

"Megan Trico! Hello, you smart person, you!"

She turned to see Jake Gruber, owner of a contemporary gallery in Soho, gray hair receding above his cheerful face, a cigar stuck behind his ear. With him stood the Englishman who had poked her with the umbrella.

"Have you met Alastair Cavendish, new Modern paintings expert at Lyndhurst and Lloyd's?"

Alastair smiled apologetically. "I've run into her once."

"Here, Megan," Jake said, handing her his champagne. "I'll get another."

Jake headed for the bar and Alastair smiled and held out his hand. "How do you do," he said formally, but his blue eyes looked kind.

His hand felt big and he reminded her of Michael York, her ideal for the big-boned, lanky blonde type. What a shame he had ruined the appeal by wearing a pin-striped suit that looked exactly like one of Ned's. But here was an auction house painting expert, right at her fingertips . . .

"I've always been curious," she began, not wanting to sound too serious at a cocktail party. "Just what is a painting's provenance?"

"You might say it's analogous to a pedigree. Rather bad form to list for people but essential for a painting." He looked at her with amusement. "Basically, it's a bit of history we provide about where the painting has been and who has owned it, which is sometimes as interesting as the piece itself. When you find out that a picture once hung in the palace of a Russian Czar, or that a banker acquired it from a foreign government in exchange for war-time loans, or that it got its start at the Salon de Refusé in Paris after having been rejected by the Academy – it can really be quite exciting. You start thinking about what the painting must have witnessed – if only it could talk!"

Megan watched his face light up as he spoke, thinking he looked almost as excited as Horvath when he scooped a story. But she needed to nail this down further, so she asked if the auction house guaranteed the provenance. He explained that the provenance was what the auction house learned from the consignor, that it wasn't legally binding, but that any reputable auction house would stand behind it.

"Do you check the provenance before you include it in a sale catalogue description?"

"As far as I can, yes."

"So then you do guarantee it."

"Let's put it this way: I hold myself responsible – and am held so by my directors – for providing an accurate provenance. But can the firm be held legally culpable? Probably not, I think *caveat emptor* applies in buying art at auction. But since art expertise accounts for a great deal at a reputable auction house, the provenance had jolly well better be right."

"What if someone claims your provenance is wrong?"

Alastair laughed. "If they could prove it, that would be rather distressing."

Megan smiled to herself, feeling grateful that it was Sotheby's that was about to be on the hot seat and not Lyndhurst and Lloyd's. The story wasn't Son of Sam, but it might keep her employed as an arts news reporter.

Suddenly feeling remiss about not having found Lizzy yet, she shook Alastair's hand and excused herself.

*   *   *

Jake reappeared with fizzing champagne flutes, one of which Alastair accepted as he watched Megan turn and go. He raised his right hand to his mouth, savoring the ghost of her palm, soft and warm in his. How very pretty she was. He had been noting this during most of their conversation, which for him was just a subtext. He had made some remarks about the chronological development of Stella's work, but in his mind he had been cataloguing her:

> 'Pre-Raphaelite School: the thick auburn hair cascading over slim shoulders, the complexion a translucent ivory, an aqua vein showing delicately at the temple, the cheeks a glowing peach. The high forehead extending down the graceful brow to a straight but distinctive nose. The full, cherry mouth curving rhythmically, the upper lip protruding slightly over the lower.'

He was quite good at this actually, carrying on a fairly lucid conversation while his thoughts were elsewhere. And then there were her eyes, her incredible eyes. Greenish-hazel, deep and crystalline, they seemed to have a light of their own. How was it that one could perceive a face so quickly? In an instant one registered the quality of the hair, the skin, the eyes, revealing age, health, intelligence. Some primitive factors must be at work, some extra-sensory honing that sparked interest, or not. In this case, his spark was clearly ignited.

Along with the champagne Jake had brought back a small, dapper man. Jake made introductions and they shook hands: Reinhold Gerhardt's hand in contrast was thin and somewhat damp. As Alastair watched Megan's auburn head disappearing into the crowd, suddenly his attention was caught by a remark of Gerhardt's.

"A tragic death, Edwin DuBois. And a great shock for her, poor Catherine."

"Yes, I'd met them both," said Gruber. "He had a real eye for business, and for art. She was lovely but seemed more to be going along for the ride."

"Indeed," said Gerhardt, "she is at a loss right now, in more ways than one. I will offer my services, of course, it's the least I can do."

An alarm went off in Alastair's head and her turned to Gerhardt with a smile.

"What kind of services do you offer?" he asked politely.

Gerhardt smiled. "I am a dealer in fine art, specializing in estates. Catherine has put her trust in me for years."

Alastair watched Gerhardt as he spoke, evenly, smoothly, his gold pinkie ring engraved with a crest sparkling in the lights. He talked about the comfort of dealing with a private dealer in these difficult circumstances, but all it impressed on Alastair was that he'd better get his bid in before it was too late. Oh, yes, it was a nasty business with them all hovering like vultures over the recently deceased, but on the other hand, someone needed to sell the remains, and sad as the circumstances were, he'd heard the DuBois collection included a splendid selection of European Modernism. Just what he needed to jump-start his department. He resolved to call Mrs. DuBois tomorrow.

*   *   *

From the ascending escalator Megan looked out into the lit sculpture garden for tall Lizzy but couldn't spot her amongst the milling figures, dwarfed by the enormous sculptures looming all around. Upstairs the galleries were less crowded and she stopped to look at the paintings, forgetting momentarily about her friend.

Standing in front of one of Stella's recent three-dimensional works, she marveled at its complexity. Looking at it was like entering another dimension. It looped and turned, leading the eye around and over and back again, continually revealing something new, some further relationship of color or form. She got lost in its interstices.

Not noticing the man standing next to her, she moved to change her vantage point and stepped right into him, stumbling on his foot.

"Hey!" he said.

"Good grief, what a klutz!" she exclaimed as she backed

off. It was the curly-haired guy who turned her around in the revolving door.

Bo looked surprised. "I know I've got big feet, but they aren't *that* big."

"I'm really sorry, I didn't see you."

She glanced at him, liking his dressed-down look in this uptown crowd – old boots, paint-spattered jeans, and a beat-up leather jacket.

He grinned. "You're sure this isn't revenge for spinning you around earlier?"

She laughed. "It is not."

She looked back at the painting. She wasn't used to talking to strangers in the city.

"You like the painting," he said.

"Oh, yes, very much. I think it's one of my favorites."

"*Fabulous?*" he asked mockingly.

"Well, yes, I might even say it's fabulous."

"I knew it. *Fabulous.* That's the ultimate New York compliment, isn't it?"

"Is there something wrong with the word 'fabulous'?"

He shrugged. "I guess not. Back in St. Louis that's how people talk about golf courses. 'A *fabulous* course, just fabulous.'"

He said it good-naturedly, but he also seemed to have a bone to pick.

"You don't like the painting?" she asked.

"Yeah, I like it, I have to admit. For abstract painting, I'd say it's pretty good."

She watched his dismissive acknowledgment with amusement; there was no harsher critic than a fellow painter who worked in a different style.

"Let me guess – you're an artist. A hard-core realist."

He laughed. "Some people would say so. It's true I think paintings are more interesting when they have some content."

"Just because you can't recognize anything doesn't mean

the painting doesn't have content. What about the emotional effect? Abstract painting is more like music, when it's good you respond like you would to a melody."

She suddenly felt uncomfortable, aware of his steadfast gaze. "You don't agree?" she asked.

He was staring at her intently and looked as if he hasn't heard a thing. "No, I mean, I hadn't really thought about it." Then he cocked his head and smiled. "You're wearing two different earrings."

She quickly fingered her ears. She'd been in such a hurry leaving the apartment that she'd put in one pearl earring set in a gold jacket, and when she couldn't find the match, grabbed another that seemed to go well enough, a cluster of baroque pearls hanging from an enameled serpent. "You're right, I do."

He looked back and forth between the two earrings. "One is formal and the other is kind of funky."

She laughed. "*Funky*? Casual, maybe."

Her mother had brought the earrings back from Japan and Megan couldn't quite think of them as funky.

He nodded in acquiescence. "Okay, casual. Anyway, it's an interesting look, I like it."

She smiled self-consciously. "I was in a hurry getting here tonight."

"They work together. Pearls and serpents, both from the sea," he said.

He looked at her appreciatively and she looked down, not sure which she was more impressed with, the fact that he liked the mismatched earrings or that he noticed them at all. Ned would have been oblivious.

Bo glanced around the gallery. "Do you suppose Stella is here tonight?" he asked.

"I should think so, although I haven't seen him. I don't know how he could miss this."

He shook his head and smiled. "Yeah, it's a pretty amazing event. To have the museum recognize him while he's still alive to enjoy it."

She looked at his teasing grin and laughed. He had such an easy way about him, his broad midwestern vowels sounded so relaxed.

Suddenly Lizzy was at her side, her long blonde hair braided down her back for the occasion, eager to spirit her away. Megan put out her hand and gave Bo's a firm, direct shake.

"Megan Trico. It was nice to meet you."

"Bo Ryder, likewise."

She shook his hand; it was small but strong.

Lizzy dragged her off, but as they stepped through the doorway, Megan turned. Bo stood looking at her, his hands in his pockets, his compact figure motionless before the enormous canvas that zigged and zagged in wild exuberance.

Chapter 7

*D*uBois – the old French name so long in America that it was now pronounced as if it rhymed with rejoice – just another of the many adjustments Alastair had to make. *DuBois, rejoice, DuBois, rejoice* – the rhythm fit his brisk walk along Central Park South, the autumn morning air crisp and invigorating, inspiring long strides and grand plans. He watched the pavement passing under his advancing feet, the hexagonal shapes fitted together in a spreading honeycomb, and hoped his day would proceed as precisely as this pavement. For no matter how well he organized his plans on the way to work, they were often squelched by unexpected crises on his arrival. But for ten minutes in the morning he enjoyed the illusion of control.

Clip clop, rejoice, clip clop, DuBois – he heard it in the horses' feet as they drew reluctant carriages into the park, vapors rising off their backs, nostrils blowing streams of white in the cool air. *DuBois, rejoice.* What a terrible rhyme, really. Was a man killing himself any cause for celebration? Although disaster was not an unusual reason for the mounting of a great collection on the auction block. Glamorous as the major sales appeared, with their celebrity names and soaring prices, the most common causes for selling were death, divorce, or bankruptcy. But one couldn't let reality get in the way of business. He had to land the DuBois collection or he might be taking a slow freighter back to Britain.

Catherine DuBois, what did he really know about her? Not enough, he must find out more. The personal touch, the social connection, could make all the difference in getting a consignment. Especially when it came down to a contest with Sotheby's or some prominent dealer. Reinhold Gerhardt, with an association already established, was clearly a contender.

"Good morning," Alastair said as the doorman swung open the brass-fitted doors of Lyndhurst and Lloyd's. He headed straight for his mailbox, across the red-carpeted reception area dappled with vases of cut flowers. He'd ask Colin, who must be familiar with such prominent collectors as the DuBoises.

At the front counter four young women stood chatting and opening mail. As fresh and pretty as the flowers, they were the first line of defense. Barely stopping, Alastair lifted his mail out of his slot and made his way through the exhibition rooms to the back elevator.

An exhibition of Old Master paintings had just gone on view and the rooms were already full of dealers. Alastair walked past a stately-looking man peering through bifocals at a painting. Leaning forward, he spit on the canvas and rubbed his finger around the surface.

"Damned varnish, can't see a thing," he muttered.

Alastair smiled and kept moving. If his sale turned out to be anywhere near as good as this Old Master collection, he'd be very happy indeed.

At the back elevator stood Hugh Haggerty, Old Master Painting expert. He paced back and forth with a picture under one arm, suit jacket rumpled, shirttails hanging out the back of his trousers. His free hand alternated between twirling his hair and pressing the elevator button. His messy clothes were no surprise but Alastair was troubled to see the hair twirling. This was not a good sign.

Alastair greeted him and he looked up, startled.

"Here until one o'clock last night hanging these bloody pictures," Hugh fumed. "The viewing opened this morning, can't find two of them. Don't know what goes on around here, typical incompetence."

Alastair watched him, thinking how remarkable that this noted authority on Old Master paintings was so distressed whenever he had a sale. Scholarly considerations of obscure Renaissance painters he greeted eagerly, but the practical logistics of organizing an auction left him quite undone. This price the firm willingly paid; Hugh's expertise was worth any eccentricity.

The elevator arrived and they stepped in, Hugh twisting what little hair he had left into a corkscrew. Alastair wondered what effect this hair twirling would have over the years, especially since he always twirled on the right side of his head. It would be bad enough to go bald, but to go bald on just one side, like a half-plucked chicken . . .

"Mr. Farmhand will have my hide if his damned Tiepolo doesn't sell, but he insists on such a bloody high reserve."

"I'll have a word with him before the sale if you like."

"Who's taking the sale?" Hugh asked in alarm.

"I am."

"Damned good thing. You're the only auctioneer over here I can trust."

The elevator doors opened and Hugh dashed off towards his office, fretting and checking his watch like the white rabbit.

Down the wide hallway of the old hotel Alastair walked to the suite of rooms he shared with Colin Plimpton. Since their areas of 19th Century European Paintings and Modern Paintings overlapped, they'd been assigned to an office together, which was quite convenient, although Alastair could think of office mates he would prefer. Windows on the street side of the large room looked out on Central Park; racks lining the inside wall stored incoming paintings. Two big desks sat in opposite corners of the room, Alastair's closer to the built-in bookcases of research books, Colin's placed for a window view. Jane, the secretary they shared, sat at a desk by the door, positioned for a quick get-away.

Bent down on his knees over a shipping crate, Colin was trying to pry off the side with a scissors. His bulky form was not suited for the task and he didn't seem to be having much luck. He had removed his jacket and was uncharacteristically working in his shirtsleeves, handkerchief stuffed into a monogrammed shirt pocket.

On his arrival in New York Colin had been appointed head of all flat art: paintings, drawings and prints. This made him Alastair's boss, which did not make Alastair particularly happy. Finding himself beholden to Colin who in London was a peer was not his idea of justice, and Colin's lofty displays of noblesse oblige didn't make it any easier.

Colin was equally fond of Alastair. Always had been, Alastair realized, for reasons he wasn't quite sure of. The fact that they both went to Eton together hardly made them school chums. If anything, Colin lorded it over Alastair because he had been two years ahead of him, and since Alastair arrived in New York, Colin seemed to have started schoolboy initiation rights all over again. So while they did their best to steer clear of each other in London, in New York they found themselves face to face. And it was Colin's advantage.

Reginald Lyndhurst sat on top of Alastair's desk. Reginald had been sent from England by his father, a viscount and head of Old Master Paintings in London, who hoped his son could learn something by assisting Alastair in Modern Paintings. At the moment Reginald was busy making a paper clip chain.

"So, Colin, can you tell me what pictures Catherine DuBois has in her collection?" asked Alastair.

"Well, she's got a terrific Tissot. But most of her collection is modern. I was only in her flat once, a huge, rambling old place on 5th Avenue, but it's full of prizes. If I'm not mistaken there's a major Degas and a stunning Franz Marc, among others."

Alastair glanced at his calendar, trying to weigh propriety with the fact that Gerhardt was already hot on the DuBois trail. "Let's see . . . the funeral was Saturday, today is Tuesday . . . ."

Colin sat back on his heels. "I'd say it's high time you rang her up. And while you're at it, why don't you organize a boardroom lunch with her? I'll co-host it with you. We'll chat her up together, kill two birds with one stone. I'll ask Jud Newton. He collects the Barbizon school. He just remarried and you know how those new wives love to redecorate. Mark their place, so to speak."

Reginald snickered and dangled the paper clip chain down to the floor like a fishing line. Colin leaned over the crate and vigorously wedged the scissors against a board. The board splintered and the scissors broke, nicking his hand. "Damn it! Reginald, make yourself useful and go find a hammer!"

Reginald trotted off and Alastair checked his impulse to ask Colin why he didn't let the porters unpack the crate. Colin didn't like to be questioned about anything.

"Blasted thing," Colin said, wiping his longish hair back from his face where a band of sweat had broken out on his forehead. He was not used to manual labor.

"By the way," he said, inspecting his injured hand, "Reginald tells me he's bored. Can't you get him into cataloguing with you?"

Alastair stared at Colin but inside he was rolling his eyes. *Please.* Reginald was always bored. He enjoyed being bored. He cultivated boredom as part of his persona.

"Quite frankly, Colin, Reginald knows so little about painting, it's faster for me to do the cataloguing myself than to correct his mistakes."

Colin raised his eyebrows. "Well, we always catch them, don't we? How else is he to learn?"

Alastair could see this was not a question, it was an imperative.

"All right, then. I'll get him cracking on it."

Colin rose and smiled benevolently. He picked up a

catalogue from the mass of papers on his desk and handed it to Alastair.

"Have you seen this?"

Sotheby Parke Bernet – Important Modern Paintings, Drawings and Watercolors. Alastair thumbed through the glossy color illustrations, page after page of impressive works, of 6-figure pictures. It was a super sale, yes. But his would be better.

Colin leaned back against his desk and crossed his arms over his generous girth. "You'll have no trouble matching that, of course."

Alastair smiled and closed the catalogue. "You know I love a challenge."

"The spring sales will be here before you know it. And we are looking to Modern Paintings as our greatest revenue producer."

Alastair stared impassively at Colin. Oh, really, sir? As if he were telling Alastair something he didn't know.

"Yes, of course, Colin," Alastair answered, his voice clipped. "I'll do my best. We will have a respectable sale." There was no point cranking up Colin's expectations; better to keep a low profile and surprise him.

Colin shifted his heavy weight to his other foot.

"Respectable? I think excellent was more what I had in mind. Outstanding. Superb. Choose your superlative. Whether it's with the DuBois collection or some other, the art world needs to know we can match Sotheby's here in New York just as we do in London, that there is no better place to buy or sell Modern paintings."

Alastair watched Colin's hand waving expansively. He was on his soapbox now, wasn't he. But Alastair had heard enough.

"Excuse my understatement. The sale will be excellent, of course."

Colin pursed his lips and looked at Alastair for a moment. Then he pushed away from the desk.

"Jolly good," he said.

He headed for the door, then stopped mid-stream.

"Oh, I almost forgot. Can you do me a great favor, Alastair, and take my 1:30 appointment? A Mr. Reiher, he's got a Burne-Jones gouache in my upcoming sale. Something has come up and I've absolutely got to run."

"Yes, I'll be here."

"Terrific. It's a bit of a problem, though, because he says the estimate listed in the catalogue is lower than the reserve. He's hopping mad about it, threatening to withdraw the piece from the sale."

"How did that happen?"

"I'm not quite sure. I let Reginald take in the painting, and he didn't list a reserve on the form. Reiher claims he told Reginald, but, who knows?" He raised his hands helplessly, palms upturned. "You know how emotional these clients can get."

"I see."

"Explain to him we can print a correction in the addendum."

"Fine, Colin, I'll manage him."

Colin flashed a smile and was off, the warrior to battle.

Alastair shook his head and hung his jacket on the back of the chair. Why on earth was Colin letting Reginald see clients, giving him that kind of carte blanche, inviting mistakes to be made? And then leaving the explaining to Alastair? Not that this was entirely surprising, not that it was the first time. But this time he was tempted *not* to bail him out, to let him stew in his own juice. But there was the reputation of the firm to consider, and that, despite any strong impulses to the contrary, must take precedence over teaching Colin a lesson. He would have to find another way.

He tossed the Sotheby's catalogue on to the desk, next to Colin's upcoming sale catalogue of 19th Century Paintings. A classic Gainsborough was illustrated on the cover, a half-length portrait of a woman in a white satin dress and matching hat. A standard society portrait, the woman was idealized into a beauty far beyond what she probably looked like. She had the usual Gainsborough complexion, an illuminated ivory. Come to think of it, she looked quite like the woman he met at MoMA the other night – Megan, wasn't it? He'd thought of her several times since then, but this really brought her back and the memory was warm and inviting. Ah, if only he had more time. *Time for the taking of a toast and tea.*

Now for Mrs. DuBois. Jane was off at the warehouse this morning so he looked around her desk for the Rolodex. He flopped the cards around to D and they fell open at DuBois. A good omen. He punched in the number vigorously. To the hounds . . . the hunt was on. She took his call.

"Mrs. DuBois, please allow me to extend my condolences. I am so very sorry to hear about your husband."

"Thank you." Her voice was somber, collected.

"If there is anything we can do to help here at Lyndhurst and Lloyd's, please don't hesitate to ask."

"It's very nice of you to offer. Every one has been *so* kind since Edwin died, I *am* grateful. Why, you calling this morning, and Terrence Young yesterday."

Alastair grimaced. Wouldn't you know it, the body still warm and Sotheby's already swooped in.

"The truth is," she went on with a sigh, "My affairs are in such disorder I really don't know where to begin."

"I'm sure this is a difficult period."

"Edwin managed all the finances." Here she stopped for a moment, and when she spoke again it was with a tremor in her voice. "We both loved collecting, but it was Edwin who was clever about the market. I really know so little about it."

"The market *is* complex. That's why most people find it helpful to call in a professional."

"I'm sure." She took a deep breath and her voice grew distant. "I appreciate your calling. But I've really got to assess just what I've got here before I can decide what to do with it."

"Yes, of course." He could tell he was losing her. He had to keep her on the line. "And don't forget we have experts in every field, not just fine art. We can help with furniture, silver – "

"Oh, silver, don't even mention silver. I've got scads of it, some we never even used. We have a Victorian tea service from my mother's family – she was English – with the Wyndham family crest. I can't imagine who would want that."

A bell rang in Alastair's head. "That's not the Cotswold Wyndhams, is it? Beech Tree Manor?"

"Why, yes, it is! However did you know?"

"My grandmother grew up nearby, at Ten Oaks. She was very close to Jane Wyndham."

"Your grandmother is . . . ?"

"Lydia Cavendish. But her maiden name was Atwood."

Catherine's voice warmed as if the sun had broken over the horizon, shedding a golden light on a gray world. "Well, for goodness sake! Lydia Atwood! I remember Mother speaking of her, they were dear friends! Well, you really *must* come over then and see the silver. How about Thursday, for tea?"

"I would be delighted."

He dropped the phone back in the cradle, a smile spreading slowly across his face. Over the first hurdle, he was now in the running. In the great Lyndhurst and Lloyd's tradition, chalk another one up for family ties.

Chapter 8

T uesday morning found Bo sitting in his broken swivel chair with the Manhattan phone book. He thumbed through looking for the girl with green eyes. He couldn't find her listed under anything: Triko, Trieceau, Treeko, Treakaux . . . Megan Trico was not to be found. How could anyone so beautiful vanish into thin air? But in truth, it was hard to imagine such an attractive woman by herself; she was probably living with some stupid boyfriend. Or maybe he just didn't have the spelling right, which seemed to have as many possible variations as those eyes of hers, their amazing shades of green, a myriad of hues splintered together like a prize marble.

But if she were unreachable the Honthorst gallery was not. So when 10 o'clock rolled around he switched gears and dialed Phil Honthorst. If he couldn't win the girl then a gallery would have to do.

When the receptionist answered, he asked for the director as nonchalantly as he could.

"I'll see if he's in," she answered officiously.

He wondered where people learned this tone of voice, as if they all took the same course, The Cool-But-Cordial Voice Makeover. Momentarily another authoritative voice spoke, this time a man's. "What can I do for you, Mr. Ryder?"

Bo paused; this was not the reception he was expecting. "That's what I was going to ask you."

"I beg your pardon?"

"I got a letter from you saying you were interested in showing my work."

"Oh, certainly." Another pause. "Could you refresh my memory? We get so many slides, you know."

Bo shook his head; how could this guy not even remember an artist he was interested in representing?

"Realistic oils and watercolors. City scenes, some portraits of people sitting in a wing chair."

"Oh, right, the red chair portraits. But we're more interested in the city scenes. Can you get us a dozen or so pieces for a show opening in November?"

Bo swiveled in the chair. Whoa, Nelly. He wanted a show but this was moving a little too fast.

"Well, I'd like to know something about your gallery policies first. Like what's your commission rate, and do you take a cut for studio sales?"

"Our commission rate is the standard fifty percent, and for our regular artists we require the same for studio sales. But you don't have to be concerned with that."

"Why not? Do you consider me an irregular artist?"

"Ha ha!" Honthorst boomed, as if this was a good joke he didn't have time for. "No, that's not what I meant. But this is for a special seasonal show we do each winter."

Special show? What was he talking about?

"Does my work have a particular holiday cheer?"

Again the mechanical laugh.

"We thought it would mesh nicely with the other works we're including."

"What other works?"

"We try to have something for everybody. So far I've got some great winter images, Currier and Ives sorts of scenes, and some country primitives – you know, Grandma Moses in the snow. With your winter city scenes, it will make a great holiday sale."

This was too much.

"Sorry. You've got the wrong guy. Sounds like you'll do just fine with a few paint-by-number sets."

Bo dropped the phone into the cradle and stared blankly at the portrait of Jeanette. He couldn't believe it. His debut into the contemporary art scene, reduced to a bargain basement Christmas sale.

He picked up a bristle brush and tapped it against the palm of his hand: up and down, up and down, staring at the portrait. Her hair needed more glints of light. He squeezed mars black onto the palette and mixed it with zinc white.

Phil Honthorst – what an idiot. Oh well. That's what he got for having high hopes. He dipped the tip of the brush and stroked the color on to the canvas. Come on, cheer up, he was no worse off than before, Honthorst wasn't the only gallery in town. Although it was the only one who had shown him any interest. He brushed a few mores strokes into Jeanette's hair, but somehow they didn't look right. He tossed the brush down. What a joke, what a fucking joke this whole thing was.

Leaning his head against the windowpane, he looked out at the street. The sun's last rays had disappeared and everything looked washed out: gray buildings, gray street, gray sky. He remembered the Honthorst gallery now; it was that place over on Bleeker that sold graphics in the back room.

He pushed away from the window and turned back to the easel, its joints mummified with duct tape, as sorry looking as his prospects. But from out of the broken-down framework shone the portrait of Jeanette, a polished gem. She was his, all his, not some compromised bit of kitsch cooked up to suit the market. So what did it matter that he lived hand to mouth as long as he could still paint the way he wanted to? And keep his loft, his studio. Which at this point was clearly in jeopardy.

So far he had been able to wing it, to get together the rent from loans, working at the parking lot, selling the few remaining savings bonds his grandmother gave him on long-ago birthdays. But he didn't know how much longer he could keep it up. The debt was gaining on him.

He picked up his unopened mail and slit open the envelopes listlessly.

In the first letter the bank informed him that he would be billed twenty dollars for a bounced check. A Con Ed notice threatened to turn off the electricity because the account was overdue. Another overdue rent notice from September had arrived from Gozzi, this time marked along the top in bright red ink, "THIRD AND FINAL NOTICE." The last letter was from his mother, saying she was sending a care package of lemon pound cake, but that his father refused to lend him any more money.

'He knows your grandmother recently lent you $400. You know, dear, how practical your father is. He still thinks it's still not too late for dental school.'

Bo crushed the letter and threw it against the wall.

"Fucking A!"

He crossed his arms, leaned against the spool table and stared at the floor patterned with dripped paint. What a goddamn pain in the ass. His father and Honthorst made a good pair – it was a tossup who was the bigger philistine.

The harsh ring of the telephone interrupted his reverie and he picked it up. Her unexpected voice sounded self-assured and upbeat. "Hi, this is Susan Jacobson. I was interested in your Matisse drawing."

"Oh, yes," he said, completely taken aback. "I remember."

"I'm calling to make one more offer for your *Joy of Life* study. As a collector, I'm sure you know that a similar drawing made a record price up at Sotheby's yesterday. So I feel it's only fair to match it. I'm willing to pay you eighteen hundred dollars."

A rush ran through Bo like a zap from an electric socket, from his chest into his fingers, through his loins, down to his toes. Was this really possible? Eighteen hundred dollars? Enough to cover all his debt in one easy sale? He was too overwhelmed to answer.

"Am I calling at a bad time?" Susan asked.

"No, it's not a bad time," he stammered.

"You want *more*? You drive a hard bargain, Mr. Ryder."

"No, no," he repeated, trying to pull himself together. "It's just that I never really considered selling it."

"I know you said it had sentimental value. But I can't get it out of my mind. I really love it. Okay. Two thousand, cash. That's my final offer."

His mind reeled. He had never done anything crooked in his life. How could he sell his own work as Matisse?

The woman's tone turned conciliatory.

"Look, I'm right around the corner on West Broadway. Why don't I stop by and we can talk this over in person."

"Sure, okay," he said. "Come on up."

"Perfect."

He hung up and stood quietly, his hand resting on the receiver, her *perfect* ringing in his ears. Damn straight it would be perfect! He walked around the big spool chewing on his thumbnail. What's the matter with you, you can't do this! said one voice. *Why the hell not? She's not hurting for money and she likes the drawing,* answered another. But it's fraud! You'd be selling a forgery! *So what? She gets the piece she wants, you get the money you need. Set you up for months.*

Bo turned and walked around the spool in the other direction. Which was better, compromising his own work for some half-assed Honthorst gallery to survive, or selling this woman a watercolor that would make her perfectly happy and support his painting from the heart?

The buzzer rang and Bo buzzed back and opened the door. Up the stairwell came two voices, a woman's and a man's.

Bo stepped back into the loft and softly closed the door, the muscle in his neck tightening. What was this? She hadn't mentioned bringing anyone. He quickly stowed a partially stretched canvas along the far wall and tried to collect himself; it was nothing to worry about, he hadn't done anything yet.

Presently a light rapping came on the door and in walked Susan Jacobson, wearing a fox coat almost the same color as her hair, which was again elegantly swept back into a French twist. She also wore the look of a woman who expected to get what she wanted. Behind her entered the small man with the close-set eyes and the black goatee who had accompanied her before.

"These lofts," he murmured, "a new kind of chic, a fourth floor walk up."

Touching a handkerchief to his brow, his face changed from annoyance to a genial smile on seeing Bo.

"Hello, Bo, nice to see you," Susan said. "Reinhold and I have been combing the galleries together this morning."

Gerhardt nodded graciously. Bo took their coats, noting that Gerhardt's velvety black topcoat didn't have a spot on it. Damn. The last thing he needed was some fey art advisor to witness this. "Would you like some coffee?" he asked.

"That would perk us up," said Susan.

Bo walked back to the kitchen and found some mugs. As he washed them he tried to steady his trembling hands. He had to get a hold of himself. The good humor he'd woken up in this morning with thoughts of finding Megan was long gone, now replaced by a chilling dread. Was he really going to go through with this, sell this woman his own *Joy of Life* study as the real thing? He dried his hands and poured out coffee, but his palms stayed moist. What had seemed minutes ago to be a solution to his problems now felt like an ominous black hole, reeling him in against his will.

Susan sat down on the couch in front of the spool table while Gerhardt walked around the loft looking everything over – the big paintings, the portrait of Jeanette, the drawings on the wall.

Bo returned and set down the coffee mugs. He glanced at Gerhardt who was peering closely at one of the watercolors on the *Ryder Museum* wall.

"How do you like your coffee, Mr. Gerhardt?" Bo asked. He wished the man would sit down and stop inspecting everything.

Gerhardt sat on the couch next to Susan, readjusting his seat when he hit the broken spring.

"Nice watercolors," Gerhardt said.

"And the young woman," said Susan, gesturing at the portrait of Jeanette on the easel. "Isn't she fantastic? And such a great setting on the Plaza fountain." She sighed wistfully. "Maybe someday my husband and I will get the nerve to buy an artist we've never heard of."

Bo laughed uncomfortably. Susan added hastily, "I'm sorry, I didn't mean it like that. I'm sure you have a name among contemporary painters. It's just that with Frank being in financial services, he can't help thinking about the investment angle."

Bo set a chipped sugar bowl on the table. This woman was a lot more attractive when she wasn't talking.

Gerhardt nodded. "Yes, there's nothing like the blue chips if you're concerned with resale. I have a client who wanted to give his daughter a yacht for her wedding present. So he sold a Van Gogh and bought a beautiful boat for two million dollars."

Bo stirred a spoonful of sugar into his coffee and said quietly, "Too bad Van Gogh couldn't always afford to buy canvas. There might have been more of them."

Susan smiled tolerantly and after a pause said, "I can't wait to see the *Joy of Life* study again."

Bo retrieved the framed drawing and handed it to Susan. Back in her hands the drawing received the same accolades as before.

"What a fabulous study! You don't mind giving it the professional check, do you Reinhold?"

Gerhardt nodded agreeably and pulled out a jeweler's-type lens from his jacket pocket. He held it up to his eye and brought the drawing close, moving it back and forth under the lens, inspecting the paper from corner to corner.

Bo crossed his arms over his chest and watched, his heart beating like a jackrabbit's. What would he say if Gerhardt declared it a fake? He'd have to play dumb, claim his mother must have been duped, that neither of them knew anything about authenticating art. He raised a hand and chewed on his thumbnail. But maybe this man wouldn't be able to tell. Don't let him discover it. *Please. I need the money.*

In a moment Gerhardt took the lens from his eye and handed the picture back to Susan.

"You won't find a finer one than that."

Bo's arms dropped to his sides, his rapid pulse subsiding. *Thank God. Hey, up there, thanks a million. I'll make it up to you, I promise, swindler that I be.*

"I'm so glad!" said Susan. "And you know, I like the tree trunks in this better than the bluish ones in the final version."

Bo smiled, his equilibrium returning. Yes, he remembered now adding a little too much raw sienna to the tree trunks. But sure, lady, it's always good to like the art you buy, no matter who created it.

Susan turned to Bo. "You'll sell it, then, will you?"

Bo looked from the drawing to Susan's carefully groomed, acquisitive face. She looked so eager, why disappoint them both? The only thing worse than being an unrecognized artist was being a copped-out artist who painted for someone else's taste. His smile broadened, his eyes crinkling into slits.

"Wonderful!" she exclaimed. "I don't care what Frank says, it's worth every penny. And how remarkable that I should find this here, after looking for so long in the galleries."

"Things have a way of turning up if you want them badly enough," Bo said.

"Will cash be all right?" she asked.

"I think I can handle it."

She opened her wallet and counted out the bills. "We always pay in cash. Funny, one dealer told us that a lot of his clients pay in cash, especially the doctors!"

She laughed merrily and handed the neat stack over to Bo, who accepted it with both hands. The bills' edges felt crisp and clean, and from the center Ben Franklin stared back steadily, lips pursed, looking eerily pensive. Not unlike his father when Bo first announced he was going to art school. Bo folded the bills against the face.

"Perfect," he said.

Susan slipped the framed drawing into a padded mailing envelope and rose from the couch. "Thank you so much, Bo. And if you ever come across any more like this, remember I'm always in the market."

She drew on her gloves with an air of accomplishment.

"Where did you find this one?" Gerhardt asked, rising also, his small black eyes fixed intently on Bo.

"Oh, a crazy story," Bo said blithely as he half-heartedly tried to remember it. Did it matter now, whatever story he told? He rolled the bills into a neat circle and stretched around a rubber band.

"With her knack for finding things, your mother could be in the business," said Susan.

Bo tossed the rolled bills from hand to hand as he walked the couple to the door, feeling like he just hit a home run. The deception was over, and in his hands was his ticket to freedom.

"That's my mom, always an eye peeled."

As Susan walked past him on the way out, Gerhardt followed and pressed a business card into Bo's hand. He patted Bo's shoulder and said, "A talented young man like you is bound to run across other marketable art. Call me."

Bo nodded and didn't reply. These people had no idea just how much talent was involved. He ushered them out the door and watched as Susan gingerly made her way down the steep stairs, holding onto the railing. She turned and waved her gloved fingers, the departing pioneer.

He took out the roll of bills and turned it over in his hands. He could not believe it was all his. An instant solution to his problems, just like that. From the single sale of a 10 by 14 inch study. She handed over the money like it was a party favor, a pittance for the hatcheck girl. What a foolish woman.

He felt a pang of conscience at this thought. She was only foolish to the extent that he'd deceived her. But so what. She got what she wanted.

She isn't interested in the work, she's interested in the name. And the fact that the *Joy of Life* is a commodity, like she said, with 'established market value'. And since the quality of the study is as good as the original, what does it matter if it's by Matisse or not? She *thinks* it is, and that's what she paid for, a name she *thinks* is good. Besides, the money was nothing to her. Spare change. And he was in debt up to his ears. *Share the wealth, that's my motto.*

He sat down and unfurled the roll of hundred dollar bills onto the tabletop. The heads of Ben Franklin seemed to dance before his eyes, melding in his mind with the face of his father, along with thoughts of his family and his dogged insistence to them that his pursuit of art was right. Suddenly with these thoughts appeared the image of the green-eyed Megan as she stood in the MoMA galleries and talked about painting, acknowledging its importance.

He forced these thoughts from his mind with the avowal that the dirty deed was done, never to be repeated. He lined up his creditors' invoices and got out his checkbook.

Chapter 9

Megan sat bolt upright at her desk typing up an article on the stolen Modigliani held up in customs for *Spotlight,* her weekly column on art world events. At the meeting that morning with the Italian consul, Agostino Celucci, she had gleaned enough for a great lead story even if some of the pieces were still missing. Her fingers flew over the keys. There was nothing like being on deadline for improving posture – her back didn't touch the chair. "Damn," she said as she hit a wrong key, then punched the backspace/correction key on her souped up IBM Selectric to white out the incorrect letter.

"Now, now," Horvath chuckled, knowing she had just begun the article. "You've got a whole hour 'til we go to press, nothing to get uptight about."

"When is someone going to invent a typewriter that knows how to spell?" she fumed, pulling out the finished page and inserting another sheet. "If we can send a man to the moon why can't we make a typewriter that beeps when you make a mistake?"

On the edge of her desk sat a row of reference books braced between a pair of winged Abyssinian lion bookends. She had begun the collection as a freshman in college with the *American Heritage Dictionary,* her favorite for its marvelous illustrations like the tortuously coiled man pictured under *contortionist.* The collection had since expanded to include Strunk and White's *Elements of Style,* a thesaurus, *The Art and Craft of Feature Writing,* a dictionary of synonyms, Fowler's *Modern English Usage, A Dictionary for Subjects and Symbols in Art*, and a two-volume edition of the *Oxford English Dictionary* with such condensed type it came with its own magnifying glass. She had become completely dependent on this last book (one might even say addicted), relishing looking up words as she wrote, getting that much closer to saying exactly what she meant.

She reached for it now to look up *contraband*, uncertain if the term applied to the detained Modigliani, as the Italian consul claimed. *Contraband, bootleg* and *smuggled* all referred to goods exported illegally, and how could these apply when Mrs. DuBois bought the painting at Sotheby's in London?

At the Italian Consulate, Agostino Celucci had been smooth as could be sitting in his corner office overlooking the chrysanthemums planted out in the meridian on Park Avenue at 69th Street. His voice was patient, reasonable, silken as olive oil as he told Megan that the Modigliani's rightful owner was a prominent Chianti producer named Calabresi who had seen the painting in Sotheby's London sale catalogue.

"Unfortunately, it was after the sale and the painting was already in transit to New York."

"How can he be sure it's the same painting?" she had asked. "Modigliani's portraits can look very similar."

The consulate laughed tolerantly, his bone-colored linen suit standing out against the green leather of his chair and the cherry paneling of the room. "My dear, it hung in his sitting room since it was painted in 1918. A good painting is like a fine wine, the connoisseur does not mistake it."

"Does he have any documentation on it? Photographs for insurance purposes?"

The consulate chuckled indulgently. "You must understand, in Italy this has never been necessary. Our thieves do not steal art. Our churches are full of paintings and sculpture by the greatest artists who ever lived – Michelangelo, Bernini, Tintorertto – no one takes them. Even our thieves respect our culture."

"I guess Mussolini had other priorities," she commented dryly.

Elbows resting on the arms of his chair, the consul put the tips of his fingers together and looked at her steadily.

"The second world war was a tragic time to be Jewish, even in Italy. The discovery of the painting is very painful to Senor Calabresi, with all the memories it brings. During the Fascist regime he and his family were removed from their beloved villa and put into a camp. After the war they were reinstated, but the portrait was missing along with the silver and everything else of value. You must understand, *bella*, these people are prominent citizens, cousins of the Fintzi-Continis. Even at this late date, they deserve justice. We have contacted the woman who bought the painting but her representative is completely unreasonable. Nor has Sotheby's been of any help. But we will not give up. Most importantly, the painting must be returned to its rightful owner. The Modigliani is an Italian painting, painted by an Italian, owned by an Italian. Modigliani's art belongs to Italy."

Modigliani tumbled off his tongue, slurred together in a sound that Megan found impossible to reproduce. Suddenly the consul interrupted himself, as if in an effort to make a personal connection.

"Your surname, Trico, is this Italian?"

"No, French Huguenot."

He smiled and tipped his long nose at her.

"Ah, French. Then of course you will understand the value of culture."

His lecture continued, never deviating from the patient, understanding tone as he denounced the black market for art, the auction houses, and the corrupt customs officials in their never-ending quest to rob Italy of its artifacts.

Megan chuckled at the memory as she typed.

Horvath turned from his tiny television and asked, "Since when is an art theft so funny?"

"Since Sotheby's has been compared to the Medellin cartel."

He boomed a big laugh. "Haven't the English been adopting Mediterranean art at least since the Elgin marbles?"

She nodded and rolled another sheet of paper into the typewriter as she looked at her notebook. Over the years she had developed a kind of shorthand of her own which consisted chiefly of leaving out the vowels. The consul had talked in quotable phrases, thanking her for doing her part in "bringing justice to bear to return a national treasure," as if he were trying to supply her with copy. But being swayed by an interviewee was not something she had ever been accused of.

With only minutes to spare before the deadline hour of four, she finished the story, pulled the last page out of the typewriter and walked the pages over to the copy editor's inbox. The piece was good, very good, and for the first time since she moved out of the apartment with Ned she had a spring in her step. She dropped the article into the in-box and pivoted back towards the front of the room. Fogelman watched her from his desk, it seemed with a new kind of interest. As she passed him he held out a letter for her.

"Here's a press release for a Contemporary Painting sale coming up at Lyndhurst and Lloyd's. From now on I want you to cover the big auctions, especially the painting sales. It shouldn't be too much of a burden since I understand you now have some extra time on your hands."

Fogleman looked at her meaningfully and she nodded.

"You could say that."

"Even though the auctions are uptown a lot of buyers live down here so I think it's of interest to our readership. Yesterday a guy in the loft above me was moving in an enormous canvas of a pair of lips as long as a sofa. A Tom Wesselman he bought up at Lyndhurst and Lloyd's."

She looked at the letter, feeling Fogelman's eyes on her all the while.

"The art auction market is hot. They're setting international records almost every week."

His look was resolute, uncompromising. Clearly there

would be no protest tolerated in his reshaping of her Arts section. And it wasn't that she objected so much to covering auctions, she just didn't like being *required* to. She tried hard to keep her expression bland. He looked at her steadily, waiting for her response.

She took the press release. "Sure, Jack, I'd love to cover the auctions."

He smiled and closed his eyes.

Back at her desk she looked more closely at the press release. It looked formal and British with its emblem, the heads of Messrs. Lyndhurst and Lloyd in back-to-back profile. Below, the company name looped along in a script-style font. Why not branch out? She had to get over the feeling that the Arts section was hers just because she'd been running it exactly as she wanted for the last two years. Better a collaborated Arts section than no Arts section at all. As long as she didn't have to write only about the Andy Warhols and the Roy Lichtensteins, giving all the publicity to the famous artists who didn't need it.

The uptown auctions *were* appealing, with their sales of marvelous decorative arts ignored by Art History classes: Japanese netsuke, Chinese bronzes, Pre-Columbian pots, Jungenstil furniture – treats from around the world, across the ages. Although seeing the best of the best tended to ruin her taste for anything she could afford. She had once succeeded in buying a Bavarian vase at an Art Nouveau and Art Deco auction. It was the cheapest lot in the sale and cost her a month's salary. But every time she looked at the emerald-green glass overlaid with copper in organic, graceful arcs, it seemed worth every penny.

A quote praised the offerings: "*An outstanding group of Contemporary Paintings, including an important Unfurleds canvas by Morris Louis, is drawing great interest from both sides of the Atlantic.*" The name quoted jumped out at her: Alastair Cavendish. Of course – the painting expert Jake introduced her to at the Stella opening. Well, now. This was another enticement. A handsome face never hurt an art auction, even if he did wear a three-piece suit. She filed the press release and turned to the stack of mail.

One of the letters, dated yesterday, was from U.S. customs, whose office she had written requesting to see the detained Modigliani. Because the Modigliani was valuable and now under international dispute, it had been moved from the steamship port in Brooklyn where it had arrived to the U.S. Customs House at the World Trade Center. From the customs inspector, the letter stated that any property lacking a customs release could not be made available for viewing and that she would need permission from a higher authority. She would have to find another approach.

By the time she answered the last piece of correspondence the newsroom had emptied out and even Fogelman had disappeared. The only sound was Horvath's typewriter still clicking away. Her stomach growled and she stretched, her muscles feeling like they'd been bound for hours. She glanced at Horvath bent over his typewriter, squinting through his thick glasses as if he were straining to see through a fog. At times like this she could forget about their rivalry and feel for the guy. He was practically blind. "Hey, Ron. Want to take a break and get a coffee?"

"No thanks. When the phones stop ringing is the only time I get anything done around here."

Good old Horvath, always putting in the hours, going for the journalism awards. Fogelman loved him even if the rest of the staff didn't.

Out on the street the night was balmy for October and she paused on the sidewalk. Down the sidewalk wafted an appetizing sweetness from the R&K Baking Company, the comforting aroma of fresh-baked cakes and pies. Her stomach growled again; it needed more than a cup of coffee. She headed over to the souvlaki place on 6th Avenue that made its own pita bread.

She entered and took a seat at a table next to the window.

Outside, the West Village evening was in full swing with hordes of people moving like busy ants under the neon lights: gathering around the street magician, peering in the lit windows of the funky shops, tossing a few coins in a fiddling musician's open violin case. Up above the four-story building across the street the moon cast a silvery light along the rooftop, silhouetting the skyline in a gray sheen against the starless sky.

The West Village would be a great diversion; maybe she should look for an apartment down here. Her attempts at finding a new place had so far been limited to scanning the classifieds; somehow she'd been unable to commit to a location. Uptown, downtown, Eastside, Westside – every neighborhood had its own appeal and she hadn't been able to settle on any one. But the clock was ticking; she couldn't stay at Lizzy's forever. Even a best friendship had its limits.

The waitress came and she ordered hummus, a kefta kebab and a coffee, and opened her newspaper. A voice said, "Make that two," and someone pulled out the facing chair.

"Mind if I join you?"

He was grinning like the Cheshire cat, his dark curls hanging over his forehead. She stared at him in surprise, knowing she'd seen him before but unable to place where.

He smiled again, this time with less confidence. "We met at the Frank Stella opening the other night. You walked into me."

"Oh, right." The revolving door, the painter. "Sure, have a seat."

He thanked her and sat down, his muscular torso leaning forward in the chair.

"It's Bo, isn't it?" she asked tentatively.

Bo's smile took over his whole face, dimpling his cheeks, constricting his eyes like Nanook of the North.

"Very good. I was afraid I was striking out there for a minute. And you're . . . Marsha?" he asked teasingly.

"Megan."

"Megan, of course." He sat back in his chair. "Some of us are visual, some of us verbal. I remembered your face, you remembered my name."

"That's a convenient way to label people."

"You didn't recognize me."

"Not so. It just took me a minute to place your face. I meet a lot of people."

"Ah, well. Maybe that explains it. I never meet anybody."

The waitress brought the food and they dug in. It was hard to tell who was hungrier. After swallowing a couple of bites of the spicy veggie balls and yogurt sauce she looked over at him, sauce dripping down his chin.

"Bo. Is that short for Beauregard?"

He swiped at his chin with a napkin. "No. Robert."

"Ah."

He took another bite. "What do you do, anyway, that you meet so many people?" he asked with his mouth full.

"I write for a newspaper. Mostly art reviews."

He pushed back from the table and grimaced as if the food in his mouth had just gone sour. "Oh my god. You're an art critic?"

"Yes."

"Really?" he asked incredulously.

"Really."

He rolled his eyes and dropped his arms. "Oh, man! And you seemed so nice."

She laughed. "Yes, believe it or not, art critics can be nice, too."

"But as a group, you so often aren't. Not in print, anyway."

She shrugged. She was used to artists being a little leery of her. "We're not really so different from you. We both love art and neither of us is exactly in it for the money."

This seemed to mollify him and they talked some about the Stella show, Bo admitting that he liked it more than he expected. "So what kind of art do you like?" he asked.

"I like anything as long as it's good."

He wiped a piece of pita bread across the plate thoughtfully, soaking up the creamy sauce. He took another bite, patted the crust around the empty plate, and glanced at her. Then he spoke haltingly, as if he were having trouble getting the words out. "Would you have any interest in seeing my work?"

"Sure, I'd love to. Do you have a show coming up?"

He laughed. "No, no, can't say that I do."

"Do you have a gallery?"

"No, I haven't managed to rope a gallery yet."

"That can take some time."

He ran the pita crust around the edge of the shining plate. "But I have a lot of paintings in my studio. Could you come and see them there?"

His eyes were hopeful but cautious, the look of an artist who wanted the world to see his work but wasn't sure of the reception, who needed help but hated to ask for it. Her heart went out to him.

"I don't see why not. Maybe sometime next week?"

He shrugged.

"How about now?"

His face was serious for a moment before breaking into a smile.

"What have you got to lose? Who knows, maybe you'll discover the next Frank Stella."

"But how can we see anything at night?" she protested, thinking of the work she had planned to do that evening and the fact that even though she admired his brown ringlets she wasn't sure she was interested in any further entanglements.

"I have a great lighting system."

She watched his face, both anxious and eager, and remembered how hungry she was when she was after her first newspaper assignment. What the hell, she'd continue her Modigliani investigation tomorrow. And she was a big girl, she could take care of herself.

"Okay," she said.

He broke into a wide grin, his sparkling eyes almost

disappearing. Taking some bills out of his wallet he handed them to the waitress with the check. "Keep the change," he said.

"No, no, you don't have to pay my share," Megan said, reaching for her bag.

"Please, let me. It's only a couple of bucks, anyway."

They left the restaurant, walking south and east.

*　　*　　*

Bo didn't know which was more thrilling, the woman coming to his loft or the art critic coming to his studio. A beautiful Arts Editor was a heady combination. He felt he was grinning like a moron, but he couldn't get over his luck, not only at having run into her again, but at her agreeing to accompany him. Good thing he had enough money to pick up the tab so he wouldn't have to look like an artist who was not only a nobody in the art world but couldn't afford to eat, either.

He was so elated he didn't feel the chill in the air until he noticed Megan hugging her arms and the end of her nose turning red. Her fitted blue blazer curved nicely around her waist but didn't look like much protection against the cool evening air, now dampened with a touch of fog.

"Want my jacket?" he offered, starting to pull the beat up leather off his shoulders. Bought years ago at an army/navy outlet, it looked like a rabid dog had gotten a hold of it. "It's a little grungy but it's pretty warm."

"No, thanks, I'm fine," she said, walking faster. From her resolute expression it was clear she wouldn't take the jacket if her nose were frostbitten.

"Is it me or is it getting foggy?" she asked.

"It is. I love this about Manhattan," he answered expansively. "Even though it's a city it's still an island, and you can almost always feel the effects of the water."

She smiled at the pavement and went on to ask him about recent art shows as they walked through Soho, down West

Broadway and into Broome Street, Bo thrilled she knew so many contemporary artists. As they crossed Greene he pointed ahead. "Almost there. Number 457."

On the front of the building's door stood the two-foot high numerals he had painted in metallic paint, shining silver in the streetlight. He unlocked the door and fumbled for the light switch. The dark stairwell flickered before springing into view, lit by naked bulbs hanging from long cords above each landing. Fog seeped in from the broken transom window surrounded the lights with halos, bright spheres of vapor hovering like beacons.

They mounted the stairs to the fourth floor and he unlocked the door. He hit the switch for the long florescent fixtures left over from the printing factory and glanced around the loft, suddenly aware that it wasn't exactly tidy. Several rolls of new canvas rested on one end of the tattered couch; partially assembled stretcher bars lay around the floor where he had been building a chassis earlier in the afternoon. He picked these up and said, "Sorry, the place is kind of a mess."

"Don't apologize, it's your studio," she said, and swung her leather bag onto the couch where it settled comfortably, taking up most of one end. Still feeling self-conscious, he changed the subject.

"That's some bag you got there. Looks like you're off on the Lewis and Clark expedition."

She laughed. "It comes in handy when I'm running around. It's my portable closet."

He stacked the stretcher bars against the far wall, being careful not to dislodge the corners, joined by tongue-and-grooves into right angles. He wondered where she went that required so many clothing changes and suddenly felt a wave of protectiveness. "Didn't Thoreau say to beware of anything you have to change your clothes for?" he asked.

"He didn't live in New York."

She walked down the wall looking up at the *Portraits of the City*. Bo threw himself into the old swivel desk chair. It was broken but teetered in a comfortable, rhythmic way. He watched her from his perch, wondering what she was thinking as she moved along, and suddenly hoped she wouldn't look around the corner at the *Ryder Museum* wall. Since the sale of the Matisse study, the wall seemed to radiate bad vibes whenever he passed it. Come to think of it, he would take the rest of the student studies down as soon as he got the chance; there was no use risking another misunderstanding like Susan Jacobson's.

"You're a great draftsman," she said, turning to him with admiration in her eyes. "I like the realist style used with the surreal settings."

"Thanks."

"And I love the wing chair set in a different place in each portrait, someplace fitting for the sitter, I would guess."

He grinned and set the chair rocking with his foot. It was always gratifying when a viewer understood what he was trying to do without him having to explain it.

"I'm thinking of calling the series *Portraits in the City.*"

"Great, I love it. Is this all of them?"

"So far."

"Have you shown these to any of the galleries?" she asked.

"I've taken my slides around but haven't gotten any bites yet."

Except from Susan Jacobson, he thought, the memory rising again like a bad dream that kept resurfacing. He quickly moved the conversation forward.

"On second thought, yeah, I did get one offer, for a group show at the Honthorst Gallery."

He told her about the Christmas show and she listened, nodding.

"It's not a big name gallery but you can't expect to start with Leo Castelli. Whatever way you can get your name out there is worthwhile."

"Yeah, maybe. But I'd rather hold out for something better."

He kicked off his shoes and put on an Otis Redding album.

He didn't mind her advice as long as she didn't expect him to take it. Women – they were always trying to tell you what to do under the guise of being helpful.

Looking over the shoulder of an art critic as she viewed his work, he saw it with fresh eyes. The portraits *were* something to be proud of, he *would* make the most of them. Hearing her praise was just the medicine he needed. But he couldn't help realizing that as far as his painting had come since he'd been in New York, he was no further along professionally.

This thought unsettled him so he got up and opened the chest of drawers against the wall. Inside sat the shoebox where he kept his stash. He picked it up along with a record jacket and sat back down in the swivel chair. Placing the shoebox cover on his knees, he angled the record jacket into it and dumped out a pile of marijuana. He tapped the jacket gently in time with the rhythm of Otis's *Pain in my Heart*, letting the seeds run into the box and the finer flakes sift down from the stalks.

Megan moved to the easel, which held the latest in the *Portraits in the City* series, one Bo was thinking of calling *Wall Street Tycoon*. It pictured a gypsy boy perched on the edge of the red wing chair set on the top step of the New York Stock Exchange. His ragged clothes were soiled and his knee was coming though a hole in his trousers. He dealt out cards on an upturned cardboard box in front of him, the building's fluted columns rising behind. The boy looked out from under a thick mop of black hair, mouth smiling, eyes wary.

"Who's this?" she asked.

"That's Ramir. He's going to make one of the great Wall Street wizard portraits, right up there with Benjamin Graham and Warren Buffet."

She smiled. "Looks like he's got a ways to go."

"He's just starting out."

She watched him with amusement as he filled the cigarette paper, nudged the flakes of grass evenly along the edge, and rolled it up. He licked the edge of the paper, wrapped it around, and twisted each end of the joint.

"He's placing his bets, just like the guys inside the stock exchange. And at least he's doing it on his own terms – he's not brown-nosing the boss, he's not a parasite."

"*Sycophant*, I believe is the term you want."

He struck a match and touched it to the joint; the papery end flared in flame. "Okay, sycophant. But give me the street trader, any day," he said and blew a smoke ring that spread slowly up towards the ceiling.

She looked back at him, her expression a mix of admiration and assessment. "Making it in the art world is a long haul for everyone, you just have to keep at it. What's important is that your work is very accomplished already and developing well – it has real integrity. Just keep painting, the rest will follow."

He wasn't sure which was sweeter, the pungent grass or the praise. As he listened the sour aftertaste of the Matisse sale began to fade; yes, surely his work was significant, there was promise in his prospects. He took a long toke and held it deep in his lungs. The smoke went to his head immediately and he stretched out his arm, offering her the joint, still holding his breath. She hesitated momentarily before taking it.

He watched her toke on the joint. She looked incredibly beautiful with her auburn hair cascading over her shoulders and the peach glow in her cheeks. He rose and stood in front of her, at just her height. He took the joint back and toked on it, then turned it around and put it to her lips, their gazes locked all the while. The grass was good and he was feeling mighty high, as if the foggy night air had seeped into his brain. Never had he seen so many hues as in her multi-colored eyes, all shades of green and brown and gold. What pigments could possibly reproduce them? The cool willow of chromium oxide, the mustards of ochre, the olive of green earth, the yellow highlights of emerald . . . and even they would be taxed to capture the depth of these eyes, like portholes into space.

She exhaled and looked at him quizzically. "So, Beauregard, is this what you tell all the girls? Come on up and see my paintings?"

He took the joint and stubbed it out on the easel. As Otis began *Try a Little Tenderness* he put his arms around her and lowered his head onto her shoulder.

"No. Only you."

"I see. First time, huh?"

He nodded and she shook her head. He raised his head and looked at her, distraught that she didn't believe him. But she wasn't miffed, only amused.

She asked softly, "So tell me – what is it you want that you haven't toadied for?"

The piney smell of her hair enveloped him and suddenly he wanted to change the subject. He was too proud to tell her how he ached to show his work, and he didn't want to think about his money worries or what he had done to forestall them. Besides, everything had slowed to a haze and none of that seemed to matter as much as her cheek, soft as chamois. "Right now all I want is you."

She was breathing softly into his neck and he sensed she was debating about this. But there wasn't a doubt in his mind. He raised his head and looked into her eyes, close and clear and infinitely deep. "I'm glad I found you again," he said.

She looked thoughtful but she smiled slowly and said, "So am I."

She raised her arms around his neck and their bodies moved together. They fit perfectly, curve for curve, limb for limb. She nuzzled into him as he ran his hand from her hips around the bend of her waist and up over her back. By the time he reached her neck he was warm all over.

"You don't mind if I call you Beauregard, do you?"

He drew back his head, trying to slow himself down. He wanted to savor this, she felt so great.

"A rose by any other name . . ."

She laughed, a wonderful open laugh. He ran his fingers over her velvety cheek to the smooth skin of her neck, then kissed her lips softly. Her cat's eyes, quick and agile before, were calm and languid now. Together, their euphoria floated them right up onto the loft bed and he felt they'd ascended into some thin-aired stratosphere. His hands explored her hills and valleys, curves and swells. "Let's take these off," he said huskily and helped pull her sweater over her head followed by his own. Their two smooth bodies slipped together, skin against skin, pulse to pulse.

Cats yowled, dogs howled, and Otis Redding wailed out his blues, but all Bo heard was the inner throb, the rhythm of two blended souls gathering and cresting like ocean swells. Cold air from Canada carried in off the Hudson blew in the open window but he felt nothing except silk against satin, back and forth and back again. Light streamed in from the street lamp, the city's moon against the shadows, but he saw nothing except the sparks that fly behind the eyes, the light of desire.

When it was over he flopped on to his back and closed his eyes against his racing heart. She let out a last, low moan and reached out to smooth the furrow of hair running down his chest to his stomach. He turned to her, soft and shadowy in the dim light, astonished at the presence of this flesh and blood muse. Clearly, with her, every success would be possible.

Chapter 10

Vines and trumpet flowers meandered in carved stone up the doorway of Catherine DuBois' apartment building on the east side of 5th Avenue across from the Central Park Zoo. As Alastair approached the marquee the doorman magically appeared. With a flash of his white-gloved hands, the heavy glass door swung open. "Alastair Cavendish for Catherine DuBois, please."

The doorman showed Alastair into the mirrored elevator and with a smooth swoosh the car rose to the third floor. He fingered his lucky Christ Church College tie, running his fingers down the navy blue silk dotted with red cardinals hats that stood for Cardinal Wolsey, the founder of Christ Church College. Not only had this tie gotten him a lot of dinner party invitations, but he'd worn it during some of his best painting acquisitions.

The elevator door opened into a foyer and a butler with white hair brushed back from a reserved face said, "Good afternoon. Mrs. DuBois is expecting you. Follow me, please."

He led Alastair down a narrow hallway. Sconces lined the high walls, light shining softly through amber veins in the alabaster, lending the paneling a reddish glow like a newly opened horse chestnut. A floor of black and white checkerboard tiles led into a grand room with a stained glass ceiling, leather-covered walls, and an enormous marble fireplace. He stopped, wanting to take it all in, but the butler was disappearing through another doorway. They passed through room after room, each grander than the last, all in the turn-of-the-century style. The taste was masculine, handsome rather than beautiful, sumptuous through materials rather than detail.

Paintings were everywhere, lining the walls in gilt frames, molded frames, plain and fancy frames, offering panoply of Modernism. It was all Alastair could do to keep up with the butler as he flew past Picasso drawings, an enchanting Franz Marc, a magnificent early Cézanne. He longed to get out his eyeglass and inspect the pictures, examine the signatures, peruse the paint. Working at Lyndhurst and Lloyd's had schooled him with the rudest impulses: he wanted to turn over every work of art and see who made it, where it was from. And then take it in for sale.

Finally they came to a set of double doors opening into a large sitting room. Tall windows swaged with crimson draperies looked out on to the autumnal treetops of Central Park. Across an enormous Oriental rug a small woman walked towards Alastair, holding out her hand. Her gray hair was drawn back in a dowdy bun but her step was sprightly; her pale blue dress matched her eyes.

"Mr. Cavendish, how very nice to meet you. I'm Catherine Dubois."

"My pleasure," he said, pressing his free hand on top of hers. "What a lovely apartment, with all the carved woodwork and the stained glass."

"Rather special, isn't it? William Morris Hunt designed it so I really can't take any credit. It was all here when Edwin and I arrived."

She smiled sadly.

"Oh, but the art you've collected does it justice," he said.

He gestured over the fireplace at a painting that caught his eye as he entered the room. By Degas, it portrayed two women in conversation at a fence. One leaned forward, a big-brimmed straw hat hiding her eyes, while the other reached out and touched her friend's arm in a confiding gesture. The figures were close to the picture plane, their bodies truncated. Alastair stroked his chin; it was never too early to demonstrate his expertise.

"Such a marvelous example of the influence of photography on Degas, the way he set the figures so close to the picture plane we see only part of them."

Catherine turned and looked at the painting. "That's the very thing that appeals to me, the intimate perspective."

"It was quite bold, stylistically, at the time."

Alastair smiled. He was off to a good start. If she knew he understood her taste she'd trust him to handle her collection. And he had to persuade her of this, because he knew that with Lyndhurst & Lloyd's behind him he could orchestrate this sale to make art auction history. And what could be better than that?

A man's voice piped up from behind him. "You don't really see this until the 1880s in Degas. It was a real point of departure, quite unlike his earlier work."

Alastair turned to see a man standing against the inside wall behind the opened double doors, positioned under a spirited dance hall scene by Toulouse Lautrec. Well, I'll be damned, Alastair thought. If it wasn't Terrence Young, Sotheby's modern painting expert.

Alastair didn't flinch an inch. All right. So they were going to play a game.

"I'm sure you two need no introduction," Catherine said brightly.

The two men stepped forward and shook hands, a quick, vigorous shake, the shake of tennis players over the net who recognize a talented opponent they are determined to beat.

Catherine rang a brass bell with a handle in the shape of a Maltese cross. The butler appeared out of nowhere.

"Yes, Madam?"

"You may as well serve the tea, Humphreys. Our other guest can join us when he arrives. And let's have some of those almond macaroons from Dumas."

Taking a seat on one end of a striped velvet sofa, she nodded at the two men. "Do sit down, gentlemen." Alastair sat at the far end next to a Chinese famille rose vase. Terrence settled himself across the coffee table in a Sheraton chair as straight-backed as himself. Dappled sunlight played across the Oriental rug, flickering over the intricate pattern of intersecting lines and abutting angles.

Alastair's watch started beeping and he quickly shut it off. "How are you enjoying America?" Catherine asked.

He cleared his throat and shifted his mode to tea talk since that seemed to be expected. "Very much indeed. Although I hadn't expected such a language problem."

Catherine gave a short laugh. "Yes, a lot of English arrivals have trouble with our dialect."

"I'm afraid it's more they who don't understand me. But I'm learning to translate. I've got to ask for jelly when I want jam, elevators when I want lifts. And then the way you call the building floors, that's quite confusing. Our street floor is the ground floor, and what we call the first floor you call the second."

Terrence crossed his leg over his knee and smiled benevolently. "We're just one step ahead of you."

Alastair smiled benevolently back. "Ah, but we're grounded, you see. A footing I prefer."

The butler set a silver tea service on the coffee table. Incised on the teapot with its sumptuously curling handle was the Wyndham family crest, its four quadrants containing a jumping stag, a turret, a crossbow and a key.

Alastair recognized the crest immediately. "What a homecoming. I feel I'm back at Beech Tree Manor."

Catherine smiled in acknowledgment and Alastair avoided looking at Terrence. He saw no reason to explain his connection, which he planned to make the most of. He would use everything he could to win this consignment.

Presently the butler announced Mr. Gerhardt, whose trim figure appeared in a dark gray suit. He glanced quickly from Alastair to Terrence, but the flicker of surprise Alastair detected was quickly replaced with a cordial smile. He bowed, showing the recession of his dark hair at the temples, and crisply clicked his heels. As it had at MoMA, Gerhardt's palm felt damp as he shook Alastair's hand. The three men seated themselves and smiled all around – the perfect tea party.

"Reinhold has been one of my best sources over the years," Catherine said as she poured the tea.

"You are too kind," Reinhold murmured.

"And your Austrian background has been a great advantage, especially for buying the European Modernists, hasn't it?"

Gerhardt stroked his goatee thoughtfully. "But not without a price, you must remember. The Third Reich – what a sad period for so many people *and* for modern art. Decadent, they termed it, as well as we dealers who sold it. So much art was confiscated, so many masterpieces vanished, just like the people."

They sat in silence for a moment until Gerhardt resumed more cheerfully.

"In my travels I *have* made some unusual finds." Gerhardt crossed his thin leg over his thigh, catching the tip of his alligator shoe behind the Sheraton chair leg.

"Like the Klee," Catherine said.

Gerhardt removed a piece of lint from his pant leg. "A stroke of luck. I found the canvas rolled up on a shelf in an antique store in Munich. I bought it for next to nothing and passed the savings right along to Catherine. This is difficult to do at Sotheby Parke Bernet."

He pronounced Bernet as if it rhymed with today.

"Ber*net*," Terrence said loftily, emphasizing the final t. "The founder wasn't French, he was a German, Otto Bernet."

"Of course, a bad habit. I, of all people should know!" Gerhardt said. "But as Mr. Cavendish can tell you, pronunciation in another country is an ongoing challenge."

Alastair nodded agreeably. He too could be magnanimous as they all sat salivating over Catherine's collection. "There's room for everyone in the art market," he said. "Where would we auction houses be without the dealers?"

"Absolutely," Terrence seconded.

"You will keep some of your collection, won't you?" Alastair asked Catherine.

She set down her cup and saucer with both hands. "I'd like to. It really depends on where I end up living. I've definitely decided on selling the East Hampton house and all of the big paintings out there. I may be staying here on Fifth Avenue, or maybe not. But in any case I do want to keep my favorite pieces, ones I'll have room for, unless I'm advised otherwise. Like the Matisse on the wall there."

She rose and walked to a pastel hanging in an ornate gilt frame. The three men followed and gathered around the picture, an interior with a figure sitting at a table. Her neck bent at an impossible angle, the woman was as decorative as the floral wallpaper around her. Every angle was flattened, every surface reduced to pattern.

"This I love, although it's not signed and I've never had it authenticated. I bought it years ago at an estate sale up in Gloucester, Massachusetts. I was just married and feeling impetuous and although my husband questioned my wisdom since it wasn't signed, I declared I wanted it no matter who painted it." She laughed and added, "I was young."

"No time like the present," said Terrence. "Why don't we have a look at it? You've got three experts here."

"Shall we?" Catherine asked.

Gerhardt's face was impassive. "Why not?"

"By all means," Alastair said, his adrenaline surging. Perfect. There was nothing like a contest to assert one's expertise. Especially with his Sotheby's counterpart.

Terrence lifted the picture off the hanger and held it near the window for all to inspect in the late afternoon light.

"It is lovely," said Alastair. "So many patterns, all different, all harmonious."

Terrence took a pair of glasses out of his breast pocket and put them on.

"But is it authentic? You'll have trouble selling an unsigned piece. And although I agree it's very pretty, I'm not sure it's by Matisse. There were many forgeries done after he died in 1954 and his work became so sought after. This one looks a bit odd, the awkward handling of the table."

"With all due respect, I disagree," Alastair said. "This is typical of his early interiors from around 1910 when he began flattening space into two dimensions. He didn't always do it gracefully."

Terrence raised his nose and looked through the bottom portion of his bifocals.

"No, I'm afraid I can't agree. It just doesn't look right. I'll bet this is one of the forgeries. That explains why it isn't signed."

Terrence looked challengingly over his glasses at Alastair and Alastair stared right back – two confronting stags in the forest.

"Do you mind if I take a closer look?" Alastair asked Catherine.

"Please do."

He took the picture by the frame, turned it over and used a key to lift the tacks out of the back. The mat board slipped out easily and he held the paper up to the light.

"Just as I suspected. Look here, in the lower corner."

With the late afternoon light behind it, a watermark was clearly visible.

"A large Arches watermark. Arches is a centuries-old French mill and has always used this watermark. But they reduced it to a smaller size in the 1930s. That dates this paper to before 1930. I find it hard to believe that a forger would have had the nerve to fake a Matisse while he was still alive."

Terrance peered closely at the watermark. He cleared his throat and adjusted his tie. "Well. You're right about the watermark."

Gerhardt nodded respectfully. "You are very observant, Mr. Cavendish."

Alastair tried not to look too triumphant as he said, "Your instincts were right, Mrs. DuBois. Signed or not, you've got a real Matisse here."

Catherine smiled slowly at Alastair, inclining her head slightly. His spirit soared – Right again! Victory! The battle was won, the foe defeated! Now he just had to make sure to win the war.

Terrence continued to clear his throat; he seemed to have caught a frog in it. Presently he explained that he had an appointment to keep. Gerhardt followed him shortly.

Catherine and Alastair returned to their seats, where he sank down into the cushions which seemed much more comfortable than before.

"More tea, Alastair?" Catherine asked. "You don't mind if I call you Alastair."

"Please. On both counts."

"And you must call me Catherine."

She reached for his teacup, her veins standing out, lavender on ivory. The cup rattled in the saucer with her trembling hand. She set down the cup and poured out the tea, the amber stream wavering in midair. "You know I've had such good luck with Reinhold over the years, he's been so attentive. In fact, he recently offered me a thousand dollars for that Matisse interior, which he said was a good price considering it wasn't signed."

Alastair looked up sharply. "Perhaps a good price for a fake, but a steal for the real thing."

Her eyes grew big and round. "But that's the whole point with Reinhold. He never pays retail prices. And when he's buying for me, I benefit from his finds."

He deferred, not wanting to speak ill of the dealer she was obviously so fond of. She continued. "I know Gerhardt has some peculiar mannerisms, but he is Austrian, after all. You can't mistrust him just because he's a foreigner."

"In my present circumstances, I should hope not."

She laughed, her blue eyes softening. A light china blue, blue like a young girl's, they didn't seem to have aged with the rest of her. She smiled warmly and handed over the tea. "When would you like to begin cataloguing?"

Chapter 11

B o's hand had started to cramp up, which it often did when he had been painting all morning. Clyde told him this was a sign of age, but he had a couple of years 'til he hit 30 so he figured it couldn't be arthritis yet. And when it was, he planned to be like Renoir, to tie the paintbrushes on to his wrists so he could still paint even if his hands were so gnarled he couldn't hold the brush.

The *Wall Street Tycoon* gypsy boy would have to wait. Instead, he switched to stretching a canvas. He didn't have much longer to work anyway, as Clyde was due to show up any minute to go down to Orchard Street and buy jeans for a buck and a quarter. He centered an assembled stretcher on a piece of slightly larger canvas, carefully eyeing the weave until it lined up parallel to the edge.

The phone rang and he halted momentarily, looking over at the answering machine sitting on the bottom of his supply shelf. Bought with money from the sale of the Matisse study, he loved letting it take calls – his own personal secretary. It was the perfect way to avoid Gozzi, who although now paid up, couldn't be trusted to leave him alone for long. For once again, Bo wasn't sure where next month's rent was coming from.

He folded an edge of the canvas over the long side of the stretcher and drove in a tack at the center of the strip. The funny thing was, by the time he used the two grand from Susan Jacobson to pay off the back rent, the bills and the loans from

Clyde, his sister and his grandmother, and bought himself a decent supply of paint and canvas, there was no money left. Of course, he'd splurged a little on an answering machine and an espresso maker. But all the expenditures had landed him right back where he started: broke again.

After four rings the answering machine picked up and over the speaker came a voice that Bo was beginning to dread even more than Gozzi's. The German accent spoke clearly, evenly.

"Hello Bo, I'm still trying to reach you. As I mentioned, I have a business proposition I think you'll be interested in. Please give me a call at . . ."

A wave of anxiety passed through Bo as the voice rang off. He caught the loose side of the canvas with stretching pliers, pulled it tightly across the opposite side and drove in another tack. This was the third time Gerhardt had called, and each time Bo felt more unnerved. Why couldn't the guy take a hint, that Bo wasn't calling back, that he had no interest in any business proposition? After turning it over and over in his mind, the only reason he could come up with for Gerhardt's calling was that he knew the study was not genuine and wanted to blackmail him. Which wouldn't get him very far – there wasn't much use in blackmailing a pauper. But this wasn't very reassuring. If Bo couldn't come up with any suitable payment maybe Gerhardt would simply expose him, report him to the police. He held the hammer still for a moment, thinking of the possible repercussions. What were the legal penalties for fraud? He would plead innocent, of course, but once that stone began to tumble, events would take on a life of their own and plunge him who knew where.

Ah, what the hell, he thought as he tried to dismiss the nagging thoughts, staring at the canvas now stretched in a diamond shape from tack to tack. It wasn't like he'd intentionally set out to deceive Susan Jacobson. And he hadn't signed Matisse's name to the watercolor, so it wasn't really forgery. Nobody got hurt, so no big deal. It was all over now, for he would never repeat the deal. Meeting Megan had made it clear that he didn't need to resort to that. But he'd gleaned enough from Buddhism to believe in cosmic retribution and it was hard to shake the feeling that somehow he would be made to pay.

As for Gerhardt, if only Bo could find out what he wanted without taking the call; what pound of flesh was he after? His messages sounded so well disposed – who knew. Maybe he was into kinky sex. But the friendlier his voice was, the more it gave Bo the creeps. Maybe he should change his phone number.

The buzzer rang and he threw up the sash of the huge paned window and leaned out just to make sure it wasn't Gozzi. Although with his recent proprietary attitude he didn't even bother to ring the buzzer anymore.

He peered down through the black slats of the fire escape to the sidewalk four stories below. He could make out a denim jacket and a head just beginning to go bald at the back of the crown. A pair of boots stuck out below like signposts pointing in different directions.

"Hi Clyde," he tried to shout, but all that came out was a croak. He hadn't talked to anybody all morning. He cleared his throat and tried again. "I'll be right down."

He grabbed his leather jacket, pulled it over his sweatshirt and clattered down the stairs. The heavy door swung open to a waiting Clyde Jackson, his red hair blown back by the wind.

"Hey, what's happening," Clyde said in his soothing North Carolina accent.

Bo greeted him, turned the key in the lock and they headed east towards Broadway.

The day was clear and blindingly bright, the kind of fall day when the light sparkled and the air smelled like the sea. Manhattan felt crisp and clean, unlike the murky days of August. Fire escapes rose in sharp diagonals up the fronts of the cast-iron buildings on Broome Street, creating a thin network of black lines against the green, gray, and blue facades. Soho sightseers meandered on the sidewalks, craning their necks for better views of the Corinthian capitals. To Bo it seemed fitting that these classical motifs were housing the contemporary art scene, since art was always built on the past, even though Andy Warhol might try to tell it different.

Clyde chattered on about his new project called ArtWeb, how his dealer was trying to get permission from the city to hang it in the middle of West Broadway. Bo listened with one ear but let his thoughts drift off to the comforting memory of Megan: her remarkable eyes in all their hues, her expressive voice, how it lilted up and down while she was trying to persuade him of the virtues of abstraction, which he had only partly heard because he had been watching the way the end of her nose moved up and down while she talked. It was hard to tell in this early stage of infatuation, but she seemed to be everything he was looking for in a woman: beautiful, smart, nice, interesting. He gave a sardonic snort; what was she doing with the likes of him?

"How did the open studio day go?" asked Clyde.

Back to reality. He kicked at a torn cup blowing up the sidewalk and smiled.

"Oh, you know these collectors. They keep beating down the door, waving cash at me, it's all I can do to fend them off."

Clyde smiled and patted his shoulder. "Gotta get a grant, Bo, get a grant."

"Yeah . . . or sell some paintings. The last decent sale I made was in the *Soho Streets* exhibit last year. I was hoping to get into the PS1 *Under 30* show, but the jurors didn't pick anything representational."

He felt a pang of conscience at these fibs, but quickly dismissed it. The Matisse sale was so minor, barely worth considering, especially since it was history. And the rest of it was all too true.

He shook his head. "My style just isn't in the right groove these days." He pulled at a hole in his frayed St. Louis Cardinals sweatshirt and gave a rueful smile. "But then, I've never been a stylish kind of guy."

Clyde laughed and they walked along in silence for a moment, bracing against the wind, which hit them as they crossed Mercer Street. Bo watched the sidewalk slipping past under his old boots. He would probably need to get another job on top of working at the parking lot. But that already ate up 30 hours a week, and more hours spent at some brainless work was not what he needed.

With the change of season the wind blew up the north/south streets, howling like a banshee. It caught paper and bits of trash from the street and swirled them up and around in the air, mini-twisters of foil wrappers, glittering plastic straws and Styrofoam, defying gravity, if only for a moment.

The tourists thinned out as they neared Broadway and turned south, making their way among the street vendors and the Latino families looking for bargains. Folding tables were covered with T-shirts for 89 cents, three lipsticks for a buck, plastic belts and shiny gold watches.

"All silver chains, only a dollar. Check it out, check it out," a vendor chanted.

"Let's hang a left," Bo said, wanting to escape the sleazy sales harangue.

"*Life is so rich in A-mer-i-ca . . .*" sang Clyde. "Which reminds me, get this: my sister saw a TV show on Gauguin about how he sometimes couldn't afford to buy canvas. So she sent me $300 for art supplies. She's a doctor so it's no sweat."

Bo shrugged dismissively. He didn't want to hear about the medical fields. He got enough of that from his father who had always wanted to add *Father & Son* to his *Ryder's Orthodontia* shingle. He still asked why Bo couldn't get "an honest job" and "paint on the weekends."

"All my old man will pay for is dental school. I suppose that would've paid my rent on time."

"Ah, c'mon, you can't think like that." Clyde put on a pompous face and mocked, "Yes, this *Night Watch* is a nice idea, Rembrandt, but will they pay you at the end of the week?"

Good old Clyde, always ready for a laugh. But Bo didn't

really want to think about it anymore. The subject of money never took him anywhere he wanted to be.

They had reached the Bowery now and the brightness of the day showed up the street in all its dreary decay. Most of the buildings were mere shells, glass broken out of the windows, stoops falling apart and sprouting weeds. Street people gathered, two and three in a doorway, smoking cigarette stubs and chugging from pints of Ripple and Richard's Wild Irish Rose. The wind blew newspapers in the street and empty beer cans rolled in the gutter with a tinny, hollow clanking like the random tolling of an offbeat bell.

The lower east side always put Bo on his guard; in these streets anything could happen.

On the corner of Chrystie Street stood a bum in front of a wire mesh garbage can heaped with old boards and torn-apart cardboard boxes set ablaze. The old man warmed his hands above the crackling flames and tugged on a cigar stub in his mouth as if it contained some sustaining substance.

He eyed Bo and Clyde as they approached. "Either of you boys got a smoke?" he asked.

He clenched the cigar stub tightly between yellowed, broken teeth. His gray hair stuck out from his head in all directions, his clothes hung on him like a scarecrow's, stiff and threadbare. Yet his hands were tough and nimble and gave the sense of a wiry body underneath.

Something about the old man intrigued Bo and he stopped. A lot of the street people were just plain crazy and talking to them was only asking for trouble. But this old man looked as if he'd seen the world twice over and was still looking around for more.

Bo pulled out a pack of Luckies from his jacket pocket and handed over a couple.

"Thanks," the old man said. "I don't ever ask for no money, but a man's gotta have a smoke to keep him going."

He took the chewed cigar butt from his mouth and stubbed it out on the rim of the garbage can, then carefully stowed it in his breast pocket along with one of the Luckies. The other he stuck in his mouth.

"Gotta light?" he asked.

Bo handed him a pack of matches and he lit the cigarette, his nails caked with dirt.

"Aren't you starting a little early with the fire?" Bo asked, knowing they didn't usually appear until the bitter cold set in.

The old man put one finger to the side of his nose and, leaning into the street, efficiently blew a gob into the gutter. He drew deeply on the cigarette and looked Bo up and down.

"This here's the first one I've built this year. Last night I nearly froze my nuggies off. Mind you, it ain't 'cause I can't get a room, they'll take me in at the Sacred Heart Mission anytime. But I got a space all set up here and once you got it you gotta stick with it."

"What space is that?" Bo asked. The old man jerked his head towards the doorway of an abandoned building.

"Can we take a look?" Bo asked.

The old man eyed Bo suspiciously but then said, "Sure, I'll show you, if you want."

He walked ahead of them, favoring his right leg and swinging his left one forward with each step. He moved surprisingly quickly.

Inside the derelict apartment building Bo paused in the musty hallway, waiting for his eyes to adjust to the dim light. Broken glass reflected from the floor; the stench of stale wine and urine was enough to make him gag.

"Jesus," said Clyde, coming up behind him.

The old man turned into a room off the hallway, a set of rusty hinges dangling loosely from the frame. The room was colder and darker than outside. A porcelain washbasin lay dismantled in the corner; ragged brown shades hung at the window.

In one corner a neat pile of cardboard was draped with a couple of tattered blankets, a cracked coffee cup sat next to a beaten up pan and a can opener. An old tuna fish container held half a candle next to several stacks of yellowed newspapers – muddied sections from The Daily News and The Enquirer. "*Thousand pound man fork-lifted out of Bronx apartment*" read the headline on top. The old man turned and faced Bo and Clyde.

"This is my place," he stated assertively. "Ain't nobody sleeps here but me." His eyes glistened territorially.

"What's the cardboard for?" Clyde asked.

"Sometimes them guys get in here when I'm not around. They take a shit anywhere, and me, I'm pretty clean. I put that cardboard down 'cause I'm never sure what I'm laying on."

Clyde poked Bo with his elbow. "And you thought your place needed work."

The afternoon sun shone through the tears in the shades, illuminating dust motes that swirled softly in the gloom.

The old man pointed to the pile in the corner. "I got everything I need, right here. I open my cans, eat my food, curl up and keep warm at night. I even got a candle to read by. And I got all the newspapers. I got the papers from when the first man landed on the moon, from when Nixon blew his wad at Watergate." The old man took a step closer and peered at Bo. "See, I got what they call dyslexia. My teachers, the nuns, they said I couldn't read. And my mum, there were ten of us so she had no time to tend to sumptin' she never hear of. But you know, I finally figured how to beat it. Took me 'til I lost my job and my house and my wife. Then I had a lot of time on my hands. But if I go real slow like, and say each word when I get it, I can read near as well as anyone."

The old man cleared his throat and announced ceremonially, "Watergate." He strutted across the bare room, one hand on his chest, the other stretched out like an orator, turning his head and shifting his voice for each quote from the period: "*A cancer on the presidency; It would be wrong, that's for sure; A second-rate burglary; Let's deep-six him.*" He narrowed his eyes and leaned toward his visitors: "*Twist slowly in the wind.*"

He stopped and grinned. "See? I know 'em all. Memorized 'em."

Bo laughed and Clyde said, "You sure would've been handy for current events class."

A slow growl came from the hall and a scruffy terrier appeared in the doorway. The old man bent down, his knees crackling like dry sticks, and called the dog. "Hey Pancho, here Pancho."

The dog scrambled across the room straight to the old man, who ran his hands over his ears.

"This here's Pancho. Won't find a better partner than him. I share my scraps with him and he keeps the rats out of this place."

The dog sat against the old man's legs, his tail thumping against the floor while the old man smoothed his wiry hair.

"Yup, he's sure been my best friend."

The old man rose, knees crackling. "I got to get out in that sunlight while it lasts, warm up these old bones."

He limped stiffly out the door, rubbing his hands together, followed by Clyde.

Bo took one more look at the compact possessions piled neatly on the floor and whistled. From here his 2500-square foot loft seemed pretty grand, even with the dripping ceiling.

Outside Clyde was giving the old man another light. He stood with his hands cupped around the match, keeping the flame away from his beard, his alert eyes focused on the end of the cigarette. Watching him, Bo suddenly had a vision. In his mind's eye he saw the old man sitting in the wing chair, his rough exterior contrasted with the rich upholstery, tattered brown cloth against the smooth sheen of the damask.

"What's your name?" Bo asked him.

"Paddy. Paddy Flaherty."

"How would you like to model for me sometime?"

First he laughed, then he peered at Bo warily. "*Model*? What do you mean? I ain't no pervert."

"No, no, nothing like that. I'm a painter. All you have to do is sit still and I paint your picture. It's real simple."

Paddy stared at Bo uncertainly.

"I'll pay you for it," Bo added. He took out his wallet and pulled out a five-dollar bill.

The old man waved it away disdainfully. "I ain't no charity case."

"It's not charity. You'd be working for me. I'll pay you three bucks an hour. What do you say?"

Paddy considered. "Well, if it's a paying job you're talking about . . ."

"It is." Bo pulled out a pencil and scribbled on a scrap of paper. "Here's my address. You want to come by tomorrow morning?"

Paddy frowned and stared up at the roof of the building. "Well, now, I don't know about tomorrow. I got a lot of stuff needs tending to, what with winter coming on and all. But I'll come when I can."

Bo handed him the address and smiled. "Good enough."

The two friends set off down the street, Bo picking up his pace, rubbing his hands together. The image was developing: Paddy in the red wing chair, his wiry body dwarfed by the elegant curves of the chair's big frame, his face composed, knowing, maybe even proud. It was clear the old man had character. What would be the setting? Maybe perched in the middle of the meridian on Chrystie Street, traffic streaming all around. Maybe at the entrance to the Holland Tunnel, headed into darkness. Or maybe on a Bowery rooftop, surrounded by pigeons and water towers.

Here was a subject he could glorify, immortalize, an Everyman for Eternity. And what a face – worthy of Carravaggio, Frans Hals, Van Dyck – what better inspiration for an homage to the older masters? Surely this would redeem his recent transgression as an artist.

Bo turned to Clyde, his eyes full of a new light. "I sure hope he comes. He'd make a masterpiece!"

Chapter 12

"What's wrong with sour cream pancakes?" Megan asked dreamily.

"Nothing. It's going to eat them for *brunch*," Bo said.

"What's wrong with brunch?"

"Oh, it's so *bourgeois*, so upper east side. Are we banned from breakfast because it's ten o'clock in the morning and we haven't gotten out of bed yet?"

He raised himself on one elbow and looked at her with a tenderness that belied his challenging words. She reached up and pushed his disheveled brown curls out of his eyes. She felt so happy waking up with him she didn't really care whether she ate or not.

"Let's call it breakfast then. What do you feel like having?"

He gently traced his finger around her mouth. Then he leaned over and kissed both her eyes, the pressure of his lips soft and warm. "You. I'll have you for breakfast."

Her heart took a swan dive but her stomach growled. She *was* hungry. All the lustful activity had worked up her appetite. "How about the diner? We can load up on bacon and eggs, keep up our cholesterol count."

He nuzzled into her neck. "Oh, let's not. It's so nice and cozy here. I don't feel like going out in that lousy weather."

"What weather?"

"It's cold and rainy."

She looked at him with good-natured skepticism. "How

can you tell it's raining when you haven't gotten out of bed yet?"

He said simply, "I can tell. Feel the air. Listen."

She sat up in the high bed and looked out across the loft space, expansive as a canyon floor, littered with stretchers, old canvases, cans of turpentine, tossed clothing and used coffee cups, towards the big paned windows that lined the street side. The glass was streaked with rivulets. The air felt raw and outside she could hear the faint sound of a car passing, its tires spattering on the wet street.

She turned to him. "You're right, it is raining. That's amazing."

He smiled. "*You're* amazing. Give me a kiss."

She met his lips and they felt like all the sustenance she needed. "Some morning I will make you waffles and ice cream and you'll see how bourgeois I can really be."

He slid one arm under her shoulder and pulled her closer. "That's not bourgeois, it's downright decadent."

"Not *decadent*, this is a culinary height. *Luxurious*, I'd say."

He looked at her tolerantly before his eyes softened. "Having you here is all the luxury I need."

She twirled one of his curls around her finger and thought of her uncle who liked to fill cantaloupe halves with champagne and refrigerate them overnight until the spirits were absorbed into the melon's sweet flesh. What a way to start the day. But somehow this didn't seem like quite the memory to share with Bo, not with his accusations of bourgeois living.

Suddenly a bell started ringing and Bo reached up to the shelf above the loft bed and tapped the top of an alarm clock. He had bought the clock the other day when he took Megan down to the flea market on Grand Street, which he told her was the best place to buy anything. He said ordinarily he didn't care what time it was, but that these days he couldn't afford to be late for his job at the parking lot. So he bought a silly clock printed with Mickey Mouse's face and two round black bells on top like Mouseketeer's ears, one of them a snooze button.

"Ten more minutes," he said and snuggled into her, closing his eyes. They lay with limbs crossed like languid puppies, basking in body warmth.

She stared up at the *Portraits in the City*, the big canvases on the same level as the raised loft bed; she loved waking up at Bo's, even with all its insouciant grit and grime. The paintings lining the walls greeted her the moment she opened her eyes, as if she were waking up in an art gallery. She didn't mind the lingering odor of paint and turpentine, or the couch that poked her with a broken spring every time she sat in it, the smudged coffee mugs, the pervasive dust. This marginal domesticity was an integral part of Bo's life, his driving focus being his art. And with any luck, he'd make some room for her.

Bo had moved one of her favorite paintings to a spot next to the window. Painted when he had been stuck for a model, he used himself. He sat in the red wing chair, ankle crossed over his knee, at the demolished midtown end of the West Side Highway. The chair was set at the torn edge that dropped off into thin air, rusted steel girders bent down under the highway into darkness. Above, the chair expanded into the infinite blue of a Cerulean sky.

She knew it was Bo only because he told her. Afterwards she recognized his compact build with the narrow hips and broad shoulders, clothed in an old military jacket with double-breasted brass buttons and fringed epaulets. But at first it looked only chimerical, for the figure wore an elaborate bird mask with bright red feathers, a long yellow beak and sequin-lined, almond eyes.

She turned and watched him as he lay on his stomach, his tousled hair a mass of dark curls on the white pillow. Looking him over as she would a painting, she admired his smoothly muscled arms, his tawny skin, his bow-shaped mouth. He could have modeled for Carravaggio. She matched his steady breathing with her own, feeling almost as if he were breathing for her.

This love affair had her flying high, drifting with the clouds.

She'd never felt like this about anyone so quickly. But how could she not? To find a man so attractive who loved art as much as she did was close to miraculous. And it was easy to forgo champagne cantaloupes for the calming effect he had on her, smoothing out her rough edges. For her professional life had become somewhat dry with her personal life so lonely, which it had been, she realized now, even before she broke up with Ned. This became clear only as she understood the emotional gap Bo filled.

Since the first night she stayed at his place they hadn't spent a night apart, although tonight she had to review a performance piece being staged in the courtyard of Lincoln Center. It would be over late, and she really had no excuse not to sleep at Lizzy's since her apartment was right down the street. She didn't like the prospect of spending the night without him, but he'd been so dismissive of performance art she hesitated to invite him.

His mouth was partly open; he was dozing off. She marveled at this ability he had to wake up and make intelligent conversation and two minutes later be asleep again.

"Hey, Beauregard, don't go back to sleep."

"I'm not sleeping," he said thickly.

"It's amazing how well you can get to know someone in a week," she said, watching the familiar way his long curls drooped over his forehead, as if they too hadn't slept enough.

"A week and a half," he said with his eyes closed. "It was October 8th and today is the 18th. I know because Gozzi said he'd give me until the 15th to pay, and that was Tuesday. I haven't answered the phone since then. Maybe I'll win the Lottery."

"Why don't you offer him one of your paintings? Tell him it's a ten thousand dollar collateral if he'll wait ten years."

He opened his eyes and looked at her questioningly.

"Why not?" she said. "This is Soho. I know lots of artists who pay fees with paintings, to doctors, dentists, even lawyers."

"He'd never go for it. He's a real plebeian. His idea of a

good painting is a day-glo Elvis on black velvet."

"Oh well, his loss," she said lightly.

"Yeah, I guess," he replied, staring moodily up at the ceiling.

Seeing his brows knit, she felt his discouragement as if it were her own. "You know, Bo," she said gently, "It's just a matter of time until you find your niche and can support your painting. And in the meantime your work is coming along wonderfully – I can see it in the city portraits. So be patient. And in the spring maybe you'll enter the Whitney Counterweight that I'm helping to organize. It's the Salon de Refusés for all the deserving artists who don't make the Whitney Biennial."

"Maybe." He turned to her and forced a smile. "What are you up to today?"

"Oh, there are a couple of reviews I have to finish by tomorrow." She smoothed the rumpled sheet. "And I've got to look for an apartment, that's definitely on the list."

He nodded and turned back to the ceiling. She snuck a look at him and, seeing his blank expression, looked quickly away. Not that she had intended to move in, but he might have offered.

She had been meaning to go apartment hunting. But she'd been so busy at work . . . plus since she'd spent every night this week at Bo's she hadn't felt an urgent need. She'd gone to Lizzy's only to restock her bag with clean clothes. And to see Oreo whom, she recollected with a pang, she was totally neglecting. But clearly now the time had come. She must find her own place.

She sat up in bed and twisted her hair off her neck, tucking the ends into a coiled bun until they felt secured.

"I'm also working on a story about a painting that's being held up in customs."

He looked at her admiringly. "I saw your article in the newspaper about the Italian who claims the Nazis stole his family's Modigliani portrait. Congratulations, it was really good."

"Thanks. It's taken an interesting turn. I got a copy of the Sotheby's sale catalogue and the provenance includes pre-war museum exhibitions in various countries. The Italian who claims to own it says it never left the villa."

He put his hand on her thigh and said, "Sounds like a new article coming."

She shut her eyes and pictured the illustration in the catalogue as Bo ran his fingers down her leg. It would be much more interesting to write about the painting now that she knew what it looked like.

The arresting portrait was entitled *Abruzzi Daughter*. A young woman wearing a lavender sweater sat in a brown chair placed at an odd angle against a mottled gray-blue background. Her elongated head with its close-set eyes, tiny mouth and long nose, sat on a slender neck that widened like the neck of a wine bottle into sloping shoulders. Her hands clasped in her lap, her pensive look bordered on apathy, as if she didn't much care who owned her. But after seeing her loveliness, Megan cared much more about finding out.

The ringing phone interrupted her reverie. Bo's eyes opened instantly but he didn't move.

"It's probably Gozzi. The machine can take it."

But the voice that came over the answering machine didn't sound like a New York landlord. It was foreign, a German accent.

"Hello Bo. You are hard to reach, a busy man. I'll try again."

He quickly took his hand off her leg and sat up, his face clouding.

"Was that Gozzi?" she asked.

"No, no. Just some jerk who was here open studio day. I don't know what the hell he wants."

"To buy a painting maybe?"

"I don't think so. He seemed a little swishy – who knows."

Megan laughed. "Nothing like sniffing down the wrong alley. Although I can't blame him for trying."

Bo grinned and his face cleared as the alarm sounded. "The dreaded time has come."

He hit the alarm button and turned back to Megan, his

eyes tender. He reached out and ran his fingers down her arm and under her breast, cupping its fullness in his hand. He smiled and said, "I could think of some other things to do but I guess we better get going." He kissed her softly, his hand warm on her neck. "Thanks for being here."

He vaulted over the side of the loft bed and began pulling on a pair of green parachute pants. She watched him, his torso long and lean, muscles clearly defined along his back, brawny shoulder cast in muted silver light. She suggested coffee, hoping to keep him for a few more minutes, but he wouldn't be detained. He walked to where she sat cross-legged on the side of the loft bed and put his hands on her knees.

"I've really got to go. I gotta catch the boss – he owes me a check. But how about if tonight I make you my pasta à la Ryder – olives, capers and anchovies over linguini?"

She hated anchovies, but anchovies with Bo sounded better than anything without him. "I'd love to, but I have to review a performance piece up at Lincoln Center at eight o'clock."

He looked down and she couldn't see his face. She hesitated a moment. "I have an extra ticket if you'd like to join me."

His eyes crinkled above his smile. "We'll have the linguini afterwards."

He blew her a kiss and was gone. As soon as the door closed she felt his absence, the loft seemed hollow, a vacuum, as if a sustaining substance had evaporated. She flopped back on the bed for a moment but it felt so empty without him she couldn't bear to stay.

Climbing down from the loft bed, she collected her clothes strewn around the floor. From high up on the walls the *Portraits in the City* looked down on her, a medley of characters, as varied in their faces as Bo's imagination. She picked up the sweater he was wearing last night and buried her face in it. As his scent surrounded her she felt a wave of softness, like falling in snow.

She was a goner, for sure.

Chapter 13

I t was standing room only in Lyndhurst and Lloyd's auction room. Dealers, collectors, buyers and sellers filled every seat all the way to the back of the salesroom. Along the walls, under the enormous canvases too big to be carried out and held up as the auctioneer sold them, stood people who lacked the status to be granted the coveted ticketed seats but were nonetheless thrilled to be in the main salesroom. Dressed in black-tie, everyone looked quite chic – men in tuxedos, women in everything from Chanel suits to strapless evening gowns. For this evening Contemporary Painting Sale was not just an auction, it was an event.

Alastair stood at the podium and scanned the sea of faces, picking out a few notables immediately. Leo Castelli, looking as polished as the pop art in his gallery, sat in the second row, his thinning hair combed back neatly from his urbane face. Behind him Estee Lauder thumbed through a catalogue. Three seats over in dark glasses and a chignon Alastair recognized a promising new collector, a Brazilian woman whose family company just won the contract to repave the country's roads. The buzzing of the crowd filled the room like the hum of insects on a summer day.

With just a few minutes to spare before he began, Alastair was feeling the proper mixture of excitement and trepidation. This was his first big auction in New York and he wanted to do well. All the major buyers were assembled; some lively bidding was in order. One of the hottest lots was an enormous painting by Morris Louis consigned by Edwin DuBois before he died. Estimated at $70,000-$80,000, Alastair hoped to nudge it over six figures. Maybe that would inspire Catherine to return the signed sales contract.

He paged through the auctioneer's book, which lay open on the podium in front of him. Prepared by the director of the Contemporary Art department, this was his bible and highly confidential. Each lot was marked with a reserve, the minimum price the seller would accept for the painting. He would open the bidding below the reserve just to get the auction juices flowing, and then essentially bid for the seller until the reserve was reached. This protected the painting from selling for too low a price. Also marked were the sealed bids from bidders who either could not or would not be present. He would bid for these clients, announced as a "bid in the book."

Just as he was about to begin, Reginald appeared.

"Florence Greene wants to add a sealed bid on the Morris Louis of ninety-five thousand."

"Terrific," Alastair said. He turned to the Louis listing and wrote, 'Greene-95' and shut the book with a smile. The painting's reserve was only $60,000 so it was now a sure sale. A California collector with a sprawling contemporary house in Pebble Beach, Florence Greene had plenty of wall space for the Louis.

Reginald grinned. "That's not all. Catherine DuBois called. She wants to raise the reserve on the Morris Louis to one hundred thousand."

Alastair looked at Reginald sharply. "That's out of the question. That's higher than the estimate."

"I'm just telling you what she said. She sounded rather loony, going on about how she had to protect the painting, that it was worth far more that she'd thought, that today was not a good day for business decisions."

Alastair braced himself against this information. "All right Reginald, I'll handle it."

He turned to check the listing again in the catalogue. *Not a good day for business decisions?* Had she read that in her horoscope? What on earth was she thinking? It was impossible for him to change the reserve now, at the eleventh hour. Suddenly his collar felt much too tight and the lights seemed awfully hot. He could not violate the printed estimate, nor could he afford to alienate Catherine. He needed her collection. He fingered his lucky Christ Church College tie and hoped to God that the bidding went over $100,000.

At two minutes past eight he tapped the microphone and the sound throbbed through the room. Two porters lifted a 3x4 foot painting on to the desk next to the podium. In it a primitive figure raised its hands in terror, its mask-like face set with sharp teeth and round eyes painted in primary blues and reds on a black and white ground. It looked like a post-war version of Edvard Munch's *The Scream*.

"Good evening ladies and gentleman, tonight we are offering contemporary paintings. We'll start with Lot 1, *Shrouded Spirit* by Karel Appel, can I have fifteen thousand to start this please, fifteen thousand?"

A paddle went up on the right aisle and the auction was off and running.

The bidding climbed and Alastair alternated between taking bids on the floor and a bid in the book. As he glanced around the room, a figure suddenly caught his eye. A young woman with auburn hair stood at the entrance to the salesroom – the newspaper reporter from the Stella opening. She leaned against the doorway looking over the crowd calmly but with interest, neither awkward nor at home, but more with the distanced engagement of an anthropologist viewing the rarely sighted ritual of some exotic tribe.

Her presence added an extra charge to the auction, especially since he'd read an excellent article she'd written about a Modigliani portrait detained after being sold at Sotheby's. Having learned she was also talented, he found her even more beautiful than before. But he looked quickly back at the crowd;

he had to keep his wits about him. The bidding climbed steadily until it stopped with a man on the left aisle whose signal had been abbreviated to a nod of the head. Alastair brought down the gavel with a wallop.

"Sold, to paddle fifty-seven for twenty-five thousand dollars."

This was a handsome price for the big Appel canvas, double the estimate and probably a record. Alastair sent a smile to – Megan, was it? – on the sidelines. She smiled back. What a capital start for the sale.

Active bidding sent pieces well over their estimates. Only a big color field painting sparked no interest. With a reserve of $15,000, he asked for an opening bid of $10,000. No one bid on it, so he took the price up himself, picking the bids out of the air, *$10,000, $11,000, $12,000, $13,000, $14,000.* Bidding up the price this way was harmless since he couldn't sell the piece below its $15,000 reserve anyway, and oftentimes someone would jump in as he took the numbers up. But this time no one did.

"I've got fourteen thousand in the book, any interest at fifteen?"

There was none. Down came the gavel, "All done at fourteen thousand, thank you."

This piece would be listed on the price sheet as 'bought in' by the auction house.

Suddenly, with a flutter of activity at the doorway, the crowd parted and in came a small woman wearing an Ermine coat who walked briskly up the center aisle: Catherine DuBois. She marched forward with dogged determination, her eyes fixed on Alastair as if he were the summit of the Matterhorn. This interruption was most irregular, but seeing that this little woman was sitting on the collection of the century and his future reputation in New York, he had no choice but to oblige her. He stepped down from the podium.

Catherine stopped in front of him, out of breath, her worried blue eyes shifting under knit eyebrows. She clutched a white leather handbag against her chest.

"Alastair," she began in a lowered but resolute voice, "I *do* apologize, but I want to withdraw the Morris Louis. Edwin gave it to me for my birthday and I'm afraid I really can't bring myself to part with it."

Her voice trembling, her right hand moved rapidly across the top of the leather bag.

Damn it. He couldn't believe her. Not only was the Morris Louis one of the most expensive lots in the sale, but selling it was going to be his final lure, proof that he could do an excellent job for her.

"If you're sure, Catherine, I'll withdraw it."

"I am. Thank you so much." She turned and walked back down the aisle, a scarf from her pocket trailing behind her.

He stepped back up to the podium.

"Ladies and gentleman, lot 37 by Morris Louis is withdrawn from the sale."

The crowd buzzed momentarily but he moved right on to the next lot. Catherine's eccentric request had thrown him somewhat but he forced himself to concentrate on selling the Frank Stella at hand. Knocking it down for a handsome $34,000 helped him to recover. He then sold Andy Warhol's "Suicide" for $72,000, a late purple-on-black Mark Rothko for $90,000, and a minuscule Jasper John's "Flag", a four-inch-square charcoal sketch, for $10,000. Way above the estimates, these figures were far higher than he'd expected. His spirits rose one notch higher with each lot sold and he was soon feeling as buoyant as the prices.

As he knocked down the last lot of the sale there was another disturbance at the doorway. Catherine reappeared and repeated her march up the aisle, more hurriedly this time, scarf still trailing. Alastair stepped down to meet her. Her face drained of color and pinched together like a hedgehog, she looked up at him with despairing eyes.

"Sell it. I must discipline myself. The East Hampton house is going anyway so I'll have no room to hang it."

"As you wish."

He sprang back to the podium, patting his Oxford tie. This was the perfect encore. The way things had gone the Morris Louis should have no problem making $100,000. And if it only came close, he'd sell it anyway and let the auction house make up the difference.

He gestured with his gavel at the Morris Louis painting whose spectacular 8 x 16 feet filled the wall to his left. Rivulets of pure pigment cascaded diagonally in from either side, staining the raw canvas in ribbons of brilliant color. Here Louis had mastered his technique, creating a classic of his *Unfurleds* style and a stellar offering.

"Ladies and gentlemen, I am happy to announce that lot 37, the Morris Louis drip painting, is back in the sale, and we shall offer it now. That's lot 37, estimated at seventy to eighty thousand dollars, can I have forty thousand to start it please, forty thousand?"

A paddle went up in the center aisle as Catherine DuBois stood off to the side, watching intently.

As the bidding climbed it got tricky. He had to stay on the right leg so that he could make Florence Greene's bid of $95,000. If a bidder on the floor bought it at 95, Greene would not be pleased. The bids sprouted up all around the floor and Alastair pointed them out, jumping in for Greene at 85 so he could take a bid on the floor at 90 and bid again for her at 95. He did, but the bidding sailed right on past, up into the hundred thousands, and he jumped to ten thousand dollar increments. *$110,000, $120,00, $130,000* . . . a hush fell over the crowd as the numbers rose. The Brazilian cement mogul stayed strongly in the running, bidding against Jake Gruber, the Soho gallery owner, who must have been bidding for a client, as Morris Louis didn't seem quite his taste. He and the cement mogul nodded back and forth like strutting chickens, taking the price up and up: 140 to Gruber, 150 to the Brazilian, 160 to Gruber, 170 to the Brazilian –

"I have one hundred and seventy thousand dollars, can I have one eighty? Going at one hundred seventy thousand dollars to the lady in the center aisle . . ." Alastair paused and looked at Gruber who loosened his tie and stared forward, lips pursed. Alastair caught his eye, smiled, and then casually, as if offering a simple solution, leaned forward in the podium and asked, "What's another ten thousand between friends?"

The crowd roared with laughter and Gruber's tense face broke into a smile. He nodded once again. Alastair called out his bid and turned to the Brazilian woman who shook her head. Down came the gavel.

"Sold, for one hundred eighty thousand dollars to the gentleman on my left. Thank you all very much."

The salesroom filled with a round of applause for the great auction, the fine entertainment. $180,000 was a fantastic price for Catherine's picture. It would keep her solvent – this month, anyway.

Alastair stepped down from the podium and Catherine came forward and pressed his hand, tears in her eyes. "What a marvelous job, Alastair. I'm so sorry for the waffling, it's just so hard to let go."

He patted her chilled hand. "You did the right thing. A fabulous price."

Standing next to Alastair, Reginald piped up with, "Lucky you decided not to 'protect the painting', like you said."

Catherine drew herself up and looked archly at Reginald. "Stuff and nonsense. I said no such thing. What I said was that I wanted to protect *myself*. Young man, I have been buying at auction since before you were born."

Reginald hung his head.

Catherine turned to Alastair. Her small face, framed with hair wisping down from her bun, shifted to a worried look and she asked to have a quick word with him. He led her through the bustling crowd to a side room and shut the door behind them.

She opened her purse and pulled out a rumpled group of pages he recognized as a Lyndhurst and Lloyd's sales contract, creased and folded several times. She clasped it tightly in her veined hand. "I've been carrying this silly paper around for days. But there's just one thing . . . . the sale date for my collection. I'm concerned about the timing. I need to sell the paintings as soon as possible."

"The next big Impressionist sales are scheduled for the spring."

She shook her head decidedly. "That's too far away. I must be frank: Edwin had everything heavily mortgaged, which was fine with our previous income but now I find that I am very much in debt. My paintings must be sold within the next two months."

"I will do my very best to accommodate you. Naturally, I'll have to check the auction schedule."

She looked at him dubiously. "Alastair, this is not a whim, it's a necessity. If you can't sell my collection before the New Year I shall be forced to take it elsewhere."

He looked at her frail face, scared and desperate, and he knew he had no choice.

"Rest assured, Catherine. We will hold your sale before New Year's."

The general manager's schedule be damned – they would have to make room for another auction. She beamed and handed over the signed sales contract, which he stowed away inside a jacket pocket. This was worth any dispute with office management.

She smiled, opened the door, and disappeared into the crowd.

As Alastair re-entered the salesroom a horde of people surrounded him with a rash of issues that always presented themselves at sale's end; a bidder who claimed Alastair didn't see him bidding, a buyer who wanted to make monthly payments, a seller who wanted to know who bought her piece. He handled them all with an easy confidence.

Then he remembered the auburn-haired reporter and realized he'd better catch up with her before she left. He made his way through the crowd to the Press office where reporters gathered after a sale to badger the staff with myriad questions: what museums had new acquisitions, which paintings hadn't sold, which lots made record prices?

Inside the room the head of the press office was speaking zealously. "De Kooning's *Woman* at one hundred and ten thousand dollars marks the highest price for his work anywhere."

The reporters scribbled furiously in their notebooks.

Alastair spotted Megan standing right inside the door. Seeing her, the real live woman he'd been daydreaming about, he slowed his pace and straightened his tie. An enormous leather bag hung from her shoulder, her hair floated in thick waves around her face, and her cheeks were flushed slightly, as if she'd just come in from the rain. He tapped her on the arm and she turned with surprise. Holding a finger to his lips, he beckoned her into the hallway.

"Would you like some information first hand?"

"Sure," she said. "That'd be great!"

What enchanting openness. Was it just the customary American enthusiasm or might she be thrilled at the sight of him?

"It's nice to see you here," he said, leaning towards her attentively as they walked down the hall.

"I'm so glad I came. What a fabulous sale!"

He couldn't help grinning. "Not bad."

"Can you tell me who sold the DeKooning?"

"A collector from Long Island who bought it from the artist just after he'd painted it in the 1950s. Quite a return on his investment."

"I'll say."

All things seemed to glow in the aftermath of his success. He couldn't imagine an auctioneer who would have done better, if he did say so himself. Nor could he imagine any lovelier reporter to brief than her. Without compromising any confidences, he told her everything he could about the auction.

As they talked he led her through the exhibition rooms. American furniture was on view with some beautiful 18th century pieces. They stopped in front of a desk and he noted happily that she was finally closing her notebook; he was off the record.

He watched as she zipped open her leather bag and tossed in the pen and notebook as if down a well. When she tried to close it, the zipper got stuck on a scarf that had wafted up from the deep. She fiddled with the teeth, trying to extract the silk, a lovely print of blues and yellows in the style of combed Italian end papers.

"Don't mind me, it's just this zipper . . ." she said.

"I do believe that is the most enormous handbag I have ever seen."

"Yes," she said laughing self-consciously, finally freeing the scarf. "It holds so much it really comes in handy for me."

She zipped the bag shut and shoved it behind her like a naughty pet.

"So . . ." she said, looking brightly around the exhibit.

He pointed out a Goddard-Townsend kneehole desk, the elegant carving of the three shells, convex above the drawers and concave in the middle. "I don't know much about American furniture," he said, "but the design and workmanship of this couldn't be better."

"It is good-looking, isn't it?"

"And this," he said as he moved to a tall grandfather clock with carved finials and a face painted with the moon and the stars. "This I covet. If I can find a place to put it I may have to bid on it myself."

"You like clocks?" she asked, seeming pleased.

"I love clocks. And these American clocks are a whole new world for me."

He noticed that the lighter grains in the wood matched the highlights in her hair. He stopped and looked at her intently.

"Yes, I've made some lovely American discoveries. And you must understand, I have very high standards."

She looked away, a smile spreading slowly behind her wavy hair.

Just then a resounding rip filled the room as a man tore the upholstery off the back of a ball-and-claw foot armchair. The material flopped in tatters while the man bent down and inspected the insides.

Megan stared in horror and Alastair touched her arm reassuringly.

"Not to worry. It's only worth eighty thousand dollars."

She looked incredulous and he laughed. "The dealers do that to get a look at the struts and see how the frame is put together. It's a way of authenticating the furniture's period. The upholstery isn't worth anything. It's the frame that makes the chair."

Suddenly Colin appeared, wearing his charm-the-ladies smile. Alastair groaned inwardly. Colin could turn it on in the most revolting way.

Colin clasped his hands behind his back and, rising up on his toes, nodded at Megan.

"Good evening. Splendid auction, Alastair." He stood expectantly, waiting to be introduced. Alastair glared at him. Why did he have to compete for everything? But there was no avoiding it.

"Colin, meet Megan Trico. She'll be covering our sales for the *Soho Weekly News*. Megan, this is Colin Plimpton." Damned if he would introduce Colin as head of the painting departments.

Colin pumped her hand vigorously. "How do you do, I'm head of the painting departments. You must be the writer of the piece I saw in the paper on the stolen Modigliani."

"*Reputedly* stolen," Megan said.

Blast, thought Alastair, he'd been so wrapped up in his sale he'd forgotten to mention it.

"Ah, yes, a curious discrepancy, isn't it," continued Colin. "Happens quite often when dealing with Sotheby's, have you noticed?"

Megan smiled. "I have no opinion yet. I'm still investigating."

Colin gave her a genteel nod. "I shall keep my eye peeled on your newspaper for further enlightenment."

He flashed a chivalrous smile and turned to Alastair. "Alastair, I need your auctioneer's book to double check some information."

Alastair handed over the spiral-bound book.

"So very nice to meet you." Colin bowed neatly and was off.

"What a gentleman!" Megan said, clearly charmed.

"Isn't he," Alastair said dryly. Why on earth didn't Colin just send for his girlfriend from London and leave the rest of them in peace? 'Gentleman' indeed. Woe the motto, *manners maketh man.*

Watching her alert green eyes, Alastair suddenly had an inspiration. A bit brash, perhaps, but why not? In these affairs, he who hesitated usually lost. Besides, this was America.

"A few of us are going next door to The Oak Room to celebrate. Would you care to join us?"

She hesitated, obviously weighing something; he hoped not him. "You know, I'd like to, but I have other plans."

He gestured at her handbag. "I can imagine. What with going off on safari and all . . ."

She laughed and looked a little regretful. He smiled over his disappointment. So much for brash spontaneity. Luckily he was still feeling good enough about the sale that his balloon wasn't burst – just slightly deflated.

Chapter 14

A cross the street from where Megan sat in the coffee shop on the corner of West Broadway and Prince Street eating the 89-cent breakfast special, a man brought out a sandwich-board-style sign and set it on the loading platform of the warehouse next to the Nancy Hoffman gallery. It read, *Everyone Passing Here Needs Something Sharpened.* As she blew across the top of her coffee cup and watched him, it occurred to her that maybe she should take in her wits – they could use a new edge.

She was having trouble figuring out why she turned down Alastair's invitation to celebrate after the auction. Really, did she not know which side her bread was buttered on? She could have had a chance at insider auction coverage, at privileged press information. She might have gained some knowledge of Sotheby's in London or tapped him for tips on authenticating a provenance, just what she needed for her Modigliani investigation. But the way he was looking at her, she knew the invitation wasn't strictly business.

In truth, she knew her problem wasn't so much that her wits were dulled as that her heart was taken – she was monogamous, constitutionally monogamous. She could not be romantically involved with two people at the same time. Or even romantically interested, for that matter. It was as if there were just one slot for a man in her life, and it was either open or closed. Right now it was shut up tight as a drum. Bo had slipped in there and expanded, filling the slot to capacity, suppressing all other desires of the heart, the mind or the flesh, for anyone else. It was actually getting a little scary; she was wanting to be with him all the time.

With him everything was new and different, every walk, every shopping excursion, every conversation. Even every meal. He was like a hound dog, sniffing out inexpensive, ethnic places with interesting food. Last week they went to an Indian restaurant off Lafayette Place where they had a feast, eight courses from pomegranate juice to sweetened cheese balls for under ten dollars apiece. On Saturday they walked to The Polish Kitchen over on Second Avenue and Ninth Street. She was as stuffed as the cabbages for next to nothing. Rutabaga and Rauschenberg were a welcome change from Steak au Poivre and the financial pages.

Last night after the auction they sat out on his fire escape drinking beer out of cans and watching the street scene below. She felt like a teenager, except that she never did that as a teenager.

But he sure was charming. Alastair, that was.

She paid the bill and left. Overhead the sky was gray with a thick cloud cover flying low over the city. Down West Broadway the tops of the World Trade Towers were shrouded in swiftly-moving clouds. The best barometer she knew, the towers promised a cold day, windy with a chance of snow. What better time to look for an apartment, to get off the raw streets and into a warm building she could try to call home.

She turned and walked up West Broadway to get a cab. The main drag of Soho was busy with trucks, vans, and a few scattered pedestrians. Eighteen-wheelers whined up the wide street, backing up to warehouse loading platforms that shared the street with galleries. Also serviced were a few recently opened restaurants, conspicuously upscale compared to the coffee shop. The Spring Street Bar provided a polished alternative to Fanelli's and Oh-Ho-So served fancy Chinese. A single storefront offered the only clothing on the street, its window displaying Indian print skirts, silver jewelry and sticks of incense.

Up on Houston yellow cabs flit along the street, weaving back and forth across the lanes like Pac-Man critters. She stepped off the curb to hail one, her hand held high. A rare old Checker cab pulled over and she climbed in. Pulling the classified ads out of her bag, she glanced at the listing circled in yellow highlighter and gave the cabby the midtown address where the apartment was being shown at 9 o'clock.

The truth was she was getting to the point where she felt she *must* take an apartment, any apartment, to get her life back on track. Two days ago Oreo had disappeared from Lizzy's apartment and was found the next morning by the superintendent in the basement. Somehow the cat must have gone down the garbage chute. Poor Oreo, and how horribly remiss of *her*. And Lizzy wasn't exactly pleased the landlord found out she was keeping yet another cat in a building that wasn't supposed to have any pets.

She scanned the apartment ads again, gravitating once more to the uptown listings. The problem was figuring out which track she wanted to be on. She just couldn't make up her mind between the stately Upper East Side with its proximity to the museums and 57th Street galleries, and the freewheeling promise of the West Village, next door to the Soho art scene.

The east side would certainly be convenient now that she was covering the auctions. It had been a while since she'd spent any time in the uptown art scene with everyone dressed for the opera, the international buyers conferring in German, French and Japanese, the museum-quality paintings coming up on the auction block, anybody's guess who would buy them or for what price. She'd forgotten how much fun it could be.

But her newspaper was downtown and so was most of the interesting contemporary art. So when she saw the midtown listing in the classifieds it seemed like a possible solution to her problem. Perhaps her vacillating interests could be satisfied by a 41st and Lexington address, placing her midway between them. The only problem was that she was not a *mid* sort of person. Nor was she easily anchored. With just one life, why confine oneself to a single spot?

She leaned back in the leather seat, put up her feet on the collapsible stool and stared out the window. Presently the wrought-iron fence of Gramercy Park came into view, a bit of urban nature announcing fall's arrival. Squirrels ran along the branches of leafless trees, nuts stuffed in bulging cheeks. How many long blocks to the next city park? Surely by now these squirrels had evolved into a separate species, isolated for generations in their urban Galapagos. That was the problem with getting stuck too long in one neighborhood.

She zipped open her bag to return the classifieds and out fell a plastic slide holder. Bo had flung it up on a shelf when he was mad at the Honthorst Gallery. The next morning while he slept she had snuck the slides into her bag, determined to show them to her gallery-owner friend, Jake Gruber. With the little influence she had she could try to open some doors for Bo, whose haunting paintings held such promise.

He had stirred as she had climbed quietly down from the loft bed, found the slides, and zipped them into her bag that was nestled into one end of the couch with its strap spread up across the arm as if it too were sleeping.

"Hey, come back here," he had called, and asked her what could be more important than snuggling with him. She had said she was looking for her auction catalogue with the prices in it, as she needed to write up the story that day.

"It's big news, a record-breaking sale," she had said as he looked at her skeptically.

"Gee, it must have made a terrible mess, breaking records all over the auction room."

What then ensued was an exchange she could only categorize as a fight. She hated to admit this because she'd been trying to figure out how to soothe his occasional irascibility, but he insisted she tell him the exact dollar amounts, which seemed only to incite him further.

"Tell me, what were the *fabulous* prices?"

She mentioned a Roy Lichtenstein comic strip painting that sold for $35,000 and he practically went up in smoke. But he refused to let go of it and pressed for more. She tried to think of more moderate sales, but it was hard to remember the prices that weren't remarkable.

"Well, there was a Morris Louis that went for one hundred and eighty thousand, and a Rothko for ninety thousand. Oh, and the de Kooning – you like him, don't you? One of his *Women* went for one hundred and ten. That was the biggest surprise."

He grimaced. "Oh, man, that is *disgusting*. Do you know how poor de Kooning has been for most of his life? And he doesn't get a red cent from this sale. He lives for years in some flea bag while the collector and the auction house are making tens of thousands on the painting he painted twenty-five years ago and sold for a fraction of that price!"

She tried to calm him down, without success. He tossed his hair like a pent-up stallion. "Don't you see anything wrong with that?"

"I didn't say it was fair."

"*Fair?* It's a million miles from fair! It's corrupt! Why don't you write your article on that instead of how much money all these art world sharks are making?"

That was hard to take. "What, are you holding me personally responsible now?" she asked quietly.

Then he turned to her, his dark eyebrows gathered together like sparring caterpillars. "You're a journalist. You have a voice. Why don't you use it for something useful?"

"Bo, if you ever read the paper, I recently did a piece promoting royalty rights for artists. Some people are *trying* to do something about it."

At that point the alarm clock rang like the bell in a boxing match. "Please don't pick a fight with me," she sighed. "I'm on your side."

Afterwards he said he was sorry, but it was clear the apology was only for upsetting her. His opinion stayed the same.

Later in the day she had taken his slides to Jake Gruber's without telling him. With his touchy pride she was sure he'd refuse to let her peddle his work. And after the morning's quarrel, she did not want to be the messenger if Jake weren't interested.

Bo's talent was so obvious she was sure Jake would recognize it. She had walked confidently into the gallery, the heels of her boots ringing out clearly on the polished oak floors of the cavernous room. If Jake could exhibit Duane Hanson's middle-aged housewives wearing pink sponge rollers in their hair, then why not Bo's realism? Surely this enormous gallery with its 13-foot ceilings and vast white walls could accommodate Bo.

But Jake, sitting behind his big desk with a cigar billowing smoke from the ashtray, had held the slides up to the light and peered at them noncommittally. His comment was, "An old-fashioned figure painter. But intriguing. This woman in the yellow dress reminds me of a Manet up at the Met." He acknowledged the work was good, but claimed, somewhat reproachfully, that he couldn't sell figurative painting, as if she should have known better.

"So – the painter is talented and intriguing, but you aren't interested," she had repeated, hoping the absurdity of the logic would bring him to his senses.

He had looked at her patiently.

"Megan, no matter how much I might like new work, I won't take it if it doesn't fit my stable. Collectors go to galleries with certain expectations. If they want to buy Pop art they go up the street to Castelli's. If they like my taste they come here. I have an investment in the style of work I show – I can't deviate too far from it."

Then he suggested the Frumkin Gallery up on 57th Street, which showed exclusively representational work. She answered with an ironic laugh.

"Bo tried. But Allan Frumkin said the background settings were too surreal."

And that was that.

She returned the slides to her bag, carefully stowing them flat against the bottom with the care they deserved. Bo would just have to keep trying. Of course getting established as an artist was hard. When had it ever been easy? Eventually he would land a gallery because he had what it took, which someday the art world would recognize.

She glanced out the window at the gray buildings flickering by, rock solid facades rising into the clouds. The city held so much, but oh how tightly it could hold it. Including apartments, which she also needed to find before she turned into a bag lady. And why not, she thought as she turned to her bulging leather bag, she already had the accouterments. She sighed at the spilled-out contents, mail she'd grabbed on leaving the office. It all looked so disorderly.

Suddenly her eye caught a manila envelope in amongst the gallery notices showing the return address of the Italian consulate. She took her feet off the stool and sat up straight. This might be some good news. She bent the arms of the metal clasp forward and out slid a letter and an old press-camera photograph encased in plastic wrap and backed with stiff cardboard. Worn around the edges, the image nonetheless had great clarity. From the bottom of her bag she dug out a magnifying lens, which folded out compactly from its case. She moved over by the light of the window and eagerly inspected the print.

A woman posed on a chaise lounge in the salon of an Italian villa. The shadowy room, accentuated by a beamed ceiling and dark furniture, was relieved by an open terrace door which sent a long shaft of golden light across the floor to the chaise, illuminating the woman and her calf-length flapper-style dress, her straight, chin-length hair held closely by a headband. She could not have been a more classic example of 1920's fashion. A standing, mustached man faced the camera in back of the chaise. On the wall behind them, also in the light, hung a large portrait painting. Megan moved the lens over the portrait. Its elongated figure and Madonna-like face, sad but serene, looked unequivocally like the *Abruzzi Daughter.*

The letter from the consul explained that he was forwarding a photograph from Senor Calabresi, which his elderly aunt had recently sent him, taken of herself as a young woman with her fiancé on a visit to the villa. The fiancé had died fighting in the war. The consul praised Megan in advance for giving the information the press coverage it deserved, clear evidence that the Modigliani portrait hung in the villa before the war.

Megan's pulse quickened. What was this, the Modigliani hanging in an Italian villa at the very time Sotheby's claimed it was resident in Paris? What great fodder for her column – maybe a lead article, with a side-by-side illustration of the photograph next to the Sotheby's provenance listing various exhibitions, including a 1925 exhibition at the Tate Gallery in London, the same decade as the photograph. Quantum mechanics aside, most people did not believe that an object could be in two different places at the same time.

The cab pulled up at the corner of Lexington and 41st and she quickly paid and walked up the street, her mind racing with possibilities. Where had Sotheby's gotten the provenance information described in the catalogue? What a great *series* of articles this would lead to. Wouldn't Fogelman be pleased, who would no doubt welcome further conflict rather than resolution, anything to get readers hooked on an ongoing story.

She stopped as she came to the crosswalk of 42nd Street – she'd come too far. Turning back the way she came she checked the numbers, looking for the right one. When she found it, with a few other people waiting at the door, she stared up at the enormous building, its facade rising straight up, flat and faceless, the only relief the rows of picture windows that looked like they didn't open. She checked the street number again to confirm that the *one bdrm riv vu* advertised was in fact in this bland monstrosity. When she saw it was, she folded up the newspaper and walked away.

Splitting the difference between uptown and downtown clearly wouldn't work, it was neither here nor there. The neighborhood didn't have a decent cafe in sight and at night the streets would be dark and empty. Added to the fact that the windows didn't open, what was the point of even going in?

And more importantly, if she got back to the office quickly she should be in time to try to call the Impressionist Department at Sotheby's in London before they closed for the day.

Chapter 15

B o stood on the edge of his rooftop under a cover of low clouds, heavy and black along the bottom, tearing across the sky with patches of icy blue between. It looked like snow.

He tossed out a paper airplane made from his latest Con Ed electric bill. The plane sailed down, dipping and gliding towards the street. Then he launched another, this one a little smaller, his AT&T phone bill. The paper planes swooped down in long arcs, fluttering white against the somber cast-iron buildings.

Sometimes it just didn't seem worth it. All the time, all the effort, all the dreams, for what? Another rejection? If he quit right now, what difference would it make? No one would miss his work, no one would feel a loss. And to think he sometimes felt such urgency, that he needed to get his work *out there now* – what a joke. As if anyone were waiting for it.

Who did he think he was, anyway? Monet? Michelangelo? Artists were a dime a dozen, there were thousands here in this city, waiting tables, pushing brooms, tending bar. And each and everyone believed they were the next Jasper Johns, if they could only get a break, a foot in the door. What vanity, what egos.

Maybe his father was right, maybe he should do something else. He didn't get paid, so who was his work for? For a public who never saw it? Or for himself, for the privilege of living in a barely heated loft? Oh sure, it was ennobling – let anyone who says so try it.

It wasn't that he was tired of painting, he'd never tire of that. In fact, the portrait of Paddy was really coming along. He had started it one night last week when he came home from the parking lot and there sat Paddy on the loading platform of the building. He was all scrunched up on the steps with an oversized coat wrapped around him, his gray head sticking out of the top like a hobbit. His bright eyes looked up and he said, "It's getting cold out. Seems to me you said something about paying." Bo was so glad to see him he threw in a meal of fried eggs and potatoes, which Paddy wolfed down as if he hadn't eaten in a week. He was going to make a great portrait – it was just a question of financing it.

The money situation was really getting serious. Once again, he owed everybody. And worst of all, Gozzi was going to throw him out on his ass one of these days. He was not a generous creditor. He had begrudgingly accepted October's rent, scraped together a week late, but now another month had rolled around again.

He folded Gozzi's rent notice neatly into a plane, giving it a downward-pointing nose like a jet fighter, and sailed it along after the others.

He pulled out his wallet and the change from his pocket and carefully counted the money. Three dollars and 87 cents. That would buy enough eggs and potatoes to hold him until the end of the week.

Good thing he'd mastered the variations on eggs and potatoes. There was the old breakfast scrambled eggs and hash browns, luncheon hard-boiled eggs and potato salad, and dinner omelets and french fries. And when he felt like really living it up, there was eggs benedict and potatoes Anna.

Or maybe he'd forget the food and go for a six-pack and some smokes.

He launched the last airplane, made from an American Express bill with a compounded interest charge now higher than the initial purchase, and watched as it dipped along after the others which lay like downed moths, specs of white on the dark potholes below.

Yeah, the artist's life. What a glamorous existence.

He walked back towards the pigeon coop, opening his arms into the wind, feeling it had been too long since he'd been out in the open. Above, the dark clouds raced across the sky in thicker clusters, squeezing out the patches of blue. Behind the chicken wire the pigeons ruffled their feathers against the wind, cooing and strutting and pecking at the floor.

Suddenly the door leading into the stairwell banged open and the photographer from the 5th floor appeared. "Bo. I thought I heard you come up here. There's someone to see you."

The photographer waved and disappeared and out on to the roof stepped Gerhardt. The door slammed shut behind him.

Bo's heart quickened. "Well, look who the wind blew in."

Gerhardt walked towards him, slowly, confidently. "Yes, I thought I'd drop by. Perhaps you didn't get my phone calls."

Gerhardt's accent seemed more distinct than before. With his black goatee, alligator shoes and trimly tailored coat, he looked displaced on the tarpaper roof, like someone from another world.

"I got them, all right. I'm just too busy right now to take on any business proposition."

"This one you may find time for."

Bo's throat tightened. "I doubt it."

Gerhardt smiled affably, his dark eyes glinting like cut glass. "You have a good eye, and a good hand. You should not waste your talent on portraits of gypsies."

"What?"

"You made your first 2000 dollars easily. You could do the same next week, and the next. With my connections, I can place your work in no time."

Bo's eyes widened with alarm. "I don't know what the hell you're talking about."

Gerhardt smiled understandingly. "My friend, we are both professionals, let us be honest with each other. The Joy of Life you sold to Susan Jacobson is an excellent likeness but it's not by Matisse. The paper is the same as the others hanging on your studio wall."

Bo stared, adrenaline pumping though his veins like water through a broken dam. He could not reply.

Gerhardt took a cigarette out of a silver case and tapped it down on the lid with his small fingers. "But I can see you have talent. With a few suggestions on how to use vintage materials and me as your dealer, we stand to make a lot of money together. There's a big demand in this Impressionist and Post-Impressionist market."

Cupping his hands around the cigarette, Gerhardt struck a match to the end. He puffed, and offered the open case to Bo.

Bo stood with his feet apart, his whole body quivering. He had stopped listening to what Gerhardt was saying, he'd heard all he needed. This fey little man had invaded his space, blown his cover, and had the balls to think he could profit from it.

Bo stepped forward and shook his fist. "Listen, I don't like what I'm hearing and if you know what's good for you you'll get out. NOW."

Gerhardt looked surprised. He raised his hands in a calming gesture and stepped backwards. "Please, don't be alarmed. I come with good will, as a possible partner. We work in the same business, we are colleagues, are we not?"

But all Bo could see was Gerhardt's smooth smile, his manicured fingers holding the cigarette, his calculating eyes. An old piece of pipe lay on the wall and he picked it up. "Get out of here!" he shouted, raising the pipe high in the air.

"All right, all right," Gerhardt said, hastening towards the door. "I'll go. I understand, you're not ready to talk."

With surprising strength, Gerhardt swung the door open against the wind and nipped inside. With his foot holding the door open, he stuck a business card in the door's molding. He called out, "I ask only that you think about it."

The wind banged the door shut and he was gone.

Bo stood staring at the gray metal door, the pipe in his hand. He was shaking and he suddenly felt weak. "Christ, what am I doing?" he said and dropped the pipe. He sat down slowly on the wall and covered his face with his hands. "What the hell am I doing?"

After a few moments he raised his head and took a deep breath of the icy air. The weight of the dark clouds seemed to press down on him. He picked up a stale end of bread from the tarpaper roof and tossed a few pieces to the pigeons. Their soft coos filled the air as they fluttered in on top of one another to peck at the crumbs. Far to the west the clouds had broken and the sun, hovering just above the horizon, sent shafts of bronze onto the underbellies of the thick cloud cover. He scanned the skyline to the south; the windows on the side of the World Trade Towers gleamed in coppery gold.

Big flakes of snow began to fall slowly all around him, enveloping him in their softness, easing his heart rate back to normal. He had to get a grip on this.

What events were now set in motion? Okay, so he'd fooled Susan Jacobson with a one-shot-deal that seemed to make everyone involved happy. Suddenly he thought of Megan; she would never allow him to get away with *'fooled'* to describe the transaction. She would require stronger language: *conned, suckered, defrauded, extorted* would be more like it.

But what now? Would it be one shot? Or would it echo and echo?

He tossed more bits of bread to the pecking pigeons as a montage of images came to him: the *Portraits in the City* lining his loft wall that he'd worked so hard on; his first oil, a dark, romantic painting of the Mississippi by moonlight; his high school art teacher who raved over it and encouraged him to go to art school; the first time he visited the Jeu de Paume in Paris and stood for hours, mesmerized by the quintessential masterpieces of French modernism, from Manet to Monet, until the guard had to ask him to leave because the gallery was closing. What was it all for, to end like this, to get caught palming off a copy of Matisse as the real thing? What good was his reverence for the masters now?

The flakes were falling faster, covering the tarpaper in downy white. The snow looked so pure, so clean. The pigeons had settled back under cover and they cooed comfortably. With his finger, Bo poked a hole in the snow. Then he drew a circle around it. And another, and another, until a dozen concentric rings surrounded one, small dot.

"Gerhardt cannot touch me. He can prove nothing. I am safe."

Chapter 16

From the middle of his office Alastair stood surveying the painting racks, tie loosened at his neck. For the first time since he'd come to New York, every rack was filled. The picture frames stuck out the ends forming a higgledy-piggledy pattern of designs from elaborate gilt concoctions to cleanly cut wood. Like a wrapped package, each excited curiosity, each invited inspection to see what treasure it contained.

Catherine DuBois and her accountant had figured out just how much of her art collection she needed to liquidate in order to keep afloat and maintain some semblance of her old life, albeit in reduced circumstances. She would be able to stay in her 5th Avenue apartment if she sold the houses in East Hampton and Palm Beach, as well as most of the paintings from 5th Avenue.

The pictures had been delivered that morning and exceeded Alastair's greatest hopes. The 43 pieces she consigned included four contemporary, three 19th Century, one old master, and the remaining 35 modern pictures were his, HIS, **ALL HIS!** What a thrill, to have the masterpieces he had glimpsed hastening through her apartment right here in his very office. They made the sale of his dreams.

He pulled a painting out of the rack and stuck on to its frame a circular identification label that Jane had just numbered. Colin sat in his chair, feet up on the desk, chewing the eraser of a pencil and studying the paper that listed Catherine's paintings and her requested reserves.

"Now wait a moment," Colin said. "This can't be right. She wants a reserve of 90 thousand dollars on the Sisley? It's a nice little picture but it will never fetch that."

"They're only suggestions," Alastair answered, returning the painting to the rack and pulling out another one. "She wants to make the most of the boom market as she no longer has any source of income. All she's got are the possessions that were put in her name."

"Which appears to have been most of them."

Alastair nodded. "Her husband was shrewd."

Jane blew on the sticky label to dry the number she had written above the printed *Lyndhurst and Lloyd's* and handed it to Alastair.

"Nonetheless, Alastair, it doesn't pay any of us to be unrealistic." Colin looked around for Reginald and spotted him sitting in Alastair's chair absent-mindedly smoothing the creases in his trousers. "Reginald!" Colin barked. "Look up last year's prices on Sisley."

Reginald looked blankly at Colin who assumed a tired expression. "Come on – in Mayer – the International Auction Prices."

Reginald stood and searched the bookshelves.

"The *blue* book," Colin said crossly.

"Oh, right," Reginald said, finally spotting it. He pulled it off the shelf.

"This is what happens when we take them just out of their knickers," Colin said in a stage whisper.

Reginald thumbed through the book. "Ah. Here we are," Reginald pronounced. "Last year, three Sisleys sold in London. Fifteen hundred pounds, thirty-two hundred pounds, twenty-seven hundred pounds."

Colin walked over with a scowl. "That can't be right, that's far too low. What are you looking at?"

Colin grabbed the book from Reginald who looked up helplessly.

"No wonder! You're in the drawing section. This is a painting, nit, a painting! Get it right, for God's sake!"

Reginald flushed beet red. The phone rang and Jane said, "Colin, Mr. Borgasian for you."

Reginald stood motionless, staring at his feet, stiller than Alastair had ever seen. He couldn't help feeling for him. He might be clueless but he didn't deserve to be publicly humiliated. "Reginald, give us a hand," Alastair said. "Help me take this painting down to Hugh's storeroom. I can't manage it by myself."

Reginald looked up gratefully. They both grabbed an end of the large painting, a full-length portrait of Saint Sebastian, naked save a skimpy loincloth and stuck through with a dozen arrows. Carefully they angled it through the doorway.

"I don't see why he has to scold me so, as if I were a blooming idiot," Reginald grumbled as they lugged the enormous picture down the hall.

"Not to worry," Alastair said, "Tolerance is not Colin's long suit."

"Plus he's in a foul mood that you've landed such a great sale from Mrs. DuBois."

Alastair stopped in the middle of the hall, banging the painting against his knee. "He is?"

"Bloody right he is. Before you came in this morning he was going off about what luck you had getting the consignment, how easy it is to collect an entire sale from a single owner."

Alastair didn't answer. So that was the bee in Colin's bonnet – what a niggardly bloke. You'd think he'd be pleased, that he might regard Alastair's coup as a positive reflection on the entire painting department, which he was so fond of reminding Alastair he headed. But no, no, dear old Colin was stuck on the playing fields, still on the opposing team, trying to block Alastair's goals. Where was the proper company spirit? "Off we go," Alastair said as he picked up the painting again, thinking how nice it would be to share an office with Hugh rather than Colin.

The last door on the hall opened into Hugh's storeroom where he did his cataloguing since his office was too small to house the Old Master paintings. As usual, it was a mess – paintings stacked against the walls, the floor strewn with piles of papers, a desk loaded with open reference books and empty coffee cups.

The only uncluttered surface in the room was the wall opposite Hugh's desk, a space he reserved for paintings that particularly impressed him. This might be paintings he loved or paintings he despised. At the moment the spot was empty but Alastair knew better than to try to hang the St. Sebastian there. So they set it down and he leaned it against his leg.

Hugh paced back and forth in front of his assistant's desk, a wild look in his eyes. Hortense, a cousin of Reginald's who came over from London to train as an old master painting assistant, sat staring at the typewriter. Little had she suspected that an apprenticeship under Hugh's tutelage included a crash course in handling a testy temper.

"Where can you *possibly* have put the receipt, Hortense?" Hugh ranted at her. "How on earth do you expect us to run this department if you can't keep the paperwork straight?"

The thin cover of hair that Hugh combed over from one side of his balding head rose when he got angry. How far it had risen was a good gauge of how upset he was. Now it stood an inch off the top of his head.

Hortense sat composed in her cashmere cardigan and string of pearls, enduring the tirade, her eyes lowered but her nose rising.

Hugh's mouth spewed flecks of spittle as he demanded, "Isn't this why we have a filing system? Or did you file it in the trash can?"

Hortense threw Hugh a disdainful look, stood up haughtily from her chair and swept grandly out of the room. Hugh shook his fist at her disappearing back while his hair rose farther off his head.

"I'm so sick of you bloody aristocrats! Why don't you all go back to the twelfth century where you belong!"

Alastair silently watched Hugh . . . on second thought, perhaps he'd keep his present office mate. But he had witnessed enough of these tantrums to know they were like small firecrackers: they sputtered and sizzled and finally blew, and then it was over.

Reginald whispered to Alastair, "I'll just make sure she's all right," and followed after Hortense to offer a few words of consolation.

"Bloody incompetence," Hugh muttered. The offending person removed, he felt the draft on his head and slapped the hair back into place. He rolled his eyes at Alastair and then knelt to the brown paper package leaning against the desk. He lit furiously into the wrapping paper, throwing the bits and pieces off to the sides with alternating hands like a dog digging a hole.

"Good God!" he exclaimed as he revealed the painting: a bucolic image of sheep dotting a tree-lined field under a cloud-filled sky. Although the composition was pleasing, the image was flat. Several sheep stood in the foreground gazing with limpid eyes out of the canvas, their gangly bodies looking more like poodles.

"How perfectly astonishing!" He looked at Alastair and laughed. "This deserves a place of note, don't you think?"

Alastair smiled charitably. "I've never seen anything quite like it."

Hugh picked up the ornate gilt frame and hung the sheep picture in the empty spot on the wall opposite his desk. "School of Constable! Quite an accomplishment! Ha ha!"

Hortense reappeared and glanced at the hung painting. She asked loftily, "You'll take it, then? February sale?"

"Why not!" Hugh guffawed, "Take it in! Let's illustrate it, front cover of the catalogue! Ha ha!"

"And here's another," Alastair said, leaning the St. Sebastian forward.

"Now *there's* something worth looking at," Hugh said, inspecting the picture.

Alastair held out the receipt, wondering if it was safe in either of their hands. "Take good care of it. It belongs to a major client, Catherine DuBois."

Hugh smoothed his hair into place and looked injured. "Of course I'll take good care of it, Alastair, what do you expect?"

Back in the office Jane and Alastair began cataloging the DuBois collection. For Alastair it felt like finding himself in the cave of Ali Baba. Even in London he never had such a marvelous group of museum-quality pictures. He picked one of his favorites to start with, a captivating Franz Marc of a woman lying in a field of blooming flowers, all in lavenders, yellows, teals and mauves. Luscious and inviting, the colors were like a trolley full of fruit sorbets.

He got out his tape and measured the picture horizontally. He began dictating the catalogue description to Jane as the phone rang. "I'm not here," he said, turning the tape measure vertically.

"Modern Pictures," said Jane. "No, not at the moment. Yes, I'll tell him you called. Can you spell Trico for me?"

His ears pricked up. Did she say Trico? "No, wait," he said, standing up. "Is that Megan Trico on the line?"

Jane nodded.

"I'll take it."

He kept his eyes fixed on the Marc while he picked up the receiver. "Alastair Cavendish here."

"Hello, this is Megan Trico from the Soho Weekly News."

He heard her voice as if from a dream. But she sounded hesitant, distant, as if she weren't quite sure about calling.

"How nice to hear from you," he said, studying the lines in the Marc, the curve of the woman's hip into a lemon-yellow thigh.

"I have your press release here about a major sale coming up in January, from a single collector. We'd like to do a story on it."

"I'd be happy to show you what's in the sale."

"Great."

His eyes traced the smooth line of the leg from the shapely hip to the slender ankle, thinking that by next week he ought to have most of them catalogued and therefore a good idea of which ones he wanted to promote. "How about Thursday week?"

"You mean a week from Thursday?"

"Yes, of course, I'm sorry," he said, laughing. He noted that her voice relaxed as they talked, easing off from its stalwart professionalism. He followed the line of the inner calf undulating upwards past the knee, between the crossed thighs to the inevitable Y. Why a Y? This was one question that needn't be asked.

"How about five o'clock?" he proposed. "That way we can talk without being interrupted."

"See you then. And thanks," she said, sounding warm for the first time.

Chapter 17

"*B*o *and Megan sitting in a tree, K-I-S-S-I-N-G . . .*" sang Clyde, his eyes twinkling.

Standing at the kitchen sink in a hooded gray sweatshirt, paint-spattered jeans and canvas sneakers with frayed holes, Bo thrust a dirty paint brush into an old coffee can, sending alizarin crimson swirling through the turpentine. Stretched out on the battered olive green recliner, Clyde switched his crossed ankles.

"Oh, come on. You've never missed an appointment?" Bo asked.

He had been supposed to meet Clyde to help him install his ArtWeb across West Broadway that morning, but he hadn't made it. He totally forgot. Wrapped up with Megan, warm and soft as a bun from the oven, it had totally slipped his mind. When he finally did remember, he figured it was too late. Getting out of bed in the morning was hard enough, but with beautiful, affectionate Megan lying next to him it was practically impossible. Incredible will power was required for him to rouse himself and leave her.

"Sure, I understand. It's all a question of priorities," Clyde said. "Hang yourself out a West Broadway window in the freezing cold or snuggle up to Miss America."

Bo wiped the brush against a newspaper, back and forth, back and forth, squeezing the reddish turpentine onto the paper.

He loved cleaning his brushes, preparing each one to perform its special task again.

"I'm sorry. I'll help you take it down when the time comes. I promise."

"I'd have had a tough time myself if I were in your shoes. Or socks, as it were."

Clyde's grin was so wide he couldn't mind too much. He had met Megan on the street the other day when the cool air had turned her cheeks the color of a dawn sky and her eyes shone like a phosphorescent sea. He kept staring at her, talking a blue streak like he didn't want her to get away.

"I guess it was too much to ask for a Sunday morning," Clyde said.

Bo grinned wryly and scrubbed the brushes' bristles on a bar of Ivory soap set on the orange-crate counter. "I might have had the same problem on Monday."

"What, is she here every night?"

"Not *every* night. I'm sure things will settle down once she gets her own place."

Clyde's jaw dropped.

"You're seeing a woman who doesn't have her own apartment? Boy, are you asking for it. She'll be moving in next thing you know. Hanging curtains at the windows."

"No, no, it's nothing like that," Bo said, rinsing the brush under the running tap water. But the truth was, although he wasn't about to admit it to Clyde, he would feel better if she had her own place. It had crossed his mind that she was getting pretty attached to him, that maybe he should reconsider spending every night with her. It seemed to be the assumption now and it was making him a little uncomfortable.

"*First comes love, then comes marriage, then comes* – hey, stop that!"

Clyde put up his hands as Bo flicked the brush at him, spraying his pants with water. He wiped at his clothing as Bo squeezed the bristles between fingers and thumb, dressing the tip into a neat point before laying it on a clean cloth to dry.

"It's just that we – we get along," said Bo. "And not just in bed. *She's* dragging *me* into galleries to see shows. Now that's a switch."

Last Saturday Megan and Bo had stopped in every gallery on West Broadway, from the 420 building to a basement co-op on the corner of Grand Street. And it was fun all the way. They stood in front of some paintings for 20 minutes or more, talking on and on about them, exploring, delving, analyzing, getting lost in them together. Afterwards it felt like they'd been to the moon. And what was he supposed to do after a day like that, send her away on some artificial notion of not getting too close to her?

"Plus which, I happen to like her. She's nice."

Clyde laughed. "Right. Tell me she's got a great personality."

Bo grinned. "She does, as a matter of fact. We're compatible, in more ways than one."

"Ah, but do you love her?"

"What kind of a question is that?"

"Well, maybe I should phrase it differently. Have you *told* her you love her?"

Bo dunked another dirty brush into the can of turpentine, circling it round and round, creating a widening spiral of sienna orange. No, he hadn't told her that, he hadn't really allowed himself to think about it. He wasn't prepared to deal with the repercussions.

"None of your goddamn business," he answered.

"Uh-oh. That's how it starts, you know, with that little phrase, '*I love you*'. An innocently-intended statement, expressing only the warmth you feel in your heart, and somehow it leads to disaster."

"What do you mean?"

Clyde stretched his long form lazily, raising his freckled arms over his head. "Oh, you know women, they always assume more than they should. No matter how unconventional they may seem, when the relationship gets serious they always start planning some kind of long-term domestic bliss. You know, up the aisle, down to the realtor. Believe me, I've seen it happen to a number of my friends. They were confirmed bachelors, sailing along with a perfectly nice life, and BOOM. They got involved with some woman, and before they knew what hit them, there they were, saddled with a mortgage and a wife who quit her job to stay home with the baby."

"Listen, we're still getting to *know* each other, for Christ's sake. I'm not about to get married, not by a long shot."

"I'm just warning you. She's no one-night-stand. I'd say she's a pretty fancy lady."

Bo wiped the brush back and forth on the newspaper, covering the newsprint with a watery orange. True enough, she was a pretty fancy lady. That was worrisome. For all her good humor of his penny-pinching and bare bones loft, she was probably roughing it. And much as he looked forward to being with her, he sometimes wondered if he could rise to the occasion. He felt like a schmuck when she paid her own way, but with money so tight, it was a stretch to fork out even his own half. She was a good sport about his home-cooked Ryder cuisine but he felt self-conscious about it. She deserved better than that.

And that was another thing, that job of hers, hobnobbing with all those glitzy art world types. How could he possibly compare to them? It wouldn't be so bad if he had a toehold himself, but her stories just made him feel like the clunky cousin from out of town. And then he wasn't exactly Prince Charming.

He sure could use another two thousand dollar shot of cash. If only that sleaze Gerhardt had come up with a legitimate deal; he had made it sound so easy, like the money would just come rolling in. What a setup that would be – then he could take Megan to the best place in town. He swatted the newspaper with the brush. Right, that'd be cozy, wouldn't it – feed her ill-gotten oysters while she praised him for maintaining his artistic integrity?

He dunked the brush into the turpentine again. The sienna orange was stubborn.

It was a bitch because he sure did like spending time with her. But the relationship seemed star-crossed. He wasn't sure what she thought about it, but he didn't want her to get the wrong idea. He would never be able to provide what most women seemed to want: marriage, kids, money in the bank. It wasn't that he had anything against families, per se. But for him they were an impossibility.

If he had another life, yes, he'd consider it. But at the moment he could barely support himself. And he certainly didn't want to find himself in the same position as Gauguin, the Parisian stock broker who up and left his family when he discovered the need to paint. Luckily, Bo had already figured that out. Gauguin's family got the shaft but he gave the world a gift he would never have achieved otherwise.

Why was he worrying about this, anyway? Would anyone like Megan ever settle for a two-bit painter like him? *Fringe lunatics*, that's what his father called artists. And the way his career was going, he barely qualified as fringe.

He lay another clean brush on the rag to dry. There was nothing like having the brushes ready, lined up slick and shining like a row of gated race horses set to take off. He stared at the shiny bristles, begging for a dip in cerulean blue, and felt a resolution pass through him. Painting was what was in store for him, that was where he should be focusing his energies, not worrying about things he couldn't control, fantasies he'd never be able to fulfill.

He looked at Clyde. "Nothing to worry about. We're just friends."

Chapter 18

Megan's high heels clicked steadily along the Prince Street sidewalk. With two hours until the Sotheby's evening auction started, she would visit Bo and see if she could encourage him to do the group show at the Honthorst Gallery as Jake Gruber suggested. Her own career seemed to be looking up and why shouldn't Bo's, too? She turned into West Broadway where the street widened to reveal the evening sky in pastel shades of sunset, salmon clouds drifting on pale blue. In the middle of the street, a giant, three-story spider web spread out between the buildings; the concentric octagons of Clyde's ArtWeb glistened in the ambient light.

Dusk in the city was a magical hour with the day ending and the evening just beginning. The shadowed facades of the buildings to the west reminded her of a painting by Magritte at the Museum of Modern Art, *The Empire of Light*. It pictured a house at dusk, its darkened stucco exterior lit by a street lamp. Above, white clouds floated in a luminous sky. The painting was classed as surrealism, but right now, before her, she saw that very sight.

Everything seemed to glow that evening, even the grimy parking lot where Bo worked on the corner of Broome Street, its cracked and broken pavement sprouting weeds. High up on the wall of the next building the billboard, featuring a looming Mack truck advertising *Sidney the Rim Man, Car Parts on Canal,* looked positively radiant. In the dimming buildings, lights came on like small promises.

She had been giving a lot of thought on how to persuade Bo to accept the Honthorst offer, since he'd been so resistant. He must know he had to get started somewhere, and who knew where it might lead? She would tell him she could make sure the show got reviewed – wasn't everyone entitled to a little favoritism somewhere along the line? Then he'd have a New York review to add to those he already had from St. Louis. What did he have to lose?

She turned into Broome Street and soon reached Bo's entrance, pushed the buzzer and pulled her arms in against the chill evening air. Yes, clearly it was a good idea, surely he would agree. Her breath came out in short puffs like a chugging train. She cupped her bare hands and breathed warm air into them while staring down at the glass bottle bottoms imbedded in the metal landing.

"Hello?" came Bo's voice, muffled through the hum of the intercom.

"Hi, it's me," she said with her hand on the door.

A sharp buzz sounded and the door gave way.

The long stairwell was dim and the sound of her boots reverberated as she trudged up the four flights. She wondered as she reached the second landing if Bo would ever give her a key. It would be handy, especially with the cold weather coming. The truth was she didn't have a clue as to whether he would want her to have a key or not. In fact, she really didn't have much of an idea of how he felt about her at all. Which was odd, really, for an artist as vocal and expressive as he was. As she approached the third landing she decided to stop thinking about their relationship and just try to support him – he had enough problems without her becoming demanding. By the time she reached the fourth landing she was determined to get Bo into a gallery. First things first.

*　　*　　*

Inside the loft Bo was in the process of capping his paint

tubes while Paddy sat on the couch with his shoe off, tying together a broken shoelace in the dim light. The sitting had gone well and Bo was pleased with the day's work. He had finished painting Paddy's head in over the preliminary pencil sketch he always did first to set the composition. He squinted closely at the portrait and resolved to add a little egg yolk to the flake white pigment he'd used for Paddy's hair, to catch its wiry quality, as bristly as its owner.

When Megan's knock swung the door open he looked up, glad to see her, this woman who in many ways seemed so right, in her hat trimmed with fur almost the same auburn as her hair. But when he saw her look warily at Paddy, the muscles in the back of his neck tightened. If she disapproved so much of Paddy, how far could she be from disapproving of him?

"Hi there," he said brightly. "Paddy's been sitting all afternoon."

Her reply was cordial, distant. Paddy snuck a furtive look at her and gulped down the last of his coffee. He bent down stiffly, slipped his shoe on, and rose, knees crackling.

"Thanks for the coffee, Bo," said the old man. "Set me right 'til I find me some supper."

His eyes twinkled at Megan but she looked away.

Bo took Paddy's coat off the hook, the gray cloth tattered and several sizes too big. He held it up while Paddy armed into it and pulled a worn cap out of the pocket. Holding the brim of the cap in both hands, he nodded to Megan as he limped to the door.

"Bit 'o chill in the air this evening, eh Miss?" he said, affecting an Irish lilt.

"Yes, there is," she answered with a forced smile.

Bo said goodbye warmly to the old man who donned his cap and clumped down the stairwell. Bo closed the door behind him, gave Megan a quick kiss and bent to pick up a long-handled fan brush lying on the floor.

She turned and laughed. "Is that where we're at now? A peck on the cheek?"

"Sorry. I'm not feeling very amorous."

"Hardly amorous, barely affectionate."

He glared at her. "Okay, okay, thanks for the word correction."

She swung her bag on to the couch. "What's the matter?"

He swatted the splayed bristles against his hand. "It's just that I hate to see you react to Paddy like that, as if he were something that crawled up out of the gutter."

She pulled off her hat and looked injured.

"I'm sorry. But it makes me nervous, seeing him making himself at home here. For all you know he might whack you on the head when you aren't looking and make off with everything you've got."

"That won't get him very far," he said wryly.

She shoved the hat into her coat sleeve and hung it on the hook. "Lots of these street people have been released from mental institutions. You don't know anything about him."

"I know all I need to know. He's a decent human being, just down on his luck. It can happen to anybody."

"I don't mean to be unkind. I'm just . . . worried for you."

He swatted his hand with the brush several times before he turned to her. "And how was *your* day?" he asked, deliberately changing the subject.

"It was okay," she said slowly. Then she smiled. "I got my article done on the World Art Market Conference."

"What a gal. No late night is going to hold you back."

"How do you know I was out late?"

"I called Lizzy's at midnight and you weren't there."

"You called Lizzy's at midnight?"

"Well, where else am I supposed to call you? Or are you having a phone installed in your bag?"

She threw him a disparaging look. "Listen, I'm *trying* to find an apartment. But they had sort of an impromptu party after the conference and I really had to go."

He thought of the scalloped potato dish he saved for her that congealed in the pot. "Sure, I understand. Professional obligations, forced to party."

She looked hurt. "Bo, it was great input for my article. I got to talk to a lot of major players in the art world."

She looked so pretty when she was in earnest, he was suddenly struck with the thought that she could take her pick of any of those major players she wanted. And if he didn't stop acting like such a jerk she just might. He smiled.

"Good thing I'm not a major player or I might have had to go."

She laughed and the air cleared for the moment. She looked at him closely then, as if gauging him, and said carefully, "Speaking of being a player, Bo, it actually *would* have been good if you'd been there. I saw Phil Honthorst – he always puts in an appearance.

He shrugged.

"Have you given any more thought to that group show?" she asked gently.

"Megan, I told you I wasn't going to do that."

"It would be good for you to have a show even if it's not with a leading gallery."

Suddenly his resolution to be nice flew off with a flare of adrenaline. "What's so good about it? To hang six watercolors with a bunch of other crap? What the hell good is that going to do me?"

She looked steadily at him, seeming to steel herself, and continued calmly. "There's nothing wrong with a group show. And if the rest of the work is lousy yours will stand out all the better."

He looked at her resentfully. She sounded like some schoolteacher, lecturing him like this. As if he were so in need of experienced advice. "Look, I'm not going to prostitute myself to some jackass Santa Claus!"

"But it's the only offer you've got. You can't expect to start at the top. I started writing for a neighborhood freebie."

He collected himself and shot her a caustic look. "Well, I'm not you."

She stood staring at him, her arms at her sides, her eyes

welling up despite her steady stance. Soft as a prayer, she said, "Please let's not have a fight tonight."

She looked so forlorn he couldn't keep it up. How could he talk like this to his wonderful Megan? He walked to her and opened his arms and she stepped into his embrace. He held her silently for a minute; sometimes it seemed like everything would be perfect if they just didn't talk. He offered some tea in an attempt at a truce, and she accepted gratefully. Together they walked hand in hand to the back of the loft.

"Speaking of chill in the air, it is freezing in here," she said.

"Gozzi wasn't very generous with the heat last winter either."

The kitchen was lit by only the meager light filtering through the grimy back windows. Objects appeared in muted shadow. He hit the light switch. The kitchen stayed dark. He flipped the switch up and down, up and down. Nothing happened.

"Those bulbs must be out," he said, looking up at the two long fluorescent tubes.

"Both at once?"

"Maybe the switch is broken."

He turned the knob on the floor lamp plugged into the far wall. It didn't turn on.

"You don't suppose the electricity is off, do you?" she asked.

He stood in the gloom, unbelieving. "Christ Almighty."

He opened the refrigerator to see a dripping freezer as she watched, aghast. He stood and stared at her incredulously, his hands on his hips.

"They shut off my goddamn electricity."

"Oh, Bo," she said softly and sank into a chair.

"I can't believe it."

"Didn't you get a notice?"

He leaned back against the refrigerator and crossed his arms. "Well, sort of. There was some kind of threat with the last billing. I sent them a check but I guess I must have missed the deadline."

"So it should be back on soon, then."

He bent down to the refrigerator. There was no way he could avoid this so he might as well just be straight about it. "I doubt it. I only paid for one month and the invoice was for three."

"Can't you go down to the Con Ed office and pay it tomorrow?"

He took out a can of beer, snapped off the top and leaned back against the refrigerator. "With what, Megan? Monopoly money? Or would you rather I print my own?"

She stared back at him, the reality settling between them like a damp fog. "Bo, this is terrible!" she exclaimed.

"Yup, it's a bitch," he answered flatly.

"I'll lend you some money."

He waved his hand at her. "No. Absolutely not." He sucked the froth off the top of the beer can and looked at her defensively; anything was preferable to showing his humiliation. She looked back sympathetically, her eyes soft but serious, and suddenly her look seemed not to hold compassion, but pity, and he hated it. His neck muscle cramped all the way down through his shoulder. He smacked the beer can on the counter. Damn it. He was not going to let this get him.

"Here," he said with forced good spirits as he reached into the refrigerator again. "Have a beer. It's a little warm – just the way the Brits like it."

They stood in the gloom, swigging on the fizzing cans.

The loft was strangely quiet. All the electrical noises were gone – the buzz from the fluorescent lights, the hum from the refrigerator, the whining of the electric stovetop. The light was fading by the minute. The high white walls had dimmed from gray to grayer, the rectangular shapes of the *Portraits in the City* seemed to have grown; they loomed large and dark as tombstones.

Bo's mind raced with possibilities. The hell with Con Ed. He'd get a Coleman stove and buy his perishables daily. He'd use candles, kerosene lamps. He could handle this. What was one more challenge at this point?

Suddenly he laughed. "I always said I was born in the wrong century. And here we are, back a hundred years. Listen, it'll be a kick."

He pulled out a cardboard box from the cupboard and opened it to reveal two layers of fat candles. He took the box and handed Megan a match pack.

"Let's use these. They're left over from the blackout. Come on. Where would Georges de là Tour have been without candlelight?"

On every flat surface in the front of the loft Bo placed a candle: on the wire spool, the shelves, the easel, the windowsills. Megan followed him, touching a lit match to each wick until a dozen flames flickered all around them, lighting the room in an amber glow. He set down the last candle and turned to watch her as she lit the rest. The candle light illuminated her hair in fiery highlights, shone on her silk sleeve in a golden sheen, sparkled off her earrings, one a silver sailboat and the other a gold scallop shell. What must she must think of him? Did she see him as some dead beat low life who couldn't pay his bills? Or would she rally to help him surmount this crisis? The trouble was, he wasn't sure it was surmountable, and how could he expect, why would he even *want*, a woman like her to get sucked under with him?

She lit the last wick and turned with a smile.

"There now. This is kind of romantic."

He switched on the portable radio, hoping for some music to lift his black mood. Out tripped Cole Porter's *Let's Do It*, the notes dancing through the darkness, light and lyrical. He tried to match his tone to the joyful song.

"What more could you ask for? Candlelight, soft music and me?"

She laughed and shook out the match. "Not a thing."

The flames flickered all around, glowing like distant suns in a dark galaxy. As Megan moved she cast multiple shadows on the walls, each in a different spot, each from another angle. Megan, Megan, everywhere, and not a one stood still.

"You look beautiful in this light," he said. "How about if I do your portrait?"

She agreed and took a seat in the wing chair.

He rummaged through the stacks of paper on his worktable and pulled out a large sketchpad. Pencil in hand, he sat on the swivel chair and opened the pad onto his knees. Looking intently from her to the paper, he began to sketch. As his hand moved his neck relaxed, his shoulder loosened like a collapsing rubber band. His face cleared of anxiety as the pencil moved with certainty across the paper.

For a while she sat quietly, watching the shadows flit along the walls, staring up at the portrait hanging on the nearest wall of two black children sitting in the red wing chair, one playing with a Rubik's cube, trying to line up the jumbled colors while the other looked on. The chair sat at the base of the Statue of Liberty, which rose like a monolith behind them. From a crack in the stone grew a cluster of buttercups. But presently she glanced at her watch.

"I don't want to rush you, but I've got to go pretty soon. The auction I'm covering at Sotheby's starts in an hour."

"This won't take much longer."

Looking down, she saw some stretchers lying at the foot of her chair. On the adjacent worktable she spotted a Swiss army knife. In one quick stretch she grabbed them both. He objected to her moving around but she said she had to occupy herself, that modeling was too sedentary for comfort. She opened the knife and began to carve lines down the side of the stretcher. Momentarily she looked up.

"How about coming to the auction with me?"

His pencil stopped on the pad for an instant and then continued, faster than before. "No, I don't think so."

"Why not?"

He thought of her last description of an auction, of the glamorous crowd, the sky-high prices for artists he didn't respect. A surge of resentment welled up in him. "It's not my scene. Besides, I wouldn't want to keep you from partying afterwards with the champagne and caviar set."

She gave him a withering look. "That's a flimsy excuse if I ever heard one."

"No, really. I don't think I could stand to see all those rich people throwing thousands of dollars around."

She whittled evenly in the wood, a neat row of parallel lines. "There are some pieces you would like. A Charles DeMuth is expected to bring $100,000."

Bo's pencil moved faster on the page. What he could do with a hundred thousand goddamn dollars – a fraction of that amount would save his sorry ass.

"That's a crazy price to pay for any one picture," he said. "I can't believe how they've inflated things."

"Who's 'they'?"

The muscle in his neck was practically in spasm. "The dealers. The auction houses. The curators. *And* the critics. It's all a big racket."

She turned the stretcher on her lap, the candles lighting her face in hues of honey and amber, and carved another set of lines, at right angles to the first, creating a whittled plaid.

"Paintings don't sell for more than people are willing to pay for them."

"Oh, come off it," he said scornfully. "The prices are arbitrary. Collectors just follow the fashion. They don't have the balls to buy work by artists who aren't certified by the art establishment."

"*Certified?* You make it sound like they're dentists or something."

He stopped sketching and scowled at her.

"What is this, the word police? Okay, endorsed, sanctioned, whatever you want to call it. The whole market is manipulated."

She looked at him regretfully.

"Really, Bo. You're so cynical."

He set down the pencil and glared back defiantly.

"*Cynical?* I'm sitting here in the cold and dark, and you call me *cynical*? I'd say I'm goddamn realistic, Megan, this is my reality!"

He tossed the sketchpad on the worktable, his heart racing.

"Okay, don't take offense," she said cautiously.

Her placating tone made him even angrier, talking to him as if he were some irascible madman who needed careful treatment.

"Well, don't act like I'm off my rocker about the art market. If they'd come down off the star system and spread the money around a little I wouldn't have to live like this."

Her face took on forbearance. It was clear she would no longer participate in this argument.

She got up and looked at the sketch. Loose in handling but fully defined, he'd caught her perfectly – sparkling eyes and quizzical smile, her face surrounded by wavy hair that softened her energetic expression.

"Bo, this is fantastic!"

He put his hands in his pockets. "Thanks."

She praised its likeness, extolled its economical but evocative lines, and marveled at the speed with which he did it. He listened gladly, but also with reserve. Would she be equally effusive about the paintings in the Sotheby's sale this evening, celebrating the famous as easily as the forgotten?

Presently she stepped back and checked her watch. "Listen, I hate to run, but it's really getting late."

He watched as she put on her warm clothes, a handsome herring bone tweed coat and the fur-trimmed hat; then eased into leather gloves, turning herself into a fashion plate. Suddenly she seemed to embody everything he was up against: all dressed up and no time for him. He felt a wave of displacement. Who was she, what was she doing here?

"So, are you going to be around later?" she asked.

He felt strange, as if he were playing a part in a play. But he'd heard his cue, he had to act. "I can't make it tonight."

She stopped and looked up. "You're mad at me?"

He turned away. "No, I'm not, but I have some other things to do." He glanced at her fallen face and took a deep breath. "Listen, Megan, I've been meaning to talk to you about something. I think I need to say this, just so we're clear. I really like spending time with you, but if you're looking for a permanent relationship you've got the wrong man."

She stared, her eyes wide with disbelief. "What on earth makes you think I want something permanent? I just asked what you were doing later, that's all."

"Yeah, I know. But I don't want to get into a thing where we assume we're going to be together. I'm not ready for that. And I may never be." She looked so shocked, he felt terrible. "I just don't want you to get hurt."

She stood looking at him with incomprehension before her expression shifted. "Don't flatter yourself."

He watched the candlelight flicker across her face. The dim light didn't hide her distress any. She looked so lovely, far too lovely for him. "I'm sorry," he said.

She stared back at him, a touch of irony in her face. But he was relieved that it seemed she wasn't going to fight him on it.

She shouldered her bag and opened the door. "All right. If that's the way you want it."

He felt like such a heel, but he fought back an impulse to console her. He never wanted to hurt her, and now that's exactly what he'd done. Was this really what he wanted, to send her away like this? But another voice counseled him, *leave it alone, let her go. You can't keep this up, it won't work.*

"Take it easy, Bo."

He nodded without moving. "I'll see you around, Megan."

Chapter 19

Lizzy held up a T-shirt printed with a doleful-looking fish eyeing a red bike. Below it read *A Woman Without a Man is like a Fish Without a Bicycle.*

"That's perfect!" Megan said, laughing.

"Maybe you should put it on. Now."

"I will keep it handy, believe me," she said, stuffing it into her bag.

Megan swirled the liquid in her glass and sipped the Lagavulin, her favorite single malt scotch, as dry and smoky as the inside of a paneled pub. Although the Spring Street Bar where she and Lizzy sat had the opposite ambiance. Painted gray, furnished in black and chrome, the room felt sophisticated but cool, like a stage set, one where you might find Lauren Bacall.

"It really was funny, in a way," Megan said. "After all I went through to break up with Ned, and there's Bo, telling me he doesn't want a permanent relationship. Nothing like a little irony to soften the blow."

Lizzy nodded sympathetically while Megan circled her glass on the bar's black granite surface. Track lighting running the length of the bar lit the amber swirling like oil and water.

"I must have been crazy to get involved with him so quickly. What was I thinking of?"

"You were on the rebound."

"I guess. His free spirit was such a welcome switch. He doesn't even own a suit!"

Lizzy nodded, her long blonde hair swaying in agreement. "That was his greatest appeal, that he was everything Ned wasn't. But I don't think he was very nice to you."

"*Nice*? What's nice? I'm sure Ned doesn't think I'm very nice."

"But at least you weren't unpleasant. You know these artists, they're a temperamental bunch. And free spirits have a way of disappearing into thin air."

"You're right, I guess I should have known better. I just enjoyed him, that's all."

Suddenly Megan felt hollow, as if some vital organ had been removed. She picked up a quarter and spun it in on the polished surface of the bar. Lizzy watched her for a minute.

"You could always call him."

Megan shook her head decisively. "No. If this is his decision I'm not going to try to change his mind."

The quarter whirled round and round, glinting in the light, winding in and out of glistening water drops.

"I just hope he isn't one of these guys who keeps coming back to hurt you."

Megan stared at the spinning quarter, wobbling now as it slowed. "I guess it was my turn to get hurt. What goes around comes around, right?"

"Now, now. Don't be so hard on yourself. Maybe you just went too far in the other direction."

The quarter was faltering now, its edge almost horizontal. She flattened it with her finger. "Maybe. It was just so much fun going around with someone who really likes art."

"There have to be some guys who like art besides flaky artists."

Megan spun the quarter again, thinking of the great openings coming up: 19th Century American Painting at MoMA, Richard Diebenkorn at the Whitney, the new Egyptian exhibition at the Metropolitan Museum.

"Wouldn't that be nice, a man who wants to go to the Tutankhamun show and can get it together to buy the tickets himself. Is that too much to ask?"

"Sounds reasonable."

Megan sighed. "But on the whole, I think I'd be better off putting my energies into finding my own apartment."

Lizzy smiled; she clearly agreed.

The quarter spun off the edge of the bar. Megan leaned down to get it and, rising, recognized the buoyant gait of Jack Fogelman approaching. His big form took up most of the aisle that ran between the bar and the low wall that divided it from the glass-topped tables and tubing and leather chairs. In the dim light his shirt's white polka dots bounced along under a black leather jacket. He stopped when he reached her.

"Megan – taking a break, eh?" He nodded at the bartender. "Another round for the ladies."

Lizzy whispered, "I told you you should have put that T-shirt on."

Fogelman, his mustache waxed in a jaunty curl, paid no attention. "I owe you one after that story on the old painting someone found stacked behind a bureau in the Mott Street junk shop. We scooped The Village Voice!" He clapped Megan soundly on the back.

"Who was the painter?" asked Lizzy, tossing her hair off her shoulder.

Fogelman glanced at Lizzy for the first time. He stared for a moment, as if registering her.

"It was an early painting by Gilbert Stuart, the colonial artist who painted George Washington," Megan said.

Fogelman leaned in towards Lizzy. "Sold for $40,000 at auction."

Lizzy's eyes grew big. "I guess I should spend more time on Mott Street."

Fogelman boomed a big laugh before turning to Megan with an assertive look. "So – what's it going to be with the Modigliani? Who's the rightful owner?"

"I'm trying to track down exactly where the painting has been for the last 50 years."

"I love the setup – the Nazi theft versus the claim of French ownership. But they can't both be true so you'd better get some answers. Readers will lose interest if they don't get the next installment quickly."

Megan tried to nod agreeably. Speaking of Nazis, Sieg Heil, Herr Fogelman. Better get right on it while there's still an Arts section to publish it in.

Fogelman winked at Lizzy and moved on down the bar.

When he was out of earshot, Lizzy leaned towards Megan with a smile and asked, "Who's he?"

"Trouble. Don't even think about it. He's got a girl in every port."

"Kind of cute, though, with the Snidely Whiplash mustache."

"And he'll tie you to the tracks, too. Hey, I thought you were giving me some sage advice here, a cautioning word about love and romance? Maybe *you* should wear the T-shirt."

Lizzy smiled slyly as she watched Fogelman cutting up with some friends at the end of the bar. "I only give sensible advice. I never claimed to follow it."

Chapter 20

Paddy sucked in a big breath, took careful aim, and sent a wad of tobacco flying through the air and into the avocado pot.

"Paddy, you gotta stop doing that," Bo said as he dabbed the paintbrush into a gob of red iron oxide. "I'm doing your face now – you gotta sit still."

Paddy ran his tongue around his stained teeth and chomped on the tobacco he gathered. He sat forward in the chair as he did in the portrait: head up, knobby hands resting on the carved wooden tassels of the armrests, bandy legs set apart on the floor. His wiry hair only partly covered his big ears, his gray beard glinted with silver. The drabness of his clothing stood in contrast to the chair's plush damask upholstery: faded grays and sepia browns against deep vermilion red.

"That avocado pot is the only thing in here to spit into, and it's so far away I gotta wind up to get anywheres close to it. How about giving me something to use as a spittoon? Any old pot will do."

"Look, buddy, you're lucky I got you the tobacco let alone a spittoon. So count your blessings chewing on that foul cud. Now hold still."

Paddy glared at Bo but stopped chewing. Bo glared right back and painted in the line of Paddy's mouth. They had come to understand each other in their developing friendship. Like a freshly baked baguette, it was crusty on the surface but warm beneath.

Lately Bo had found himself looking forward to Paddy's sittings. Since he broke up with Megan he didn't see much of anybody except Paddy and Clyde. Paddy seemed equally glad to see Bo, especially when he threw in dinner.

"Yup, them nuns down there will drive a body 'round the bend," Paddy said matter-of-factly.

Bo kept painting and listened. Paddy frequently started a conversation somewhere in the middle, as if Bo were privy to his train of thought.

"They act all pious and forgiving and then they damn near torture you to death. They got these Sunday morning breakfasts, see, at the Sacred Heart Mission. But before they let you eat they make you sing hymns and listen to the priest carry on. And the whole time you gotta keep kneeling and standing and sitting and kneeling again – damn near ruins your appetite."

Capturing the old man's expressions had been hard because they shifted continually as he talked, but in this afternoon's session Bo had finally caught Paddy's spirit. Like the wakening of Pygmalion, the image on the canvas had suddenly come alive. There he was in all his motley glory – raggedy Paddy, every proud inch of him.

Bo stood back with satisfaction. Painting a face that conveyed true personality was the hardest part of portraiture. And this rendition of Paddy's intelligent face – good-humored but discerning – forced the viewer to wonder why this man of character was dressed in tatters. The background would be easy once he figured out what it should be. But what a bummer that the light was fading so early on these November afternoons.

"Okay Paddy, we're done for today, I can't see well enough anymore. Can you come back tomorrow? Maybe in the morning, since it's getting dark so early."

Paddy scratched his beard. "Well, now, I can't come first thing, because tomorrow morning they's having biscuits and gravy at the Mission. But I can be here mid-morning if that will do."

"Great. Afterwards I'll make omelets."

Paddy smiled agreeably as he rose stiffly from the chair. He ran his knobby fingers through his wiry gray hair but it still stood out around his head like a matted mane.

Bo took some bills from his wallet and handed them over. "Thanks for coming. I'd offer you something to eat, but I'm a little out of commission with my refrigerator off."

"Con Ed turned off the juice on you?"

"That they did."

"Damn companies. Ought to be illegal, turning people's kitchens off so they can't even cook a decent meal."

"I borrowed a Coleman stove which works pretty well but I haven't gotten down to the store yet today to buy food."

Paddy looked a little disappointed. "Yup. I know it must be hard to keep a refrigerator so well-stocked."

Bo set the brushes in turpentine. "What, mine?" he laughed. "All that's ever in there is eggs and beer."

"That's well-stocked, Bo, well-stocked."

"I wouldn't exactly call it high living."

Paddy set his scrawny hands on his gaunt hips. "Well, now, it's better than pulling supper out of the garbage, ain't it?"

"Yes, I guess it is."

"Why, you got it great!" Paddy went on. "Nice big place, all to yourself. And you – practically a boy yet."

"Twenty-eight is a little past puberty."

Paddy waved his hand dismissively. "Twenty-eight's a young 'un."

Bo gathered up the mugs around the loft and Paddy followed after him, talking all the while. "I was rich once, too. Had me a Cadillac. Had the damnedest times with that car, tearing around town. Finally totaled it, though. Bounced off a curb and broke the drive shaft." He chuckled and then clucked his tongue. "That was a long time ago, though. Times change."

Bo looked at the thoughtful old man and wondered what it must have felt like to have his whole world vanish, to wake up one morning in a flophouse on the Bowery, clean sheets nothing but a memory.

The buzzer rang and Paddy said, "That'll be that girlfriend of yours. She'll be wondering what kind of friends you got with me hanging around."

"You don't have to worry about her anymore," Bo said with a sudden pang of loss, but at the same time feeling relieved she wasn't around to see him in this reduced state.

"Now don't you fret," Paddy said, pulling on his coat. "This happened to me plenty of times. You'll get yourself out of this."

Bo looked at the old man standing in his moth-eaten coat, a leathery hand holding the buttonless lapels together, dirt caked under the nails. Suddenly a chill ran through him. *Would* he come out of it just like this old man had?

Paddy said goodbye and his uneven gait sounded down the stairwell as the buzzer rang again. Bo walked quickly to the intercom; maybe it was Megan, come to broach a reconciliation. That would be just like her. He drew in his breath sharply and held down the intercom button. *Please*, don't let it be Megan.

"Hey Bo, what's happening?"

Clyde; thank goodness. Although if it had been her, he would have gone to meet her halfway down the stairwell . . .

"Hi Clyde. Come on up."

Bo buzzed Clyde in and flopped onto the couch. Yes, it was better that Clyde had arrived instead of Megan. But damn, it would've been nice to see her, the real flesh and blood woman instead of the intangible Megan who'd been haunting his dreams. He stared at the darkening wall, lit only by the twilight from the windows. *Don't miss your water 'till your well run dry.*

If only things were different. But as it was, he couldn't face her. First the electricity, and any day now he would lose the phone service. Yet another domino down in his advancing collapse. And wasn't that really the reason he discouraged her, because he knew all this was coming? *The Decline and Fall of Bo*

Ryder, now there was a story she could write, first hand. So what if he was painting a masterpiece? Was it consolation or not that Rembrandt died a pauper?

A shaft of sunlight suddenly appeared on the floor, momentarily illuminating the studio in a pale, winter light. Ah yes, he remembered, this happened last November. The angle of the sun had shifted and for a week or so in the late afternoon it would shine up Broome Street, hit the big paned windows across the street and reflect into the loft. He watched the white light, swirling with motes of dust, a single shaft as in a Renaissance *Annunciation*. Now there was a thought. Maybe some heavenly apparition was about to appear, a haloed angel, lily in hand, come to deliver some blessed news, the art world was at hand. With a wave of her blossom the collectors would line up at the door. Now that was a creation myth he could get into.

"Hey, Bo. What's the good news?"

Clyde walked into the loft with a wide grin, toothpick sticking out the side of his mouth. Bo looked at him askance; sometimes Clyde was so cheerful he could wring his neck.

"'Good news'? You came to the wrong place for that."

Clyde turned the toothpick around in his mouth. "What's the matter?"

Bo shook his head. "Nothing. Don't mind me."

Clyde handed over a packet of mail and Bo fingered rapidly through the envelopes, hoping for a cheerful word from someone. But no such luck, just another stack of bills, and at the bottom, an envelope from Gozzi. Bo slit open the envelope and scanned the letter. He dropped his arms and closed his eyes.

Clyde walked around the wire spool table sniffing the air. "Smells like you've had that Coleman stove on again. What do you say we go down to Chinatown, give you a break from this camp food?"

Bo raised the letter and re-read it to make sure he wasn't misunderstanding anything. Then he crumpled the paper into a ball and tossed it on the floor.

Clyde took the toothpick out of his mouth. "What's that?"

Bo's head fell back against the back of the couch. "My eviction notice."

Clyde looked over quickly. "You're kidding."

"No, no, no, this isn't happening," Bo said, covering his face with his hands, pressing his fingers against his eyelids. This was impossible, this could not be. He parted his fingers and opened his eyes. The shaft of reflected sunlight on the floor had narrowed to a thin strip and as he watched, it disappeared.

"Fucking A," Bo said. Then he laughed, a big laugh, a crazy cackle that bounced off the walls, rising up to the high windows and the *Portraits in the City*. "What the hell am I going to do?" The question filled the loft, resonating in the vast space.

He got up and tossed the rest of the mail onto the table, his mind flashing with options. He would need to move, to a smaller place, maybe in Brooklyn. But with his negative bank balance, where would he get the money for that?

"You can always come and camp out with me if you don't mind sleeping on the couch," Clyde offered. Bo shook his head. His thoughts were charging down a long dark corridor, slamming doors as he considered each unworkable alternative. But there had to be an answer.

"Come on, Bo," said Clyde, handing him his jacket. "Let's get out of here. Dinner in Chinatown, my treat."

*   *   *

Several hours later, their stomachs full of sesame noodles and gingered fish, they climbed back up Bo's stairs. Their footsteps sounded as hollow as his prospects.

"Come to a party with me tonight," Clyde said. "Get your mind off your troubles."

"No, thanks. You go. I don't really feel up to partying."

Clyde looked at his friend regretfully. "I've got time to hang out here for a little while, then."

Bo opened the door to the loft. Inside it was dark and still as a tomb. Clyde struck a match and lit a candle.

"How about a warm beer?" he asked Bo, who nodded.

Clyde carried the lit candle back towards the kitchen.

Bo lit the candle on the spool table. The single flame glared in the surrounding blackness. He dropped onto the couch and watched the tiny flame flicker, wavering to and fro in the cold air currents. A host of possible solutions to his eviction churned in his thoughts, but all seemed flawed, and at this point he could neither settle on any options nor dismiss them. His mind felt muddled, overloaded.

Maybe he should go back to St. Louis, eat his pride and accept defeat. No, anything was better than that. What about Hoboken? Get a job on the docks, sleep anywhere as long as he could find a studio. But weren't the dockworkers unionized? Or what if he became a watchman, a caretaker for some place that needed a guard at night? But that still wouldn't give him any studio space. Where would he store his paintings? Where would he work?

Or maybe he'd just stay where he was. Refuse to leave. Let them come and drag him out. *I'd prefer not to.*

The telephone rang, startling him out of his worries. He stared at the phone. Who could he possibly want to hear from now?

"Hello?" he answered quietly.

"Finally, the real person," came the Austrian accent.

Bo froze.

"I'm calling because I've had a request from a client and, given its specific nature, I thought immediately of you. He's looking for a Max Ernst drawing, one of the Dada bird pictures. I know this is a subject you could easily provide. He's fronted the money already. Your portion is in my pocket and waiting for you – fifteen hundred dollars."

Bo steadied himself against the spool table. *No, no, no, he couldn't do this.*

"So my friend, what do you say?"

"Like I told you, that's not the kind of work I do."

"But you are perfect for the job, which of course will be kept strictly professional, totally confidential. He wants just one."

Just one, you can keep your loft if you do just one.

"I'll have to think about it," Bo replied.

"Fine. But you must let me know tomorrow, my client is eager. I will contact my other resources if you aren't interested."

Bo dropped the receiver back into the cradle. *Fifteen hundred dollars, in his pocket . . .*

"Who was that?" Clyde asked.

"Oh," Bo said uneasily, walking around the spool table. "An old friend from the Art Students League."

"Who wants to buy something from you?"

"So he says. He was in here on Open Studio day. Liked a drawing of mine." *In fact, liked a lot of my drawings, showed more interest in my talent than anyone else has.*

"Terrific! Just the ticket, right?"

"Yeah, maybe." *Just what I need all right, a ticket to jail.* Bo began chewing on his thumbnail.

"Say, this portrait of Paddy is really shaping up," Clyde said walking over to the easel.

"Thanks," Bo answered mechanically, turning to walk around the spool in the other direction.

Clyde watched him dubiously. "You know, you gotta get your mind off this. How about watching the game? The Giants are playing the Redskins."

Bo stopped pacing and shrugged helplessly. "With what? Telepathy?"

Clyde knocked the side of his head with his hand. "Of course, *stupido*, I forgot, the electricity is off. Jesus Christ, Bo, how are you gonna live here?" He stared at Bo as his eyes widened. "Oh, *right*, you're not, you're evicted. Oh, man. Listen, maybe it's best if you get the hell out of here. The place is falling down around you."

Bo watched as Clyde's expression shifted from dismay to

regret to pity. To see his friend, his peer, his fellow artist, feeling sorry for him was worse than eviction itself.

Slowly a smile spread across Bo's face. He raised both hands above his head in the quick shake of a victorious athlete, then vaulted over the couch. "C'mon. Let's blow this pop stand! Fanelli's, my treat."

"But Bo, you're broke!"

"No, I'm not. I've got six bucks left from my last paycheck."

"But you're in debt up to your ears!"

"So what, it's only money."

Bo suddenly bent at the waist and rushed at Clyde, ramming his shoulder into Clyde's hips and lifting him into the air. He ran with Clyde over his shoulder down to the pitch-black kitchen, imitating a sports announcer as he went. *"And here comes Ryder in for a touchdown!"*

Then he turned and carried Clyde back to the front of the loft, straight towards the tiny flame dancing in the darkness. *"And here he comes again in an unheard of move, scoring at both goals!"*

"Hey, let me down! What, are you crazy?"

Bo laughed breathlessly and lowered Clyde to the ground.

Clyde straightened his shirt. "Boy, you are in some serious trouble. You are losing your mind."

Bo grabbed his jacket from the hook and opened the door to the stairwell. "Maybe. Maybe I am."

Chapter 21

M egan turned to the last page of the article she was
editing, one of her own reviews on Robert Vickrey.
What a brilliant, underrated painter he was, one who might be
highly acclaimed in the future if he wasn't now. A master of
egg tempera, his enigmatic images stayed with her long after
the exhibit, like the one she would illustrate of children standing
with transparent umbrellas on a wide expanse of pavement,
slick with rain. She stared at the words on the page in front of
her. Did she want *serene mystery* or *mysterious serenity?*

Fogelman appeared, interrupting her concentration. Today's
polka-dot shirt featured nickle-sized lemon-yellow circles on
forest green, but above the zany shirt the lines in his rugged
forehead were deep.

"Listen up, you two," he said, including Horvath in his
glance. "We're having a little problem this week with advertising.
We may have to cut a sheet so be prepared to hold a few
articles."

Horvath peered up through his thick glasses. "Real news
doesn't hold."

"True," said Fogelman. "So put aside the human interest
pieces and the arts stuff."

Megan looked from Horvath's triumphant smirk to
Fogelman, whose usual mild condescension seemed today to
be tempered, less certain, as if he thought she might warrant
reassessment.

"Unless, Megan," Fogelman added, "you have any further developments on the stolen Modigliani. That we'll definitely make room for. Good job, by the way, on that last article illustrating the catalogue description next to the villa photo. That's the way to raise some interest."

"I'm glad you liked it," she said looking at him steadily. So – he *was* reevaluating her.

She bent to numbering the pages of her finished article, thrilled to think he might actually be giving her a chance. If only Sotheby's would return her call she might have some further developments to write about. In the meantime she would finish up the Vickrey review and an arts editorial on the misguided penny-pinching in the state commission on the arts and hope that they wouldn't get cut. Now that Bo had stepped out of her life, she felt oddly protective about the rest of it.

She walked over to drop her copy in the editor's box and stopped at the coffee pot on her return. This cup had to be her last for the day because she had already drunk far more than she should. But some days got so crazy she lost track of how much she had had, she just kept drinking it to keep up her pace, then drinking more to keep from crashing, stoking up the adrenaline until by 6 PM she was flying so high the only way to come down was to pour a scotch.

As she stood spooning sugar from a cardboard container into her mug, Horvath approached and peered curiously through his thick glasses.

"White sugar? How déclassé. Don't you know brown sugar is the *correct* sweetener these days?"

She looked at his patronizing expression and carefully stirred in the sugar.

"I know, I'm a social throwback. I like my tea black and caffeinated. I like my meat red and preferably prepubescent – veal or lamb." She tapped the stirrer on the edge of the mug and leaned towards him, lowering her voice. "And I like my *men* as refined as my *sugar.*"

She turned from his appalled face and walked away. Little did he know she was practically a vegetarian. *Real news* indeed.

Back at her desk she checked her watch and wished the phone would ring. She was due at the New School at six to cover a symposium so she couldn't wait too much longer for the return call she was promised from the Modern Paintings expert from London who happened to be in New York this week. She looked down at the clogs she wore, scuffed and worn and thoroughly comfortable, as close as she could get in the office to wearing bedroom slippers. They would not do.

Strewn around under her desk was a collection of shoes that had grown since she'd been staying at Lizzy's. She sighed at the sight of them. Feeling bad about imposing on Lizzy, she'd practically moved into the office. A pair of sweats hung now on the hook in the women's room. But Fogelman would draw the line at Oreo, she knew, and after the cat got lost in the garbage chute, Lizzy left the classifieds on her fold-out couch with a number of apartment ads circled in red. The time had come. In fact, she was supposed to see one of them this afternoon but when the receptionist said the expert from Sotheby's would phone back after lunch, she really had no choice but to wait.

Alongside her beat-up sneakers sat pumps for interviews, sling backs for gallery openings, high heels for evening receptions. She reached down and pulled out the high heels. They were a little more formal than the calf-length rayon skirt she wore but at least the color was right. Now all she needed was stockings.

Hoisting her bag up on the desk, she groped around inside. Out came a white plastic egg containing a pair of 'Barely Black' nylons. She shoved them back in the bag with the high heels. Clearly recovered (he was annoyingly resilient), Horvath watched with amusement. "Can you pull a rabbit out of there, too?"

She shot him a disparaging look. "Aren't you on deadline, shouldn't you be finishing your article?"

Picking up the high heels, she headed for the bathroom.

Inside, she leaned against the edge of the sink, pulled on the nylons and wedged her feet into the shoes. The heels immediately made her stand straighter, taller, more elegantly. She rooted around in her bag and pulled out several accessories. A black silk scarf with a gold fleur-de-lis design dressed up her white sweater. A barrette fastened the loose hair she pulled up off her neck. A stick of Ruby Red lipstick turned her mouth the color of bing cherries, a translucent shade so she wouldn't look like a painted doll.

From her ears shone two different earrings, one a gold sun ringed with flames and the other a quarter crescent silver moon. Since the first time she wore the mismatched earrings when she was in such a rush getting out of the old apartment, she had taken to wearing mis-matched pairs deliberately. She always chose two that were harmonious, whose designs, no matter how different, complemented one another. Bo had once said they were like the two of them, yin and yang; so much for oneness.

She looked at her reflection in the mirror with satisfaction and shouldered her bag. As she walked back towards Fogelman's desk he watched her coming.

"Step right up, step right up, see the Chameleon Woman, capable of instant transformations before your very eyes."

As she passed his desk he gave her the first hint of a smile she'd seen since he'd arrived in the office. Amazing. And all from a few juicy little articles. If that was all it took to keep Fogelman happy, maybe she could manage.

Back at her desk she looked at her watch. It was well past lunch now, in fact, practically teatime for an Englishman; it was time to be more assertive. She picked up the phone and dialed Sotheby's on Madison Avenue. A minute later she had the visiting head of the London department on the other end. The polite tone of his greeting changed markedly when she introduced herself.

"Ah yes, a lovely pair of illustrations you had in your

newspaper. A shame you couldn't have gotten them on to the front page."

She ignored his sarcasm and asked about the provenance.

"Of course the provenance is legitimate. This is Sotheby's you're speaking to."

"So you verified the exhibition listings yourself?" she asked.

He sighed audibly. "*Ms.* Trico, I have no reason to doubt Monsieur Garnier's statements as to his ownership of the Modigliani. He was an honorable man and a client of our firm for years and if he documented the painting as being owned by his mother since 1910, I take him at his word. As for the exhibitions the painting was loaned for, there have been quite a few, even on your side of the pond. This is a matter of public record, for heavens' sake. And now I really must go. If you have any further questions I suggest you take them to the Parisian law firm handling the estate. They're called Resiliere et Tesson, on the Boulevard St. Germain in Paris."

She hung up and grinned, a burst of excitement running through her. This was a great lead – the Parisian firm should be able to provide positive substantiation on the provenance. The apartment viewing would have to wait; she would go up to the Alliance Française and find a translator.

Chapter 22

The hell with Bo, Megan thought as she climbed the steps up out of the subway at 59th Street and 5th Avenue into the clear but cold afternoon. The air had a sharp bite to it, the bite of winter coming. High overhead the sky was streaked with the long, gray clouds of November.

On her left stretched the handsome old high-rises of Central Park South, the street level peppered with stone steps, elegant marquees and gleaming hotel lobbies. On her right rose the trees in Central Park, their bare limbs lit by the street lamps that had just come on. Gusts of wind rattled the few remaining leaves that clung stubbornly to the branches.

She shouldered her bag more comfortably and walked past the hansom cabs and snorting horses, their nostrils flaring with steam. Up in the next block the Lyndhurst and Lloyd's green canopy extended like a welcoming arm. Her hands felt clammy, a sure sign of nerves. Why should she be nervous? This was just an interview like any other.

Although she had initially called Alastair about the DuBois collection with purely professional motives, she had since found herself looking forward to the interview, hoping it would cheer her up. Why should she spend her time mourning the loss of Bo when other men were nice to her? It had taken her a while to arrive at this conclusion, reached only after many days of mooning around the office, chiding herself for pushing Bo about the group show, resenting her job for keeping her preoccupied with the Modigliani story, kicking herself for not lending him money when he was so broke, regretting the stories she'd told him about fancy receptions that had no doubt made him feel bad. But when she woke up one morning wishing she hadn't written such a rave review of Ben Schonzeit's show, an alarm went off. She pulled up short like a horse at a fence and realized her thinking was wrong. Did she really believe that undermining other people's success was the answer? Obviously not. And from here her feelings swung back in the opposite direction, which she decided was definitely healthier.

If Bo really cared about her, he would be happy that she was doing well for herself. And if he were going to exist as an artist – a sane one, anyway – he would have to learn not to be so bitter about the art establishment. She had not been able to persuade him of this. And how he could dump her after what they had found together – well, that was unfathomable. So the hell with him. It was time to move on.

The traffic turning around 6th Avenue was jammed to a standstill and Megan wound her way between the honking cars. Up ahead she could see the well-lit lobby of Lyndhurst and Lloyd's. She picked up her pace; this would make a good story.

As she opened the door a uniformed attendant appeared with a set of clinking keys. "Just in time," he said in a soft Caribbean accent as she walked past him. He locked the door behind her.

Reginald lounged foppishly across the front counter in a blue blazer and gray flannel trousers, his long hair hanging down over a typewriter where a young woman sat typing from a stack of papers. He straightened up as Megan approached and pushed his hair back from his ruddy cheeks. Another young woman standing behind the counter in a peach sweater asked if she could help Megan, who told her she had an appointment with Alastair Cavendish. The woman picked up the phone and suggested Megan have a seat while she waited, but she didn't feel like sitting and walked to an exhibition case displaying porcelains. On the glass shelf stood a group of 18th century

Commedia dell'Arte figures, eight-inch-high porcelains of ladies and cavaliers, masters and servants. Beautifully molded, the ornamental forms posed in stances from capering frivolity to courtly elegance.

Out of a corridor wandered Hugh, holding a corn muffin. He stopped at the counter and took a bite, dropping crumbs on the surface. The young American woman sitting at the typewriter asked, "Is it *The* Right Honourable Earl of Seafield, or *The* Right *the* Honourable Earl of Seafield?"

Reginald sniffed. "Neither. It's *The* Right Honourable *The* Earl of Seafield."

"Thank you, Reginald. I knew I could count on you."

"What are you doing there, anyway?" he asked.

"I'm helping out James. His secretary is sick so he asked me to type up these consignor's receipts."

"Are you becoming an expert in European furniture, then?"

"No, Reginald. That's why you need to stay here. I have no idea how to address these people."

Megan inspected the mincing Harlequin figure with his mask and suit of colored triangles and wondered what one had to know to address them.

A moment later the typist asked, "What about this Princess-Duchess? Is it The Princess of Gloucester, Duchess Alice, or does she take her husband's name?"

Reginald snorted scornfully. "She's called Princess Alice, Duchess of Gloucester, of course."

"You'll have to excuse my ignorance, Reginald," the typist said. "Hereditary titles are illegal in America."

Reginald's jaw dropped. "No!"

Hugh guffawed, spattering muffin crumbs across the counter. Reginald turned to him for confirmation.

"Quite right, Reginald. Guess I should be glad I don't have a title to lose."

Reginald smoothed his hair back from his face and said, "Well. These people *do* have titles and you've got to use them properly. After all, we're not some Portobello Road dealer."

"By all means," Hugh said with a sly grin at the young woman in the peach sweater. "We must be proper. After all, we're just gentleman trying to be auctioneers."

The elevator doors opened and out walked Alastair. He approached Megan with an easy, confident stride, his head up, shoulders back, his carriage poised but comfortable, and she instantly understood why he was chosen to head this department in America.

Around her hand closed his, strong and warm. "So glad you could come."

"So glad you invited me," she said, smiling back.

"Let's take a look at the pictures, then," he said, and led her into the elevator. They stood on opposite sides of the car, each with hands clasped in front. It had been a long time since she'd seen him, and she noticed in the bright elevator light that at the temples his straight blonde hair was turning gray.

A smile played around Alastair's mouth. "You're going to love the paintings. It takes a very strong collection to be offered as a single-owner sale," he said as the elevator rose. "Now that they're all here it's clear that the DuBois pictures constitute one of the finest post-war collections in private American hands."

As he talked she watched his eyelashes. As straight as his hair, they angled down from his eyelids like a window awning. She wondered if he ever had trouble seeing out from under them. But since Alastair was clearly launching into his public relations speech, she rummaged in her bag for her notebook, realizing that she'd better takes notes before her only memory of Alastair's DuBois collection spiel was of his curiously slanted lashes.

"The most brilliant thing about the collection was that they bought what they liked," he continued. "Although their fortune wasn't made until some years later, they weren't concerned with resale."

The elevator doors opened and he led the way down the hall to his office, talking enthusiastically all the while. She noted with disappointment his professionalism; The Expert was evidently at hand.

As they entered the office Reginald came in on their heels. Colin was standing in back of his desk adjusting a silk scarf around his neck.

"Hello," Colin greeted them cheerfully.

Alastair stopped as he saw Colin. "Working late, are you?" he asked somewhat accusingly.

"I'm just going."

"You remember Megan Trico?"

"Indeed I do." Colin walked around the front of his desk and offered his hand to Megan along with a smile. "Alastair is going to show off his prize lots, is he?"

"That I am," Alastair said vigorously. "Let's begin at the beginning."

He pulled the first gilt frame out of the rack, a large oil by Joan Miro of a woman whose whimsical form, reduced to bright blocks of color connected by wafting appendages, was barely recognizable. As he lifted it he nodded towards his desk. "There's a list of artists and titles there if you'd like a copy."

Megan picked up the sheet and as she did, a book caught her eye, a large volume with one of Gauguin's Breton women pictured on the jacket. Across her white winged hat read the title: *Modernism and the French Tradition,* by Alastair Cavendish.

"You wrote this?" she asked with surprise.

"What's that?" Alastair said as he leaned the Miro against the wall.

"This," she said, picking up the book.

"Oh, yes." He looked pleased and reached for another painting, a dreamy Paris scene by Marc Chagall in which a bride and groom and a green horse wafted in the night sky over the Eiffel Tower. "I did write that, once upon a time."

"Alastair, I hate to interrupt," Colin said disdainfully as he pulled on a camels hair overcoat, "but I wonder if you could take my 10 o'clock appointment in the morning?"

"Didn't you know Alastair is a writer?" Reginald asked Megan as she opened Alastair's book.

"I had no idea!" Megan said, admiring the handsome color plates.

Colin continued, his voice louder. "Something has come up and I won't be able to see Mrs. Tuthill, so I would appreciate it if you could see her for me."

"Oh, yes," Reginald said to Megan, "Alastair is a regular scholar."

Colin glared fiercely at Reginald. "Reginald, *I* am talking!" Reginald looked away.

Colin cleared his throat and turned back to Alastair. "Can you see Mrs. Tuthill or not?"

"I can and I will," said Alastair, setting another painting along the wall.

Colin smiled quickly at Megan. "Nice to see you again," he said and walked quickly out of the room.

Reginald waited until Colin was gone and then snickered. "Colin can't bear hearing about Alastair's book."

Alastair leaned an anxiety-ridden street scene by Kirchner up against the wall, the buildings and figures in garish hot pinks and turquoises set at dislocating angles. "All right, mate, let's get these pictures out of the racks so Megan can have a look at them."

"Nothing will get Colin to leave a room faster than mentioning Alastair's book," Reginald said as he lifted a large Max Beckmann out of the rack, the heavy, black lines as foreboding as the portrait.

"I don't think that's it, Reginald," Alastair said. "He had an engagement he was running off to."

"He always has something he's running off to."

Alastair straightened up with a grin. "He doesn't want anyone to get the wrong impression, that he might actually be working in the trade."

They all laughed as Reginald leaned a Picasso up against the wall, the three-eyed Cubist figure fragmented at impossible angles. The wall was now set with leaning paintings, a stunning array of European modernism.

"I love that one," Megan said, pointing to a landscape by Yves Tanguy in which strange yet solid forms sharpened by shadows stood against an opalescent, infinitely receding ground. The disturbing image had the odd clarity of a dream.

"It is rather fetching, isn't it?" Alastair said.

She smiled at the excitement in his voice. *Fetching*, yes, what a great word, that's exactly what it was. "I can't believe one couple amassed such a collection!" she said momentarily.

"It is remarkable, isn't it?"

"And that they had such impeccable taste!"

He looked at her closely. "That surprises you?"

"Well, wasn't he a banker or something?"

"An institutional investor." He smiled. "They can have good taste, too."

She flushed with embarrassment. What was she saying? Had spending so much time with Bo turned her into a reverse snob?

Reginald put on his coat and consulted with Alastair about some arrangements while Megan faced the row of paintings, realizing that Bo had influenced her more than she wanted. And in ways that were contrary to her own inclinations. How nice it was with Alastair not to feel the need to repress her fondness for abstraction. Or for wondering who had owned a painting before, or might buy it next. And then there was the surprising pleasure of not feeling the urge to correct Alastair's use of English. And it wasn't just the snake-charming effect of his accent, but the pleasure of his vocabulary, so varied and precise and full of unusual words.

As Reginald excused himself, the door on the other side of the hallway opened and Hugh Haggerty backed out of his office. His rumpled shirt hung out of his trousers and he was shouting back into the room at his secretary.

"I don't care what you tell him, give him Lloyd's address in London! Let him write a proper letter of complaint! It doesn't matter anyway, I'm going to be sacked by the end of the week!"

As he walked backwards he collided with Reginald. Hugh

pivoted, turning to Reginald angrily. His eyes grew wide and he said scathingly, "I'm sorry! I didn't *go* to Eton or Harrow! I don't have a *rich* daddy to support me like the rest of you! I don't go to the *best* dinner parties and say the *cleverest* things!"

He was practically dancing, his body pent up with frustrated rage. He turned back to his secretary while Reginald escaped into the stairwell. "What do I care? Let them sack me! I'll make it easy for you! Get a packing crate and ship me off to Australia with the rest of the undesirables!"

Alastair sighed and walked into the hallway, Megan behind him. Hugh turned and froze, staring at Alastair and Megan incomprehensibly as if they were from Mars. Then he raced off down the hall, his shirttail flapping behind him.

Hugh's secretary appeared in the doorway. Blond hair teased up on her head, she clacked her pink chewing gum. Smoke wafted lazily from a cigarette holder, which dangled from her fingers, her arm bent at the elbow.

"What's the matter?" Alastair asked.

"Nothing special. A client called up asking after a painting she left for appraisal a couple of days ago. Hugh hasn't looked at it yet." She blew a long stream of smoke into the hallway. "Nothing to worry about. Happens all the time in the six months I've been here."

Alastair patted the secretary on the shoulder. "Yes, Shirley, you've almost broken the record."

Shirley clacked her gum and smiled toothily. She had lipstick on her teeth. With a shake of her head, she returned to her desk. Alastair beckoned Megan back into his office.

"*Who* was that?" Megan asked.

"The man or the woman?" Alastair asked with a grin.

"The man, of course!"

"Oh, that's just Hugh. He does Old Master pictures here."

"But he needs help! He's on the verge of a nervous breakdown!"

"Hugh has been on the verge of a nervous breakdown ever since I've known him."

"But those things he said!"

"Well, they're not *all* true. He's not about to be sacked, he's much too good for that. And as for the rest of it . . . well, he does tend to exaggerate."

She stared uncomprehendingly. "But how can he work here if he feels like that?"

He shrugged. "He loves paintings. But he doesn't do well with the rest of the business, he takes it all too personally. Working here is rather absorbing, you see, it can be hard to maintain a healthy distance." He flashed a quick grin. "*I* don't even *try.*"

She laughed as he smiled at her.

"Now then. Let's have a look at the collection." He turned to the pictures leaning against the wall and his whole face lit up. "Quite something, wouldn't you agree? I can't remember a better collection coming up for auction, not since I've been in the business."

"They do make an impressive line-up."

Alastair brushed his hair out of his eyes and surveyed the row of pictures happily. He gestured at Jean Dubuffet's image of a goat, whose humorous and awkward form filled the picture frame.

"This one I expect to do *very* well. I have a client who says she will die happily only if this is hanging over her fireplace."

She hoped so, too – the clever goat deserved it. Looking beyond to the few pieces still left in the rack, she pointed to a lively collage still-life of a table top made with pieces of torn cardboard, newspaper, and a cigarette box.

"What about that collage there," she asked. "Is that in the sale?"

"No, that will be going to L&L's East, our secondary rooms."

"Really? I love the way the different pieces combine into the bigger design."

Alastair smiled understandingly but without reconsidering.

"I agree the form is pleasing, but it's by a minor artist who never really made a name for himself. Here we offer only the established, only the best."

Megan thought of Bo with a pang and asked, "Don't you ever take a chance, maybe discover a artist who hasn't been recognized yet?"

"If I ran a gallery I would. But auctions are a resale market."

She nodded with some disappointment. Moving on, she asked, "Which one is your favorite?"

"I have so many favorites here, it's hard to choose, but if I had to pick, I might choose this," he said, pointing at a hilly landscape of vibrant colors: golden yellows and cherry reds and forest greens, rollicking across the canvas.

"I like Kandinsky, too," Megan said.

"Isn't it fantastic? Such movement, it practically rolls off the canvas."

He gestured at the cubist portrait at the far end of the row and said, "And that Picasso is fantastic, one of the best of this mistress. Look how he's given her three eyes, but he's done it so *lovingly*."

Alastair looked with delight at Megan and they both laughed.

She pointed to a Renoir portrait of a young girl holding a bouquet of flowers, her pink face hazy as if seen through a soft-focus lens. "That's a nice one, too."

"Yes," he said, turning thoughtful. "Although I liked it better when I first saw it. Sometimes, you know, you fall in and out of love with the pictures, find you like one better than another you preferred before."

She looked at the girl in the painting and was suddenly struck by a wave of sadness. "Do you do that with people, too?" she heard herself ask.

Alastair turned to her quickly, his surprise shifting to pleasure. "I'm sure I wouldn't do it with you."

His eyes were tender, his smile gentle, and her disappointment melted away.

He put his hand on her shoulder. "Maybe we should see more than the inside of Lyndhurst and Lloyd's together."

"I'd like that."

"Wonderful. Come to think of it, I have an invitation to the opening of the Tutankhamun show at the Met next week. I'd love to take you if you'd like to come."

A rush passed through her and she wasn't sure if she was about to laugh or cry. "Nothing would please me more."

Chapter 23

B o took a deep breath and blew a long jet of air towards the sailboat. The small sail swelled and glided off towards the end of the tub, wavering in and out of bubbles, its tiny flag wobbling. He wasn't sure of the nationality – a white star on a blue ground – but he liked the image. One wish in an open sky.

One wish – what would he ask for? What else would he want now that fortune had arrived? Accompanying fame? The household variety would probably get to be annoying. When he was growing up in St. Louis his best friend's father was a famous basketball player who would never take the family out to eat because he spent his whole meal signing autographs.

How about professional recognition? Now that was something else. A retrospective of his work at a major museum? He squirmed at the thought. Which work would be shown? The Portraits in the City? Or his copies after the masters? *Will the real Bo Ryder please stand up?*

In truth, what he would like most was Megan. But at this point he couldn't imagine her being back, walking around the studio. Forthright Megan in a factory for fakes – the combination was too incongruous.

He paddled his feet and the currents swirled around the end of the tub. The sailboat rocked precariously on the waves, turned, and dipped unevenly back towards him. It bobbed through the steam rising off the hot suds like a mythical vessel in a bubbling sea.

On the practical side, he was pleased with the improvements he'd made around the loft, thanks to his arrangement with Gerhardt. Like the bathtub. It had always held potted plants because he couldn't afford to hook up the plumbing. But now it gurgled and drained with the rest of the fixtures. The lights were back on and so was the stove. The heat was up and running with no sign of abating since he'd actually paid December's rent in advance.

He'd gone ahead and done the Max Ernst bird drawing for Gerhardt, and once again the money had gone through his fingers amazingly quickly. There were so many bills to pay, so many supplies to buy. When Gerhardt came around the following week, this time with an ongoing offer guaranteeing safety, secrecy and big profits, Bo couldn't say no. It was such an easy end to all the struggle.

Once he got out the first few forgeries, the others came more easily. He stopped worrying so much about the fact that he was a forger. Whenever he started feeling bad about it, he reminded himself that he was just filling a gap in the market for rich people, that this sideline was all for a good cause with no harm done because the money he made would allow him the freedom to do his real work.

Besides, he wasn't really a forger, not technically, because he didn't sign them. Gerhardt had asked him to, but he had flatly refused. He had drawn the line. He might be bending the rules temporarily but he wasn't totally corrupt.

Now he was on a roll, cranking out the fakes quickly and profitably, raking in his share from the middleman. Gerhardt's thin hands accepted the forgeries eagerly: he would smile behind the trim goatee, his forehead rippling slightly under the widow's peak like Dracula in an old silent film. Bo had begun to think of him as The Count. The skinflint had originally offered him 30%, which Bo turned down. But with a 50% cut he was in pretty good shape. Hell, he was loaded.

And it sure felt great. What a feeling, to walk into the art supply store and be able to buy anything he wanted – canvas, paints, brushes, just like that. The other day he spotted a fantastic easel, big and sturdy with an adjustable back that would probably expand to hold a life-sized *Last Supper*. It made his old easel look like something he pulled off the street, which was exactly what it was.

He also had his eye on a set of track lights at an electrical store. Sleek and shiny black, they moved in any direction and would hold a new kind of daylight bulb designed to mimic the sun. Just what he needed for these winter months. The harsh, bluish light from the florescent bulbs was having a strange effect on the portrait of Paddy. It was almost finished, although it had been slow going in recent weeks. Since he'd started supplying Gerhardt, it was hard to find time to work on the portraits.

To make his time more efficient, he started mixing cobalt drier in with his paints. Pretty amazing, because he had always scorned drier in the past as a crutch for quick-and-dirty painters. But hey, life was demanding, he had to adjust. The ideals of his student days simply weren't practical anymore.

He settled down further in the tub, letting the suds surround his ears. As he cleared his thoughts the portrait of Paddy formed in his mind's eye, and suddenly he saw the background: Paddy sitting in the wing chair at the top of the long set of stairs that rose from the avenue to the entrance of the Metropolitan Museum of Art. His eyes snapped open. Of course! The setting Paddy deserved!

He smiled and closed his eyes again. Yes, that would work very well. Paddy would be as thrilled as when Bo gave him a raise. He started as the sailboat bumped his chin.

"So, you've come in, my little ship," he said, watching the flag waver from side to side. "But don't stay in port too long." He blew and off it tottled. Leaning his head back against the tub, he could feel the heat penetrating his bones, relaxing him all over.

What else would he like? As long as he was daydreaming . . . What about a country place for him and Megan . . . a farm nestled in rolling hills, long fences and grazing horses. Yes, that was it, a horse farm, maybe out in Bucks County. Big-cloud skies and grassy fields, a barn studio and her. What a dream, to get away from this crazy rat race and paint in peace. Surely she would eventually understand it from his viewpoint, she'd see that it was all worthwhile in the end.

The buzzer sounded, breaking his reverie. He quickly sat up. He was getting a little carried away here, anyway. The money coming in was far short of affording a country place.

The buzzer rang again, more insistently.

He dunked his head to revive himself, raised up and shook, sending out a spray of water and suds. He hopped out, quickly wrapped a towel around his waist and padded out to the intercom. Over the crackly system came the dulcet tones of Gerhardt.

"I am sorry to come unannounced. But we have some new business to attend to."

The muscle in Bo's neck constricted. Wouldn't you know it, just when he was starting to relax, who shows up but the Count with his unctuous smile. But business was business. Bo buzzed Gerhardt in and dashed back to his bath. Maybe he could sedate himself if he ran enough hot water.

"Come on in!" he yelled at Gerhardt's knock. The door squeaked open and Bo smiled at the sound of hesitant footsteps – he thought vampires could see in the dark.

*　　*　　*

Gerhardt walked slowly, letting his eyes adjust since this ruffian of an artist had such bad manners he couldn't even turn on a light for an arriving guest. He moved towards the lozenge of yellow light shed by the cracked bathroom door. Pausing outside, he listened to the running water before carefully pushing open the door. He knew better than to move too quickly with this irascible fellow. From out of the mound of bubbles in the tub he saw the back of a head plastered with wet hair. With surprise he noted the thickness of the neck, usually hidden by a mass of dark curls.

"I am sorry to disturb you."

Bo turned a wary eye. "Yup. Caught me in my five o'clock bath."

Indeed. This young man did have a taste for the good life, perhaps even more than he knew. Gerhardt looked with disdain at the grimy toilet seat lid. He gingerly lowered his slight frame on to the edge and crossed his legs. Bo watched, his dark head disembodied above the bubbles.

"Looks relaxing," Gerhardt said, trying to divert his distaste for the bathroom.

"It was. What can I do for you, Mr. Gerhardt?"

Gerhardt smiled superciliously. Of course painters couldn't be expected to have any social graces. But it was preferable to maintain an agreeable footing.

"I need a Miro. The client is very eager and I know a good one is coming up at auction soon. So we need to act quickly. And by the way, I'm very pleased with the pieces you gave me last week. The small Klee pen and ink went immediately to a collector on Park Avenue for four thousand dollars. And a private dealer is interested in the Gauguin drawing, I believe for an interior designer – "

Bo sat up swiftly, the water sloshing out of the tub. "Thanks for the update, but I'm really not interested in what you're doing with them. Just give me my cut, that's all I want."

Gerhardt stared at him. Such hostility was not good in a business partner. Especially in this kind of racket. He sat silently for a moment before he spoke again.

"All right. But there's another issue we really must address."

"What's that?"

"I was all set to sell one of the Picassos yesterday but the buyer backed off because it wasn't signed."

Bo threw him a sharp look. "We've had this discussion."

"You need to reconsider. The market is getting more sophisticated, better documented. Buyers want the painter to be validated."

Bo snorted defiantly. "I see. I should sign them so they're sure they're getting the real thing?"

Gerhardt looked back questioningly. How could this painter have such contempt for his own enterprise?

"As long as you're in this business you may as well make the most of it. It really is in your interest."

Bo stared back steadily without answering, the vaguely hostile expression returning. Gerhardt smiled again, hoping he hadn't pushed too far. He didn't want to alienate this supplier; he was a gold mine, a definite winner.

"I told you before, I'm not signing them. If the fools want to pay thousands for *my* drawings, let them. But I'm not going to seal myself in forgery by faking the name. You sign them if you want them signed."

Gerhardt looked back steadily. "My friend, with all due respect, you are kidding yourself if you believe you are not in the forgery business."

Bo's jaw set stubbornly; he didn't reply. After a moment he said, "If you don't mind, I'd like to get out of the tub now."

Gerhardt rose with a steady smile, rubbing his hands together. "Of course, I will respect your wishes. But you must realize that we could have gotten twice the price for the Klee had it been signed."

He headed out of the room and stopped with his hand on the doorknob. "Perhaps I will sign them myself," he said, raising his eyebrows.

Out in the loft, Gerhardt peered into the gloom until he found the light switch. He wanted to see what else Bo had hanging on the walls. He walked quickly past the irrelevant *Portraits in the City* to the back wall where the drawings used to hang. But the wall was bare, except for the fancy lettering that read "RYDER MUSEUM – Modern Masterpieces."

Where had they gone? What a shame, some of them were quite salable.

He returned to the front of the loft, stopped in front of the portrait of Paddy and shook his head. Why did such a talented painter bother with these portraits? They had no market value whatsoever.

As he scanned the walls a book on the shelf drew his attention. The title, *Toulouse-Lautrec*, looped along the spine in longhand, the artist's signature. Well. Why not try his hand now? He reached for the book, propped it up on the spool table and sat down with a sketchbook and pencil. He looked from the signature on the book to the paper and tried to duplicate the slanted script. He gave it several tries, but the imitation wasn't easy. He scowled at the clumsy renditions. This would take some practice.

* * *

Bo inspected the two razors on the washbasin and chose the cleanest. He squirted shaving cream into his palm and lathered up his dark stubble. His face looked out from the rococo mirror, dark curls twisting away from his head, echoing the baroque turns of the ornately carved frame. Yes, with this spiraling mop he was a fair match for Louis XV himself. *Apres moi, le deluge.*

He shaved leisurely, in no hurry to go out and talk to Gerhardt. Although a comment of Gerhardt's stuck in his mind . . . *twice the price for the Klee.* That meant his cut would have been four thousand instead of two. That would have bought the easel, the lights, and then some.

He began to the pull the razor rapidly across his jaw. On second thought, it probably wasn't such a good idea to leave Gerhardt alone in the studio. The guy was such an operator, who knew what he would be up to, snooping around out there. In fact, this whole business left a bad taste in Bo's mouth. But if he were making more money . . . the faster he made it, the sooner he could get out. Just a little bit more.

When he emerged from the bathroom Gerhardt was sitting in the broken swivel chair looking with mild condescension at the portrait of Paddy. Bo stiffened at the sight. He didn't like seeing Gerhardt anywhere near it.

In his bare feet Bo walked up behind Gerhardt and said, "That one you cannot have."

Gerhardt turned with an oily smile. "It's not quite ready for the market. But soon you won't have to pull your models off the Bowery anymore."

"He happens to be one of the best models I've ever had and I don't *want* another."

"Suit yourself, of course. I'm only making a suggestion."

"Thanks, but I'm not looking for advice," answered Bo dryly. Walking over to the closet next to the front door, he said, "All right, let's get on with it. What did you say you wanted?"

Gerhardt's face brightened. "I need a Miro, a simple one, for a lady who has something quite specific in mind. 'Lyrical' she asked for. You know the style, dreamlike, with fishes and birds."

"I think I can manage that."

Bo took a key from his pocket and opened the closet. Racks of horizontal shelves stacked with drawings filled the bottom half of the closet. The top half was lined with vertical dividers for canvases. He sorted through the drawings, pulled one out and held it up. Biomorphic figures in chartreuse and teal frolicked under a midnight blue sky studded with stars.

"Fantastic!" Gerhardt said. "Lyrical as a song." Eyeing the shelves he asked, "What else do you have in there?"

"More of the same. Just keeping you supplied."

"Excellent. But you're not supplying *me*, my friend. It's *us*. We are a team, are we not?"

Bo shot him a disparaging look. "Please."

Gerhardt looked archly at the watercolor for a moment before sliding it into a portfolio.

Bo locked up the closet and then spotted the sketchpad where Gerhardt had practiced signing the signature, *Toulouse-Lautrec.* "Christ Almighty, what is this?"

"Just trying my hand."

Bo looked at the awkward scrawl and laughed. "*That's* your copy?"

"I never was much good with a pencil. But someone needs to sign them."

Suddenly Bo felt an odd sense of propriety. How could he let Gerhardt blow all the trouble he was going to with a crappy signature like that? He shook his head. What a travesty.

Gerhardt watched Bo intently, like a cat eyeing its prey. "I don't have your talents, you see," Gerhardt said.

Bo sighed. Man, who did he think he was kidding? Here he was painting flawless fakes and telling himself he wasn't a forger because he didn't sign them?

Gerhardt stepped closer. Nodding at the sketchpad, he laid a hand lightly on Bo's arm. His voice was silky, encouraging. "It would give the final touch to what you've already perfected. Bring them up to the market value they deserve."

Unexpectedly, across Bo's mind flashed the image of the fancy new easel standing in a sky-lit barn studio. He saw himself painting, set up with plenty of money, not beholden to any of these assholes, living a free and independent life.

He picked up the sketchpad and turned to a clean sheet. "All right, you win."

Gerhardt stood back, his forehead rippling under his window's peak. "You are a wise man, Bo." He quickly pulled the Miro out of the portfolio and placed it on the spool table. "Why not start with this?"

Bo looked at the drawing reluctantly. He'd always had great admiration for Miro. "I guess so."

Under the harsh glare of the fluorescent lights, Bo pulled out a book on Miro and inspected several signatures closely. He chose a charcoal pencil and practiced the signature on the sketchpad several times. Then he leaned over the drawing and slowly, carefully, signed *Miro*. As he raised the pencil from the paper a shudder passed through him.

His complexion sallow in the harsh light, Gerhardt's smile broadened and his lips drew back over pointed incisors. "Fabulous. Bo, you are a true professional."

He picked up the black portfolio and continued smiling at Bo who did not smile back. "We'll be in touch," Gerhardt said, slipping the drawing under his arm and heading out.

Bo closed the door behind Gerhardt with relief. He turned off the glaring fluorescent lights and headed back to the refrigerator for a beer. Goddamn, how did he ever get mixed up in this con game? And today he burned the last bridge. Now he wasn't just a copier anymore. He was a signature-wielding forger.

Beer in hand, he slumped into the swivel chair, pulled off the tab and tossed it on the floor. He stared up at the ceiling. Man oh man. How had he dug himself in so deep, when all he ever wanted was enough money not to worry about where he was going to sleep at night?

Good thing Megan wasn't around to see this. She would have nothing to do with him if she knew what he was up to; she'd hate him for it. So now he had money but he didn't have her. What good was that?

Damned if he'd keep this up for long. Sure as hell, when he had saved up a nest egg big enough to stabilize himself financially, he'd quit this nonsense and get Megan back. The only problem was, it was turning out that the nest egg needed to be a lot bigger than he'd first thought if he was going to be certain of real independence.

He rummaged around on his workbench until he found the sketch he drew of Megan the last night he saw her. Setting it up on the shelf, he lit a candle alongside, and sat looking at the drawing. It captured her wavy hair, the turn of her ready smile, the unflagging spirit in her eyes. But it was only a sketch, and the dark strokes on the white paper lent her a ghostly look. It was just a likeness, a mere reminder, a mirage.

His memory, however, was anything but sketchy. The piney smell of her hair, the way it shrouded them when they were making love. Her pert nipples, surrounded by pink sidewalls. And the way she called him Beauregard, like he was a Three Musketeer or something: *Hey Beauregard, don't steal the covers*; the way she snuggled into him at night, *Beauregard, my nose is cold*. The look in her crystalline eyes when she wanted him as much as he wanted her, the lushness of being inside of her, ambrosial as Eden.

He sipped the beer and stared listlessly at the ceiling. Then he noticed the drip. Would you look at that. The ceiling had been plastered up last week, but damned if it wasn't coming through again. Watching the water gather, he crushed the empty beer can in his hand.

Chapter 24

A lastair heaped a cracker with caviar and glided it through the air and into Megan's mouth. Her tongue exploded with the cool saltiness of the tiny black eggs and she washed them down with a sip of vodka.

The crimson, horseshoe-shaped banquette where they sat was surrounded by poinsettias, their cheery red vibrant against the deep green walls. The colors reflected brightly in the antique samovars, winking and shining in red and green like a lit Christmas tree.

"This is such a treat, coming here," she said.

He smiled across the table. "For me, too. I'm glad you suggested it."

After a lovely evening at the Tutankhamun show, he had asked her out for dinner the next week. He wanted her to decide where, and she suggested The Russian Tea Room. It always looked so festive and inviting when she walked by, and it seemed fitting that she should visit this legendary restaurant with Alastair. Who knew whom they might see.

No sooner did the vodka cleanse her palette of the salty canapé than she was ready for another. This one she spread herself, sprinkling the shiny mound with chopped egg and onion.

"Have you always worked at Lyndhurst and Lloyd's?" she asked looking across the table at Alastair, his ash-blonde hair as straight as his suit's pinstripes, his silk tie a pattern of small brass keys on an olive-green ground. He looked about as handsome as she could imagine.

"When I first got out of university I thought I would do advertising. But my mother used to have to drag me out of the National Gallery, so a friend of hers who knew Horatio Lyndhurst got me a summer job at the auction house when I graduated. And I never left."

She took another sip of vodka, cool and fresh as a mountain stream. She was starting to warm up like the samovars, to glow like the lamps. In fact, the whole room had taken on a radiance, suffusing her with a sense of well-being.

Alastair spread another cracker with caviar just as a burly man with graying hair stopped at their table. With a clap on Alastair's shoulder he said, "I hear those DuBois paintings are something to see!"

Alastair rose from the table, dropping his napkin on the chair. "Hank, how are you? I've been meaning to call you. You'll come for a board room lunch, won't you, and have a look?"

"Love to."

"There's a fabulous Ensor, a street scene that's got your name on it. If you don't buy it a museum will."

"Call me."

Hank winked at Megan and was gone.

Alastair grinned and sat down, returning his napkin to his lap. "Didn't I tell you I almost did advertising?"

He picked up his utensils and from across the vase of budding roses she noticed his hands, strong but fine, squarish with well-trimmed nails.

"It must be fun, selling wonderful paintings," she said as the waiter set down a steaming plate of chicken Kiev in front of her, the parsley-sprinkled breast plumply stuffed with butter.

"It is, although selling is the operative word. It's one job to get the paintings in, it's another to find the buyers."

She cut into the tender chicken, flooding the plate with melted butter as Alastair continued.

"It's a bit of an adjustment for me, you see, selling pictures in America. I have to get so many people I barely know to trust me. I've no London contacts here."

She sipped the Mersault and smiled wryly, thinking of all the painters she knew who had trouble selling anything ever.

"So back in England you just call your friends and family?"

He gave her a reproachful look and forked a piece of beef Stroganoff.

"Most of them can't afford these prices."

"It sounds like your grandfather could."

"My grandfather was very well off when he was a boy. But we now have ninety percent inheritance taxes in England. Primogeniture no longer gets one very far."

"But I thought your mother still lived on the family estate . . ."

"My mother lives in the east wing. Ten Oaks is now run by the National Trust, a sort of Historical Society. Tourists traipse around the house six days a week and on weekends we hold medieval festivals with jousting matches on the front lawn. That just about pays the property taxes."

She blushed, realizing how cocky she must have sounded. How much vodka had she had?

"I've seen too many old movies, I guess. I think of English manors as places where wealthy aristocrats sit around after the hunt eating cucumber sandwiches."

"Your stereotypes are a bit out of date, I'm afraid."

A man passing their table stopped suddenly and greeted Alastair. This time Alastair kept his seat while he introduced Terrence Young, who greeted Megan politely before turning to Alastair.

"I understand you're offering the DuBois collection at the end of December. We need to get together on dates."

Alastair maintained a steady smile. "Call me and we'll figure it out."

Terrence put his hand to his chin and turned curiously to Megan. "Megan Trico . . . I know the name." His expression clouded and he glanced quickly at Alastair and back again. "But surely that can't be you . . . the Trico who's been writing the articles suggesting the Modigliani we sold in London was stolen?"

"That's me."

Terrence stared at her for a moment before turning to Alastair.

"How very convenient for you, Alastair, to have a friend in the newspaper trade. What a clever way to undercut the competition." Then he faced Megan. "I suggest you try fiction, since you clearly have a talent for it."

Terrence walked swiftly away before Alastair had time to reply. He raised his napkin to his face. Megan looked in alarm at his shaking hands, but when he lowered the napkin she saw he was laughing.

"What's so funny?" she asked, reaching for the wine to settle her nerves.

Alastair waved his napkin in the air. "Don't take him seriously. I don't give a fig what he thinks. Actually, it's rather gratifying to get such a rise out of my rival, especially over a suggestion of fraud. Makes one wonder, don't you think?"

He chuckled again and she felt her calm returning. She smiled over at him and bit the tip off an asparagus spear.

"How is your investigation coming along, by the way?" he asked.

"Very well, thank you. My current stumbling block is that I want to verify the provenance listing with the executors, but they are a law firm in Paris and I don't speak French."

"Which one?"

"Resiliere et Tesson, I think it's called."

"I know them well. We frequently use them ourselves because they've got a number of Americans on staff. Talk to one of them."

She bit the asparagus in even segments down the spear. This *was* turning out to be an excellent evening.

They talked on about art and the art world, the entrée finished and the salad served. Against the muted clink of utensils and the murmuring from nearby tables in the narrow room, the only voice she heard was Alastair's. And he looked as if nothing could be more captivating than watching her nibble on lettuce leaves. Finally, his thoughts clearly elsewhere, he reached across the white linen tablecloth and covered her hand with his.

"Would you like dessert?"

His hand was warm and snug on top of hers; what could feel better than this?

"I don't have room for dessert."

Outside on 57th Street concertgoers poured down the steps of Carnegie Hall as Megan and Alastair stood on the corner waiting for the light to change. Storefronts lit the street brightly on its eastward descent and skyscrapers rose on either side, disappearing into the night sky. He looked at her, his eyes a mix of admiration and appreciation.

"It's nice to walk with a woman who's almost my height."

She looked down at her boots. "I must be about five ten with these heels on."

"Just right."

The traffic inched across the intersection and he took her arm in his, weaving deftly between the cars as they crossed the street to head north on 7th Avenue. They walked quickly in the cold night. Alastair joked about New York drivers as Megan laughed and watched their feet stepping swiftly along the sidewalk beneath them, her black boots and his cordovan wing tips matched in eager unison. As they approached Central Park South a horse and buggy pulled up in front of them, the bay horse stepping high, his long mane blowing in the breeze.

Alastair bowed in mock chivalry. "Would you care for a ride, my dear?"

"Really?" She'd never ridden in a hansom, it always seemed so touristy.

He opened the cab door. "After you."

They climbed up the narrow step. Inside, the black hood surrounded them like blinders, leaving only the front open to the back of the driver's seat.

"Up around the reservoir, please," he called to the driver

who snapped the reins and off they went, crossing into the canopy of the park.

"You must be cold," he said, looking at her. In the darkness his eyes shone from the passing streetlights.

"A little."

He raised his arm and she moved over under it.

They turned to face one another and he said, "You're very beautiful."

"Don't tell me that."

"Why not? You are."

She looked at his handsome jaw, at his kind eyes, and the thought that she must be crazy flickered across her mind: all she needed now was to fall into another relationship. But the hesitation disappeared as quickly as it came. With a man as great as Alastair, was she going to let some sense of incorrect timing interfere? That would be even crazier.

"Thank you," she said.

His free hand gently stroked her cheek and he suddenly looked serious. He leaned towards her and she met his lips, opening hers slightly, his mouth supple and full against hers.

"May I touch you?" he asked huskily.

"Yes."

He kept kissing her as his hand fumbled with her coat buttons. His mouth pressed against hers, now with some urgency as he struggled to free first one button and then another. When her coat fell open and his hand found her breast his whole body relaxed. He pulled her closer while his hand moved up and down her torso, tenderly exploring. Enveloped in his warmth in the cold night air, her heart beat in time to the steady gait of the horse.

* * *

Boom, boom, chink chink, bong, bong . . .

"What on earth is going on?" asked Megan, turning in alarm

to Alastair. She stood in his bathrobe, the hemline brushing the floor.

He laughed and opened the curtains at the window, throwing on the wall a bright rhomboid of light. How marvelous that the vastly distant sun could throw a ray of sunshine right here on this very wall. He couldn't remember the last time the bedroom looked so cheerful.

"The clocks are striking. Didn't you hear them during the night?"

"Not really. I'm a pretty sound sleeper."

He put his arms around her and said, "So am I, especially when I have such a delicious nightcap."

She smiled. The sun caught the reds in her lustrous hair and the radiant greens in her eyes and she looked more beautiful in his baggy robe than ever.

"How many clocks do you have?" she asked.

"Enough to keep me on time."

"No, really."

He pursed his lips and looked at the ceiling.

"Three upstairs and four down. Plus my wristwatch."

She laughed. "Why so many?"

He shrugged. "I like to know what time it is."

Her hands slid down his arms and pressed his palms. She walked to the dresser and looked curiously at the mystery clock.

"How does this clock keep time?"

"It's a mystery clock."

She turned and gave him a half smile. "Don't tease me."

"No, really. It's called a mystery clock. The French invented them."

"But how do the hands move? They aren't attached to anything."

"You mean they don't *appear* to be attached to anything."

She looked inquiringly at him. Putting his hands on her slender shoulders, he looked over her head at the clock's gleaming onyx hands, each graceful tip studded with a diamond, suspended inexplicably in the center of the jade circle.

"The clock was a gift to me from my grandmother, Lydia Atwood. She loved secrets."

"Lydia Atwood. What a great name."

"Yes, or, as she was also known, Duchess Lydia."

Bong, bong, bong, . . . The grandfather clock in the hallway began.

She turned and faced him. "Why is that one chiming now?"

He brushed her hair away from her neck and noted her small gold earrings, one shaped like a jumping dolphin, the other an anchor.

"They don't all keep the same time. I synchronize them every so often, but eventually they get out of sync again. Rather like your earrings."

She laughed and shook her head self-consciously.

"What good is having all these clocks if they're all telling a different time? How do you ever know what the real time is?"

He brushed her hair away from her forehead, noting the resilience of the wave as it sprang back. Moving his hands to her narrow waist, he smiled at her questioning look, one eyebrow cocked higher than the other, her cheeks the color of ripe peaches, her eyes as deep and full of greens as a moss agate. He felt as if he were in a dream; was this really she, standing in his bedroom?

"I know it's high time I met you."

Chapter 25

Roger Greaves, the managing director of Lyndhurst and Lloyd's, sat in his office off the reception area, his big desk covered with auction catalogues and upcoming sales notices. He looked over his half-glasses at Alastair and smiled, a rare occurrence in his usual gruff demeanor.

"Congratulations on landing the DuBois collection. I knew you could do it."

"Thank you."

Greaves cleared his throat uncomfortably, his salt-and-pepper eyebrows working like wiry brushes. "I'd like you to accompany Hugh to an appraisal this morning over on Park Avenue. When you leave make sure Hugh keeps his one o'clock appointment at 77th and Madison with a Dr. Dimm. I'm sure you've noticed Hugh has been under a great deal of stress and I think he could benefit from some professional help. I've made him an appointment with a psychotherapist."

He looked significantly at Alastair and handed him a business card.

Alastair laughed in surprise. "Since when do we send our staff to psychotherapists?"

"Hugh broke his toe on Monday when he kicked in the storeroom wall in a rage. Joel Greene is concerned and he recommended this doctor. Said he might give Hugh some medication to keep him on an even keel."

"Ah, Joel Greene," said Alastair. The head of the press office must be worried about the impression Hugh was making on clients. "But rushing off to a *therapist*, it just sounds so – *American.*"

"That may be, but it's worth a try. There's Hugh now."

Alastair turned to see Hugh limping past the open door, pulling on his coat, his shirt tail hanging out the back of his trousers.

Greaves called out to him. "Say, Hugh, wait for Alastair. These clients have got a few Modern pictures someone needs to look at."

Hugh stopped, looking startled. "Coming along then, are you?" he flashed a crooked grin. "Jolly good."

Two hours later Alastair and Hugh stood on the sidewalk outside the Park Avenue apartment building, the appraisal finished. The owner had had more to look at than they expected, and it was now almost one o'clock.

"Care for lunch?" Hugh asked.

"I'd love to," Alastair answered. "But Greaves said I should remind you about your appointment with Dr. Dimm."

"Oh, blast. Sent you to mind me, did he?"

Alastair smiled and turned into 73rd Street. Hugh stood looking down at his shoes.

"It's not as bad as all that," Alastair said. "Come on. I'll walk you over."

The storefronts on Madison Avenue were full of their usual array of remarkable art and artifacts: Chinese porcelains, Japanese netsuke, Classical busts, Cambodian Buddhas. Hugh was captivated by them all. He stopped in front of a window displaying an Indian Shiva, the large bronze figure sitting cross-legged with a dozen hands extending from the torso.

"Now *there's* an assistant for you," he said, turning to Alastair with a smile.

Out of the office, away from the ringing phones and piles of paperwork, Hugh seemed calmer to Alastair than he had in weeks. Maybe a holiday was all he needed. Or a date with a nice girl.

"Say, Hugh, have you met any American women you like?"

"Can't say that I have. Although I do rather fancy Janine at the front counter."

"She's married."

"Bit of a stumbling block, that."

They both laughed.

"How about you?" Hugh asked.

"Yes, I have, actually. A newspaper reporter."

Hugh stopped and peered through a window at a black and red Grecian urn picturing mighty chariot horses viewed from a frontal perspective.

"Oh? One of those muckrakers?"

"No, no. She writes on art. She's not the hard-boiled type at all – in fact, I find her rather ethereal. She looks a bit like that Gainsborough portrait in Colin's sale."

Hugh's smile broadened. "Aren't you lucky."

"She's so beautiful it's hard to believe she's on her own."

Alastair looked at his watch. He had made a promise to Greaves. "We've got to get along here, Hugh. It's nearly one o'clock."

"My foot is not fully cooperating, I'm afraid," Hugh said, limping heavily. His toe seemed to have taken a turn for the worse. He dawdled up the Avenue, full of admiration for every passing shop, Alastair making offers to speed him along: his arm, a taxi, a cane from one of the windows. But nothing Alastair said would induce him to hurry, and by the time they arrived at Dr. Dimm's building it was 1:18. They stepped into the foyer to see the glass door of Dr. Dimm's office firmly shut. A sign hung behind the glass: *Out to Lunch.*

"Oh, drat!" Hugh exclaimed with a grin. "What rotten luck."

"Isn't it," Alastair said, laughing. He couldn't get too upset about missing the appointment; it seemed like such an odd thing to do, anyway.

Hugh stooped down and peered at Dr. Dimm's name, etched in black lettering on the glass door. Below in bold black letters was printed, "LICENSED REGISTERED THERAPIST."

With a mischievous look he said, "Well, as long as we're here . . ."

He took out a black marker from his pocket and neatly penned over the first three letters in THERAPIST, changing the lettering to read, "LICENSED REGISTERED RAPIST."

He chortled with glee.

"Come along, you mad man," Alastair said. "I've got work to do."

Chapter 26

Alastair sat alone in his office, ruminating. He reached for the phone, then pulled his hand back. Oh come on, don't be daft, of course it's all right, he told himself. After all, she wasn't a nitwit, she knew discretion. He reached for the phone again but his hand rested on top of the receiver. He wavered . . . she was a reporter, after all, a member of an infamously loose-lipped bunch. But no, no, don't be silly, this was Megan, lovely Megan. He picked up the receiver and punched in a number. It would be fine, just let her know the ground rules.

"Megan, hello! I'm so glad I caught you. Listen, I know this is very late notice, but I've had a cancellation for my boardroom lunch today at one o'clock and I wondered if you might like to come. Round out the table."

A pause. "Me? Aren't these lunches reserved for courting wealthy collectors?"

"Usually. But I've got a table set for twelve and one of my clients just canceled."

"Are you sure I won't stick out like a sore thumb? The lowly writer?"

"You're anything but lowly."

"Well, I'm flattered you asked. Sure, I can't resist."

"But you must promise me, anything you hear is off the record. I'm inviting Megan the art lover, not Megan the reporter."

"Yes sir."

Alastair smiled as he returned the phone to the cradle. He looked at his watch. Great. Only two hours until she arrived.

He picked up the morning's *New York Times* obituary listing, cut out from the newspaper and circulated daily. Scanning it quickly, he verified that no Modern painting collectors had died during the night, although he did recognize the name of an old dowager he remembered who bought a painting in Colin's last sale. He scribbled a note on *Loretta Rowe Dickerson*. Then he checked off his own name on the list of department directors stapled to the sheet and carried the paper over to Colin's desk, whose name was next on the list. Colin had always been better at ambulance chasing anyway, keen on the kill if not on the follow-up. He looked at his watch again – time seemed to crawl whenever he was waiting to see Megan.

As usual when he co-hosted a luncheon with Colin, he had to take care of most of the arrangements himself. Relying on Hugh, the third host, wasn't even a possibility. But inviting collectors almost always proved worthwhile. Along with wining and dining they would get a private showing of paintings from the DuBois collection. And a good bottle of wine never hurt a client's interest in a work of art.

As an added bonus Alastair had invited Catherine DuBois herself, to give them an idea of just what a DuBois provenance meant. Buying a painting from a prominent collector always added a certain cachet, and a living owner as colorful as Catherine would only boost the attraction. Add Megan, and who could ask for better company? Why on earth had he hesitated?

Out in the hall the aroma of the luncheon preparations wafted down from the kitchen. The long corridor leading back towards the middle of the hotel was filled with the appetizing aromas of butter, garlic, and savory herbs. He passed a front counter woman on her way to the Chinese department gingerly carrying a Yung-chêng period bowl decorated with flying bats and succulent peaches. He greeted her and pushed through the swinging kitchen door across from the dining room to see how everything was going. The small kitchen was made even smaller by the presence of bulky Colin, who stood scowling over the shoulder of the middle-aged cook as she stirred an enormous pot of soup.

"Watercress is *not* the same as sorrel, and I specifically asked for sorrel soup."

He glared at the dismayed Giselle.

"But Mr. Plimpton, I tell you there was no sorrel in the market. It was either watercress or leek, and watercress is closer in taste."

Colin clicked his tongue impatiently. "I requested this last week. With a week's notice I should think I could get what I asked for."

He shot her an admonishing look and pushed out the swinging door, muttering to Alastair as he passed, "Bergman is *mad* about sorrel soup."

"Let's hope he's as mad about the DuBois collection," said Alastair.

Colin was about to retort but stopped short as three people rounded the corner from the elevator: a tall, good-looking man arm-in-arm with a short woman escorted by Lauren from the front counter. Colin's annoyed expression shifted to genial warmth and he adjusted the white triangle of handkerchief sticking out of his breast pocket.

"I brought the Bergmans up since I knew you were expecting them," Lauren said.

"Couldn't be better," said Colin, flashing a smile at the older man with the youthful face and his wife who wore a pillbox hat with black netting strung across the front. Alastair remembered Bergman from the last 19th Century auction where he was the under bidder on a Harlanoff landscape that went for a record price to the Kuntshistorishe Museum in Munich.

"Do come and see the pictures," Colin said and they followed him down the hall, the wife taking two steps for every one of her husband's.

Alastair headed back into the kitchen to ask Giselle about the Floating Island he requested for Catherine, a dessert that was the former house specialty at Beech Tree Manor. He wanted to keep her happy during these emotionally draining days of divesting herself. Her capricious behavior had him a little nervous. If she could withdraw a painting during an auction, what else was she capable of?

Giselle stood at the counter chopping onions with quick, short strokes. She turned to Alastair with a skeptical look. "And now I suppose you want something?"

"What's the matter?"

Giselle waved the knife in the air. "Oh, you directors! You are never satisfied! I make you five-star lunches but it's never enough. Always more demands, always making trouble for me."

"I'm sorry Colin was rude to you."

"Storming around here like Louis the Sixteenth – that's the problem with you English, you never had a revolution! Mr. Plimpton and his airs, nothing a guillotine wouldn't cure!"

Alastair couldn't help smiling. "You needn't take it out on me. We're not all the same, you know."

Giselle chopped furiously and said nothing.

"Listen, Giselle, you are the best chef we've ever had. Don't be upset about Mr. Plimpton, he's just nervous about his clients."

Giselle's chopping slowed. "Fine. I make this lunch for you, then, not for him."

Alastair poured a glass of wine and slid it along the counter to Giselle. "Here. It all smells delicious."

Giselle smiled, her wide face relaxing. "Later. Not while I'm working. And by the way, the Floating Island came out perfect. It will carry you like a cloud."

*　　*　　*

Megan entered the stately boardroom and pulled her suit coat down firmly over her skirt. A crystal chandelier hung over a table set with gleaming china, shining silverware and silver candlesticks. Finely woven taupe draperies on the street-side cast the room in a honey-colored light. Leafy palms in porcelain jardinières stood in the corners of the room, the long walls lit by standing torchieres in between which hung paintings from the DuBois collection.

Placed closely, one behind every couple of chairs, the stunning paintings seemed almost like guests themselves. Except that none of the figures had dressed for the occasion: the elbow of Picasso's guitarist poked through a tear in the sleeve, Ensor's street revelers hid behind garish masks, Renoir's bathers wore nothing at all.

At the head of the room hung a sizeable interior by Van Gogh: five thin peasants sat at a plain board table under a hanging kerosene lamp that lit their faces lined with hardship. Painted with broad, confident strokes, their gnarled hands poured tea and served potatoes with the grateful reverence of taking wafers and wine. The canvas of humble grays and browns was housed in an ornate frame of resplendent gilt.

The guests stood chatting cheerfully with one another, drinks in hand. Megan recognized no one among the sleek suits and silk blouses, and suddenly she wondered if she should have come. She looked around and spotted Alastair just as he saw her, and the way his face lit up reassured her. Turning to walk around the table to him, she practically bumped into Colin.

"What a nice surprise!" Colin said. "How have you been?"

"Fine, thanks, how are you?"

"All the better for seeing you," Colin said with a gracious smile.

She felt her face flushing; he *was* charming. She glanced at Alastair who was watching them steadily from the far end of the table. "There's Alastair, I'd better say hello."

Colin inclined his head slightly.

Alastair stood with Reginald and a small, silver-haired woman. Her red plaid suit jacket, trimmed in green braided cord, sported a gold butterfly pin, glinting jewels marking the dotted pattern on its wings.

Alastair took Megan's arm behind her elbow. "Catherine, this is Megan Trico. Megan, Catherine DuBois." His voice was warm, as if it were a special introduction.

Catherine's eyes sparkled. "I am so glad you could come. How nice to have a member of the press, you will keep us honest!"

"What would everyone like to drink?" Colin asked, stepping up next to Reginald.

"You're doing the honors?" Alastair said archly.

"May I ask, what is the white wine?" said Catherine.

"Puligny-Montrachet."

"Marvelous! I'll have a glass of that."

"And you?" Colin turned to Megan, who wasn't quite sure what she wanted and looked to Alastair.

"I'll have a Tangueray martini," Alastair said.

Colin looked back to Megan. She was tempted, but there was the article waiting to be written this afternoon, which she had to do a good job on. Fogelman had been giving her the evil eye lately, asking where was the beef. But refusing didn't seem in keeping with the spirit of the luncheon.

"A white wine spritzer, please."

Reginald grimaced. "You're going to dilute the Puligny-Montrachet *with soda water*?" His scorn was palpable, as if she'd proposed putting ketchup on her eggs.

"It's just that I don't usually drink at lunch," she said, wishing she could melt into the rug.

"Quite right," Catherine said. "I'm sure this young lady has a busy afternoon ahead of her. A spritzer sounds like just the thing." Catherine leaned towards Reginald and Colin with a reprimanding look. "You know, *some* people work for a living."

Colin clapped his hand on his heart as if wounded, and he and Catherine laughed.

"Reginald, help with the drinks," Alastair said curtly.

A newly arrived couple approached and Megan turned to them gladly.

"Hank Campbell!" exclaimed Alastair. "How nice to see you. And Heddy, aren't you looking well!"

Alastair made introductions all around. Megan noted that the genial man from the Russian Tea Room appeared as unassuming as his wife looked flamboyant. She wore a form fitting knit dress showing every curve in her svelte body. A fuchsia boa twisted around her neck and hung down her back to practically sweep the floor. Her blonde hair, chin-length and crimped, was parted on the side and waved over one eye. The other eye looked out from under suspiciously long and curly lashes. Her extended hand shook Megan's as firmly as a dead fish.

Colin and Reginald returned, hands clinking with glasses. Hugh sidled up alongside Colin and lifted a martini from his hand.

"Hugh, have you met Megan Trico?"

"'Lo," Hugh said, glancing shyly at Megan. Then he looked down. When he saw Megan's outstretched hand he shook it abruptly, as if he were not used to shaking hands with women. "How ja do."

Heddy turned to Colin, her crimson lips moving as if they had a life of their own.

"We're *so* looking forward to the St. Luke's hospital fundraiser. We're gotten some fabulous donations and with you as auctioneer we're expecting to break our record!"

Colin's eyebrows knit. "Yes, I've been meaning to talk to you about that. You see, being the week before Christmas, it's quite a busy time for me and I wondered if you might let Alastair take the auction instead?"

Heddy looked alarmed and Alastair shook his head. "Ordinarily I'd love to, but I'll be in London that week."

A flash of displeasure crossed Colin's face before he quickly smiled. "Not to worry, Heddy. I'll make sure you get another of our excellent auctioneers." He looked questioningly at Alastair and said, "I didn't know you were off to London, Alastair."

"Yes, it just came up. The BBC wants me to host a show they're doing on Turner. It will be a few days filming."

Megan smiled in surprise. In talking about English artists, they had agreed that Turner's tumultuous seascapes were some of the best, especially those he painted after having himself strapped to the top of a mast during a storm.

"Congratulations," Colin said, his lip curling slightly. "We've always known we had a star in the department." He set his drink down and said brightly, "I'll just see about the soup."

With Colin gone Hugh guffawed loudly and handed his glass to the bartender.

"Once again, please."

The waiter pushed through the door with steaming bowls of watercress soup and the guests took their appointed places. Megan shook her white linen napkin into her lap and settled herself between Jack Bergman on her left and Hank Campbell on her right. Across the table the high cheekbones of Hank's blonde wife become apparent with the frontal view. In the center of the table between them sparkled a silver candelabrum, its two arms crossed in graceful curves over a central stick. The fortified guests had at least three conversations going at once and their voices rose above the table, mixing with musky perfumes and delectable vapors from the soup.

A bottle in each hand, the waiter bent and asked Megan, "White or red?"

"White," Megan said with abandon, the spritzer having eroded her resolve. What the hell, why miss this chance to try the Puligny-Montrachet unadulterated? Her article would get written somehow or other.

"How do you like the black trumpets?" Jack Bergman asked her with twinkling eyes.

"The what?"

"The mushrooms in the soup – a variety of chanterelle we find right up along the Hudson River. Aren't they tasty?"

Catherine poised her soupspoon in mid-air. "Are you still mushroom-hunting with Jasper Johns?"

"I am. He's still got the best eye of the lot of us!"

Megan sipped the wine, a perfect complement to the savory soup. She felt lulled into luxury, like Oreo lapping up warm milk in front of the radiator. She would have purred if she could.

"Scotland has the *best* bird hunting," Colin stated unequivocally from the head of the table. "I saw more grouse there this season than you could shake a stick at."

"You may change your mind after hunting quail with me in Georgia," said Hank. "I guarantee you'll bring one back for Christmas dinner."

Megan saw Alastair shoot a challenging look at Colin, who blithely ignored him. So that was why Colin couldn't take the St. Luke's auction.

Next came the entrée – veal in cognac, cream and tarragon, with green beans almondine. Megan reached for the butter and in retrieving it accidentally clinked her wine glass, sending out a clear, resonant ring.

She heard a similar tone, lower in pitch, from the end of the table. She looked to see Hugh grinning conspiratorially at her, holding his knife upright in his hand. His face flushed like a lobster, he looked as if he were enjoying himself immensely, sitting down at the end of the table talking to no one. His guests, the elderly Simpsons, sat to his left, but he spent most of his time stealing glances at Megan.

He suddenly brayed, "Please pass the butter, thank you veddy much," accenting his words by tapping his knife on his wine glass.

Colin glanced at him scornfully but everyone else was talking so much they didn't seem to notice. Megan giggled and passed the crystal butter dish. She glanced at the Monet hanging on the wall behind Hugh and thought that if she had the money she would bid on the painting herself, as a memento of this remarkable meal.

With everyone engaged around her, she looked more

carefully at the painting, which offered a view into a pond as deep as the heavens. Blues and greens shimmered in a dazzling reflection of water and light. Lily blossoms in satiny pinks and yellows sat on teal lily pads, suspended on the surface of the deep turquoise water like stars floating in the infinite. The watery image seemed weightless, undulating, blurring the line between reality and reflection, as if the vision had been caressed from a genie's lamp and might just as quickly disappear.

Jack Bergman leaned towards Catherine. "It's great to see all your collection together instead of pieces here and there at the various houses."

Catherine nodded. "I just hope the new owners enjoy the paintings as much as we did."

"You have an open invitation to visit any I buy," Bergman said.

Catherine smiled regretfully and pushed her green beans around her plate. "Needless to say, this has all marked quite a turning point for me. Although my astrologer says that simplifying my life was in the stars all the time. I've been reading *Siddhartha* and I'm starting to feel ever so much better. Once I've sold the houses I think I'll find an equilibrium – I'll just have to adjust to living year-round in the 5th Avenue apartment."

"Catherine, you are very brave," said Bergman.

Megan suppressed a smile. As sorry as she was that Catherine's husband jumped out a window, it was difficult to work up a lot of sympathy for her plight of being constrained to a 5th Avenue apartment.

"How are you going to sell the other houses?" Bergman asked.

"Well . . . since you asked . . ." Catherine lowered her voice and gave a furtive glance to Alastair who was busy talking. "Apparently Sotheby's is getting into the real estate business, selling the better properties, of course. The nicest young woman has been calling me, and I must say I do feel comfortable with her."

Bergman nodded understandingly.

"You see I've got to work with people I can trust. I feel so vulnerable now."

"Absolutely," Bergman said.

"Now you, my dear," Catherine said to Megan, "You are young and have your whole life ahead of you. My advice is trust your instincts and consult the stars."

Megan smiled agreeably but didn't answer. Astrologers were not high on her list of mentors but she didn't want to offend Catherine. In fact, she didn't want to offend anyone at this lovely luncheon. But wine did have a tendency to make her speak her mind; therefore, it would probably be best to simply keep quiet when tempted to disagree. This resolution adopted, she found herself silent for some time. But floating along on the Puligny-Montrachet high, she thoroughly enjoyed listening to the guests. Even with her deep immersion in the New York art world, this was her first intimate view of the collectors. And the glimpse was fascinating, although they might have talked a little more about art.

"Do you have any children?" asked the blonde woman across from her.

Megan was trying to remember the name of this natural beauty but the only one that came to her light-headed mind was Jean Harlow. "No, I'm not married."

Heddy laughed gaily. "That doesn't necessarily exclude you these days. But enjoy your motherless freedom while you can. I'm having such trouble."

"Oh? Aren't they well-behaved?"

"Oh, not *them*, darling, it's the nannies. They hate each other. They sit on opposite benches in the park and the children can't play together. We have one for each child, you know, because it really is *so* difficult to cope with both at once, goodness knows I can't." She gazed forlornly at the tablecloth for a moment, and then, smiling again, offered Megan a dish of hot rolls. Megan took the dish and wondered

if Heddy's perfectly manicured fingers had ever chang
diaper.

Julio set a crystal cup of golden liquid topped with wh.
froth in front of Catherine, who gasped with delight. "Alastair,
you didn't! Floating Island, my very favorite!"

The waiter lowered a cup to Megan. The glistening dessert
reflected as a yawning stretch of yellow and white in the silver
candlestick. She dipped her spoon into the egg-white foam
and let some custard sauce flow into it. Sweet and lemony on
her tongue, it melted as quickly as a cloud.

"Divine, isn't it?" said Catherine.

For the first time she could remember, Megan felt the word
fit.

Heddy gestured at a painting hung in back of Megan, an
abstraction in which sensuous, body-like organisms with
suggestive crevices and protrusions capered on a mustard
ground.

"Catherine, your collection is *marvelous*. We're so hoping
for the Arshille Gorky. I love those languorous forms of his –
so sexy, aren't they?"

"If we bid successfully on that we'll send it straight to the
St. Barts house," said Hank, putting his arm around Heddy
and giving her shoulder a squeeze. "Get you in the mood for
vacation."

Heddy laughed, her ruby-ringed fingers adjusting her
diamond necklace which flashed with prismatic color against
the dark painting hanging on the wall behind her, a dance hall
scene by Toulouse-Lautrec picturing a dancer's garishly lit
raised leg and several absinthe drinkers, arms bent despondently
around their milky drinks.

Heddy smiled across the table at Megan. "That late style
of Gorky's is my favorite. I wish he had painted more."

Megan looked at Heddy's glittering form and thought of
Arshille Gorky and his life of poverty from Armenia to Union
Square where he finally killed himself. How astonished he would

have been to see this diamond-draped woman effusing over his art. She was suddenly swept with a wave of sadness. Why couldn't these people ever notice sooner?

Simpson, the old Master collector down at Hugh's end of the table, raised up his wine glass. "So many of the Contemporary artists, they're all style, no substance. And the styles they do choose change all the time. They're like fashion designers, trying for one that sells."

Megan's pulse quickened. The painters she knew never considered the market when they painted. With her heart hammering her reserve disappeared. Who was this Simpson, with his ignorant opinions and dismissive attitude? Surely someone should stick up for the artists. But no one replied.

"Good artists aren't driven by the market," she said in a voice clear enough to travel. "But when they have a lot of dimensions, they keep expressing themselves in different ways, which accounts for evolving styles. Like Picasso's."

The table grew quiet. Simpson's watery eyes looked at her challengingly. "Picasso? He just proves my point. He had no trouble selling."

"He was lucky. But many artists aren't, and when they change styles collectors sometimes stop buying. Take DeKooning, for instance. His paintings from the 1950s sell much better than what he's painting now."

"Not much of a businessman, I'd say," Simpson said decidedly and several people laughed.

Megan looked straight back at him. "But for him art isn't a business. It's a way of life."

Her words hung in the air above the quiet table. Simpson smiled skeptically and Heddy looked blankly across at Megan, her face a vacant stare. From the candlestick a drop of wax dripped on to the tablecloth.

Heddy turned to Colin. "Could you pass the cream, please?" she asked.

"Absolutely. Would you care for more Floating Island?"

"Oh, no. I've got to watch my figure."

The table broke into small talk and Simpson's wife patted his hand.

Megan felt her face burning and tried to collect herself by concentrating on the custard remaining in front of her. When her flush had subsided, she looked around at the crystal-stemmed cups shimmering with half-eaten desserts, at the jeweled women, at the ruddy-faced, well-fed men, and suddenly she thought of Bo, notching in his belt and inventing yet another way to cook potatoes.

"I hate to break up the luncheon," Hank said, "but I have an appointment on Wall Street in 30 minutes."

The other guests murmured in accordance and moved to go. They stood, gathered purses, shook hands. Hank smiled kindly at Megan as he pushed in his chair, and she felt she ought to respond.

"Good luck with bidding at the sale," she said as she pushed in her own chair. She smiled at him, but his large form had turned to Colin and she found herself smiling at his back.

The hosts made the rounds with good-byes while she stood behind her chair, adjusting the strap on her bag, which suddenly seemed to need attention.

"I saw your nephew's beach house in *Architectural Digest.* What a fabulous place!" Heddy exclaimed to Catherine.

"It *is* lovely. But what possessed him to spread it out in a consumer magazine for all the world to see I cannot imagine."

Heddy laughed and they exchanged pecks on the cheek.

The guests filed out of the dining room and into the hall to the coat rack. Megan's herringbone hung between the furs. The men helped the women into their minks and chinchillas, and Alastair held up Megan's coat for her to don. Instead she took it by the collar and tucked it under her arm. It was all she could do not to grab it and head for the staircase. She could barely look at Alastair.

"I'll put it on downstairs," she said.

Alastair glanced at her with concern. "What's the matter?" he whispered.

"Nothing at all."

"Make sure they distribute that BBC show over here," Bergman said, "We'll look forward to seeing it."

Alastair ushered them all into the elevator. His face slightly flushed, he was nonetheless gracious to each departing guest. Megan watched him; how good he was at all this. Catherine stepped into the elevator and winked at Megan.

"I'm so glad Alastair has found an American to keep him company while he's working so hard at this auction business. It is *so* exhausting."

Megan smiled wanly. "Yes, it can be a tiring business."

Alastair glanced at the full elevator car and then at Megan. "I don't think you'll fit."

She gave a little laugh. "No, you're right about that."

Everyone called good-bye and the elevator door closed.

Alastair stepped closer, his face worried. "Megan, I hope you found the lunch enjoyable."

She laughed and hoisted her bag up onto her shoulder. "*Enjoyable?* I'm not sure that's the word I would use. Enlightening, perhaps, illuminating, maybe. And certainly tasty, I'll credit you with that."

His face fell. "Darling, what's wrong?"

She didn't answer. How could he ask such a lame question?

"You're not upset about Simpson, are you? Don't mind him, he's an opinionated old plastic surgeon who just started buying art."

She took out her mittens and pulled them on. How could she possibly express her feelings about these wealthy collectors while standing in the hallway of one of the oldest bastions for selling art to the upper crust?

"I've got to go. I'm on deadline this afternoon."

He sighed. "All right. Listen, I'll be working the next couple of nights to get this catalogue to the printer, and then I'll be up in Boston all Friday on an appraisal. But let's get together over the weekend."

He leaned over to kiss her but she turned her cheek.

"Thanks for inviting me. It was . . . an experience."

Chapter 27

November passed into December and the New York winter pulled the sheets up. Sleet, snow and driving winds assailed the streets and nature asserted its supremacy by covering the concrete city in a blanket of white. Megan walked along Prince Street avoiding patches of ice and climbing the knee-high snow drifts that rose at every corner. The cone of light shed by the street lamp danced with falling snowflakes.

Her weekly newspaper assignments were finished, but instead of feeling satisfied, she was restless, she couldn't sit still. Fogelman had pressed her today about why the Modigliani story was stalled. Why couldn't he be patient?

This morning (although it only seemed to cloud the issue) she had finally gotten through to the Parisian law firm who were the executors of the Garnier estate, which had supposedly included the *Abruzzi Daughter*. An American lawyer at the firm had provided some interesting news. Yes, he told her, their firm was the executor of the entire estate, everything from investments to the house and all its furnishings. As they always do in these cases, he explained, they called in experts to evaluate the art. But the connection was crackily and she couldn't hear well.

"I'm sorry," she said, "You called in *Dear Heart?*"

"No, *Gerhardt*. The paintings were handled by Gerhardt Fine Art."

Megan had sat still, confused. How could that be? Gerhardt was the buying agent, not the seller. "Gerhardt, you say?"

"Yes, Gerhardt Fine Art of Monte-Carlo. He's a modern art dealer with offices in New York and Palm Beach. He organized selling the paintings through Sotheby's in London."

She had the lawyer repeat himself until he must have thought she was an idiot, she was so perplexed by the news. Gerhardt had bought the painting for Catherine DuBois, and was also linked with its sale?

She walked along the snowy street, mulling it over. Just what kind of operator was Gerhardt? Or was he? Realtors sometimes represented both the buyer and the seller, so why not art dealers? Was this underhanded or not? She needed to talk to someone. The person who came to mind was Alastair, but he had been busy for days.

Alastair. The thought of him produced a confusing mix of feelings. How awkward it would be to see him again, after that boardroom lunch. What a disaster. All those rich collectors talking about buying paintings as if they were expensive wines. Except for the Bergman fellow and Catherine, they were all so lofty, so airily superior. Maybe that's why they bought art at auction, so they wouldn't have to lower themselves to entering an artist's studio. No Puligny-Montrachet there.

She was finding it difficult not to group Alastair with the rest of them. She knew this was not fair, but it was hard not to. As open-minded as he seemed, how could she know what he really thought? How could he operate in that world and not be part of it? Of course, that's what Bo had thought of her . . . But she wished she could talk to Alastair about it, or someone who knew the auction world; this information about Gerhardt was more than she could sort out herself.

A car passed on the street, its wheels plowing heavily through the deep snow. The drift at the corner was too high to climb so she cut out into the snowy street where two tire ruts ran down the middle. She chose one of them and walked along towards West Broadway, feeling disconcerted. Directly overhead shone a full moon, so bright and clear she could see its craters like veins in a Gorgonzola. The snowfall had quieted the streets, the cold night air hung hushed and still.

At the intersection of Wooster Street a voice called out clearly.

"Hey, Megan!"

In front of her the street was empty.

"Up here."

She looked up to the top of the single story building on the far corner, and there on the roof stood Bo, a bright light behind him.

"Bo!" she exclaimed delightedly. What a welcome sight!

He stood with paintbrush in hand grinning down at her like the Cheshire cat.

"Hey, girl."

"What are you doing up there?"

"Moonlighting," he said, his voice carrying clearly through the still air. "That mural job finally came through."

"Congratulations."

He grinned. "I'm a working man." He stared down at her for a moment and then asked, "Want to take a look?"

She hesitated. Wasn't this the guy who told her to get lost? But she was so pleased to see him, and so surprised to be pleased, she couldn't say no. "How do I get up?"

"There's a ladder over at the end."

Carefully she climbed the ladder to the snowy roof. At the top Bo grabbed her hand and pulled her up with wool gloves, the tips cut out of the fingers. His rosy cheeks and eyes shone in the moonlight.

"Hello stranger," he said, his smile warm and endearing.

"Hi Bo." She felt her resentment momentarily returning. How dare he smile at her like that, as if everything were fine between them?

They stood staring at each other, neither knowing quite what to say.

He gestured with the paintbrush across the rooftop to the

adjacent wall, lit by a floodlight. She looked up to see a building mural – of a building. Finished except for the bottom corner, the enormous, tromp l'oeil image pictured a cast-iron facade. The mural depicted rows of windows flanked by columns, and in the upper stories, incorporated into the painted design, light shone out of two real windows. At a quick glance the effect was deceptively real, impressive enough to make her forget her grievances.

"Amazing!" she said. "If the shadows weren't going the wrong way, it would look like a real building."

"Thanks."

He reached into his jacket pocket and pulled out a pint of Calvados. He tipped it back and drank, then blew out a stream of steaming breath. "Pretty remarkable, isn't it? Representationalism finally gets me a paying job."

He looked at her with a rueful smile and they laughed. But as he turned to an angle where his face caught the torchlight, she noticed he somehow looked older, his face held a world-weariness she'd never seen in it before.

"Why are you painting at this time of night?" she asked.

"Oh, these city bureaucrats, once they finally decide, they want it done instantly. The project is funded by a state grant and some cultural commissioner is showing up tomorrow to see what's happening with the money. This is the third night I've been up here." He glanced over at the mural. "It's the last, though. I'm almost done."

He offered her the brandy and she took a sip, the heat spreading instantly though her stomach. "Boy. Strong stuff. No wonder those poor bums freeze to death, they never feel it coming."

He grinned, his eyes crinkling happily. "Want to help?"

"Me?"

"Why not? It's all cartooned on the brick already. You just have to fill it in."

At the base of the wall sat two gallons of paint and a smaller brush, which he handed her.

"See these lines?" he said, gesturing to the unpainted brick. "Just follow them. Bring them right down from above, like this."

He dipped his brush into the paint can and drew a long, vertical stroke downwards, continuing a window frame. The floodlight at his feet threw a giant shadow of his form against the spotlit wall. She watched the shadow move in tandem with him as he dipped and stroked, dipped and stroked, the enormous arm of the shadow reaching down to the spot where he worked, the dark shadow stroking the paint on quickly, vibrantly, with skilled determination. And suddenly it seemed as if the energies were reversed, as if the giant shadow were moving him.

He picked up the other brush and handed it to her. "Here. Give it a try."

She dipped the brush into the soupy, pale yellow pigment and stroked in the next column. The paint layered on easily and she filled in the decorative lines of the column.

"Excellent," he said with a smile. He took the Calvados out of his pocket and offered it again. "Have another hit. Keeps the blood running."

This time the brandy didn't burn her stomach, it just added to the warmth.

She dipped the brush again, following along next to him. She felt cheered, just why she wasn't sure: from the brandy, from seeing Bo, or maybe from being back in Soho having fun painting instead of worrying about her social status. But she felt as warm on this dark and frozen night as if she were basking on a summer beach.

When she finished another window she stood back and surveyed the mural. It was looking good, but it seemed too much like an architect's drawing – it was as still as the air.

"I have an idea. How about adding some life?"

"Like what? A few roaches crawling the walls?"

"No, no." She walked over into the dark to a painted open window. "How about a cat? Curled up in this window over here?"

"But Natasha, it is not in ze plans," he answered in a mock Russian accent. "Ve must follow ze approved plans."

"Oh, come on, since when did you ever follow any rules? It'll be a nice touch, I'm sure the commissioner will love it."

He looked at the window, blowing into his hands. "Okay, a cat."

Picking up the floodlight, he walked across the snowy roof and set down the light to illuminate the window. Rubbing his hands together briskly he said, "I'll draw the outline and you can fill it in."

He dipped the brush and drew the neat form of a seated cat curled up on the sill, paws tucked in. He handed her the brush and she carefully filled in the outline, leaving two unpainted almond shapes for eyes. He nodded approvingly. "Very nice."

"Just one more thing."

She bent back down and drew whiskers on each side. She stood and beamed at Bo who looked amused.

"Now people will have to watch for the cat to move to see whether or not it's real," she said. "Crowds will gather, admiring your work."

"*Your* work," he said, his eyes softening. "Or, more accurately, *our* work."

They stood staring at each other, their dark forms lit by the moon above and the floodlight below, the two light sources casting crossing shadows on their faces. Bo's eyes mixed affection with apology. "I've missed you so much, Megan, I can't tell you how I've regretted what a jerk I was."

"Is that right?" she answered, her hurt returning.

"Yes. There's no excuse, really, except that I was going through a rough time, and I guess I don't have to tell you that when I'm feeling down I can be pretty moody."

She snorted. "*Moody?* That's putting it mildly. Contrary. Irascible. Downright disagreeable."

He laughed. "Yeah, that'll about do it."

He stepped towards her, the snow crunching underfoot

until he stood so close she could feel his warm breath. He put his hands on her shoulders. "Would you take me back, schmuck that I was?"

She was so happy to see him looking genuinely sorry and hopeful, her heart went out to him. But at the same time a small voice piped up with Lizzy's warning about men who keep coming back to hurt. "Well, gee now, I don't know. I wouldn't want you feeling *cramped*, like you were *obligated* to see me."

He looked at her with such remorse she almost regretted her words. "Megan, forgive me. That night you walked out left a hole in my life. Please give me another chance."

His words passed over her heart like a warm spring breeze, carrying away all resentment. She couldn't believe her ears, to hear him declaring himself. Wasn't this exactly what she had wanted? She had to believe him. Her face broke into a slow smile.

"Okay. But only if you promise not to put anchovies in the pasta anymore."

His eyes filled with gratitude, followed by a smile so big his eyes practically disappeared. His arms encompassed her, and with the taste of his kiss she was pleasantly flooded with familiar associations, as if she'd put on a jacket from last season, a season she enjoyed, a season when she'd felt at home.

Suddenly came the question: *What about Alastair?* But the thought slid away like egg white off a spoon. She couldn't worry about Alastair, he and his boardroom-lunch world felt so distant, and this here and now was just too comfortable.

"Listen," Bo said, drawing back. "As soon as we're done here, some payment is in order. Can I take you to dinner? Any place south of 14th Street."

She smiled. Nothing like a separation to bring out the chivalry. "Okay. The Charcuterie. A dozen blue points on the half shell."

"You got it."

She laughed. "Just kidding. Why don't we walk down to Chinatown?"

He shook his head. "No. We're going to the Charcuterie. That's what you asked for and that's where I'm taking you."

"Bo, you've drunk too much Calvados. You've got delusions of culinary grandeur."

"No, I'm serious. The Soho Charcuterie. Tonight."

She looked at him curiously and saw he meant it. As far as she knew he could barely afford Ray's Pizza.

"Really. I'm loaded from this job. Don't you worry about a thing. I'm going to take you to the best dinner you've ever had in about" – he glanced at the unfinished wall – "five feet."

He kissed her again, his lips moist and appley with brandy. "Everything is going to be different now. No more Mr. Tightwad. My fortune is changing and I want to share it with you. You deserve the best that money can buy."

Chapter 28

M egan lowered a paint stirrer into the open can, swirling the purple pigment as thick and viscous as blueberry yogurt. Oreo sauntered over, tail waving like a ceremonial plume, rubbed against her leg and switched his tail into the paint puddled in the rim of the can. Normally tipped in white, the end of his tail turned as purple as a Scottish thistle.

Megan looked at him approvingly. "Oreo is now officially inaugurated."

Lizzy laughed. "Black and purple. Suits the neighborhood."

"Which, by the way, is great, Lizzy," said Megan. Then she added somewhat sheepishly, "I couldn't have found a better apartment myself."

Lizzy shrugged. "I could not in good conscience stand by while you got involved with a new man without having a place of your own."

Megan smiled without replying. Yes, the apartment would make her love life much more manageable, especially since she now seemed to have more than one man to manage.

The clincher had come the other day when Lizzy had accompanied Megan on the subway and shooed her out of the car at Sheridan Square with a classified ad in her hand for an apartment being shown that morning on 11th Street. Megan had had no choice. And when she came through the square at the corner of 6th Avenue and 10th Street, the gargoyles glaring down from the lofty Jefferson Market Courthouse clock tower, the bell had struck eleven times, her lucky number. It seemed like providence. Off bustling 6th Avenue on a quiet, tree-lined block of stately townhouses, who could guess there would be an apartment in her price range?

True, the four-story townhouse had fallen into disrepair, but that accounted for the affordable price. A graceful set of stairs rose to the handsome doorway, flanked on either side by fluted pilasters with Doric capitals. But the curve in the bottom step was broken, a railing was missing, and the wooden door was badly cracked and peeling. At the top of the building a broken window winked down from under a cornice half hidden by swallow nests.

But what did that matter, or the faded wallpaper of ribbons and roses on the staircase that peeled away in patches to a motley green beneath? The apartment itself was perfect.

She had climbed up the worn marble stairs with the rest of the crowd, around the landing with the stained glass sailing ship in the window to the third floor, where they filed into the apartment on the front of the building. They entered a good-sized living room made light and airy by tall windows and high ceilings, with a kitchenette separated by a counter on the inside wall, and in the far corner a door led to a bedroom just big enough for Megan's bed and bureau.

The state of the housekeeping left something to be desired. The gray-white plaster of the living room walls rose unevenly to carved wooden moldings. Victorian wall fixtures with zany cranberry glass shades were covered in dust. A circle of grimy molded flowers surrounded the ceiling light. On the wide floorboards two lozenges of sunlight from the windows on the street side lit the dingy room in irrepressible brightness. Megan tried not to look too eager; all the place needed was a little t.l.c. and it would be home.

The landlord had planted himself in front of the fireplace, his arms crossed over his big belly, sizing everyone up. "Okay, first things first. To rent this apartment you'll need three months rent up front: the first month, the last month, and a month's security deposit. In cash."

That had emptied the room of half the people.

"No fires, the fireplace doesn't work. And no families moving in with you," the landlord continued. "If you want the place painted, I'll buy the paint but you do the painting. Okay? You still interested?" He looked around at the circle of nodding faces, and stopped with a toothy smile at Megan. "Looks like we draw straws then."

He pulled a bunch of straws out of his pocket and turned his back while he adjusted them in his hand. Then he faced the half-dozen applicants and held out his big fists, one above the other, the straws sticking up like a blossomless bouquet. He passed his fists around, starting with Megan, who took the closest. When everyone had chosen, they all held up their straws. Megan's was the long one.

The landlord had turned to her with a lecherous grin. "Well, what do you know! Welcome to the building!"

Lizzy looked up from where she was almost finished painting the third window frame, the last of the tired white disappearing under strokes of brilliant purple. The shade was light but rich like a soufflé, an Easter purple, worthy of dyed eggs and frivolous bonnets.

"I'm sure my mother is very grateful to you, Lizzy, although she doesn't seem to know if she should endorse my moving in or not," said Megan.

"What did she say?"

"Well, it's sort of a bind for her. She's glad I've got a roof over my head. I think she was worried that I might end up pushing my belongings around in a shopping cart. But at the same time, she can't really congratulate me because she still can't believe I broke my engagement."

"I see."

"But I've got to hand it to her, she did try to stay upbeat. When she called me to see if my new phone was working she told me, Dear, maybe you'll just be a career girl."

Lizzy dropped the paintbrush and howled with laughter. "Thank you, Mrs. Cleaver, for your enlightened opinion."

"She can't imagine me not getting married and having children."

"Why, so you can quit being an arts editor and stay home and try to figure out how to get the Saran Wrap unstuck from the roll?"

Megan laughed but didn't want to pursue the subject further. Her mother said she had heard from Ned's mother that he was accepting a transfer to San Francisco. Then she had asked hopefully, did Megan remember how much she had liked the city when she attended a summer session at Berkeley? Megan had gotten off the phone in short order. But the next day when she saw a calendar for the new year in a bookstore with the Golden Gate Bridge stretched across the cover, she realized that she wanted to end on a good note, if at all possible. She bought the calendar and sent it to Ned with a card wishing him well.

"I wasn't sure you would take the apartment," said Lizzy. "It's so far downtown."

"Oh, no, it's great being able to walk to work. And what I love most is that nook," she said, nodding towards a corner of the living room where the wall recessed into a space just big enough for her desk and typewriter. "I finally have a place to write away from the office."

In the nook's high window she had hung a prism. On clear afternoons when the sun moved west above the townhouse rooftops across the street, tiny rainbows played along the wall, dancing lozenges of pure color. This was a singular commodity in the city, one more easily found down in the low-lying blocks of the Village where the buildings stopped at single-digit stories, away from the looming skyscrapers and their shadowed, canyoned streets that knew sunlight only at noon.

In that nook she planned to write the next article in the Modigliani series. A phrase from the American lawyer in the Parisian firm stuck in her mind: *the dealer has offices in New York and Palm Beach.* She hadn't known about Palm Beach. And with a hunch that there was more to be learned, she had searched old art magazines until she found a Florida listing for Gerhardt Fine Arts. When she called she reached a different art gallery, but after talking with the owner, Jack Drury, discovered that Gerhardt had rented the space ten years ago from this very man. He had no trouble remembering Reinhold Gerhardt.

"A sleaze bag. Worst tenant I ever had. Ditched me for the last month's rent and left the place a mess. Not only that, but it turned out the guy was mixed up in some pretty shady stuff. The day after he left a nice Jewish lady came in from Miami Beach. Told me Gerhardt had hung a painting in the gallery that was her father's in Munich 40 years ago. She said the Gestapo snatched it just before the war broke out and they hadn't seen it since. She told Gerhardt she wanted it back or she'd go to the police, but then he disappeared and she never followed up on it. It turned out she'd lost her parents to the camps and couldn't worry too much about a painting."

That was all Megan needed to hear. This testimony erased the last of her doubts – Gerhardt was unscrupulous and more. Now she just had to prove it. She had called back the American lawyer in Paris to try to get an original list of all the paintings in the French estate's collection, but he told her there was no list except the one catalogued by Gerhardt. Which meant half the collection might be bogus.

"By the way," said Lizzy, "How's the investigation going on the stolen painting?"

Megan laughed. "Gee, did Fogelman put you up to asking me that?"

"Of course not. I just wondered, you got my curiosity going."

"Well, since you ask, it's actually taken an interesting turn. The focus is shifting from the painting to its Madison Avenue dealer. He seems not only to have bought the painting for a New York client, but also to have set it up for sale. I think he's probably been feeding Nazi-stolen art into the market for years.

When I figure out exactly what he's done and how he does it, you'll see it in the paper. In the meantime you can read about his Florida dealings."

Lizzy grinned. "Can't wait."

Megan put the cover on the paint can. Lizzy stood and they surveyed the newly painted woodwork, its satin finish gleaming in a glorious hue somewhere between lavender and lilac and the last light of the sunset.

"It does just the trick," said Lizzy.

Megan nodded with satisfaction. "I agree. I hope the landlord doesn't mind."

"Will he see it?"

Megan pushed in the edges of the paint cover with the end of the stick.

"I certainly hope not. He's pretty creepy. Yesterday I blew the fuse by plugging in the iron and the hairdryer at the same time. I had to go find him in the deli he runs over on 6th Avenue. He's big and fat with oily hands from making sandwiches. He followed me back here, wheezing and reeking of garlic and stale coffee. Before he went down in the basement to change the fuse, he leered at me and asked, 'Anything need fixin' up in the apartment? Anything you want me to look at?'"

Lizzy shook her head. "Maybe you'd better plug in only one appliance at a time."

Lizzy put on her coat and gave Megan a hug. "Thanks so much for coming, for all the support, painting and otherwise."

"Listen, you're starting a whole new life. It's going to be great."

The front door closed after Lizzy and Megan sat down on the couch. She took hold of the alabaster ball set halfway up the shaft of the brass floor lamp and rocked the lamp gently on its base while she studied the effect of the newly painted window frames. They brightened not just the outer wall, but the whole room. The color was the same shade as the lavender sweater worn by the *Abruzzi Daughter*. And just as this lavender brightened the apartment, that painting was going to brighten her career. Her column would soon sparkle like these windowsills; she would be as redeemed as the woodwork in the eyes of Fogelman.

Chapter 29

A lastair hurried east along Central Park South trying not to get his feet wet. Last night's deep and powdery snowfall had turned by mid-afternoon to slush, drifts blackened at the curb by dirt thrown from passing cars. He stepped gingerly around a puddle. What a change from a pristine blanket of white to a slippery, mucky mess.

His watch read just past three; he was late for his appointment at the Plaza. With the overload of work he had to do, he wouldn't be leaving the office at all if it weren't that Catherine called and said she had found some interesting provenance papers. She sounded nervous so he humored her and accepted her offer for tea.

At the entrance to The Oak Bar he caught himself and turned up the steps, taking the shortcut through the side of the hotel to save a minute. He walked quickly down the corridor outside the paneled bar and around into a cheery hallway.

The old hotel was dressed in its Christmas best. Down the red carpet under sparkling chandeliers he turned the corner towards the lobby where an enormous Christmas tree towered, draped with so many strings of faux pearls and ornaments he could barely see the branches. At the entrance to the Palm Room a gingerbread house dripped with frosting sat across from a table laden with delicacies – fruitcake, plum pudding, cranberry torte.

The maitre d' approached wearing a felt bowtie of green

holly leaves fastened in the middle with a cluster of red berries. Alastair explained he'd be joining a lady for tea and looked around the room with its mirrored walls reflecting potted palms reaching towards the lofty ceiling until he spotted her. He made his way past sipping and munching guests to the table where Catherine sat against the wall, her face lively and alert like a mouse poking out of a baseboard hole.

"Hello Catherine, sorry I'm late."

"Not at all, I know you're busy but I thought it might do you good to get out and have a proper cup of tea. I've already ordered, I hope you don't mind."

"You're very kind."

He took a seat and looked at the battered portfolio tied with a frayed ribbon.

"The papers are right here," she said, patting the portfolio. "But before I show you them I do want to tell you how much I enjoyed meeting Megan."

"Oh?" he said, surprised but pleased.

"She's charming. Pretty and smart, and speaks her mind. A girl after my own heart."

He smiled. "Thank you." He felt oddly grateful at the compliment.

"And I loved the way she stood up to Harold Simpson, he can be such an oaf."

"She does have her own opinions."

"As well she should. Tell me, I hope you don't mind me asking, is it serious?"

He laughed. "I don't know."

Her question was amusing partly because it was so personal and partly because he was tickled at being considered a couple with Megan. The waiter set down a pot of tea and a platter of assorted confections.

"I hope you don't feel I'm prying. I think of you practically as family, Alastair, with your grandmother growing up with my mother. Anyway, I just wanted you to know I approve wholeheartedly."

He considered his response: just what was his public stance on the relationship? "I guess it is somewhat serious, on my part at any rate."

She beamed. "I'd love to see you anchored to an American, for purely selfish reasons."

He poured the tea and tried to calm his surfacing feelings. "We haven't quite gotten that far," he said. The notion of marrying Megan hadn't really crossed his mind.

"No?"

"We haven't known each other very long."

"Ah. Well, this old lady's unsolicited opinion is that she is a jewel, to be treasured, before someone else snaps her up."

Catherine looked the plate over and chose an almond macaroon. She nibbled at a cluster of encrusted nuts while Alastair's thoughts reeled with this possibility.

Megan, as his wife? He pictured her standing in his bedroom on East 67th Street like she had the other morning, his satin robe pulled around her trim body, his wool socks sticking out the bottom, the knotted sash trailing on the floor. What if she were there every morning, asking him questions about his clocks, telling him his tie didn't match his shirt, closing the window she cracked at night?

Catherine watched his distracted face for a moment and then sat back decidedly.

"Would you like to see what I've brought?" she asked.

He snapped back to attention. "By all means."

She untied the portfolio and lifted out a handful of yellowed receipts, some written in French, and a photograph. "I found these out at East Hampton. I was organizing things out there yesterday, getting ready to put the house on the market, you know, and there in an old chest in the attic was this portfolio with invoices and an old photograph picturing some of our first acquisitions. I thought they might be useful for the catalogue."

He inspected the photograph. It pictured a large room hung with modern paintings. In the foreground stood a much younger Catherine DuBois with an also much younger Paul Mellon and Roland Balay of Knoedler's. On the wall hung two paintings from the sale: the Toulouse-Lautrec dance hall scene and the Degas double portrait of two women.

"This was taken by the local newspaper when we held a fund-raiser at East Hampton. Edwin and I had just bought the Toulouse-Lautrec and the Degas from Knoedler's. Since they're both in the sale I thought it might be interesting to use the photograph as a frontispiece for the catalogue."

"Let me think about it."

"Is it too late to include illustrations?"

"No. We go to the printer Friday week."

"Good. I was afraid I might have missed the deadline."

He shook his head and chose a pfefferneuse, leaning over his plate to catch the confectioner's sugar. "No, no. For you the deadline is the eleventh hour. If you want to include any other paintings in the sale, let me know. We'd like everything you feel you can part with."

She stared at him fixedly for a moment as if considering something. "Well, I do think I'll keep the paintings still left in 5th Avenue. I don't want to completely denude the apartment if I can help it."

"Of course not."

She sighed and selected a piece of fruitcake, chock-full of candied fruit nuggets.

"My astrologer tells me my stars are at a turning point, that this is the time for me to make a fresh start. Who knows what the future may bring, there's always the possibility of collecting again."

He rubbed his fingers together sending a fine sifting of confectioners sugar onto the plate. "You may be very well set to do that, Catherine, considering the interest in your collection. You may end up making enough money to start all over."

He grinned at Catherine, but she looked suddenly serious. "To tell the truth, this is a concern of mine. It would be nice to know how much money I'll make. Sotheby's mentioned that in these sorts of single owner sales they often guarantee a final sales total."

He looked up sharply. "You're still talking to Sotheby's?"

She looked apologetic. "I must be frank with you, Alastair. I've decided to let Sotheby's sell my houses, both East Hampton and Palm Beach. You know they've expanded into real estate. And a very nice young lady I've been talking to – she knows about my painting sale with you, of course – she has offered to handle all the houses' furnishings: furniture, rugs, whatnot. She said they would assure me of a bottom dollar amount despite what prices the houses bring."

Alastair slowly lowered his cup into the saucer. Catherine fumbled with the fruitcake and dropped it into her tea. "Oh dear, now look what I've done."

She fished around in the cup with the spoon and pulled out a sodden mass of disintegrating cake.

He stared at her with great concern.

"Don't worry dear," she said. "I'll ask the waiter for some more."

"I don't care for any more cake, Catherine. Are you asking for a guaranteed profit, then? Is that what you want?"

She set the runny mess into her saucer and looked at him, her small face furrowed with worry. "It would help tremendously. Please understand, Alastair, I'm not trying to be difficult; it's just that my houses and paintings are all I've got. Having to sell them off to make ends meet, well . . . it's awfully nerve-wracking when I have no assurance of the outcome."

He picked up the teapot and poured her another cup of tea. "All right, Catherine. We will be happy to offer you a guarantee. Let me sit down and work out the numbers and I'll have a figure for you by tomorrow. We can do the same for your furnishings."

Her eyes brimmed with tears. "Thank you Alastair, you are a darling."

*   *   *

Walking back along Central Park South to the office, Alastair's thoughts were a jumble of concerns. Sotheby's! How could she? Sell her artwork with Lyndhurst and Lloyd's and her houses with Sotheby's? What an embarrassment! And all without a word to him. If only she had told him what she was considering maybe he could have talked her out of it. Just when he thought he was getting to know her ... and now what? If one stick of her furniture sold at Sotheby's, Greaves would have his head.

Goodness knows it wasn't the first time hard-pressed clients had behaved bizarrely about their beloved possessions. Like the last estate sale he did in England where the owner, at the last moment, insisted on taking all the glass doorknobs that years of sunlight had turned a pale amethystine.

And she started off by endorsing his relationship with Megan. Nothing like kissing him on one cheek and slapping the other. He glanced up at the darkened sky, still heavy with clouds, and sighed. Catherine. She *could* be a dear, and she did seem to have a certain amount of loyalty to him. At least, he thought she did.

Then this notion of marrying Megan ... what a titillating thought. How nice that Catherine had noticed her. In fact, he'd been missing her terribly the last few days. Suddenly he stopped in the middle of the sidewalk. What if Catherine were right, what if someone else did snap her up? What if he lost her? How could he have gone so long without seeing her? Where were his priorities, for God's sake?

The streetlights suddenly came on in the winter gloom, lighting the snow that lay like a sugar topping on the tree branches across the slushy street. He looked at his watch. It was just past four o'clock, and Thursday, her deadline afternoon, so she would be at the newspaper office. He glanced at the street and saw an empty cab coming towards him, its free light shining like a beacon in the darkening afternoon.

"Taxi!" he called as he waved his arms and bounded into the street. The yellow cab careened to a halt in front of him, sending a spray of dirty water over his shoes. Alastair swung open the door and jumped in. "Prince and Mercer Streets, please. And quickly."

* * *

Megan sat at her desk, receiver to her ear, staring at the photograph of the Italian villa interior hung with the supposed *Abruzzi Daughter*. She was now almost certain it was the same painting. The question was, how much did Gerhardt have to do with its alleged history of being part of the French collection? The time had come to ask.

She dialed a number and waited as the receptionist put her on hold.

"Yes, Ms. Trico, this is Reinhold Gerhardt," came a cool voice on the other end. "What can I do for you?"

He must have seen her articles. She explained that she'd been in touch with the Parisian executors of the Garnier estate.

"Would you like to comment on the fact that you acted both as a buying agent for Mrs. DuBois on this side of the Atlantic and also as the selling agent in London who consigned the *Abruzzi Daughter* to Sotheby's? Some might regard this as a conflict of interest."

Gerhardt laughed, but not without annoyance. "Did I not tell you, my dear, that my business is international? I was retained by Resiliere et Tesson to catalogue the Garnier estate's paintings; you must know I am well regarded as a specialist in the modernist period. Several months later Catherine DuBois saw the Modigliani in Sotheby's catalogue. She has been my client for years, so of course I couldn't refuse when she asked me to bid for her since I was in London for the sale anyway. Surely there is no conflict here. With all due modesty, it is simply a result of my extended business connections, and my long association with Mrs. DuBois."

"Did you also acquire artwork for Mrs. DuBois when you worked out of your Palm Beach gallery? Jack Drury tells me you had quite a network around Miami."

Silence on the other end.

"And another thing, Mr. Gerhardt, I'm finding hard to explain, is a photograph sent to me by Senor Calabresi taken in the 1920s and showing the *Abruzzi Daughter* hanging in his Umbrian villa. But according to the provenance, the painting supposedly spent those years in the Garnier house in Paris."

A contemptuous laugh. "If you knew anything about Modigliani, you would know that he painted many portraits, some stylistically quite similar. An old photograph is no assurance. And besides, young lady, there is no question that the painting has been part of the Garnier collection from the time it was purchased from the artist in 1918. The provenance papers are incontestable. The painting has appeared in many exhibition catalogues, including one right here at MoMA in 1936. Now, if you don't mind, I have a client waiting and I really must go."

The dial tone was loud and insistent. Megan hung up.

Incontestable? Very little in this world was incontestable. Yes, the copied provenance papers the Sotheby's expert had sent her did appear to be in order. There were copies of listings in exhibition catalogues, a noted collector's mark, a bill of sale. But these were just papers, after all, certainly not incontestable, possibly counterfeit. But who supplied them? Sotheby's, Gerhardt, or one of the heirs to the estate? And how could she contest these authorities?

She stared hard at the green ink blotter and suddenly Gerhardt's phrase came back to her . . . *an exhibition right here at MoMA in 1936* . . . now *that* she could check. Her pulse quickened. What a prize story if she could prove Gerhardt had pulled off a brilliant scam . . . it would make her journalistic career.

Suddenly out of the corner of her eye she saw a lanky figure in a long coat enter the newspaper office. Then, as if her ear had a homing device, she faintly heard the man asking for her. She put down the photograph and looked towards the entrance. Standing at the reception desk was Alastair. He cut a handsome figure, but she'd been so consumed by her musings his appearance seemed oddly displaced.

She rose and walked towards him, feeling a strange mix of pleasure and misgiving. His face was lit with excitement and he asked her to come outside for a moment. She buttoned up her long wool sweater and they walked out into the dusk of the snowy street lit by the yellow glow from windows. Underfoot the refreezing snow crunched on the sidewalk. Alastair stopped before the next doorway, his back to the building, his face lit from the streetlights in an unmistakably happy expression.

"What's up?" she asked.

He smiled bashfully. "I missed you. I had to come and see you."

"Really? Just like that?"

"I know, such spontaneity. So unlike me."

"But you look so happy, what's the good news? Did you land a new collection?"

He laughed ironically. "No, as a matter of fact, I've just found out Catherine DuBois is selling her houses through Sotheby's."

"Ummm," she nodded. His eyebrows rose.

"You knew?"

"She mentioned she was thinking of it at lunch the other day."

Her face clouded at the thought of the luncheon while he looked dismayed.

"You didn't tell me!"

She looked at him askance. "I was under strict instructions from my host to keep whatever I heard to myself."

"I meant out of the newspaper, not from me!" he said reprovingly.

She shrugged. "You weren't specific. And besides, I haven't heard from you."

He stared at her fixedly for a moment. "You aren't angry with me, are you?"

"No . . ."

She looked down at her hand and fingered a small paper

cut. She *was* mad at him and she hadn't forgiven him and why hadn't he called and consoled her after that dreadful experience?

"Oh, but you are," he said.

"No, not at *you*, really."

His look softened and he took hold of the loose lapels of her sweater. "Don't hold me responsible for old scalawags Simpson. I don't like him either."

His eyes were as blue as a sky after a storm, as open and clear. He lowered his head and touched his nose to hers. She felt her hard edge crumbling. She raised her hands to his scarf. She'd never wanted to be mad at him. He nuzzled her nose.

"You can't stay angry with someone who loves you."

She froze. "What?"

"I said, you can't stay angry with someone who loves you."

She held still as a stone as the words sunk in. *Wait a minute! What's going on here? What about Bo?* Presently she raised her eyes to his searching expression, hopeful but tentative. She gave him a long look before smiling. Her smile broadened and she began to laugh. He looked relieved.

"You see, my mystery alarm clock went off today. I'm not sure why, but I'm hoping it's telling the right time."

She brushed his cheek with her own. "Don't ever question mystery timing."

Chapter 30

An arm crossed over Megan's shoulder and a hand closed around her own. A body nestled into her curled shape from behind until they fit together like two spoons in a drawer.

She stirred slightly, hovering in the realm between sleep and consciousness. As she surfaced, waking enough to feel the warm body next to her, she wondered, was this Bo or Alastair? Opening her eyes, she focused on the hand in front of her. Short dark hairs covered a compact, muscular hand.

Of course it was Bo! How could she possibly have been unsure? She closed her eyes again, wishing to return to the comfort of sleep, but was now fully awake with the realization that the body next to her could be one man just as easily as the other. She shifted her hips, trying to get comfortable. Boy oh boy, how did she ever get herself into this? Two lovers? For Ms. Monogamous? The thought with all its complications distressed her and she turned over to find Bo to talk to.

"Hey Beauregard," she said softly. "Yoo-hoo."

His eyes opened sleepily. "Who are you yoo-hooing? I've been busy here, watching you dream."

"I see. Is that why you've had your buzz saw going?"

He pulled her closer. "I'll buzz your saw if you don't watch out."

"Is that a promise?"

"I don't promise, I deliver."

He moved her nightgown sleeve up her arm and kissed her bare shoulder. She turned and slid her leg over his hip, eager to get lost in him.

*   *   *

Bo sipped the coffee and asked, "How come it always tastes better at your apartment than at mine?"

"It's an old family secret. Leave out the Raid and you'll be surprised how good a cup of coffee can taste."

He made a face from where he sat on her living room couch, balancing a coffee cup on his thigh, lit by a stream of morning light from the window. His hair, sticking out in unruly curls, glinted purple in the sun. She stood at the kitchen counter spooning sugar into her cup and noticing how together he looked this morning in his brand new jeans with stiffly turned up cuffs and a spotless tan pullover. She couldn't remember when she'd seen him in clothes that didn't have a single fleck of paint.

"Don't speak too soon," Bo said. "You never know, after the new dishwasher is installed you may find yourself missing that certain something."

She looked up in surprise. "You're getting a dishwasher?"

He stretched his legs out leisurely. "Yeah, I decided to go for the whole kit and caboodle. As long as he's doing the cabinets and the stove I decided I might as well get a dishwasher too."

She looked at him uncomprehendingly. She knew he had been doing better financially, but did it go as far as renovating the loft? "Sounds expensive," she said.

"Yes, but Gozzi agreed the place could use a little work."

"What, Gozzi is so pleased you paid your back rent that he's putting in a new kitchen?"

He laughed. "Not quite, but he knows the zoning is changing so he's splitting the cost with me."

"That's surprising."

He sipped his coffee, raising his eyebrows over the stylized

Grecian waves that curled along the edge of the cup. "Yup, we're regular buddies now. Amazing what paying the rent will do to improve landlord relations."

The cardboard pint was empty when she turned it up to pour cream into her coffee, so she looked for another in the refrigerator. Taking it out, she glanced at Bo questioningly, still wondering where he got the money for such costly home improvements. But his gaze had shifted and he was staring with a far-away look at a museum poster on the wall picturing one of David Hockney's Los Angeles pools, the aqua water glinting with the bright southern light, the white lounge chair invitingly empty.

"So the mural job paid pretty well," she said.

He looked up quickly, as if startled. "What's that?"

"The mural job must have paid well."

"Oh, yeah, the mural job did pay pretty well. But that's not what's got me in the chips. See," he hesitated and picked at the corner tassel of a cushion. "I got lucky. You know those stocks my grandfather bought for me when I was a kid?"

"No. What stocks?"

"Oh, didn't I tell you? Yeah, my grandfather, he bought me some stocks when I was born. And they've really taken off lately. Through the roof with some new technology stuff. I sold some shares and I'm riding high."

"No kidding, Bo, that's great! What a stroke of luck!"

"I'll say. Just in the nick of time, huh?"

He smiled, but it was a wan smile, as if he had a pain in his stomach. She had noticed this since they got back together again. Although he seemed at times more relaxed than ever, his good moods alternated with periods of preoccupation; his anger had been replaced by brooding. She wished she could cheer him up.

"By the way, I got a notice from the Art Students League yesterday at the paper, a call for submissions for their spring painting contest. This year it's going to focus on realism."

"Oh?" he replied, looking somewhat uncomfortable.

"It sounds perfect for you. You could submit one of the *Portraits in the City.*"

"Yeah, maybe," he said, looking away.

She sighed inwardly and decided to let it go. Lately, any mention of art world subjects seemed to depress him. So although she had wanted to talk to him about the latest developments in the Modigliani story, it seemed best to stick to neutral topics. "Did I ever tell you your hair has purple highlights, just like in the comic strips?"

"Matches my personality," he said, swinging his leg over the arm of the couch as the phone rang. "Oh, let it ring," he said with a wave of his hand. "Who else can you want to talk to but me?"

She shot him a questioning look and reached for the phone. "Don't tell me you're getting possessive on me now . . ."

He stared at her as she answered the phone.

Hearing the voice on the other end, her heart leapt up almost at fast as she clapped it down.

"I'm such an idiot, I forgot to ask," came the self-effacing voice of Alastair. "The Lyndhurst and Lloyd's Christmas party is this Friday night and I'd like to take you, if you're free."

Oreo jumped up on the counter, tail waving like a ceremonial plume.

"I am. I'd love to," she said as she pet the cat, running her hand along the arched back and up the curving tail. Alastair apologized for not calling before and she listened to his voice, hearing more the timbre of its rise and fall than the words he was saying. They hung up shortly. She tried her best to keep her expression bland, to suppress her pleasure and uneasiness alike.

"That was brief," Bo said dryly. He stared at her fixedly.

"Just a last-minute appointment," she said, picking up the coffee thermos.

"A martini lunch, perhaps?"

She raised her eyebrows and stared unflinchingly at him. "Another cup?" Refills were available, explanations were not.

"Okay, be mysterious," he said with a shrug.

She filled his cup and set the thermos on the end table. "If you recall, you're the one who didn't want to be accountable," she said.

He stirred his coffee quietly and then set the cup on the end table. He caught her wrist and pulled her down on the couch as she cried out in surprise. Pressing her down on the cushion, he kissed her fiercely, his overnight stubble grazing like sandpaper on her chin. Then he drew back, his eyes resolute. "I don't care who you have lunch with as long as you have breakfast with me."

She brushed her hair away from her face and looked at him. "To what do I owe this assertiveness?"

He smiled. "I don't know. But I've been thinking how nice it would be to have you sit for the *Portraits in the City* series."

She sat up and considered this flattering proposal, not entirely sure whether to take him seriously. He looked at her earnestly. "Really, it'd be an honor for me, to capture your pale skin –

"Not pale, *fair*."

He rolled his eyes. "Pale, fair, what's the difference?"

"There's a big difference. Pale means drained of color, like when you're sick. Fair means light-skinned. You can be fair and still have color in your cheeks."

"Okay, okay. *Fair* skin. Really, Megan, you can be such a nit-picker."

She sipped her coffee, thinking that she was no more exacting about words than he was about brushstrokes, and a very good thing it was, too, for both of them. But she didn't want to pick a fight so she kept quiet.

"Anyway, I hope you'll consider it," he said. "And to make it easier for you to show up for your sittings . . ."

He pulled over his leather jacket from the far end of the couch. From the inside breast pocket he took out a shiny brass key and placed it on top of the cushion between them, woven with a design of a bearded unicorn sitting behind a fence in a field of flowers. She stared at the key in astonishment. "You're giving me a key *now?*"

"What's wrong with now?"

"I'm just surprised. You've always made such a point of preserving your independence."

His hand gently smoothed the fringe on the pillow's tassel. "I found out what it was like being independent from you. I'm trying to keep that from happening again. So now feels like the right time to give you a key."

She looked at his conceding expression and her heart dipped. Oh, Bo, if only your timing were better, for your painting or your heart. She picked up the key.

"Better late than never."

Chapter 31

Lizzy laughed and kicked a chunk of ice. "Yeah, it's a tough gig, I gotta admit. Two great guys courting you, I don't know how you can handle it."

The bright sun shone blindingly on the snow of the defunct West Side Highway, the elevated road packed firmly by joggers, dog-walkers and cross-country skiers. Snowy sand flats expanded westward in a pristine plateau to the choppy Hudson River. To the south the World Trade Towers rose gleaming into a porcelain blue sky.

Megan squinted over at her friend to see how she was taking all this, and Lizzy smiled back. Good. It was a little uncomfortable talking about her predicament to her mate-less friend, but she had to talk to someone. "I know. Two men. It is kind of embarrassing," she said.

"Anytime you're done with one of them you can send him my way. I have a feeling Jack Fogelman is going to turn out to be just another ship passing in the night."

"Really?"

"I think so. We have a great time when we're together, but he never says when he wants to see me next. He seems to exist only in the here and now. He's like an extended one-night stand. Which is actually an improvement from the summer, when I couldn't connect with anybody. They were either jerks I didn't want to see again or else I'd like them and they'd never call."

Megan laughed. "The dating game. It almost makes marriage look good."

"Either marriage or celibacy," said Lizzy as she scooped up a handful of snow, packed it into a ball and sent it sailing high into the air. The snowball soared in a graceful arc before disappearing over the edge of the highway. "So enjoy these doting men while you can."

"*While I can* is right. I don't know how much longer I can keep it up. And it's not that I'm really trying to keep it up, I never planned it this way in the first place."

"Frankly, I don't know how you keep them juggled."

"Alastair is busy a lot in the evenings, with auctions and social dinners and cataloguing, so I don't see him every night. And Bo is used to my running around to art events, so he doesn't question me when I'm not with him." After a second thought she added, "Not usually, anyway."

"Sounds ideal," Lizzy said with a smile.

"Maybe it sounds good, but I actually feel pretty lousy about it. I feel like I'm sneaking around on them. That's because I *am* sneaking around on them."

They laughed and walked along silently for a moment, listening to the squeak of snow under their boots. The sound annoyed Megan, like the sound of nails on a chalkboard. Or maybe it was just the conversation. She let out a long sigh.

"Luckily, the Modigliani story is heating up so I don't have too much time to worry about my love life. This gallery owner Gerhardt I'm investigating is turning out to be even sleazier than I thought. I talked to an older dealer in Monte Carlo yesterday who spoke wonderful English. He told me he knew a Reinhold Gerhardt painting dealer in Vienna before the war who was under suspicion for a long time, even though no one ever got anything solid on him. But he said that whenever artists were rediscovered and in demand, Gerhardt always seemed to be able to come up with their prime paintings. He also said Gerhardt kept a stash of American cigarettes and whiskey to trade to German soldiers for war loot. It all sounds pretty suspicious. I'll bet anything he's not clean on this Modigliani business. I just have to figure out how to flush him out."

Lizzy looked admiringly at her friend. "Yes, Jack told me you were working on the art exposé of the year."

Megan nodded eagerly, looking ahead, the day so bright and cold the snow sparkled like diamonds.

"That's what it's looking like. As long as I can keep track of whose apartment I left my latest notes in. If it weren't for my bag my belongings would be dispersed over the length of Manhattan."

Lizzy laughed and pulled her hat cuffed with circling reindeer down against the frigid gusts blowing across the highway. "It sounds complicated."

"It *is* complicated. And lately, I've been so focused on the Modigliani story I feel like I don't have enough real estate in my brain to also keep track of my nefarious scheduling: who am I having dinner with, what excuse did I give the other one, where am I sleeping . . . really, it's ridiculous."

"You could always choose one of them."

"I've tried to do that but I *can't*," Megan said vehemently, her pace quickening. "I know it sounds greedy, but I can't bring myself to give up either of them. I like them both so much, and they're so completely different. They're like opposite ends of a spectrum and my problem is that I love the whole rainbow."

Megan caught up a handful of snow and packed it into a ball. She threw it at one of the lampposts and missed.

"You could always tell them about each other. See if they would share you. It worked pretty well with *Jules and Jim*."

Megan shook her head decidedly. "Not a chance. Not these two."

Lizzy shaded her eyes against the blinding light and looked over at her friend. "So what do you think is going to happen?"

"I don't know. I really don't. I suppose eventually one of them will figure it out and then there will be a big blow up." Megan sighed deeply. "I guess that will solve the problem."

The two friends trudged along thoughtfully and Megan

swung her arms out against the open space of the elevated highway. It helped to see the snow and sky spread out in every direction, to be away from the skyscrapers that rose so high they squeezed the heavens to a distant strip of amorphous blue.

"But if you don't choose," said Lizzy, "then it's out of your hands. Anything could happen. Events have a funny way of taking on a life of their own."

Megan watched an ocean liner passing out of the harbor. "You're right. But *I* can't make a move, so fate will have to decide for me."

They squinted at the sunlight flashing off the angled surfaces of the approaching twin towers. Lizzy packed another snowball. "Come on. Let's see if we can hit the lamp post."

Lizzy threw the snowball and it smacked onto the metal pole and stuck.

Megan packed the snow as tightly as she could and hurled it at the lamppost. The ball curved up and hit the square edge of the top, where it split and the two halves fell to the ground.

The two friends' laughter carried like pealing bells across the frozen tundra.

Chapter 32

S he was getting the hang of it now.

As soon as she was aware of being awake, Megan snapped her eyes open. In the half-light of dawn objects appeared only in shades of gray; she could just make out the shape of the wardrobe and the Queen Anne chair. Okay, she was at Alastair's. She exhaled and closed her eyes.

As long as she knew where she was, she could handle it. It was that momentary displacement, the odd feeling of limbo when she wasn't sure who she was with that was so unsettling. She turned over and looked at Alastair sleeping. Her heart dipped at the sight of his straight lashes, the fringe falling flat against his honey-colored skin.

In fact, this morning she had a hunch where she was even before she opened her eyes. She could hear the ticking of the mystery clock, the faint click of its cogs and wheels in their inexorable advance. Also, the sheets were cleaner and the bed wider at Alastair's, she never found herself hanging precipitously at the edge. There was no odor of paint and turpentine lingering in the air. No, she didn't really have to open her eyes.

Oh, so was that what it boiled down to, a preference for material comfort? She turned back in the other direction and stared into the disorienting swirls of the wardrobe's burled wood, the reddish grain becoming more perceptible in the increasing light. No, that wasn't really true. The view from the top of Bo's loft bed, surrounded on all sides by the *Portraits in the City*, was always a wondrous way to start the day.

But she was having trouble juggling the two men. Yesterday she had already made plans with Bo, and when Alastair asked her for dinner and she declined, he had looked at her oddly. She made up an excuse about having to work, but he was familiar with her schedule now and knew the paper had gone to press in the afternoon. He accepted her refusal, but not without disappointment and, she thought, some suspicion. At that moment she realized the time was approaching, the jig would soon be up.

She stared at the ceiling, her feelings pulling her in different directions. How had this ever happened? She never would have gotten involved with Alastair if Bo hadn't been so flaky. But he dumped her, and Alastair had been too good to refuse. But now, with Bo's change of heart and her own suppressed feelings revived, what was she supposed to do? Her mind churned, overloaded.

Alastair stirred, moaning slightly. Oh, if you only knew, you would *really* moan. Turning over, she tried to dismiss the thought and snuggled into him.

"Umm," he murmured, pulling her closer.

"Are you awake?" she asked.

"Getting there."

Her eyes poured over the ash blonde hair falling across his closed eyes, the stubble of beard, the strawberry mark that spread over his big-boned shoulder. When she first saw the birthmark she was surprised. Not that she found it repulsive, but he looked so completely handsome in a suit, she had never imagined the rest of his body to be anything but perfect.

"You haven't moved since you fell asleep," she said. "You were out like a light last night."

"*Out like a light.* What a charming colloquialism. Does that mean you find me electric?"

"Charged, I'd say."

"I do feel quite electric, when I'm plugged into the right socket."

She laughed. "You're the only man I know who can make such bawdy comments out of my innocent remarks."

He pulled his head back and looked at her questioningly. "Oh? And how many others are in the position to be making them?"

She buried her flushing face under his chin. "I didn't mean that. I just meant I like your style."

He stroked her hair. "Sorry. It's just that I'm emotionally opposed to double sockets."

"Me too," she said with a little laugh, and then began to intently study the hairs on his chest. This was not a subject she wanted to pursue. With her fingers she combed his wiry hairs upward from the taut chest muscles to his neck, where his light skin erupted with the strawberry mark, which at the moment seemed darker than usual. She gently kissed it.

"Ugly, isn't it," he said.

"Not to me," she said and kissed it again.

His fingers traced the line of her collarbone out to her shoulder and then pulled the mustard-yellow sheet up over their heads, bathing them in a golden light.

"Come into my cocoon."

*　　*　　*

The ringing phone roused Alastair from his euphoric drowsiness. Returning to reality was not something he really wanted to do, but he disengaged his arm from under Megan's shoulder and picked up the receiver.

"Alastair, it's Catherine DuBois." She sounded rushed and nervous. "Do forgive me for calling you at home, but I tried the office and they said you wouldn't be in until tomorrow and I absolutely must talk to you today."

"Hello Catherine. Yes, I'll be up in Connecticut on an appraisal all day."

"Then you've finished the catalogue?"

"I have. It's gone to the printer."

"Oh my lord . . ."

"Why?"

Catherine's gasp was audible. When she spoke her voice was distinct but shaky. "Alastair, there's another painting I want to include in the sale."

He sat up and swung his feet onto the floor. "I'm afraid it's too late, Catherine."

"Oh, dear. Whatever shall I do? I've got to sell it, now is the time, I'm sure of it. I wonder if Sotheby's would take it."

He winced. "What painting is it, Catherine?"

"A Gauguin, a Tahiti scene."

He stood and pulled on his bathrobe, switching the phone to the other ear. "I don't remember it."

"You wouldn't. You haven't seen it. But it's an absolutely stunning image of an island woman with horses. It's rather large – about three by four feet, oil on canvas. You'll love it."

"How did this escape me?" He never would have refused a painting of this caliber. Gauguin's Tahiti scenes were done at the height of his talent and brought enormous sums in the market.

"Well," she said, clearing her throat, "It's been hard to remember everything, Alastair, with my affairs in such disorder. But you wouldn't believe what's been squirreled away out here in East Hampton over the years. I was cleaning the house out and, lo and behold, there it was. You did tell me I had until the eleventh hour."

"Yes, but it's the twelfth hour now."

"Couldn't you just squeeze it in?" she pleaded.

He didn't answer, his thoughts were spinning. How could she have forgotten a painting like this? And now that it was so late, how could he give it the attention it deserved?

"I'll call the printer this morning and see what he can do. It's really a matter of getting the painting properly cataloged and photographed, and whether he can still fit it in. Can you bring it in today?"

"I can't, I'm out here for my niece's wedding this afternoon. But I can bring it in tomorrow morning."

"I won't be here. I'm flying to London tonight. I have a filming with the BBC tomorrow."

"Can't someone else take care of it?"

He hesitated. How could he include a painting in his sale he hadn't seen? This went completely against his grain, totally defied his training of making sure everything in the sale was right. But Catherine's nerves sounded so frayed, he couldn't risk refusing. Knowing her, she *would* take the painting up to Sotheby's.

"Don't you have some other painting expert there who can catalogue it? I've got the provenance papers, it seems straightforward enough."

"All right, Catherine. But be sure it's here tomorrow and see that Colin gets it."

She sighed with relief. "Thank you, Alastair, I knew I could count on you."

He hung up. "For God's sake," he said, running his hands through his hair and sitting down on the bed.

Megan looked at him curiously. She raised her hand and touched his strawberry mark, now a deep scarlet.

He glanced at her inquiring look. "Yes, it turns brighter when I'm upset."

He explained Catherine's reason for calling and Megan asked why the painting was so important to include. He raised his hands and quivered them in the air.

"She says, *'Its time is now.'*" He dropped his arms and gave her a skeptical look. "Her astrologer probably put her up to it. Normally I wouldn't mind, but it's just that it's so late now, we're paying a hefty rush premium to the printer as it is." He looked away. "And I'll have to let Colin catalogue it. But if the painting is as good as it sounds it will be a real gem to have, one of the most expensive in the sale."

"Can't turn that down," she said with a grin.

He brushed a stray lock of hair away from her face. "That's not the only reason I'm taking it. It's because Catherine has been very jumpy lately and today she sounds like she's right on the edge, ready to go off the deep end. I don't trust her. I can't have her canceling the sale on me."

"Do you really think she'd do that?

"If it's *in the stars*, she just might."

The mystery clock struck the hour, its silvery chimes running up and down the scale. Megan widened her eyes in mock alarm. "Oooo. A sign from the mystery clock. Maybe Catherine is right, this is the time."

He smiled. What a wonderful woman, she could always make a situation seem better, even one like this that was a royal pain in the ass. He stroked his fingers down her soft cheek and she blinked slowly and leaned into his hand. Sitting there with her crystalline green eyes looking calmly into his, he suddenly felt an intense identification with her, as if he were staring at himself.

"When are you going to tell me how the mystery clock works?" she asked.

"I'm waiting for you to guess. Then I'll give you a prize."

"What's the prize?"

"Can't say."

"Ahh. A double mystery."

He looked at her good-humored face, her auburn hair set off by the warm walnut wood of the bed's headboard, and wished they didn't have to get up at all. "I can't wait to take you to the Christmas party tonight. I quite honestly don't know how I'm going to manage in London without you."

Chapter 33

B o stood away from the easel and studied the portrait of Paddy. Chin up, gaze direct, the soft sheen of his silvery beard set against the dull sepia-brown coat, Paddy's face reflected the full measure of his dignity.

As envisioned, he'd placed Paddy in the wing chair at the entrance to the Metropolitan Museum of Art. In the background, the museum's classical columns rose on either side, massive bulwarks of established culture. He liked the confrontational suggestion: Art of the ages, what did it take to qualify? Being a Nefertiti or a Virgin Mary wasn't necessary anymore although, with some of the curators he'd met, it probably wouldn't hurt. But if Carravagio's commoners could make the grade, why not Paddy?

In the shortened winter afternoons he plugged away at forgeries for Gerhardt, since nothing but natural light would do for Impressionist and Post-Impressionist styles. That left few daylight hours for working on Paddy's portrait, so he'd broken his rule and sat Paddy under the florescent light. At first he'd hated the effect, but now, surprisingly, he found himself drawn to it. With the cool, blue-white light the image took on a surreal quality, and inspired him to fool around with the rest of it, to follow the feeling that the painting was not quite what it seemed. This altered the style from the other portraits in the series, but at this point he saw no reason not to. Since he was only painting them for himself, what did it matter?

Lately he had come to terms with the fact that he wasn't a recognized artist and might never be. And it was probably just as well. To hell with all those boring cocktail parties and dinners – he'd never be any good at them, anyhow. Knowing him, he'd end up saying the wrong thing to the wrong person, insulting the curator or collector who was about to take an interest in his work. And so what? He was a painter, not a socialite.

The florescent lighting lent an eerie silver-gray cast to Paddy and the chair; they appeared to be floating in front of the museum like an apparition. Was Paddy really there, or did he just appear to be there, a milkweed wish carried on the wind, hovering only momentarily?

The odd effect seemed fitting. As it grew on him he began to see other possibilities, and in a moment of inspiration added some extravagant architectural elements to the museum, borrowed from post-Renaissance Italy. He painted the column's capitals upside down, and instead of placing the pediments above the windows, he put them below, inverted. These outlandish elements added to the feeling of displacement.

But now he was done; he would add nothing more. He didn't want to steep his consciousness in any further strangeness, not with the bizarre visions that had been appearing to him lately. They were unlike anything he'd ever experienced: his own hands, severed; his eyes, with razors slicing through them. He'd be doing something mindless, like cleaning brushes, and the terrible images would flash across his mind's eye, unannounced, unprovoked. Whenever it happened he made a point of changing his activity, of concentrating on a specific task to try to distract himself, but it didn't seem to help. They came anyway. It was always his eyes or his hands, being violently dismembered.

Paddy's portrait sat on the easel, still wet from the morning's work. It was almost finished, with just a little left to do on the background, and if he made no changes when Paddy came next it would be ready for varnishing. The portrait was out because Megan was coming for lunch to celebrate the new kitchen. Although he'd had to practically beg to get her to come, she said she was so busy. Which was pretty ironic, really. Just when he was feeling needy, wanting her around to steady him, she was often unavailable. Half the time she couldn't make it, and when she did, her mind frequently seemed elsewhere. Her distance made him wonder if perhaps she had some suspicions of the forgeries; sometimes her comments seemed fraught with double meanings, to hint at nefarious doings on his part. And when she complimented him, commending his diligence, praising the integrity of his work, it was all he could do to look her in the face.

The buzzer rang. Luckily, even though she had a key, she always buzzed first, probably to save herself walking up the four flights if he weren't home. He put down the paint tube and buzzed her in, then looked quickly around the loft. Good thing those stairs were long flights.

Leaning up against the wall, varnish drying, sat two paintings: his first large oil forgeries. Gerhardt had encouraged him, said he was ready for the big time, and justified the greater risk of scrutiny with the substantially higher profits. And why the hell not, Bo figured. As long as he was breaking the law he might as well make it worth his while. And he had to admit, the money felt good. He liked having new paints, new clothes, a new loft. Plus, he told himself, the bigger his profit the sooner he would accumulate his nest egg and could be done with the nasty business. Although he'd done some refiguring, and the amount he would need to retire was larger than he'd first thought. After all, if he was going to be financially independent, it might as well be in style.

He picked up an oil after Degas of dancers stretching in a studio, and next to it a landscape Gerhardt requested specifically, Mont Sainte-Victoire à la Cezanne. This had been particularly difficult to work on, as Bo had always regarded Cezanne as the paramount modern art authority, in a class of his own, a painter's painter. How could a disciple forge an idol's work? What kind of Judas was he? Or maybe this was the ultimate compliment, wasn't that what they said about imitation? But duplicating the shelving planes of Cezanne's purple mountain in the bright light of Provence only made him feel like the ultimate charlatan, a painter's putz.

He carried the paintings to the closet. As he slid them swiftly into the top rack, he saw his own eyeball, a blade slicing cleanly through the iris. He shut the closet door. No. Go away.

He ran his hand across the top of the door jamb, feeling for the key, but it wasn't there. Damn. Where had he put it? He checked his pockets – empty. His pulse quickened as he heard Megan's footsteps approaching. He pushed securely on the closed closet door. It would be okay; she never went in there anyway.

* * *

Megan trudged up the last few steps, her bag weighing on her shoulder as if she were climbing Mt. Everest. She was carrying yesterday's clothes from staying over at Alastair's, a hairdryer, and a pair of shoes from the office she wanted to wear to the Lyndhurst and Lloyd's Christmas party that night. She wasn't crazy about coming to Bo's for lunch because she felt pressured to follow up on a new lead that might link Gerhardt with a painting which, when recently donated by the owner's estate to the Boston Museum of Fine Arts, was turned away as a forgery. But Bo sounded so eager for her to come, she couldn't turn him down.

She pushed open the door to see him dabbing with a brush at the portrait of Paddy, which lay flat on the spool table. He dropped the brush as she entered.

"Hey peach," he said and gave her a long hug, pressing her body to his as if he wanted them to fuse. "You're early," he said after a moment.

"You're still working."

He sighed with mock resignation. "Gotta do something to fill up my hours away from you."

She smiled and hung her coat on the hook. These recent avowals of his were amusing; maybe she should have been less available before. She swung her bag on to the couch and it hit the wooden arm with a clunk.

"What was that?" he asked.

She looked warily at him. "Just some shoes I need for tonight."

"I think your bag has gotten even bigger lately, if that's possible. Maybe you should mount it on wheels, like a mobile home."

She ignored this remark and walked over to the portrait of Paddy. Her face lit up as she looked at the painting.

"Wow, Bo, it's really come together. Are you done?"

"Pretty much. I'm just finishing the surface texture of the building. See, I can get the variegated tone of the stone like this." Picking up the fat badger blender brush, he tapped its dry bristles on the wet paint, blending the different tones of orangey-brown and sandy-beige into a fine stipple. "Burnt sienna is such a great pigment. Mixed with white, it has an incredible range of hue."

Megan smiled and kept looking. "I like the way you've changed the architectural elements."

"Ah, yes."

"It has a disconcerting effect on first glance. Something's not right but you don't know exactly what."

"*What's wrong with this picture?*"

"Exactly. 20th Century Mannerism." She continued looking. "It's really terrific, Bo. Fresh, original, and beautifully painted."

He smiled appreciatively; she didn't give out high praise often. She stared thoughtfully at the picture. "You've made Paddy look noble."

"I just painted what I saw."

She crossed her arms and looked intently at the portrait, trying to see if this were true. To her, Paddy always looked like a down-and-out street person, but the dignity staring out of the canvas was impossible to deny.

"It's come a long way since I last saw it," she finally said. "Oh, which reminds me, I think I left my green sweater here. Have you seen it?"

He put the brush down and looked around the loft. "Yes, I did see it somewhere."

The loft was so big it was often hard to find things. She looked up on the loft bed, under the couch cushions, in the laundry box, with no luck. She wanted this sweater back because it was the only one big enough to keep her warm sitting around the drafty newsroom. She was sure she left it in the loft because she remembered the bottom button had raveled loose and she'd stowed it away in the pocket.

He looked under the couch. "I tried to get things out of the way while the workmen were here."

She looked through the clothes hanging on the wall rack, but it wasn't there. She glanced around the big room and stopped at the closed closet door. "Maybe you hung it in the closet," she said.

"No, I didn't," he answered decidedly. "Your sweater's not in there."

He said it with such certainty, she shrugged and looked through the laundry box. He went to the dresser and rooted quickly through the drawers, and then began pulling back the quilt on the loft bed.

"It's not up there, I already looked," she said, walking towards the closet. "I'll just take a look in here, maybe you forgot."

He moved faster than she'd ever seen, sliding instantly across the floor in front of her. His eyes were intense, forceful. "I'm telling you, it's not in there."

"What's the harm in looking?" she said, reaching for the doorknob. "It doesn't seem to be anywhere else."

His hand slammed against the door. "No!"

She stepped back as he looked wildly around the room.

"There it is," he said, bounding towards the shelves where a telltale sleeve hung down. Sweat beading along his forehead, he handed her the sweater with a look of great relief.

"What on earth has gotten into you?" she asked in bewilderment.

He forced a laugh. "Nothing. It's just that I cleared the clothes out of the closet to keep work in there and I don't want to disturb it."

She shook her head. Right, as if she were going to disturb it. "You'd think you were hiding away masterpieces."

He looked at her sharply.

"Not that your work isn't masterpiece quality," she added hastily, "I mean, you never know what they'll be worth some day."

He took a big breath. "No, you never know."

He took her hand and led her back towards the kitchen, telling her he had a surprise for her. She walked quietly. Bo – what a madman. Relaxed one minute, hyper the next. Why was he so erratic, now that things were looking up for him?

Her thoughts were interrupted as she looked ahead and saw the back of the loft, a cooly-lit contemporary kitchen. Three pool-table style lights with green shades hung above an oak-topped island. A six-burner gas stove sat in the middle of the wall next to a built-in dishwasher on one side and a full-sized refrigerator on the other.

She looked around in wonder. "Bo, I can't believe you!"

The island housed a shining chrome sink, next to which sat a platter of freshly shucked oysters. He picked one up and tipped the shell towards her. The slithery oyster slid straight off and into her mouth.

She gulped and laughed. "I think it went down whole."

He grinned and turned the barnacle-encrusted shell over in his hand. "I picked these out this morning on South Street – the biggest, fattest ones they had. I wanted to get something special to inaugurate the kitchen with you."

She smiled. He really could be sweet. She slid another oyster into her mouth and watched as he began to make the pasta. He lifted out a big pot from the cupboard under the island and filled it. The running water sparkled in the overhead lights, the curved chrome faucet gleamed. She looked around and saw there was even a new phone mounted on the side of a cabinet. How surprising, how incongruous. Bo – a well-heeled artist? Landed gentry? The notion was jarring. "What a great job," she said.

"Yes. Now all I have to do is pay for it."

"It's not paid for?"

"Not yet. That's how I know I'm coming up in the world. I'm in debt, but it's acceptable now, it's called a home improvement loan."

She laughed and turned the oyster shell over in her hands, inspecting the two divergent sides. The rough exterior looked like it came from the dark side of the moon with its shadowy blues and grays, while the inside shone, as smooth and lustrous as mother of pearl.

He began chopping garlic and she slid another oyster down her throat. What a treat, they'd never eaten so well. The phone rang and he wiped his hands on his jeans and answered it. She picked up another oyster and half-listened to his conversation, still trying to reconcile these new changes with the old Bo.

"Not bad, I'm kind of busy at the moment." Pause. "But it's not ready."

She picked at the barnacles on the outside of the oyster shell but couldn't dislodge them. He turned his back to her and kept talking.

"What? What do you mean I have to? Is this an ultimatum?" His voice turned tense. "All right, calm down. I'll do it. I'll see you tonight."

He hung up and glanced furtively at her.

"What's the matter?" she asked.

"Oh, nothing. Just an anxious buyer. Wants a painting from me that I haven't finished yet."

"Well, isn't that great! It's nice to be in demand."

"I guess. But I'm going to have to hurry up this lunch and kick you out of here because I really have to rally this afternoon.'"

She looked at his stressed expression and wondered what could be so pressing. "Who is it for?" she asked.

"No one you know. Someone I met last month when you weren't around."

She dropped the oyster shell with a clunk. "Oh, I get it. What's her name?"

He laughed feebly. "No, Megan, it's nothing like that. It's a consignment I'm committed to. I have to finish it, I can't afford to lose the job."

He sounded so stressed that she decided to say nothing more. She wasn't exactly in a position to be grilling him about whether he was seeing someone else. But she wouldn't be totally surprised if he were. Come to think of it, maybe he freaked out about the closet because some other woman's clothes were hanging in there.

Really, how could he be so capricious, begging her to come to lunch and then handing her her hat as soon as she got there? What a flimsy excuse, that someone needed a painting *immediately*, as if any buyer were in such a hurry. What could be so urgent? Would the wall space for the painting disappear? Did he really expect her to believe that?

She watched as he chopped the garlic vigorously. And as she looked she noticed something disturbing, a quality in his face she'd never seen before. He looked haunted. Clearly something more was bothering him than a rushed request for a painting. A sinking feeling passed through her. Yes, he must be seeing someone else.

"Sure," she said. "I certainly wouldn't want to stop you from making a sale."

Chapter 34

A lastair sat down at his desk, pulled the scarf off his neck and let out a long sigh. All right. Just one more picture. He thought he'd put the DuBois catalogue to bed, that this fabulous sale was finally on its way to clients around the world. But first he had to arrange the inclusion of Catherine's Gauguin in the sale without missing his London shooting with the BBC. On returning, he would relish spreading out the collection before the art world like a royal flush.

"Don't get too comfortable there," said Colin as he walked in the office. "You've got a party to go to."

"Ah, Colin," Alastair said, sitting up. "Just the man I wanted to see."

"Yes?"

"I've got a favor to ask of you."

"Ask away."

Alastair explained about Catherine bringing in one last painting which the printer had agreed to squeeze in if he got everything by noon tomorrow, including the negative the photographer was going to shoot in the morning. He spoke eagerly, not trying to hide his enthusiasm.

"If Catherine is describing it accurately, it should be one of the best lots in the sale, a late Gauguin from Tahiti."

Colin raised his eyebrows. "That sounds like a prize." He picked up the Lyndhurst and Lloyd's Upcoming Sales brochure whose cover pictured a lot from the 19th Century American

Painting sale. *Coming Storm* by Martin Johnson Heade depicted a cove with lapping waves and a stormy sky. Tapering piles of stones enclosed the beach with slender arms, a questionable shield against the approaching white caps and black-bottomed clouds.

"The problem is," continued Alastair, "I'm taking the night flight to London tonight after the party, so I was wondering if you could take in the painting and catalogue it for me."

Colin peered closely at the brochure cover. "Look at this foolish thing. You'd think they could get the colors right."

Alastair watched him. Wouldn't you know it, the one time he really needed some help. Damned if he'd ever ask again.

Colin looked up from the catalogue, his eyebrows innocently raised.

"Sorry, Alastair, what's that? What would you like?"

Alastair picked up a pencil and tapped it against the desk. "If you could take in and catalogue Mrs. DuBois's painting in the morning."

Colin pursed his lips and nodded. "I'll be in and out tomorrow, but I should think we could manage that."

"Don't go too high on the estimate. She wants to sell it."

"Not to worry. Now, what is it you're off to London for?" Colin asked, thumbing through the brochure.

"To host the BBC special on Turner."

"Of course, how could I forget."

Colin turned back to the cover and stared at it again. "Blasted thing."

"Thank you Colin, I appreciate it."

Colin looked up and beamed brightly. "Least I can do."

Alastair picked up a stray pencil and dropped it in the holder. Good old Colin, never one to let go of a rivalry, not even when it would serve him well.

The strained atmosphere was broken by Reginald, who banged through the door carrying several plastic-sheathed garment bags, his ruddy cheeks glowing from the cold.

"Hello. Bloody costumes, I've dragged them all the way from Broadway."

"Who's using those?" Alastair asked as Reginald hung the bulky garments on the door.

"Mr. Greaves sent me to get them, they're for the skits tonight."

"Jolly good, I'm all for skits," Alastair said.

"I'm in one myself," Reginald said, smiling mischievously.

"You're not?" Colin asked Alastair.

"They asked me, but I didn't feel I should desert my date."

Colin looked up with interest. "A date, eh? Who's the lucky lady?"

Alastair hesitated before answering. "Megan Trico."

"Oh really?" Colin asked, his voice rising an octave. "I didn't know you two were dating. A couple now, are you?"

Alastair smiled. "I guess you could say that."

Colin nodded thoughtfully as the phone rang. As he reached for it he looked at Alastair. "She is rather pretty. And the social gaps are not such a problem anymore. Not over here, anyway."

*　　*　　*

The entrance to Lyndhurst and Lloyd's was swaged with festive greenery; ropes of spruce and hemlock trimmed with holly and wintergreen adorned the doorway. As Megan approached she spotted Alastair sitting in the lobby under a wreath. When the doorman ushered her in Alastair stood and welcomed her with raised arms. "Hello darling. I'm so glad to see you."

He hugged her and kissed her cheek. "Can I take your coat? You look lovely."

She laughed. "Really, Alastair. Such a public display of affection!"

He kissed her again. "I could blame it on the mistletoe. But it's actually that I'm honored to have you as my guest tonight."

He took her by the elbow and lead her down the hallway lined with an upcoming sale of Persian miniatures, immaculately painted in glorious colors like exotic birds, beckoning viewers into their fairy-tale worlds. But tonight Alastair had no time to stop; he hastened her along the hallway and up the few stairs into the main auction room.

Cleared of chairs, the enormous room was filled with dinner tables and milling staff members and their guests. Tribal art figures, masks, shields and spears had been moved against the walls. Alastair tucked Megan's hand inside the crook of his arm and made the rounds, eager to introduce her to everyone. He was as gracious as could be and everyone seemed glad to meet her.

"You're making me feel like queen for a day," she said when they were finally alone for a moment.

"You should feel like queen for a lifetime," he said, his face full of affection as he covered her hand with his own. A waiter approached with a tray of fizzing champagne flutes, and to Megan the wine tasted like Christmas itself: sweet, effervescent and intoxicating. Her bare shoulders, milky and supple above the spaghetti straps of the midnight blue evening dress, felt warm as toast as Alastair's hand rested lightly on one of them.

"Let's say hello to Hugh," she said as she spotted him standing awkwardly next to a Benin bronze bust of a woman with a dozen necklaces circling tightly around her throat.

"If you like."

A smile played around Hugh's mouth as Megan offered her hand. He shook it and then nodded at the Benin bronze. "This here's my date for the evening. You know I always go for the natural girls." He chuckled throatily.

"You've chosen one of the oldest and finest, I'd say," said Alastair. "They've been doing bronze casting in Benin since the 12th century."

"Just the thing, then, since I'm a bit of an Old Master myself."

He smiled shyly at Megan, smoothed the thin layer of hair over his bald top, and gulped the last of his drink.

Colin appeared and inclined his head towards Megan with a solicitous smile. "What a nice surprise," he said.

"Hello Colin, Merry Christmas," Megan said.

"And Merry Christmas to you. Although what a shame you two will be separated at the holiday season," Colin said with concern. "I'm surprised Alastair's not taking you with him."

Alastair glared at him.

"I don't really have the time off," she said. "The newspaper is so busy this time of year."

The thought that he never asked her flashed across her mind.

Colin raised his glass in a toast. "Cheers. A very merry to everyone, wherever we are, whomever we're with."

At dinner Alastair sat Megan at a table between himself and Ivan Yoblonsky, the expert in Russian works of art. Ivan kept his hand tightly clasped around a glass of vodka, which he sipped frequently. Intermittently he hummed a tune that she vaguely recognized as *The Song of the Volga Boatman*.

Alastair rubbed her thigh under the table. "You know I'm going to miss you dreadfully. Even though I'm only going for a week, from here it seems like an eternity."

He took her hand and she looked at his tender expression and agreed.

"I wish you were coming with me."

She laughed. "I might have if you'd asked me."

"I should have. I wasn't thinking. I've really had my hands full, and I'm going to be flat out filming that BBC show while I'm there. Plus, things with us have happened so quickly . . ."

He looked at her remorsefully.

"It's okay."

"Next time," he said earnestly.

As the meal was served and the wine poured, spirits rose in the room until it was filled with merriment. In between the lively conversation, a realization came over Megan. The end of December was approaching, advancing hands would soon ring in the new year; it suddenly struck her that her coach might soon turn to a pumpkin, leaving her stranded at the roadside, mice scurrying away. Fate could only be allowed to play so big a part; she was not willing to stand by and allow for self-destruction.

Alastair. She would have to choose Alastair. He was so adoring, so enjoyable, so *stable*, the alternative would be crazy. Alastair was not subject to fits of rancor, he had never broken up with her, he wasn't incapable of saying he loved her, he didn't get mysterious phone calls that he wouldn't explain. And she was as sure as could be that he wasn't seeing anyone else. Yes, it was time for chance to take its bow and cede the stage.

Ivan raised his glass and pronounced to no one in particular, "One hundred years ago on my grandfather's estate you would all have been serfs!"

Reginald rolled his eyes from across the table and Megan hid her smile by taking another bite of the Lobster Thermidor; the sauce was perfect. Ivan seemed to want some attention so she asked him about life in the Soviet Union. He treated her to an enthusiastic monologue on the wonders of Novgorod, its gilded onion domes, sacred icons, mosaics of fierce and holy deities.

While dessert was being served Reginald set up a microphone at the open end of the room and the skits began. The head of the Silver department did imitations of Margaret Thatcher, the expert in Art Nouveau and Art Deco staged reenactments from Monty Python, and Roger Greaves played Thisby from *A Midsummer's Night Dream.*

Megan leaned over to Alastair and said, "It's wonderful to see all these proper people letting their hair down."

He smiled and put his arm around the back of her chair. "We're not complete stiffs, not all the time, anyway."

Next came Hugh's turn. Reginald had set up a folding card table, which Hugh staggered up to carrying the large painting of sheep in a field.

"Are we going to have a lecture?" Megan asked.

"I don't know. He's had that sheep picture hanging in his warehouse for months now."

Hugh cleared his throat ceremoniously and tapped on the painting with a wooden pointer. "Here we have an absolute masterpiece from the 18th Century Dutch school," he announced exuberantly. His cheeks were flushed, his speech slightly slurred. "But no picture is perfect, and this one lacks a sense of depth. Nothing that can't be fixed, however." From his pocket he pulled a can of aerosol shaving cream. "For instance, these sheep here could use a bit more volume."

Alastair sat up straight. "Oh no."

Raising the can to the canvas, Hugh squirted shaving cream over the bodies of the sheep, the creamy lather rising in mounds off the surface of the canvas. He continued spraying enthusiastically, his hair lifting off the top of his head with each vigorous squirt. All the while he kept talking, pointing out the problems of the painting. When every sheep was covered he turned to the audience.

"Being highly evolved as we are, I think you'll all agree that the kindest thing we can really do for this poor picture is to put it out of its misery. So with the help of my trusty assistant Reginald, who can always be counted on to use his head – "

Hugh swung the painting up in the air and brought it crashing down over Reginald's head. The canvas tore with a resounding rip. Reginald stood grimacing, the lopsided triangles of canvas rising stiffly from his shoulders.

Hugh and Reginald both turned towards the tables and began to sing.

"*All we like sheep, have gone astray . . .*"

Chapter 35

The archives at the Museum of Modern Art reminded Megan of her grandfather's study, the rich smell of leather preservative mixed with a faint odor of mothballs. The room was lined on one side with wooden file drawers and on the other with shelves housing volumes of books, manuscripts and catalogues from a host of 20th century New York exhibitions. At the end of the room, under a window, an old radiator clanked and rattled with the effort of distributing heat.

Alice Beatty carried a pile of catalogues to the worn oak table. Her hands, skin as papery as velum, set the volumes upright on the table, lining up the bottoms before laying them in a trim, flat stack.

"These are all our exhibition catalogues from 1936. You sit right here and help yourself and I'll be in the next room if you need anything."

She looked from the stack to Megan, as if assuring herself that the 50-year-old booklets, dating from exhibitions she might have seen herself, were in good hands, and then bustled out, as neat and tidy as Mrs. Tittlemouse.

Megan had had no trouble gaining admittance to the MoMA archives as a reporter. In fact, she was surprised at the scanty security, but Ms. Beatty had explained that the policy at MoMA was to allow researchers as much access to the archival documents as possible. With a twinkle in her eye she said, "We're happy to help everyone understand that New York is the capital of the art world."

Megan turned through the various catalogues, sheathed in plastic to prevent damage, each dated 1936 on the cover. She smiled; there was nothing like efficient records for checking wild claims. Okay, Sotheby's, let's see if your provenance is correct, let's try to verify the information supplied by the grand vizier Gerhardt. And when it could not be corroborated, they could decide which one of them would return the Modigliani to Senor Calebresi.

She looked through several catalogues with no luck, then thumbed through the stack to see if any others looked more likely: near the bottom was *African Influences in Modern Art: An Exhibition of Paintings and Sculpture.* It was in remarkably good condition, the pages only slightly yellowed. Original photographs illustrated the works included, tucked into triangular corner pockets. She began with the first page, turning carefully past art by Picasso, Giacomitti, Matisse, Brancusi, Arp. With each page turned she felt she was advancing the Calebresi case, until suddenly, with a shock of recognition, she saw it. There it was, staring right out at her, ethereal as ever, the *Abruzzi Daughter.* In clear Times New Roman font below was listed the title, artist, and lending source: *The Garnier Collection, Paris.*

Megan sat back in the chair, stunned. How could this possibly be? Jesus . . . were all her deductions wrong? She suddenly felt that she'd been under some strange influence. Consul Cellucci, Senor Calebresi, were they in league in a spurious claim? Had she been duped by them both? Or played for a pawn in some larger game?

She turned back to the *Abruzzi Daughter* again, staring so long that when she looked up she saw the complementary colors on the white wall. There was no question that this was the same painting. It was just hard to accept. Amazing, how wrong-headed she could have been. And to think that she had been about to falsely accuse Gerhardt, to say nothing of

Sotheby's. She pushed back her chair, which squeaked loudly on the wooden floor, walked over to the window and stood staring out across 53rd Street with her hands in her pockets. So much for her exposé. So much for saving her career.

Alice Beatty poked her head around the corner and asked, "Are you done with those, miss? And if you wouldn't mind, we ask all our visitors to log the references they've used. She disappeared and came back with a large green ledger, which she set open on the table. Megan picked up her pen in a daze, for what did any of it matter, now, and began to fill in the data. As she finished, she glanced at the *Name* column, at the true scholars who had come before her. Suddenly a line jumped out from the topmost row: Reinhold Gerhardt. She followed her eye along the row and read the listing under *Reference*.

Alice Beatty bustled back in, offering help as if it were a cup of tea.

"Is there anything else I can get for you, miss?"

"No, no thanks. I see from the log, though, that the last person to look at this particular catalogue was a colleague of mine, Mr. Gerhardt."

Ms. Beatty's eyes lit up. "Oh you know Mr. Gerhardt, do you? Such a lovely man. He's been a regular visitor here for years. He's quite a scholar, he'll be in here for hours. And *so* thoughtful. He always brings me a nice pen. They used to be the cutest little palm tree pens when he was down in Florida, but now he brings Parkers." She looked decidedly at Megan. "They're the best, you know. Now, are you all done here?"

"I'm not quite done with this catalogue, thank you."

Megan looked once more at the date of Gerhardt's visit in the logbook – he'd taken the book out in August, a month before the Sotheby's sale in London. What a coincidence.

She turned once more to the catalogue as Ms. Beatty spirited the logbook back to the other room. In examining the triangular pockets holding the corners of the *Abruzzi Daughter* photograph, one came loose. There appeared to be two kinds of glue, one yellow and crusty, the other smooth and white, much like Elmer's glue when dry. She checked the font of the Modigliani description carefully: the letters were identical to the print throughout the catalogue. But that would be no great trick to duplicate since Times New Roman was one of the oldest fonts in printing.

She turned the book up on its spine and saw that it was composed of a dozen or so gatherings. The page the *Abruzzi Daughter* appeared on was at the center of the gathering, where the threads stitching the pages together were visible. The thread was white, much brighter than the yellowed stitching at the top of the spine, or in the middle of the other gatherings. She counted the pages of the gatherings. They all had four leaves, except for the one in which the Modigliani appeared, which had five. The page holding the illustration was the same off-white shade as the others, but when she held the page up to the light of the window, she saw that the pattern of fiber in the paper was not nearly as dense.

So, he *was* clever, wasn't he. He'd sewn in a new sheet of paper, making two new pages and room for the *Abruzzi Daughter*, then restiched and reglued the binding. And added a few other bogus paintings to the additional pages in the process.

Megan sat staring at the serene eyes of the Modigliani. The old radiator hissed with a release of steam. The evidence might be circumstantial, but it was enough for her. But would it constitute conclusive proof for the authorities, was it beyond a reasonable doubt?

She stood and called for Ms. Beatty, who appeared immediately, her cheerful face glad to be of service.

"Ms. Beatty, I'd like to show you something."

Chapter 36

"Thanks so much for coming over, I know it will make a splendid show," said the producer as he saw Alastair out of the London BBC studio.

Alastair smiled and shook his hand. "My pleasure. I'd love a copy of the tape when you've finished."

"Absolutely. Cheerio."

Alastair turned out of the flagstone entrance and walked along the wrought iron fence. What a treat it had been filming the Turner special, exploring the essence of the great painter and his work. He held his folded London Times to flap along the vertical iron bars, grateful the anticlimax he might have felt was totally absent due to the anticipation of the event to come: the indisputably *Fine and Important collection of Modern Paintings of Mr. and Mrs. Edwin DuBois.* He welcomed returning to New York tomorrow like a spring rain, especially since along with the promise of the auction was an equally promising Megan.

Megan. Her image floated into his mind and he let it hover there: soft, lovely, luscious Megan. He reached the cross street and, looking to his left, stepped off the curb. A horn blared from the other direction and a car swerved around him as he hopped back on the sidewalk. Good God, he looked the wrong way. He'd been away longer than he realized.

Watching more carefully, he made his way through London's back streets – cleaner, smaller-scaled and more uniformly handsome than Manhattan's – to the West End offices of Lyndhurst and Lloyd's. Reaching the stately Neoclassical building, he took the front steps two at a time. The doorman, expressionless as those at Buckingham Palace, opened the door and Alastair entered the front hall, its stone floor and lofty coffered ceiling reminiscent of his dining hall at Oxford.

Two colleagues standing at the front desk hailed him.

"How about a drink before you're off?" asked Jeremy, an old school friend from Christ Church College.

"Love to. Let me just check the telex."

"How are you getting on over there?" asked Ian.

"Not badly," Alastair said with a grin. "I'm surviving."

"Looks like more than that, I'd say," said Jeremy. "I haven't seen you glowing like this since you and Amanda went punting up the Cherwell together."

Alastair smiled and shifted the newspaper to the other arm while his friends looked at him curiously.

"Cat got the canary, it looks like," Ian said.

Alastair laughed but didn't answer.

A man approached them. Tall with rounded shoulders and a rug-like head of hair, his bulbous nose tilted slightly upward. The three younger men straightened up as the older man stopped in front of them.

"Cavendish, nice to see you," the older man said.

"Hello Mr. Brompton, very nice to see you, sir," said Alastair.

"How are you making out over in the outpost?"

"Very well indeed, thank you."

"I've had some good reports. By the way, I understand an urgent phone call came through from Greaves in New York. You're to ring him back. I'd see to it straight away if I were you."

"Yes, sir, I shall. Directly."

Alastair took his leave and looked at his watch: 4:30. That made it 11:30 AM, New York time. Greaves should be in his office. He hurried up the wide stairwell bustling with people coming out of an antiquarian books auction. He nipped past the small groups talking quietly outside the double doors of the sales room, wondering what Greaves called about and why he would be ringing up instead of telexing. He turned past the salesroom and down a labyrinth of narrow corridors, doors closed beneath reticulated pediments. He found his old office empty, the secretary gone home.

He sat down at the desk and dialed the New York office. An overseas operator came on.

"I'm sorry, all lines are engaged, please stand by and I'll ring you back."

He hung up, sat back in the chair and looked around the office. Not much had changed – an asparagus plant hanging in the window, a poster of Monet's *Notre Dame* reduced to light reflections, a walnut bracket clock ticking from atop a bookcase. But somehow the room smelled musty and the lights weren't bright enough. The effect was gloomy and uninviting. He sat distractedly, tapping a ruler against a stained ink blotter.

The phone rang and he jumped.

"Ringing through to New York for you," said the overseas operator.

"Lyndhurst and Lloyd's," came the muted receptionist's voice.

"Roger Greaves, please."

"That line is busy."

"It's Alastair Cavendish here, I'll wait."

"Oh, Mr. Cavendish, calling from England? I'd love to go to London, see the changing of the guard and all."

"Yes, it's worth a trip. Can you try Mr. Greaves again please?"

"Sure, sure."

The phone clicked and Greaves' voice came over the line. His genial tone turned severe as soon as Alastair identified himself. "About time. I've been looking for you. You're in quite a jam, young man."

Alastair's throat tightened. "What is it?"

"If you were in New York I wouldn't have to tell you. The story is all over the morning newspapers. The prize lot in the DuBois collection is a fake."

Alastair dropped the ruler and sat bolt upright. "What!?"

"Yes. It's staring right out of our advertisement in *The New York Times*."

"I'm sorry, but I don't know what you're talking about," said Alastair, his body turning rigid with the shock.

"Don't be so clueless, Cavendish," Greaves snapped. "The Gauguin, the Tahiti scene. Terrence Young up at Sotheby's has declared it a fake because it's dated 1889 and Gauguin didn't go to Tahiti until 1891!"

His voice had gotten louder and louder until he was shouting.

"Oh my God," Alastair said, covering his face with his hand.

"You'd better start praying or come up with a damned good explanation."

"But I haven't even seen the picture," Alastair said weakly.

"Then it has no business in your sale!"

"Colin took it in. Reginald probably helped," he said, searching wildly for an explanation.

"I don't care if your secretary took it in. It's your sale and you're responsible. Now I suggest you get yourself back here and straighten out this mess before the whole firm is slurred with incompetence."

"I'll be on the next plane. Look, I'm terribly sorry," he said, knowing how lame he sounded. "I don't know how – "

"Well you *should* know," Greaves interrupted irritably. "Being sorry doesn't help a blasted thing. Offering fakes is not our business here at Lyndhurst and Lloyd's. I must say, I am surprised. We expect more of our people than this."

"Of course, sir."

"Come and see me when you get back," Greaves said brusquely, followed by a click.

Alastair slowly set the receiver back in the cradle. The bracket clock ticked loudly, a relentless, metallic tick. He sat immobilized, staring at the *Notre Dame* poster, the cathedral's shimmering image practically dissolved. His mind raced with questions. Who advertised the painting in *The New York Times* without asking him? Why didn't Colin check the date? Where the hell had Catherine gotten the painting? And how would he ever recover from this scandal that made him look like a total jackass?

"What a cock-up!" he said, pushing angrily away from the desk. He stormed out the door and headed blindly down the hall, his solitary figure marching past the gray marble pilasters that lined the corridor like stationed sentries. But he saw nothing. No matter how this had happened, damned if he would let it ruin him.

Chapter 37

S o you've heard the sorry story," Alastair said glumly over the phone.

"It was hard to miss," Megan said, setting down her coffee cup next to the stack of city newspapers. Yesterday she had lined them all up on her desk. Alastair's story had the distinction of appearing in every one.

"It was on the front page of *The New York Times.*"

She spared him the fact that it also made the 11 o'clock news, gleefully announced as *the late-breaking art world scandal: Lyndhurst and Lloyd's touted DuBois collection offers a million dollar forgery.*

When she first heard the story she didn't believe it. Even seeing it shouting from the headlines, she had had a hard time accepting it as true. Now she waited intently for his exonerating explanation. Obviously there had been some kind of mistake, but she couldn't imagine it was his. She could not believe he was capable of any kind of professional incompetence, much less duplicity. Unless her emotions had her totally deceived, which, if she thought about it historically, was entirely possible.

"Who took in the painting?" she asked.

"Reginald, the morning after I left for London. Our master in knickers," he said sarcastically, a tone she had rarely heard in him.

"Didn't Colin look at it?"

"He was supposed to have catalogued it." His voice was clipped and edgy. "He knows perfectly well Reginald isn't experienced enough to handle this. I don't know. I've only just got back. I haven't seen either of them."

She stared at *The New York Post* headline on the top of the stack: *Going, going, oops . . . A million dollar fake.*

"It must be an incredibly good forgery to have gotten as far as it did," she said.

"That's exactly right. I must say, it's so good I wouldn't have known it was a fake myself if the date weren't so glaringly wrong." His voice rose angrily. "That's what's so inexcusable, how these nitwits could have been so inept."

She had stared at the headline so much the word *fake* was beginning to look strange and meaningless, and she swapped in other letters, trying to make sense of it: million dollar *cake, take, jake, rake, snake.*

"Alastair, I'm so sorry. What rotten luck. And you had nothing to do with it."

"Yes, but it lands in my lap, doesn't it? This is my department, this is my sale."

He sounded tight and tense and she was silent, thinking of the repercussions.

"Look Megan, I've got to go try to sort this all out. I'll be damned if I'm going to stand by and let my reputation be destroyed without finding out who's responsible."

She felt helpless but, hoping to comfort him, she offered to come over; he said to come at five.

"You can have a look at the impostor and we'll go get a drink. I'll need one by then."

"Okay. Try not to worry," she said encouragingly without feeling much confidence herself.

She turned back to her typewriter and the article she'd been editing, pushing Alastair's predicament from her mind to pick up the thread of her story again. The piece was a full profile on Gerhardt, his underhanded past, his likely present, his dim future. She had validated the Viennese suspicions of fraudulent dealing with several quaking old art dealers, she had reported the full story of Gerhardt's Florida exploits told to her by Jack

Drury and confirmed by Miami police records, and she had described the various roles he'd played in selling the *Abruzzi Daughter* at Sotheby's in London, including the evidence of the doctored catalogue. This had been proved unequivocally by Alice Beatty when she produced from her own home archives (she never discarded a single flyer from any show she'd attended) the very same exhibition catalogue which included neither the *Abruzzi Daughter* nor three other modernist paintings on the added leaf.

Megan's exposé amounted not only to an excoriating indictment of Gerhardt's past frauds, but called for an investigation into his nefarious activities at present. Like the best newspaper muckraking, this was a case in which the police would have to come to her for information. Fogelman read the draft and gave her an enthusiastic thumbs up. "Way to scoop 'em, Meg," he'd said, and approved an expansion of the section to make room for the whole story, including illustrations.

Megan returned the typewriter carriage to the right with a deft flick of her wrist and then stopped momentarily, wondering about the repercussions of exposing Sotheby's lack of expertise in verifying the Modigliani provenance. Not that Terrence Young could damage Alastair much more than he had already. Would he have been so quick to accuse Alastair of incompetence in the Gauguin dating if not for her allegations against Sotheby's in the first place? And how unjust, what terrible timing, that Alastair should be getting creamed just as she was writing her prize-winning piece. Her stomach churned as she returned to typing.

*   *   *

5:10 PM found Megan at Lyndhurst and Lloyd's front desk. Alastair had left word with Lauren, who accompanied her up in the elevator.

"You know the way from here, don't you?" Lauren said as the doors opened.

Megan nodded and headed towards Alastair's office. She glanced briefly at the framed prints hung along the hallway reflecting two hundred years of the firm's history: sale catalogue title pages proffering everything from emperors' libraries to fabled poet's love letters; 18th Century auction advertisements for Dukes' and Duchesses' collections of books, wines, and firearms; humorous cartoons set in Lyndhurst and Lloyd's London auction rooms from printmakers as notable as Thomas Rowlandson. She tried to take the long view: surely mistakes like this had been made before; surely there was room for granting the benefit of the doubt. But a phrase she'd heard repeatedly at the auction house kept reverberating in her head: *get it right.*

As she approached Alastair's office door, raised voices inside carried into the hallway. She recognized Alastair's and stopped in surprise. She'd never heard him shout like this.

"How could you be so *bloody* stupid, Reginald! Any beginning textbook will tell you when Gauguin went to Tahiti!"

"But it looked so perfect," came Reginald's voice, "I just didn't think . . ."

"You're *supposed* to think," retorted Alastair. "We *hired* you to think, strain as it must be for you. *How* could you not check the date, that is *so* fundamental!"

"But Mrs. DuBois had all the proper papers!"

"That's no excuse for not covering the basics. This is a first-rate department we're running here, your job is to get it right." His voice had a desperation to it. "*Why* didn't you check it with Colin, especially since you were advertising it as a million dollar picture, the most expensive lot in the sale?"

"I *did,*" Reginald insisted. "I showed it all to him and he said it was fine."

"Now, wait a minute," said another voice. "Don't point your finger at me, this isn't my department."

A silence followed. Then Alastair said slowly, "Right, Colin, but you are a nineteenth century man."

Colin's voice was aloof, assured.

"Indeed, the nineteenth century is my specialty. And although your picture is dated 1889, I am not responsible for Gauguin. He is a modernist, wouldn't you agree?"

"*Of course* Gauguin belongs in Modern Pictures, but I wasn't *here*, Colin, and it's not as if you're in an unrelated department! You could have checked it!"

"He did check it," Reginald blurted out. "He looked it up and everything and he told me to put it through."

Megan heard someone get up from a chair and walk towards the door. A cavalier voice said, "You can't expect me to detect mistakes in Modern Pictures. After all, Alastair, you're the expert, aren't you?"

Rapid footsteps approached the door and Colin came barreling out of the office. He pulled himself up with surprise when he saw Megan. She flushed with embarrassment, realizing she must have looked like an eavesdropper.

"Do you make a habit of lurking in corridors?" he snapped.

"I didn't want to interrupt."

He smiled superciliously. "It's quite all right. There are ringside seats inside."

He stalked off and she stood paralyzed, his words vibrating in the air with the twang of an arrow hitting a target. Was that really *Colin?* The perfect gentleman?

Gathering herself, she walked through the open doorway. Reginald stood in the middle of the room with his hands at his sides, facing Alastair. She halted just inside the door, not sure if she should enter. Alastair saw her and said coolly to Reginald, "We'll talk more about it tomorrow."

"Right," Reginald said, and bolted out of the door with a curt nod to Megan.

She entered the room slowly. Alastair stood looking at her, his clothes full of trans-Atlantic-flight wrinkles. He didn't move, but just stared, his face rigid with restrained emotion, his nostrils flaring slightly.

"Hello Alastair," she said, walking up to him.

He didn't answer but put his arms around her. She hugged

him back, wishing she could melt the world away. He held her silently for a moment before dropping his arms.

With a wan smile he said, "So. Now that I've been vilified by the press, what's next? Will I be tarred and feathered?"

He ran his hands through his dirty hair, his fingers leaving lines like furrows in a field. His loosened tie exposed the strawberry mark, flushed bright crimson.

"Oh, Alastair," she exclaimed. "Can't you print a retraction?" she offered helplessly.

"It wouldn't do any good. The damage is done. The headlines say it all: *Alastair Cavendish, modern painting expert and blooming idiot.*"

He looked so done in, she felt she would do anything to right this. "There's got be some way to fix it."

"Oh, it will get fixed, all right. I'll be fixed straight out of my job." He sighed and walked over to the racks. "Would you like to see the little gem?"

She nodded and he pulled out a picture from the rack and propped it up against the wall. She let out a low whistle.

Rich, earthy colors depicted a south-sea island woman in the foreground holding a melon. The curving shape of the ripened fruit was echoed in her bare breasts, her body soft and sensual. Dark eyes wide and open, her full lips were closed but inviting. Behind her stood two horses, one pale green and drinking from a stream, the other a shadowy maroon looking off into a verdant tropical forest. The mood was compelling and mysterious; this was a painting you wanted to enter, to become part of, to discover its secrets.

"Incredible," she finally said. "The forger has certainly done Gauguin justice."

"Yes, it is a perfect forgery. Gauguin himself would be flattered. Look at the juxtaposition of the saturated colors, the way the horses are foreshortened, just as he would have painted it. It even captures Gauguin's haunting, spiritual quality."

"No wonder Reginald was fooled."

"Yes, but look here in the corner, Megan," he said, his voice rising, "Right here. *P. Gauguin, 1889!* You couldn't ask for a more obvious flaw! Gauguin didn't go to Tahiti until the spring of 1891! It may as well say 'Made in Tokyo.' It's amazing that anyone so talented in forgery could be so brainless about the dating."

She shrugged. "Most painters aren't art historians."

"He certainly took enough trouble with the other details. Extensive provenance papers, exactly what any reputable dealer would provide. And here," he picked up the canvas, "look at the surface. He must have rolled it up while it was still drying to get all the tiny cracks in it. He even used cheap, old canvas. Look." He turned the canvas over and pointed to a round, black seal on the back of the canvas. "Here's a pre-war French gallery seal."

"Let's see."

He handed her the painting and walked away in disgust. "Such a clever trick he's played," he said, a bitter note creeping in. "A trick that may cost me my career."

She looked at the seal and then turned the canvas back to the front. Suddenly she had an odd feeling, more than wonder at the forgery. Something felt familiar here, beyond the knowledge of Gauguin's Tahitian period. She turned the canvas over and stared at the back. Next to the French gallery seal, shallow cross-hatchings were scratched into the surface of the stretcher. The scratchings make a pattern of widening bars, a whittled plaid.

Recognition came over her slowly, like a break in the clouds. A beam flit across her brain, grew lighter and clearer, sending a jolt through her body. The realization sank in despite her resistance. These were her scratchings in the stretcher, the ones she made the night Bo sketched her portrait. She stared, incapacitated. No, this couldn't be. She tried to shake the reality, unable to accept it. Bo couldn't be the forger.

"It's just unbelievable," Alastair's voice came to her as if from a great distance. "What a waste of talent. Whoever the painter is, he was extremely accomplished. Why didn't he paint his own damned pictures?"

"I don't know," she said flatly, thinking, he can't sell his own. Everything around her had retreated into a haze, but she herself was at an apex of clarity. Her memory fired rounds of evidence at her, supporting the new knowledge. That's why Bo had been buying old canvas lately that he used to scorn. Nor had he been complaining so much about the art world and how screwed up it was. No wonder he'd been so slow finishing the portrait of Paddy. And what about the money he'd been spending lately – new clothes, installing a kitchen? Everything made sense now, as if she had been seeing the scattered pieces of a jigsaw puzzle that just now fit together.

"Nobody paints like that without being trained in the style of the period," Alastair said from where he stood at the window. "And he's had a hell of a lot of practice to pull it off so well. What a racket, palming off fakes as the work of great painters. What scum."

"He must like the French school," she said, thinking, of course, there must be others.

"A good choice," he said tartly, "considering they're bringing the highest prices in the art market."

"A good businessman too, then." Bo the penny-pincher, yes, he would make a good businessman.

The phone rang and Alastair answered it. She paid no attention, she was in such turmoil. How could Bo have done this, and what would happen to Alastair? And how absurd, what a bizarre irony, that the two men in her life should come together like this.

"Be straight over."

Alastair hung up. He clapped his hands on her shoulders, barely able to conceal his agitation. "Look, darling, I'm sorry, but I've got to skip the drink. That was Catherine. I'm going over there to ask her where she got this picture. I've got to find this shyster. Somebody's going to jail here and it's not going to be me."

She stared at him without speaking. Yes, of course, there would be an investigation. Bo would be caught.

Alastair didn't notice her preoccupation he had so much on his own mind. "If I'm going to be ruined he can bloody well go down with me."

"Don't worry about me," she said, pulling herself out of her trance. "I'll see you later."

She couldn't meet his eyes.

Chapter 38

Alastair stepped out of the elevator and rapped sharply on Catherine DuBois's door. Light footsteps approached rapidly on the other side, and for the first time since he had been coming to see her, Catherine opened the door herself.

Her hair wisped about her worried face, escaping on all sides from her bun.

"Alastair, dear, come in."

Her forced smile didn't hide her distress, and she led him down the paneled hallway lined with alabaster sconces, her long lavender skirt swinging from side to side. The butler approached from the other direction looking astonished.

"Humphreys, take Mr. Cavendish's coat please," Catherine said curtly.

Alastair handed his coat to the bewildered Humphreys and followed Catherine into the library. A fire crackled in the fireplace, the logs popping and sizzling from behind a pair of dragon-shaped andirons. The firelight glinted off the bindings of gold-leafed books, winked in the Wyndham silver tea service waiting on the coffee table. This cozy ambiance would ordinarily have had a soothing effect on Alastair, but this evening he barely noticed.

"Do have a seat," said Catherine, sitting down on a velvet sofa of richly colored stripes.

"Thank you, but I think I'll stand."

Catherine perched on the edge of the sofa and crossed her legs. Alastair stared into the fire, pondering how best to approach the delicate subject of how the famed DuBois collection came to have a fake in it. This thought was only slightly less disturbing than the one that consumed him on the dark walk over, which was how the forgery made it across the lines of expertise and into his sale. Competitive as he and Colin had always been, he'd never dreamt the bile was bitter enough for deliberate sabotage.

But there was more than one villain here. And since he had no recourse with Colin (in the end, it *was* his sale), he had no choice but to go after the other: the forger.

He raised one arm and pressed his fingers to the bridge of his nose. Catherine watched him uneasily.

"First of all, Alastair, I want to apologize from the bottom of my heart. I feel absolutely awful that I've caused you so much trouble. I simply can't imagine how it happened."

"Rather messy, isn't it?" he said, crossing his arms and turning to her. The flames danced in fiery reflection on the Wyndham tea set, lighting the jumping stag and the crossbow in blazing red and orange.

"And dreadful of that Terrence Young up at Sotheby's to be so smug about it."

"That's no surprise. It's a two hundred year old rivalry."

"I just can't believe the painting is a forgery. I've never bought a fake in my life, at least, not to my knowledge." She shook her head incredulously. "I've bought only the best from people I've trusted."

He dropped his arms and faced her squarely. "Catherine, where did you get the picture?"

She clasped her hands around her knee, the veins showing in her hands, their color almost matching the lavender of her cashmere cardigan. "From Reinhold Gerhardt."

"When?"

She fidgeted uncomfortably on the couch. "Well, recently. Last month."

Alastair looked up sharply. "What?"

"Yes, and here Alastair, I really do feel culpable. But you must believe me, I had no idea the painting was a fake. You see, Reinhold knows what terrible financial pressure I've been under, and since the collection had been getting such positive notice in the newspapers, he proposed that I make the most of it. Being a Taurus, he's gifted in financial matters. He thought buyers would pay far more for a painting as part of my collection than they would ordinarily. So when he showed me the Gauguin, which I absolutely *adored* and is the sort of thing Edwin and I would have bought anyway, it seemed like a good idea to include it. With the price he was giving me, it was clear I could make a handsome profit."

"Oh Catherine," Alastair said, shaking his head.

She crossed her legs over the other way and looked pleadingly at him. "Alastair, I am *so* sorry. And poor Reinhold. He's had the wool pulled over his eyes, too. And he being a professional dealer – well. It looks very bad for him."

"He's not the only one it looks bad for," Alastair said dryly, leaning up against a mahogany breakfront, its glass doors glowing in the firelight.

"I know, Alastair, I know. It's a terrible situation."

"Can I ask what you paid for it?"

"Of course. We have no secrets, have we?" She smiled hopefully, but he stared fixedly at her; at this point he wasn't interested in camaraderie. "One hundred thousand dollars."

He leaned forward at the waist. "But Catherine! That's an absurdly low price!"

"That's exactly why I bought it," she said simply, her eyes big and open. "It was such a good deal. But then, Reinhold has always found me bargains."

He stared at her incredulously. "But Catherine, don't you see?"

She reached up and patted the stray hairs from her bun. "Surely, you don't think . . ."

"What else? Gerhardt knows he could easily have gotten five or even ten times that if it were authentic."

Her face drained of color as the implication dawned on her. The loosened hairs wisped back down around her ears. "But Alastair! I've known Reinhold for years! He's always been honest with me. I can't believe he would deliberately deceive me!"

He looked over at the tiny woman blushing in the firelight, her frail form bolstered by the velvet cushions, her eyes innocent and pleading, and suddenly he thought of the tiny Meissen figurine of the courtly lady. He sighed and decided to get on with it. "I don't suppose you know where he got it."

"Well, I assume it was from the owner listed in the provenance papers. Apparently she died recently."

"How convenient. And how was it delivered to you?"

"Reinhold brought it out to East Hampton himself."

"He transported that enormous painting alone?"

"No, no. A young man was with him. I noticed him because he didn't look like a moving man. In fact, he reminded me of an old film star with longish curly hair who used to play in westerns. And I remember his name, too, because it was so unusual: Bo, the same as my great grandfather, Beauregard DuBois.

"Did he tell you his last name?"

"Well, *he* didn't exactly tell me. It was the funniest thing, really. I had my house painter, Pete, touching up the woodwork and it turned out he's also a real painter, an artist from the city who knew the young man. Pete was working away on the baseboard in the front hall, quiet as a mouse, when Reinhold and the young man came in the door. Suddenly Pete stood up and said, 'Well, if it isn't Bo Ryder. Fancy meeting you out here.' He startled me, quite frankly. It seems they knew each other from a Soho bar that artists frequent. Anyway, Bo isn't a name you hear often and I was curious to see if it was short for Beauregard, so I did ask – you know I'm a Francophile at heart. But it seems Bo is a nickname for Robert, which was in fact more fitting with Ryder and my Western impression. Come to think of it, I remember that for some reason Reinhold seemed quite agitated at my inquiries. Anyway, I invited them for tea but they declined and left shortly." She sighed deeply. "I don't know anything more than that. One doesn't like to ask too many questions."

Alastair pushed away from the breakfront. "Well, here's one who's going to start asking, right now. Do you know where I might find Gerhardt at this hour?"

"The gallery will be closed by now. But I have a home number for him," she said, rising and walking to the phone. "I'm sure he'll have an explanation."

"Please don't call. I prefer to go see him. Forgery is not the sort of thing I like to broach over the telephone."

She turned resignedly towards the door. "As you wish. I believe I have his address on an old receipt from when he ran his business out of his apartment. As I recall it was over on the West Side."

She returned momentarily with a yellowed receipt in her hand, which she meekly handed to Alastair, who pocketed it.

"I'll be in touch."

"Yes, please. And if there's anything I can do . . ."

"Thank you, Catherine. You've done quite enough already."

Alastair looked at the slip of paper on his way down in the elevator, the paper penned in small but precise lettering, listing a Renoir entitled *Le Déjeuner*, a thoroughly authentic and lovely painting in the DuBois sale. So at least some of Gerhardt's goods were legitimate.

The receipt was printed at the top with a West 77th Street address. He had only a vague notion of the neighborhood, and confronting Gerhardt was not something he wanted to do alone. What if he stored forgeries in his apartment? What if he were armed?

Down in the lobby the doorman sat behind a marble counter reading the newspaper, his black and white uniform blocked by the opened *Daily News*.

"Can I use the telephone, please?" asked Alastair.

Deeply engrossed, the doorman looked up blankly. "What's that?"

"Can I make a phone call?"

"Sure. Help yourself," the doorman said, lifting the phone on to the counter.

Alastair picked up the receiver and dialed.

"Them dog tracks over in Jersey, they sure are sumptin'," said the doorman, nodding his head in approval. "People making some real money out there."

Alastair drummed his fingers on the edge of the counter, waiting for the connection. He finally got it.

"Hello, police?"

Chapter 39

T he cab ride was one red light after another. All the way down 5th Avenue, rush-hour congestion from 59th Street to Washington Square, the taxi was out of sync with the rhythm of the changing traffic lights and hit a red light every few blocks. The cabby stopped, started, honked, yelled, but none of it did any good. They moved with trickling slowness.

Megan vacillated between gratitude and annoyance. For at the same time she felt she must confront Bo immediately, she dreaded hearing his answer. But there was no avoiding it; she had to know.

She kept turning over the evidence in her mind, coming up with other explanations. Maybe she wasn't the only restless model who whittled stretchers. Or maybe Bo gave that stretcher to someone else. But as quickly as she came up with excuses, other memories counteracted them: his recent slowness in answering the door, his desperate reaction to her almost opening the closet, his change in spirits, from angry protesting against the art establishment to resigned acquiescence.

The cabby yanked the wheel to the left and surged forward to pass a downtown bus spewing clouds of black exhaust, then jammed on the brakes as he rounded the bus and the traffic light at 23rd Street appeared, shifting to red. The cab idled impatiently and she stared out the window at the Flatiron building, its profile squeezed to an improbable wedge with the effort of accommodating the crossing of grand 5th Avenue and the old cow path, Broadway.

And then there was Alastair. How absurd, that this painting should have found its way to him. As if fate, in a moment of whimsical humor, decided to bring her life full circle since she hadn't. And that Bo's foolhardy act might wreck Alastair's career – it was just too much to think about.

The cab turned around the corners of Washington Square and she looked out at the ever-present chess players in the southwest corner. She recognized a bearded man with granny glasses who was often playing, and his challenger, a mop-haired boy of not more than 11 or 12. Then there was the black man with the Brooklyn Dodgers hat, and the old guy who always wore a suit and a pocket watch with a gold chain. And when these regulars weren't present there were others, and when they stopped coming they would be replaced by more. The cement tables, built slab on slab with stone chessboards inlaid into the top, impervious to fire and ice, wind and rain, would always have players, ever different, ever the same.

"Five-forty," said the cabby as he pulled up to Bo's corner. Megan shoved some money through the window, jumped out of the taxi and slammed the door.

She turned her key in the lock and pushed into the dank hallway. Fixing her eyes on the naked bulb hanging like a distant star above the fourth floor landing, she took the stairs two at a time, her footsteps reverberating up the cavernous stairwell, her hand pulling her along the damp railing. By the time she reached the fourth floor landing her heart was racing, from exertion or anticipation, she wasn't sure.

She knocked on Bo's door and it swung open. Slumped in the cockeyed swivel chair, he faced away from her, his long curls lying limply on the frayed collar of his blue work shirt. Above him, sitting in the same position with ankle crossed over knee, his masked self-portrait in the red wing chair sat precipitously at the broken edge of the West Side highway.

"Come on in, Paddy," he said without turning around. He was staring at the portrait of Paddy and his voice sounded distant and forlorn.

She walked into the loft, stopped, and glanced around. It looked different, as if she were seeing it in a new light. How strange if Bo had really been painting forgeries right here where she had spent so much time, without her ever knowing.

He turned around and sat up straight. "Oh, Megan, it's you. I was expecting Paddy."

She stood where she was, put her hands in her pockets, and looked at him. Her face was sober, solemn.

After a moment he said, "You look like you're here on business."

"I guess I am." No, this wasn't happening, how could she say it?

He looked back at her, waiting.

Mustering all her courage, she said, "I was up at Lyndhurst and Lloyd's this afternoon."

"Oh?" he replied, an edge to his voice.

"There's quite a mess up there."

"Yeah, I saw the story in the paper." He looked away. "Those people are always getting themselves into trouble." His tone was dismissive but uneasy.

"I saw the Gauguin, Bo. It's good. You would like it."

"Oh yeah?" he said with forced nonchalance. He stood and picked up a paintbrush from the easel and swatted it against the inside of his palm. He walked over and looked out the window. His half-turned figure was framed against the glass, big and alone.

She watched him, her nerves pitched as tightly as an acrobat on a high wire. "In fact, it looks like the sort of piece that you could paint."

He whirled around and stared at her, his eyes fierce like an animal backed into a corner. When she saw the answer in his face, the wire snapped and she closed her eyes.

"Oh, Bo," she cried, her voice falling to a moan.

"How did you know?" he asked intently.

Once released, her feelings tumbled freely. "How could you? How could you do it?"

"What do you mean, how could I?" he answered vehemently. "How could I not? I couldn't go on living like that. It was killing me."

She looked at him, her face fallen with disappointment and disbelief. He stared back defensively. "Is that plain enough English for you? It was killing me."

"Why didn't you tell me you were so desperate?" she implored. "I would have lent you some money."

"I owed everybody already." He threw the paintbrush on the floor and paced back and forth between the wall and the easel. "I couldn't go on borrowing. Where would it end? My work will never sell, I was born in the wrong century. It was either paint like Gauguin or give it up completely. Sell shoes or something."

She walked forward and clenched the back of the chair. She couldn't believe this. She thought of Bo's talent, of what he'd done with it, of the consequences to himself and to Alastair. Suddenly she was really angry.

"Yes, you could have sold shoes," she retorted. "It would have been a lot better than this. Now you've sold your integrity as a painter."

She was losing control now but she didn't care; she let herself go. Half of her retreated and watched the other half play this out. She heard her tone change to scorn.

"Here you sit, talking about how corrupt the art world is, how all they're interested in is money, and now you've gone and joined them! And worse, because you're not even selling what's yours. You've sold out to the very system you despise!"

"Don't hand me that moralistic crap! I haven't given anybody anything they didn't want. They can't tell my paintings from the real thing so what difference does it make? I gave them the name, that's all they're after. Why do you think Picasso could put his signature on a blank napkin? Because he knew the mindless public would still buy it! How long did you expect me to sit down here with no light or heat while your champagne and caviar set spends tens of thousands of dollars on paintings they barely know how to look at?"

He was furious but his words only made her angrier.

"I'm so tired of your contempt for the rest of the world!" she shouted back. "Not everyone is as mindless as you think. You're so superior, sitting down here acting virtuous, the unrecognized artist! You refuse to wait, you refuse to compromise, so what do you do? You prostitute yourself! You've sunk to the cheapest trick you can turn – fakes! Fakes for money!"

"Goddamn you!" he yelled, his voice shaking with fury. "Do you think I wanted to do it?" He picked up a can of turpentine and threw it at the locked closet. The can dented the door and banged to the floor. "There! They're all in there! Burn them, I don't give a shit!"

He grabbed a mug of coffee and hurled it at the portrait of Paddy. Megan screamed as it hit the middle of the picture, splattering murky brown liquid across the canvas. The mug fell to the floor and shattered while the coffee ran down the painting, dripping down Paddy's face like tears.

"Burn them all, burn the whole goddamn place down!" Bo cried, his face contorted with rage. "What does it matter in this hell hole of a world?"

He stormed out of the loft.

Sobbing, Megan collapsed into the chair.

Sometime later – a few minutes, an hour, she had no idea – a hesitant knock came at the door. She looked up slowly to see Paddy enter. He approached tentatively and asked, "No sitting today?"

Chapter 40

A lastair braced his foot against the floor as the police car screeched around Columbus Circle and up Central Park West, missing a parked car by inches. The officer at the wheel grinned, his smile almost as broad as his heavy black eyebrows.

"We don't worry about getting tickets." He floored the accelerator.

"Hey McBride, keep the pedal off the metal," said Detective Conroy from the back seat. "We're not chasing a getaway car."

McBride smiled at Alastair, a smile full of hubris but not without respect.

"I'm not used to this kind of job, see. It's usually some junkie hauling a stereo out the fire escape. We don't get too many calls for art forgeries."

"I wish I could have avoided the theatrics, myself," said Alastair.

Beyond the stonewall that ran along the sidewalk, Central Park extended into blackness. Presently, through the thicket of leafless trees, he spotted the twinkling lights of the Tavern on the Green, a sparkling oasis. He sighed and hoped the evening would be as illuminating. Finding the forger seemed the only way to redeem himself. The lights receded and Alastair stared once again into the inky foliage. Up the street on the left, the stone portals of the Dakota yawned like a medieval entrance to Hades.

The trick would be getting the information out of Gerhardt, who was most likely just the middleman, doing the backup provenance work to support feeding the forgeries into the market. It was highly unlikely he had the talent to actually paint them himself. The young man who helped deliver the Gauguin would know something; Gerhardt was too cagey to allow someone uninvolved to witness any part of the transaction. But Alastair needed some confirmation, instead of just a hunch. Given the mess he was in, he didn't need to compound it with any false accusations.

McBride slowed down and glanced out the window at the street signs. Spotting 77th Street, he careened around the corner and pulled into an empty space outside the Museum of Natural History. The three men piled out.

The night was bitterly cold and the wind howled through the treetops in the museum grounds, sending the boughs thrashing to and fro against the sky. Beyond the blowing branches the conical turrets of the museum rose like witches' hats.

The three men crossed the street to Gerhardt's building and into the modern foyer.

"Keep your lip buttoned when we get in there," Detective Conroy said to McBride. "We don't have a warrant, we're just asking a few questions."

"Who, me?" McBride asked with mock innocence. "Since when do I jump the gun?"

Conroy winked at Alastair. "Trigger-Joe here."

Conroy found Gerhardt's name next to 5B and pushed the button. No answer. He waited, his small face patient under his wool cap. He stood a head shorter than McBride's burly form, and instead of a police uniform he wore a non-descript overcoat. He looked like he could fade unnoticed into the woodwork.

After another moment with no response Conroy began pushing buttons indiscriminately. Alastair looked at him in surprise as the door buzzed open.

Conroy shrugged. "You learn these things."

Their footsteps rang hollowly on the tiled floor of the once elegant lobby, now faded, its aqua walls dingy at the corners. The large room dated from the 1920's, with Art Deco style wall fixtures and a large mirror whose silver backing had begun to peel away in spots. Overstuffed chairs faced each other, their cushions sagging as if they'd been sat in too many times.

An elevator in the far corner squeaked its way down. As they stood waiting Alastair noticed the turquoise floor tiles rimmed with dirt, the air that smelled stale as if the building needed a cleaning.

On the fifth floor the elevator opened to a brightly lit aqua hallway. The mauve carpet, worn brown down the middle, led them around a corner to 5B.

Alastair rang the buzzer and Conroy and McBride stood to one side. Alastair's ears were primed to every sound behind the door. Adrenaline pumping like mad, he was sure the policemen must be able to hear his heart pounding.

After a seemingly endless silence, footsteps approached behind the closed door and a voice asked loftily, "Yes? Who is it?"

"Alastair Cavendish. I'd like to see you for a moment, if I could."

One lock slid back, then another, and the door opened several inches, a link chain still fastened across the door. In the narrow crack Gerhardt's dark eye appeared above the pointed end of his mustache. "Mr. Cavendish! What a surprise! One moment."

The door closed and the chain clanked against the metal plate. Gerhardt opened the door, wider now. He stood in a burgundy bathrobe with velvet lapels and leather slippers, his hair disheveled and an uncertain smile on his face. When he saw the police his face fell.

"Detective Conroy," Conroy said, flashing his badge. "We came along with Mr. Cavendish to ask a few questions."

"What about? Is there a problem?"

Conroy put his badge back in his pocket. "We need to ask

you a few questions and we can either do it here or up at the station house."

Gerhardt looked them over warily and backed into the room. "Come in, then, come in."

The three men entered the living room. There was not a square inch on which the eye could rest. Covered with striped red and gold wallpaper, the walls were hung with everything imaginable: mirrors, photographs, candleholders, prints and paintings. Every tabletop was covered with objects, from turtle-shaped ashtrays to tiny brass Indian animals to Rookwood vases filled with dried flowers. All the colors in the room were red or a variation of, from hot pink to rusty orange to deep crimson. Alastair felt as if he were standing inside an enormous mouth.

"Bronx renaissance," whispered Conroy as he looked around the room.

Gerhardt straightened his bathrobe in a dignified way, but his eyes were guarded. "Would you care for coffee?" he offered.

"No, we won't be here that long," said Alastair, swiftly taking a seat on a low-lying orange divan with a curled headrest at one end set with an imitation leopard-skin pillow. He glanced toward the far end of the room where a window looked out onto darkness, a welcome relief from the busyness of the decor. McBride and Conroy sat down and Gerhardt slowly lowered himself on to a sofa. He looked apprehensively at Conroy.

"You watch the news much, Mr. Gerhardt?" Conroy asked.

"I confess I am usually too busy to watch the news."

"We had some interesting news last night.

"Oh?"

"Yes. It seems that one of the paintings in the DuBois sale at Lyndhurst and Lloyd's is a forgery. A million dollar Gauguin."

Gerhardt turned to Alastair with an unctuous expression of concern. "I am sorry to hear that, Mr. Cavendish."

Conroy looked skeptical and said, "It may be bad news for you too, Mr. Gerhardt, because Mrs. DuBois says you sold her the painting."

Gerhardt looked surprised. "She said that?"

"You didn't?"

Gerhardt cleared his throat. "Well, yes, I did, of course I did. But to the best of my knowledge it is a genuine Gauguin."

Alastair could not contain himself any longer. He didn't even try to keep the disdain out of his voice. "*To the best of your knowledge*, right. That won't get you very far."

Gerhardt looked defensively at Alastair. "I am sorry, but if the painting is a forgery, it is news to me too. You must admit, Mr. Cavendish, you were fooled by it yourself."

"Don't be daft. You sold the piece to Catherine last month for a damn sight less than you would have if it were genuine. Although $100,000 for a fake is not a bad profit."

Gerhardt drew himself up haughtily and stared at Alastair. "Mr. Cavendish, I am surprised at you. A man of your standing, resorting to cheap accusation to defend your own mistake . . ."

It was all Alastair could do not to pin him to the wall.

"Now, now, calm down, boys." Conroy said. "This isn't a trial, we're only asking a few questions. Where did you get the painting, Mr. Gerhardt?"

Gerhardt cleared his throat repeatedly, as if something were stuck in it. "Well, I have many contacts. We all do, all dealers. We get our artwork from all over the world."

Conroy looked sternly at Gerhardt. "Where did you get the painting?"

"I am trying to remember. It was a while ago. I think I got it in France. Yes, on a trip to Marseilles two years ago, in a flea market."

Alastair stared icily at Gerhardt. "You got a million dollar painting in a flea market and you've been sitting on it for two years? Really, that is the most transparent – "

"But you know it is not always easy to find the right buyer!"

Conroy put up his hands in a time-out signal. "Okay, okay. There will be plenty of time for accusations, Mr. Cavendish." Conroy pulled out a pen and put his clipboard on his knee. "Mr. Gerhardt, let's start with your name and address. I'm going to have to file a report on this."

Gerhardt clasped his hands together and assumed an air of injured innocence.

Alastair got up and walked towards the window. A supreme effort was required for him to control his temper. To think that this pretentious little gnat of a man could ruin his career, this quack of a dealer, insinuating himself and his pointy mustache into Catherine's life. He stopped at the far end of the room in front of a roll-top desk and looked back at the group. Gerhardt, stroking his goatee, his leg elegantly crossed, delicately adjusted the bathrobe over his knee . . . If he were any smaller Alastair would squash him like a bug.

Alastair looked away in disgust, his eyes resting on the open desk. He stared blankly, thinking of the mess he was in, but suddenly his attention was drawn to a book lying in front of him: *Gauguin, The Tahiti Years: 1891-1903*. Stacked next to this book were books on Miro, Matisse and Picasso. On the top of the pile lay two rubber stamps. Alastair looked over at the threesome who was still engrossed in the interrogation. He picked up the stamps and looked at the bottoms: one he recognized as the authenticating seal from the Jeu de Paume Gallery in Paris, the other bore the turn-of-the-century insignia of the French gallery that was stamped into the stretcher of the Gauguin.

Alastair stared at the symbol and his spirit soared, releasing with it any doubts he'd harbored as to Gerhardt's guilt. He slipped the rubber stamps into his pocket. Even though his next card was a bluff, he was now confident enough to play it. He approached the three men, his heart racing triumphantly.

"I think we've about wrapped things up for tonight," said Conroy, rising.

"Yes, I believe we have," said Alastair with a smile.

"You'll need to find the receipt for that painting," Conroy told Gerhardt. "If you managed to hold onto the other papers you should be able to come up with the receipt."

Gerhardt nodded cooperatively, his eyes half closing. "I will find the receipt."

"Naturally," Alastair scoffed. "What's a receipt to a forger of provenance papers?"

Gerhardt stood looking nervously at Alastair. "Please Mr. Cavendish, do not jump to conclusions. I am as unhappy as you about all this."

"I'm sure you are. But I'm actually feeling a bit better now, and I'm sure I'll be right as rain after we visit our next suspect: Bo Ryder."

Alastair watched with fascination as Gerhardt's face transformed. Always held so tightly, his expression shifted from poise to panic.

"Isn't that right, Reinhold?" Alastair continued. "Not only will we find the answer to who forged the Gauguin, but probably to a few other fakes that have surfaced in the market recently."

Gerhardt's eyes widened with fright and he rushed over to the roll-top desk. "What have you been looking at? How dare you pry into my affairs!"

He pulled down the roll-top with a bang.

Alastair put his hands in his pockets and smiled. "You *are* clever. I've always admired a man who can improvise when he can't find the real thing."

Gerhardt rushed towards Alastair, losing a leather slipper on the red rug. "But, but, you cannot prove anything!" he stammered, grasping his goatee wildly. "You do not have a warrant! Anything you find here is illegal!"

"We don't need to find anything here. I expect we'll find most of the evidence at another address."

"What the hell is going on?" Conroy asked.

Losing all composure, Gerhardt looked desperately between the men. Like an old, worn canvas that, when touched, disintegrates, his facade crumbled before their very eyes. "Please, there is more to this story! Ryder, he blackmailed me! He made me do it!"

"Did he now?" Alastair said snidely. "Forced you to provide the gallery seals, too? And you can't even get the dates right when you've got a book on the subject."

Gerhardt's eyes narrowed. "He dated the Gauguin. The damned fool used the wrong date! But he signed them, he is the forger, he tricked me into selling them for him. I was trapped!"

"The only thing you've ever been trapped by is the meager limits of your own talents," said Alastair. He beckoned to the two bewildered officers. "Come on. Let's go find the forger."

"Wait, please," Gerhardt pleaded, grabbing Alastair's arm. "I can help you! With immunity I can tell you more! You must understand, all my life, the persecution, first the occupation, the Nazis confiscating modern art, destroying my business, then as a foreigner here . . . I have been forced to live by my wits, to play whatever game I can . . ."

He writhed like a snake, his thin hands clutching Alastair's arm, his black eyes almost popping out of his head.

"Let go of me, you parasite," Alastair said. He shook Gerhardt off and walked out, the policemen following. They left Gerhardt at the door, fuming and cursing.

"Damn that fool Ryder, I told him the right date!"

*   *   *

Pulling out from the 20th precinct on West 82nd Street, Conroy tapping the search warrant on his knee, Alastair repeated the address he'd found in the phone book for Bo Ryder as if it were a mantra. McBride cut back through Central Park, past the frozen lake, its skated surface dulled like pewter in the lamplight. The car shot out the south end of the park and down 7th Avenue, sailing through green lights all the way to Herald Square.

"Wow," said McBride, "from 82nd to 34th without stopping. That's a lucky sign."

"Let's hope so," Alastair said. He sat forward in the seat, watching out the window. To his right the *Macy's* sign looped in script across the storefront, shining out in neon splendor. A snarl of traffic moved glacially at the south end of the square and Alastair fumed in frustration.

"Isn't there any way to get through this a little faster?"

McBride looked over and shrugged. "Why not?"

He turned on the police siren and the logjam of cars in front of them parted like the red sea. Alastair smiled as the car surged forward, siren wailing like a banshee. He noted each passing landmark as a hurdle in a race. His only concern was reaching their destination. He was primed, ready for anything, thrilled at the thought of catching the forger, edgy at the possibility that the tip would lead nowhere.

The traffic cleared below Bleeker Street and they zoomed down the empty avenue and turned left on to Spring Street.

"Let's kill the siren," said Conroy. "No need to let him know we're coming." They drove the rest of the way in tense silence.

Broome Street was dark and empty. McBride stood looking up at the cast iron buildings, their looming facades barely lit by the streetlights, recesses shadowed in blackness. "Here's 457," McBride said, "but this can't be right, it's a warehouse platform."

"Where've you been?" said Conroy. "This is a loft, the latest craze for artists."

"Oh, yeah, I heard of them. Even a fake artist gets a loft?"

Alastair was already up the steps and inspecting the names by the buzzer. "Here it is. Ryder, 4th floor."

He tried the front door and found it wasn't closed all the way. He swung it open and the three men entered.

The hanging bulb lit the steel-gray entrance just well enough to see the rusted old elevator shaft, the torn rubber mats lying at cockeyed angles on the stairs. From somewhere overhead water dripped with a faint but insistent plop, landing in a puddle on the floor. Alastair reached out to the glistening wall; it was wet to the touch.

"This ain't no loft, it's a cave," said McBride.

Alastair started up the stairs. The light on the first landing had burned out and the stairway rose into gloom, dank and dark. Far up on the second landing another naked bulb shone, weakly lighting the way.

"Hey, look at this," McBride said, inspecting the broken elevator.

"Come on, McBride, get the lead out," said Conroy, mounting the stairs.

They finally reached the fourth floor landing, winded. Conroy said, "I better go first. The warrant makes this official business."

Conroy stepped up to the door and rapped sharply. From behind the door came creaking and shuffling. Conroy knocked again, this time louder. "Open up in there."

McBride stepped in behind him, his hand moving to his pistol. The shuffling grew louder, stopped, and the door swung slowly open. A bearded man stood in his stocking feet. Alastair stared at him unbelievingly. Could this withered old geezer be the forger?

"Well, hells bells!" Paddy said in surprise. "What can you boys be wanting?"

"We're looking for Bo Ryder," said Conroy.

"And so am I," answered Paddy staunchly.

Paddy stepped away from the door and eyed the threesome suspiciously. Conroy walked into the loft and looked around. Then he turned to Paddy. "What are you doing here?"

"Like I told you, I'm waiting for Bo," Paddy answered cautiously. "I ain't him, if that's what you're thinking. I'm just the model. Bo's 'sposed to be giving me a graduation dinner. See here, he painted my portrait." Paddy gestured at the portrait and added wistfully, "Looked pretty good, too, 'til something got spilled on it."

The painting was streaked with milky coffee drippings.

McBride walked cautiously around the bathroom wall, his hand still on his gun. Alastair began to search the loft. He glanced briefly at the portrait of Paddy and dismissed it. That wasn't what he was looking for. Nor were the paintings lining the walls. The loft was so open it was hard to imagine where anything could be hiding. Conroy rummaged around in the kitchen, McBride in the bathroom. Alastair searched the shelves and worktable, finding scraps of drawings, brushes and books. Against the wall behind the table a cardboard box full of dirty clothes was heaped with shirts and socks, one with a design like a pair of Megan's, he noted absently.

He spotted a small stack of matted drawings leaning up against the wall. Kneeling down, he flipped quickly through sketches of the city, some of the Staten Island Ferry, gulls dipping in the air alongside the boat, others of people scattering crumbs to pigeons in Battery Park. In the middle of the stack he came to a charcoal portrait of a spirited-looking young woman with wavy hair and vivid eyes. Alastair stopped and did a double take. Curious; she looked remarkably like Megan.

"Hey, what about this closet?" McBride called out. "It's locked."

Alastair let the stack fall back against the wall and rose, dismissing the odd coincidence. McBride stood in front of a closet door; Paddy had disappeared.

"This is the only private room in the joint."

McBride grinned at Alastair, who tried the locked handle for himself.

"Let me in there," said Conroy, coming back from the kitchen with an oyster knife. He stuck it into the lock and fiddled, turning it every which way but the door didn't budge.

"Screw it," McBride said and Conroy stepped back. McBride took a karate stance and kicked the door swiftly. The door panel split with a resounding crack. He kicked it again and the whole panel caved in. McBride reached through the splintered hole and turned the knob from the inside. The door opened to reveal the neatly stacked shelves, drawings below, canvases above.

Alastair slid out a pile of drawings. On top was a sketch of a cubistic bull and matador. Lifting it onto his chest, he turned to a richly patterned domestic interior. Next came a native girl, lying prone on a bed, colored in strong earth tones. "Jesus," Alastair said softly. "He surely knows his modern masters."

"Is this the stuff?" Conroy asked.

"Indeed it is – Picasso, Matisse, Gauguin."

Conroy took the stack of drawings and put them on the spool table. Alastair reached in for another batch. Glancing over them quickly, he was amazed at how good they were, each one a classic, textbook example of the artist imitated.

"At a couple of grand a piece this guy was on his way to being a millionaire!" said McBride.

"To say nothing of the paintings," Alastair said, sliding out the Degas dancers and the Mont Sainte-Victoire à la Cezanne from between the sheets of corrugated cardboard. "These bring six figures."

They removed everything from the closet and the police set to work recording the paintings. McBride systematically attached identifying stickers and Conroy listed each one on a form on his clipboard.

While they were busy Alastair walked around the room under the *Portraits in the City*, the large figures looking down on him from the same height as the portraits of his ancestors in the great hall at Ten Oaks. They had an eerie effect on him, as if he were being watched from both the present and the past. He tried to shake the feeling. Why should he feel uneasy about searching the studio of a low-life forger?

But he couldn't dismiss his strange mood and he wasn't sure why. Catching the forger was exhilarating, and at least partially exonerating. Now the real criminal would take the rap for this, the press could lay the blame where it was deserved. However, he was awed by the forger's prodigious talent. Why was such an accomplished painter wasting his time in a criminal sideline? But something else was also disturbing him, a strange feeling he couldn't put his finger on.

The phone rang on the table next to Alastair. Without really thinking he answered it. "Yes?"

"Hi, Bo?" asked a woman's voice.

He didn't answer.

"Bo, is that you?"

"No," he said quietly.

"Paddy? Can I speak with Bo, please?"

Silence.

"Come on Paddy, don't play games with me. I need to know if Bo is there."

He said nothing. He couldn't have replied if he'd wanted to. He knew the voice on the other end.

"Are you going to answer me or not?" Megan demanded. After a pause she exclaimed in irritation, "Ohh!" The receiver clicked.

He stood still, the receiver droning monotonously in his ear. His mind stalled. He had some vague notion that she'd pick it up again and continue talking, that she'd explain to him how she happened to be calling the man who had ruined him.

He hung up and his frozen thoughts chugged slowly into low gear. One by one, the facts come at him as if in a procession of single-file mourners. The socks, the portrait, the voice on the phone. And then, more distant evidence, of nights he couldn't reach her, of attractive invitations she turned down, of her unwavering support for current, underrated artists.

He stood still, unaware of his surroundings, until he finally heard Conroy.

"I said, *who was it?*"

Chapter 41

Megan slammed the receiver back into place. Damn it! What was the matter with that old man? Where was Bo? What was Paddy doing in the loft without him? It didn't seem like Paddy not to talk to her, he was usually so friendly. Maybe it wasn't Paddy, maybe it was Clyde, but why wouldn't Clyde answer her? In fact, who would pick up the phone and be so mute?

In the kitchen she emptied a cup of cold coffee into the sink. A pot of coffee had seemed in order when she first got home from Bo's, initially so shaken that it took a concerted effort to find the key in her bag to let herself in. After the shaking stopped she had felt oddly numb. She'd moved around the apartment doing everyday chores, going through normalizing motions. A shirt needed ironing, the bed sheets changing. But now she realized that she just changed the sheets a few days ago and the cotton shirt was not warm enough to wear anyway. The coffee sat in the cup until it was cold.

Back in the living room she dropped into a chair, exhausted. In the last few hours she had mulled over every aspect of the situation, turning events over and over in her mind. The reality of Bo being a forger was extremely difficult to accept, as if she had been asked to believe that the world was flat. He, of all people, one of the most gifted young painters she'd met, with a vision utterly his own, what an incredible waste of talent. And to actually resort to selling forgeries – how could he have? Her perception of him had undergone a radical shift, her feelings for him irreparably changed.

She had called him to ask just one more question: at what point had he begun his sideline? If he had been producing forgeries since before she met him, she felt it invalidated their entire relationship, all their early conversations about his work and what it meant to him. Maybe it was only a matter of degree, because clearly he had deceived her, but she wanted to know just how much and when. If it wasn't too late to ask.

The room was lit only by the floor lamp next to the chair where she sat. Gripping the brass stand by the marble ball in the middle, she gently rocked the lamp on its circular base. The shadow from the wavering shade swept back and forth across the rug. Watching it mindlessly, her mind felt blank, her psychic energies depleted.

*　　*　　*

"No, it's quite all right. I think I'll walk," Alastair said.

"Suit yourself. But it's cold as hell out," McBride said.

"I'm used to it. English blood."

"I'll be in touch when we know anything," Conroy said. "With any luck, it won't take us long to catch this guy."

"Right," Alastair said, shaking Conroy's hand. McBride and Conroy looked so pleased with themselves, Alastair forced a smile and added, "Good show."

Digging his hands deep into his pockets, Alastair walked up West Broadway, the wind at his back. He barely knew where he was going, but he headed in the general direction of Megan's apartment. He was desperately resisting the idea of her involvement with the forger, despite the evidence to the contrary. Surely she deserved the benefit of the doubt. This *must* all be some crazy coincidence, it wasn't feasible that she had another lover, that she had any part in a forgery ring, especially one that had deliberately defamed him. No, no, no . . . not Megan. It was impossible.

He turned left on West Fourth Street and, with head bowed, paying little attention, crossed 6th Avenue. His mind reeled with irreconcilable thoughts, and before long the short blocks and diagonals of the West Village streets seemed a labyrinth; he was lost. He looked up at a street sign that indicated the intersection of 4th Street and 10th Street. He stared uncomprehendingly at the sign; Manhattan was a grid, how could 4th Street cross 10th Street? Was he going crazy, too?

He turned right and plunged on, hoping to come to a street he knew. Several blocks along he found himself at Greenwich Avenue. Up on the far corner of the triangular park the clock in the Jefferson Market Courthouse tower began to toll. From out of the tall tower the bell bonged deep and long, striking the hour of ten. Alastair stopped momentarily and stared past the gargoyles to the clock; how had it gotten to be so late? He walked up to 11th Street and turned into Megan's block. Striding up the street he saw a light on in her window.

He stood at the door of her building staring at the buzzer buttons. Anything was possible at this point. If she did know the forger, what if he were up there with her? He began to push the buttons randomly, pressing every one but hers. Presently the buzzer sounded. Pressing his shoulder against the door, he entered as it opened.

*　　*　　*

Megan started out of her trance-like state at the sharp rapping. She jumped up from the chair. It must be Bo. With trepidation she opened the door.

"Alastair!" she exclaimed. "What a surprise!"

He had never come to see her without calling, but she felt she had never been so happy to see anyone in her life. How gratifying, that this was the man she had chosen to be with. Her instincts were right, and she welcomed his presence as she would blue sky at the edge of a storm front.

He said hello and walked past her into the room. She

noticed his jaw muscles working; poor lamb. She cheerfully offered him coffee or tea.

"Coffee's fine."

She turned on the light in the kitchen, glad of the occupation. "How was your meeting with Mrs. DuBois?"

He unwound his scarf but left his coat on. "It went well. She told me which dealer she bought the picture from and the police and I went to see him."

Megan bypassed the mugs in the cupboard and brought out cups and saucers, which she knew Alastair preferred. She lifted the pot off the burner to take out the grinds. She could hear him approaching behind her.

"From there we got the name of the forger. A Bo Ryder. I've just come from his loft."

Her hand slipped, knocking the top of the coffee maker into the sink with a clatter, spilling the grinds all over the stove. He leaned his arms on the counter, his face close to hers. "Or am I telling you something you already know?"

She turned and looked into his demanding eyes and tears welled up in her own. Her face collapsed. He dropped his head and groaned as if she'd kicked him in the groin. They stood silently for a moment, heads bowed, his face clenched in a grimace, hers dropping tears onto the counter.

When he raised his head his expression had hardened. "Maybe you will be so kind as to fill me in on the rest of it, then, since you have first hand knowledge of this forgery operation?"

Her eyes widened in disbelief. "What?"

He leaned his elbows on the counter, his fists gripped tightly. His voice was low but full of intensity. "Don't stand here and lie to me."

"Now, wait a minute – " she stammered.

"No. I won't wait a minute. It seems I've waited far too many minutes, long enough for you to make a complete fool out of me."

"Alastair, please, you don't understand!"

His voice rose and he backed away from the counter. "Oh, balls! Are you going to try to tell me you don't know him, that you're not his lover, with your clothes lying all over his place?"

"Yes, I have known him, but I met him before I met you, and he has nothing to do with us, with how I feel about you."

"You are *so* liberated!" he spat, "How convenient that you have enough love to go around!"

"Please, let me explain," she pleaded.

He pulled the scarf away from his neck and his strawberry patch showed vividly through the open collar, a green vein pulsing through the fiery patch of red.

"Yes, please do tell me, tell it all! How you coached him right along, told him just how to paint the Gauguin to fool me and the rest of the world! Which makes perfect sense, since Gerhardt is far too clueless to have been of any help."

She stared, confounded. "Gerhardt . . . Reinhold Gerhardt? What does he have to do with this?"

Alastair stood back, his eyes full of disgust. "Spare me, as if you didn't know. How despicable! You not only cheat on me in love, but you help to ruin my reputation!"

"No, Alastair, you're wrong!" she answered, trying to keep her wits about her under this barrage of accusations and the news that Gerhardt was involved. "If I had known it was a fake I would have told you," she pleaded.

"Right, sure you would have," he retorted. "But instead you stood by while Gerhardt slipped the fake into Catherine's collection. What a clever way to get back at all of us."

"Alastair, you're being unfair! I never knew about the forgery until today!"

His voice sounded like someone else's, hard and unforgiving. "Oh, please! What kind of horse's ass do you take me for? You were practically living there and you didn't know what he was filling the closet with?"

"I didn't, I swear I didn't! He hid it all, he never told me!"

He walked towards the door and turned, with one last wrathful look. "You're such a snake. I only wish I'd seen it sooner."

The door slammed shut behind him.

She fell a little to one side so she was propped up by the wall. The steam knocked in the pipes and a car honked faintly from the street. She stared at the door, at the overlapping design of wooden panels that looked at once like a coffin and a cross.

Could lives be ruined in a single day? she wondered weakly. Two people, fallen, just like that? The two men who meant the most to her, with two slammed doors, both gone? Was it two lives undone, or was it three?

She became aware that the old coffee was boiling over. Mechanically, she turned off the flame and let the dark puddles settle on to the top of the stove.

So, Gerhardt was Bo's distributor. What an ending for her story . . . unveiling Bo as accomplice in Gerhardt's latest scam. She leaned against the counter for a moment, watching the lampshade still swinging slightly from where Alastair had knocked it going out, casting a bobbing circle of light on the rug. She stood there, hands braced against the counter top, for quite some time, thinking about her story and its ramifications, of who it would now expose.

After several minutes she pushed away from the counter and walked slowly over to her desk and typewriter. Gathering up a stack of papers and a notebook, she carried them into the living room and set them on the floor. She took a match pack off the mantle and knelt in front of the fireplace.

The first page of the stack was typed with the title she had planned to use for the headline: *From Nazi Vienna to Chic New York: Established Madison Avenue Dealer has Tarnished Past, Questionable Present.* The paper crumpled stiffly in her hands, then futilely tried to straighten out when she placed it on the grate. Adding a few more wadded-up sheets, she struck a match and touched it to a wrinkled corner. The paper flared, flames catching at the edges and eating into the pages like a hungry beast. One by one she fed the remaining typed sheets into the blaze, then the neatly penned pages of notes. The paper curled with the flames, shifting from white to red to gray. When all the papers were consumed, she reached forward and touched the warm shards lightly with her finger; they crumbled into ash.

Then she rose and sat into the chair, resting her head against its back.

Presently she heard footsteps coming down the hall. They grew louder and closer until they stopped in front of the door and were followed by a gentle knocking.

Springing to her feet, she then froze. Was this Alastair, returning to hurl some further accusation at her? Or could it be Bo, come to lament his cause? Standing still, she stared at the door; she had no defenses left.

"Megan," called a voice softly, "Megan, it's Clyde."

She stepped towards the door as if in a dream. What could he want?

Opening the door, she found Clyde standing breathlessly in the hallway with a large, narrow package wrapped in brown paper under his arm. Cold and nervous looking, he asked to come in. He entered and carefully leaned the package up against the couch. From his look it was clear he knew about Bo.

"I don't know what's going to happen," he said, pulling off his gloves. "He's in police custody. They were outside the building when we came back – they nabbed him at the door." Clyde shook his head. "But I gotta hand it to the guy. He told them I knew nothing, then said this was mine." He gestured at the package. "The cops knew it was no forgery so they let me have it. The last thing he said as they put him into the patrol car was that he hoped I'd take it up to 11th Street where it belonged."

She looked at the brown paper package tied up with string, then glanced helplessly back at Clyde. Seeing her immobility, he grabbed the package and untied the knotted twine. Tearing back the brown paper, he revealed a canvas.

It was the portrait of Paddy.

Chapter 42

"Next stop, Saint Lambert, Quebec," called the conductor. "Last stop before Montreal."

Bo looked out the window at the snow-covered wheat fields, stretching out in long arcs towards the horizon. The train whistled over a river, its banks glistening with layers of crystalline ice, brown stalks rising from frozen hummocks of grass. He had always liked Canada, ever since his father took him fly-fishing there as a kid. A wave of sadness passed through him at the thought of his father. He would go through the roof when he heard the news. Just when the old man thought he'd hit rock bottom with an artist for a son, he gets a felon.

Being a convict on the run didn't make Bo proud, but the prospect of jail was intolerable. One night in a precinct station had taught him that. So he'd be out of touch, out of sight. If his profile were low before, it would be non-existent now.

He stared blankly out the window, unable to rid himself of the thoughts that had plagued him in the nine hours he'd been on the train. He hadn't made much progress in reconciling his feelings, which ranged from rage to remorse. The only thing he was sure of was that the farther away he got from New York, the better he liked it. What a viper's nest, that city.

Leaving the country did have its advantages. It would be good to wipe the slate clean, to start over again. Making all that money had created more problems than it solved, except perhaps for his creditors. The forgeries had made his head thick, he couldn't think clearly. He sighed. Maybe that was why he screwed up and put the wrong date on the Gauguin.

Now that he thought about it, he did remember Gerhardt telling him to sign the year 1898. He remembered because at the time he couldn't help thinking how amazing that Gauguin was painting in such an advanced style right on the eve of the 20th century. But somehow, he had transposed the last two numbers and signed 1889 instead. Who knew – it was late, he was feeling pressured. Numbers never were his thing.

The rhythmic motion of the chugging train was soothing and had helped to settle him from the panic he'd been in when he'd slipped on to the Canada-bound train minutes before it pulled out of Penn Station. He'd just made it. World's roughest 36 hours, since yesterday morning's newspapers hit the stands. Although, after so much bad luck, yesterday the fates seemed to turn in his favor: the window in the station house bathroom had been just big enough for him to squeeze through. Crawling out onto the fire escape, he had dropped to the alley behind the precinct station. From there he'd slipped through the dark streets four blocks to the subway stop and caught the C train to Penn station. Nothing like the subway for a quick retreat.

He put his hand to his pocket to check that his wallet was still there and, feeling its bulge, took it out and unfolded it. Lying neatly in the leather was a wad of bills, packed in tight and crisp. Good thing he'd emptied his bank account before the police nabbed him. When the news of the Gauguin forgery broke, he'd planned to leave town anyway. Fingering through the bills he counted under his breath, "one thousand, two thousand, three, four, . . ." He reached six figures by the end of the stack. Dirty money, but it would serve to get him started again. He looked at the cash for a moment and thought about all it had cost him – far more than the worth of what he held in his hand.

Megan. No price was worth losing her. The thought of her tugged at him, bothering him so much he couldn't bear to think about it. Gerhardt, the collectors, the auction house – them he could dismiss without regret. They were playing the game, they took a risk, they lost. But Megan didn't deserve his deceit. His thoughts kept returning to that last awful scene, especially since he couldn't get around the fact that so much of what she said was true. And to think that he had somehow believed, after having rejected her, that he could win her back again as long as he was flush . . . well, the money had done more than clog his mind, it had choked his heart. But these thoughts only led him back to why he began it all in the first place, and that he preferred not to start again.

The thought of what he did with his art was equally painful. Would he ever feel like an artist instead of a charlatan again? *Prostitute*, Megan had called him. That was the charge that hurt the most. *'Tis pity he's a whore*. No wonder the last painting he started was a scene of working girls lined up for inspection in a brothel, à la Toulouse-Lautrec. That was exactly where he belonged. Ah well, it was all over, all behind him. Never again would he paint a copy of anything. Time to change the tune, play a new song.

The train chugged on. A red barn came into view followed by a rambling old farmhouse tucked under the wing of an enormous oak tree, its bare branches forming a latticework against the sky. How peaceful it looked. He would never have guessed that these rural outposts he'd hated back in Missouri would someday look like paradise.

Suddenly an image formed in his mind's eye. He saw the huge tree, its branches reaching gracefully upwards, and beneath it, in a surreal cross-section of the earth, a woman lying naked in amongst embracing roots. It was Megan. Bo smiled. This was the first pleasant vision he'd had in weeks, a definite improvement over severed eyes and hands. Mangled body parts weren't particularly appealing, especially when they were his own. This was a good sign; maybe now he could clear his head and get back to his own painting.

Change the tune, change the tune, the train chugged as it slowed down.

"Saint Lambert!" the conductor called out as the train pulled into a small station.

Passengers gathered their belongings and filed off the train. Bo couldn't wait to get to Montreal. What better place to lie low, to blend into the cobbled, baguette-baking streets. It wasn't quite Paris, but close enough.

He watched as a woman took her place in line on the platform. She wore a long black coat that almost reached her ankles and a black hat with a fur-trimmed brim. Boarding the train with the rest of the passengers, she looked left and right, then walked towards him carrying a briefcase. She stopped at the empty seat next to him and asked if anyone was sitting there. He pulled his backpack to the floor.

"No, have a seat."

She sat down and took off her black kid gloves as he looked out the window. The train pulled away from the station and from the field a flock of Canada Geese flapped up off the ground and rose into the clear sky forming a wavering V, headed north.

He looked back at the woman who still wore the hat, its shortly cropped fur rim sporting a red velvet rose. She pulled out a French arts magazine and leafed through the glossy illustrations. He rested his head against the seat and looked over her shoulder at paintings very different from what he was used to seeing.

Presently she turned to him and smiled. "Are you interested in contemporary art?"

"Sort of. I'm a painter myself. But lots of people don't consider me contemporary."

"Why is that?"

He shrugged. "My style. It's not exactly trendy."

"I try to avoid trends."

"Well, it's hard to when you're in the business."

"I am in the business. I run a gallery in Montreal."

"Ah."

"What's your work like?" she asked after a pause.

"It's kind of hard to describe. Representational. With a twist."

She smiled. "A picture's worth a thousand words."

He laughed and bent down to his backpack. He pulled out a plastic sheath of slides and handed it over. She held them up to the light of the window and inspected them closely. "These portraits are great, I love the settings. Is this the New York stock exchange in the background?"

"Yes, they're all set in Manhattan."

"And you weren't well received there?"

He gave a little laugh. "Not particularly."

Shaking her head she said, "Those New York galleries, they're so provincial." She looked a little longer and then put down the slides. "I'd love to see them in person. Where is your studio?"

He returned the slides to his backpack. "I'm in the process of moving to Montreal. A friend of mine is shipping my work up as soon as I find a place to live."

The woman handed him a business card. "Come and see me when you're settled. I have a branch gallery in Paris and we've had a lot of interest in American painting lately, especially in work that portrays the other side of America, the one that Hollywood doesn't show. As these seem to. With a twist."

They both laughed and he tucked her business card into his pocket.

Twist and shout, twist and shout, the train barreled along the tracks and blew a long clear whistle into a brilliant cerulean sky.

Epilogue

5 months later

Megan shook the glass of ginger ale and caught an ice cube with her tongue. She crunched it into small, melting pieces, cooling at least her mouth on this unseasonably warm May day. The double doors of the museum were set open to let in the breeze but the air still felt stifling. Looking up, her eyes followed the spiraling ramps of the museum upwards to the glass dome at the top. She imagined it lifting back like an escape hatch, releasing the stuffy air.

"Since when did they decide to hold this at the Guggenheim?" asked a voice, and Clyde appeared in front of her. He was out of breath and beads of sweat stood out across his forehead.

"Clyde! I was afraid you wouldn't make it."

He pushed up the sleeves on his gray waffled shirt. "I thought it was at the Arts Students League, so I went there first."

"They moved it up here, there was so much interest."

Clyde nodded, pushed his damp hair back from his forehead and looked around at the milling crowd, dressed festively for spring in everything from the Hawaiian shirts of artists to the linen and seersucker suits of dealers and curators.

Megan was always glad to see Clyde since he was her only link to Bo, her only confirmation of his existence, which these days often seemed more like a dream. Clyde had proposed entering the *Portrait of Paddy* when the call for submissions came out for the contest, billed as *New Trends in Realism*. He had taken the painting up to the sponsoring Art Students League to enter it.

"I'm sorry, I should have called you," she said. "I got the change notice, for some reason."

Clyde lifted a glass of champagne from a passing tray. "I put your name and address down as the contact on the submission forms."

"You did?"

"Well, I wasn't about to list Bo, considering his wanted status. And I didn't want to give my name, this isn't my work. So I listed the painting as care of you."

She nodded and crunched another ice cube, thinking that since Bo couldn't be named the artist it didn't much matter who was listed. Clyde looked away wistfully.

"What are you going to do with the prize money if it wins?" he asked.

"It should really go to Bo. But I wouldn't know where to send it."

He looked at her questioningly. "You don't know where he is?"

"I was hoping you would tell me."

He put his hand to his chest. "Me? *I* don't know where he is."

They sipped their drinks silently, the sounds of clinking glasses and animated voices filling the air around them. In the five months since Bo had left, Megan had thought over what had happened from every possible perspective. And although Bo could no longer hold the same high place in her esteem, she had reached a point of clemency. With all he had endured, with his undeniable talent, she would try to redeem his fraud by proffering his art.

She glanced over at the wall where the seven finalist paintings hung. From the center shone the *Portrait of Paddy,* all spit and polish after Clyde cleaned it, set like a jewel on the white wall. Wouldn't Bo be flabbergasted if he knew. But the only clue to his whereabouts was a postcard she got a few months ago, postmarked from some town in Quebec. All it said was, "I'm all right. I'm sorry. I miss you."

"Hey, great review on the Elmyr de Hory paintings," Clyde said, and then added, "It's good to see your byline again."

She smiled, glad he saw the magazine story she so enjoyed writing. Although she couldn't quite accept that her newspaper days were entirely over, it was wonderful to be writing for a publication whose focus was art for art's sake.

After her exposé went up in smoke, she had run one more story in the *Soho Weekly News,* snuck in at press time the day before Fogelman fired her. After the news broke that Lyndhurst and Lloyd's was offering the fake Gauguin, every other city newspaper had covered the art world scandal except hers. Instead, Megan had written up the latest claim on the *Abruzzi Daughter,* made by the curator from the Museum of Modern Art whom she had brought in for an assessment. He had looked over the painting with a lens for several minutes and then declared that stunning as it was, it was not by Modigliani at all but was a brilliant forgery by Elmyr de Hory, the infamous Spanish forger of modern masters. This opinion had since been corroborated by several Modigliani experts.

Sotheby's then held a press conference saying they could not be held liable for listing an incorrect provenance if the painting was not in fact by Modigliani. The Calebresi family dropped their charges against Sotheby's in London of knowingly providing false provenance papers. Senor Calebresi declared he loved the remarkable beauty of the pensive *Abruzzi Daughter* no matter who had painted her and would welcome it back in his Umbrian villa with great pleasure. In an act of atonement, Catherine DuBois had relinquished all claims to the painting. The Calebresi family was overjoyed.

Gerhardt had been indicted immediately and an investigation of his holdings revealed a significant stash of European modernist pictures, German Expressionists in particular, many of which had disappeared from noted Jewish collections during the Third Reich. Gerhardt, under the weight of irrefutable evidence and in exchange for a lighter sentence, had confessed to creating phony provenances to support his feeding of both stolen art and forgeries into the market. The *Abruzzi Daughter* was one of them.

Apropos of these developments, and in memory of Elmyr de Hory who had committed suicide when the French authorities tried to extradite him for trial, a 57th Street dealer in May opened an exhibition of de Hory paintings, some of which were selling for hefty prices. With the permission of Senor Calebresi, Megan was instrumental in including the *Abruzzi Daughter* (not for sale).

Then she wrote a magazine article exploring the whole notion of art forgery, entitled, *Forgeries: homage or purloining?* With great gusto she laid out the full chronicle of Elmyr de Hory, past and present: a forger of paintings, legally a criminal, on his death embraced by the art establishment for his exceptional talent, his forgeries exhibited as notable works of art. She only wished she could send a copy to Bo.

Clyde clinked her glass with his and laughed. "An exhibit of fakes by a forger. I love it. It's almost conceptual art."

As Clyde turned to talk to someone else, Megan walked over to get a closer look at Paddy's portrait. Paddy floated like some otherworldly royalty on a shimmering throne before the architecturally converted Metropolitan Museum. His lively face and eyes sparkled in fluorescent silver above his tattered clothes.

"I'm so glad to see a critic here," said a voice beside her. She turned to see a smiling Diana Drexler, the chairperson of the contest. Smartly tailored in a hound's tooth suit, she wore earrings shaped like lions heads that could have passed for doorknockers.

"*Fabulous*, aren't they?" said Diana.

Megan nodded tolerantly. She had stricken the word 'fabulous' from her vocabulary. "Yes, I'd say they're all very accomplished."

"We were swamped with submissions, I had no idea there

were so many artists working in realism. And the caliber of the work – the judges will have a hard time deciding."

"They will."

"Oh, and just in case you're writing about this, we lost one of the judges to appendicitis yesterday, but we were lucky enough to get Alastair Cavendish to serve instead."

The bottom of Megan's stomach dropped.

Diana smiled at a passing man. "And speak of the devil – "

*   *   *

Alastair felt a tap on his shoulder and he turned questioningly to see Diana Drexler. A reserve rose in him at the sight of this overly manicured woman, but he smiled graciously, conscious more then ever of the importance of building good business relationships. Although his good will didn't always come as easily as it used to. He turned his genial expression to the woman next to Diana; his smile froze.

"I want to thank you so much for standing in on such short notice," said Diana. She leaned confidentially towards him. "You know, two is just *not* the right number for judges, a third is really needed to act as tie-breaker."

He cleared his throat and addressed Diana. "Actually, that's just what I was. If I hadn't had such a strong opinion you may have had a different first prize."

Diana looked with interest. "Really?"

"Yes. I think one succeeds best in combining classic influences into something new. As with most American realists, there's clearly a European influence. This painting fits right into the tradition of Winslow Homer and John Singer Sargent, but at the same time it is thoroughly contemporary. Fresh but familiar."

He looked down self-consciously, hearing himself sound like some Sunday afternoon BBC talk show on art appreciation. But what choice did he have, really, except sticking with the professional?

"I'm glad you felt so strongly," Diana said with a smile.

Alastair looked fully at Megan for the first time. She couldn't have looked lovelier. A bit thinner, perhaps, her cheeks a little wan, but beautiful nonetheless. With her wavy auburn hair pulled back in turtle shell combs in a style he'd never seen, he also saw she wore matching earrings, a pair of hand-hammered silver stars whose surfaces glimmered with every movement.

"I have strong feelings about things I like," he said

"That's just the sort of enthusiasm we were hoping for," said Diana.

"Mind you, not that the others aren't good," he quickly added, not wanting to sound overly critical, reminded suddenly of his thorough denunciation of Megan. In the long months since the crisis, his harsh view of her had softened, especially after reading Gerhardt's deposition in which he described the subterfuge Bo put him through when Megan once arrived unexpectedly and Bo insisted that he hide in the bathroom until she was gone. *Definite paranoid tendencies,* Gerhardt had claimed, trying to make a case for Bo's madness.

Diana lowered her voice. "Just between us, beyond a certain level of competence, these choices of which is the best really are personal, aren't they? By the way, do you know Megan Trico?"

He turned to her, bittersweet feelings flooding him. Know her? Yes, he knew her, certainly in the biblical sense. But did he truly know her? Or did he think she was someone she wasn't? And at which point, if ever, was his opinion correct?

"Yes, we've met."

"Please excuse me then, I need to make sure the microphone is ready."

Diana whisked off, leaving them face-to-face.

*   *   *

To Megan, the sight of Alastair was as remarkable as if she were seeing a fan-tailed peacock standing on a snowdrift.

Longer than he used to wear it, his straight blonde hair hung over his forehead, following the downward line of his eyelashes. He still looked handsome, but also somehow older, more serious than before.

He smiled hesitantly. "How are you, Megan?"

She blinked rapidly, suddenly overcome with feeling. He was such a fine man, how had things ever gotten so out of hand? "Not bad. Keeping busy, you know, same old thing." Then, realizing that whatever her life was now, it was not the 'same old thing', she blushed and added, "I've got a new job as editor at ARTS Magazine. It's a monthly, so a little saner pace."

"Congratulations." He nodded at her bag. "I see your bag has lost some weight."

She laughed with relief and patted the leather bag that hung flatly at her side. "It doesn't hold so much these days. All I really need is my swimsuit. Lizzy and I rented a beach house out on Shelter Island for the summer."

His face clouded, his expression retreating to a distant place. "It is always pleasant to get out of the city in the warm weather."

She looked down uncomfortably. "And how are you?" she asked momentarily.

"Fine. Getting organized to open my gallery in September," he said impassively.

She put her hand to her shoulder strap and hiked up her bag, which didn't need hiking. "Yes, I heard you were going out on your own. That's terrific. Where?"

"I'll be on Madison, between 75th and 76th."

"Great location," she said, thinking how odd for him to choose a place right down the block from Sotheby's.

He smiled wryly. "I figure I can use the overflow from those people up the street."

"You'll be showing Modern Paintings, of course."

"I will. But also some new work, I think. I'd like to showcase some sleepers, to dig up some painters who were overlooked in their time." He looked at her significantly. "Just to make it more interesting."

She looked at his expression, open to new possibilities in a way she'd never seen, and suddenly, more than anything, she wanted to be forgiven, for him not to think badly of her, for him to understand that she never meant him any harm.

She reached out and lightly touched his arm. "Alastair, I wish you the very best. You have every reason in the world to succeed. All you need is a little luck."

His eyes softened. "We can all use a bit of that sometimes."

The twang of feed-back sang through the room and Diana Drexler stepped up to the microphone.

"Ladies and gentleman, we are ready to announce the awards. And please remember that we will have a discussion of the paintings with the judges afterwards."

"I'd better take my seat," he said, brushing his hair away from his forehead and looking towards the judges' table. But he turned back to her abruptly. "By the way, would you still like to know how the mystery clock works?"

He asked with concern, as if inquiring about a scarf she'd left.

"I'd love to know."

"Each hand is embedded in a circular glass plate, and the two plates are turned separately by cogs hidden in the base."

The information was delivered considerately, as if it were an explanation she was due. She could barely muster a thank you. He tried to smile casually but his eyes were profound. "Nice to see you, Megan."

He made his way through the crowd to the chairs on the riser and took a seat with the other two judges.

Clyde sidled up to Megan and gave her a wink. Diana put on the half-glasses hanging on braided silk around her neck and opened a manila envelope on the table in front of her. She announced two honorable mentions, then cleared her throat and put her hand to the microphone. The crowd fell silent. "And the first prize goes to . . . Portrait of Paddy."

The room filled with applause and Megan covered her face with her hands.

"Goddamn it, he won!" cried Clyde.

"Could Beauregard Rye please come forward?"

Her eyes widened at Clyde. "*Beauregard Rye?*"

He shrugged. "Isn't that what you used to call him?"

Diana peered more closely at the form in front of her.

"Oh, I see he has a representative. Megan Trico, will you please step up to accept the prize for Mr. Rye?"

"But Clyde!" she protested in a whisper, "This is too obvious, the name is so close – "

People turned to look, smiling expectantly and clapping. She saw Jake Gruber giving her the thumbs up sign. Clyde nudged her forward with a grin. "Go on. It's all a game anyway."

She made her way through the applauding crowd to Diana Drexler, who handed her an envelope. "What a shame he couldn't be here!"

Megan stammered in confusion, "Yes, he's away, painting out of the country right now."

She took the envelope and as she turned she caught Alastair's eye. He was staring at her in utter astonishment.

As Diana made announcements, Megan stuffed the envelope into her bag and headed for the door, intent on making her escape as quickly as possible. Out of the building, she crossed the street and headed down 5th Avenue on the cobbled sidewalk, past the spraying fountains in front of the Metropolitan, the expansive concrete radiating heat, across 79th Street and into Central Park.

Down off the street and under the trees the air was cooler, the light green new leaves shimmering overhead. She passed babies in strollers, roller skaters and sleek city dogs, yet she noticed little. She couldn't get over the look on Alastair's face. But what did it matter at this point, when he'd been so ready to think the worst of her before? Her pace slowed and she turned down towards the bronzes of Alice in Wonderland. What a day. In fact, what a year. She sighed and thought of the rented summer house on Shelter Island. No vacation had ever looked so good.

She sat down on a bench, set her bag on her lap and patted it fondly. Flat and roomy, the bag was now reduced to carrying the standard necessities: wallet, brush, keys, a lipstick. The only significant addition was a full floor plan of the Metropolitan Museum of Art. In the last few months she'd used her spare time to visit the museum's permanent collections. And she'd discovered all sorts of art – Jungenstil silver, American weathervanes, Grecian red and black vases – delightful displays she'd never seen that were there all the time. And in doing this she had come to see that she couldn't split herself amongst the dozens of special exhibitions and visiting collections and understand any of them fully, and that in trying to she had missed appreciating the depth of character of her favorite museum of all.

Small children clamored over the big bronzes. A little girl grasped the far side of the toadstool and with a grunt pulled herself up. She turned around and arranged herself in the middle, dangling her feet over the edge, her tiny face beaming with pleasure. Megan watched her and smiled. Yes, it was a great perch, but be careful. Don't fall. It's a long way to the ground.

She let her thoughts drift, wishing they would all empty right out of her head. First of all, what would she do with the money? She looked inside the envelope, neatly packed with ten crisp hundred-dollar bills. Should she put it in the bank until Bo's return? What if he never came back? Did he need it? Would he want it?

Suddenly she noticed an old man digging around in a trashcan. He pulled up paper bags and opened them. Some he discarded, others he emptied into a black plastic bag hanging on his shoulder. She watched him curiously; his wiry gray hair looked somehow familiar. He investigated one last bag, tossed it back, and turned away from the basket. He limped slowly up the path towards her. As he came closer she recognized Paddy.

When he was about ten feet from her he stopped and looked at her curiously. He took a step closer and his face lit up. "Well, bless my soul," he said, tipping his hat. "If it ain't Miss Trico!"

"Hello Paddy."

When he saw her smile he stepped up and said, "Beautiful day, eh?" His wrinkled eyes were watery and he seemed to be moving with some difficulty, but he smiled cheerfully. He scratched the top of his head and looked towards the model boats sailing in wide arcs across the pond.

"Ain't been up here in a coon's age. I always try to make it up once during the spring, see the trees come out and all. Don't have too much of that down on the Bowery."

He grinned good-naturedly.

"I guess not," she said.

He shuffled his feet, looked at her hesitantly and took a step back, as if afraid of getting too close. Then he spoke up brightly. "Seen Bo around?"

She shook her head.

He clicked his tongue and frowned. "Sure do miss that boy. Never ate so good as when I was working for him."

From the longing look in his eye she knew it was a lot more than food he missed.

Suddenly she said impulsively, "Paddy, what would you do if someone offered you a lot of money? Like a thousand dollars?"

"*Me?*" he asked incredulously. Then he laughed, his eyes small sparkles of blue. "God knows what they'd be wanting from me for that kind of money!"

"No, you wouldn't have to do anything. Free for the taking."

He stroked his beard and looked into the treetops. "I don't expect I'll have to decide this anytime soon, but if I did, I reckon I'd have to turn it down."

He looked at her decidedly.

"But why? Just think what you could do with it."

"Well, Miss Trico, the way I figure it is, what would it do to me? Complicate things something awful. Probably have to pay taxes on it, for starters, and I always hated filling out them damned forms. Then, they wouldn't let me in at the Mission for meals anymore, so I'd have to cook. And that bloodhound of an ex-wife of mine, she'd probably hunt me down and fight me for it." He shook his head and waved his hand at her. "Naw, I don't need it. Cost me more than it'd be worth."

She looked at his frail form, barely discernible beneath the worn rags, and smiled. "Paddy, you're a prince."

The old man's face lit up and he chuckled. "Me, old graybeard? A prince?"

Megan cocked her head a moment. "Okay, then, how about king? Yes, that's better – Paddy, you're a king."

"King of the Bowery, eh miss?" he said, his faded eyes twinkling.

Tipping his hat to her, he turned and hobbled up the path.

BVG